Before she knew what was happening, Merrick tugged her into his arms and captured her mouth with his.

Never had she been kissed, and never, in her most lustful daydreams, had she imagined this. The taste of him. The scent of man and leather, horse and salt air. The sensation of his strong arms about her, holding her close.

This could not be right, because no matter how good it felt, this man kissing her was Merrick, Wicked William's son.

She struggled to break free. "I'm an honorable woman!"

"You're my betrothed," he replied. "There's no harm in a kiss."

"Betrothed or not, I didn't give you leave to kiss me!"

"Then I humbly beg your forgiveness, my lady," he calmly replied, bowing like the most chivalrous of knights. He looked about to smile and his eyes seemed to glitter.

"There is nothing humble about you, my lord, and I beg you not to touch me again unless I give you leave."

The little half smile melted away, and his expression settled into an impassive mask. "As you wish, my lady—until you give me leave."

MARGARET MOORE

The Unwilling Bride

HQN™

ISBN 0-373-77065-0

THE UNWILLING BRIDE

www.HQNBooks.com

Printed in U.S.A.

With many thanks to the recappers and posters at TelevisionWithoutPity.com, for the entertainment and enjoyment. You never fail to make me smile!

The Unwilling Bride

PROLOGUE

Oxfordshire, 1228

MORE THAN ANYTHING, THE BOY wanted to go home. There he knew every rock and path. There he could breathe the fresh salt air blowing in from the sea, feel sand and pebbles beneath his bare feet and the rivulets of water running between his toes. There he was happy. There he was safe.

Here, riding through this strange country, he was afraid.

He was afraid of the soldiers who surrounded him, with their terrible scars and big, calloused hands. Of their weapons. The long, heavy broadswords. The maces. The daggers they tucked in their belts and hid in their boots.

He hated the smell of them—sweat and ale and leather. He hated the way they cursed in their foreign tongue.

The nobleman leading the cortege was even more frightening than the soldiers. With his hawklike beak of a nose and narrow, dark, fault-seeking eyes, Sir Egbert bore no scars or other marks of battle. He didn't smell like the soldiers, and he usually didn't raise his voice—yet he could make the boy quiver with just a look.

He wanted to go home!

They came to a fork in the muddy, rutted road. One way led to a dark wood of oak and ash, elm and thick underbrush; the other veered away from the forest, although still heading north.

Sir Egbert raised his hand, bringing the column to a halt, and gestured for the leader of the soldiers, who had a horrible red welt of a scar marring his already ugly face, to join him.

The boy sat motionless and silent, wondering, worrying about why they had stopped. His hands trembled as he did his best to control his prancing pony. The tall grass bordering the road swayed and whispered in the breeze, sounding a little like the sea. The soldier nearest him hawked and spit, then said something under his breath that made the others sneer and laugh.

What was wrong? Was Sir Egbert unsure of the way?

Sir Egbert gestured down the rutted road that led toward the dark wood. The leader of the soldiers frowned, muttered something and pointed the other way.

Please, God, not into the wood, the boy prayed. The close-standing trees, the dense bushes, the shadows…it was like something from stories told 'round the hearth, the dwelling place of ghosts and evil spirits.

Please, God, not into the dark wood.

Please, Jesus, let me go home!

Sir Egbert's voice rose to an angry, insistent shout, including what had to be curses, and he made angry gestures. The leader of the soldiers nodded and, frowning, turned his horse back toward his men.

Sir Egbert raised his hand and pointed to the wood— the murky, scary woods full of terrible things. The scarred man barked an order, and his men drew out their swords.

The boy prayed harder as he nudged his pony forward. *Please God, keep me safe. Please, Jesus, let me go home. Mary, Mother of God, I want to go home!*

WITHIN AN HOUR THE ATTACK WAS over. All in the cortege lay dead or dying in the wood.

Save one.

CHAPTER ONE

April, 1243

THE BOAR'S HEAD TAVERN boasted the prettiest, cleanest serving wenches for miles around. The young women were all eager to please their customers in a variety of ways, too, especially the boisterous knights and squires currently making merry in the taproom. Carrying pitchers of wine and mugs of ale, the wenches moved deftly between the tables, laughing and joking with the men, and sizing them up as to their worth. They could easily earn a month's worth of income in a single night from drunken revelers like these.

Only one man sitting silently at a table in the corner seemed uninterested in the women, or celebrating. He had his back to the wall and stared down into his goblet, completely oblivious to the merry mayhem around him.

Two other knights, equally young and muscular, shared his table. The handsomest of the pair, brown haired and with a smile that held a host of promises, delighted in having the women compete for his attention and hurry to fetch his wine. The second knight, more sober, with shrewd hazel eyes, a straight, narrow nose and reddish brown hair, seemed more inclined to view the women and listen to their banter with a jaundiced eye, well aware that they were calculating how much they could charge for their services between the sheets.

"Here, m'dear, where do you think you're going with that jug of wine?" the comely Sir Henry demanded as he reached out and drew the most buxom of the wenches onto his lap.

She set the jug of wine on the scarred table beside him and, laughing, wound her arms around his neck. It was a miracle her bodice didn't slip farther down and reveal more of her breasts, but then, she wouldn't have cared if it had. "Over to that table there, where they *pay*," she said pertly, and with unmistakable significance.

"Egad, wench, will you besmirch our honor?" Henry cried with mock indignation. "Of course we'll pay. Didn't my friends and I win several ransoms at the tournament? Aren't there many young men who had to pay us for their horses and armor after we triumphed on the field and forced them to cry mercy? Why, we're rich, I tell you. Rich!"

The silent knight in the corner glanced up a moment, then returned to staring into his goblet as if he was expecting it to speak.

Henry turned to the cynical knight beside him while his hand wandered toward the wench's fulsome breasts. "Pay the girl, Ranulf."

Sir Ranulf raised a sardonic brow as he reached into

his woolen tunic and drew out a leather pouch. "I don't suppose there's any point suggesting you be quiet about our winnings? You're making us the bait of every cut-purse between here and Cornwall."

"Fie, man, you fret like an old woman! No man would be fool enough to try to rob the three of *us*!"

With a shrug, Ranulf pulled out a silver penny. The wench's eyes widened and she reached out to snatch it from his grasp, but Ranulf's hand closed over it before she could. "You can have this if you bring us some good wine instead of this vinegar."

She nodded eagerly.

Sir Ranulf's eyes danced with amusement. "*And* if you'll share my bed tonight."

The wench immediately jumped up from Henry's lap.

"Hey, now!" Henry protested.

Ranulf ignored him. "Off you go," he said to the wench, holding out the coin again.

"What about him? Does he want any company?" the young woman asked, nodding at their companion.

The dark-haired man raised his head to look at her. He was undeniably good-looking, but there was something so stern and forbidding in his expression, the wench's smile died and she immediately took a step back. "I didn't mean no offense."

"Don't mind Merrick," Henry said with a soothing smile. "He's in mourning for his father, you see. Now fetch the wine like a good girl."

The wench cast another wary look at Merrick,

smiled at Henry and Ranulf, then hurried to do Henry's bidding.

Henry smacked the table in front of their grimly silent friend. "For God's sake, Merrick, this isn't a wake."

Ranulf frowned. "He's got a lot on his mind, Henry. Let him alone."

Henry paid Ranulf no heed. "It's not as if you cared for your father that you should be upset over his death. You haven't even been home in fifteen years."

Merrick leaned back against the wall and crossed his strong arms that could wield a sword, lance or mace for hours without tiring. "Ruining your entertainment, am I?" he asked, his voice deep and gruff.

"As a matter of fact, you are. Granted, it would give any man pause to think he's not just inherited an estate but also has to get married to some girl he hasn't seen in years, but if you ask me, that's all the more reason you should enjoy tonight. Given how many knights you defeated, I wouldn't be surprised if one of these wenches would do it for nothing. Come, Merrick, why not have a little sport? I know you, and once you're married you won't stray, so all the more reason to—"

"No."

"You're going to save yourself for a girl you haven't seen since you were ten years old?" Henry demanded.

"Yes."

"Then I hope what we've heard is true, and she's a beauty."

"Her looks don't matter."

"But supposing you don't suit each other?" Henry asked with exasperation. "What if you find you don't even like her? What will you do then?"

"I'll manage."

"It's a question of honor, Henry," Ranulf interjected, giving Henry another warning look. "The betrothal agreement means they're as good as married already, so it's no easy contract to break. Now for God's sake, let it alone."

"If there's honor involved, it's his late, unlamented father's, not his," Henry replied. "Merrick didn't make the betrothal agreement."

"His bride's lived in Tregellas since they were betrothed, so she'll know the household, the villagers and the tenants," Ranulf pointed out. "That'll be a help to Merrick when he arrives to take possession. Plus, she's got a sizable dowry…" He glanced at Merrick. "There *is* a sizable dowry?"

The knight inclined his head.

"So he'll be even richer. He'll also be wanting heirs as well as a chatelaine, so he *needs* a wife."

Henry frowned. "I don't know what it is about men once they get an estate. Suddenly it's all about finding a woman who's a good manager, like a steward."

"You'll be the same, should you ever get an estate," Ranulf replied. "Responsibility changes a man."

"God help me, I hope not!" Henry cried, the skin at the corners of his eyes crinkling as he grinned. "When

I marry, I'm going to find the most beautiful woman I can and to hell with anything else."

"Even if she's poor?" Ranulf skeptically inquired.

"My brother claims his wife has enriched his life in a hundred ways although she brought barely a ha'penny to the marriage. So, yes, even if she's poor."

"And if she's silly and insipid, and can't run your household?"

"I'll make sure I have excellent servants."

Ranulf raised a brow. "How do you plan to pay these servants?"

That gave Henry a moment's pause. Then he brightened. "I'll win more tournament prizes, or find a lord who needs a knight in his service."

"Surely you'll want a woman you can talk to, who doesn't drive you mad with foolish babble?"

Henry waved his hand dismissively. "I won't listen and I'll keep her too busy to talk." He grinned at Merrick. "Is that your plan, too? Keep Lady Constance too occupied to talk? You *do* intend to actually have some conversation with your wife? Otherwise, she's liable to think you're mute."

Merrick shoved back his stool and got to his feet. "I speak when I have something worthwhile to say. Now I'm going to bed."

Henry shrugged his shoulders. "Well, if you want to leave so soon, Merrick, farewell. All the better for us, since we won't have to compete with the new lord of Tregellas and tournament champion for a woman's favor." He shook his head with bogus dismay. "For a man who barely says ten words at a time, I don't know how you manage to attract the attention you do."

"Perhaps because I barely say ten words at a time."

"Since he doesn't usually go lacking, there must be some truth to that," Ranulf dryly affirmed.

Henry looked indignant. "I'll have you know many women consider me charmingly well-spoken." Then he raised his voice so that those around him could hear. "Merrick may outshine me on the tournament field, but I believe *I* carry the honors in the bedchamber."

The rest of the merrymakers in the tavern fell silent, while the women eyed him with speculation.

"If it pleases you to think so," Merrick said, and there was a look in his eyes that told Ranulf that Merrick's temper, slow to rouse, was rising.

"Gentlemen, gentlemen!" he cried, likewise getting to his feet. "Since the lord of Tregellas and champion of today's tournament wishes to leave us, let's allow him to retire from the field with honor intact and declare a draw in matters of the bedchamber."

Henry stood and bowed to Merrick. "I'm willing to agree that we're evenly matched."

The buxom serving wench sauntered toward them, a carafe of wine balanced on her hip. "I could try you both," she offered, "and choose a winner."

"No need. My friend is just leaving," Henry said as he grabbed the carafe out of her hands. Tipping it back, he let the wine pour into his open mouth, while with his free hand he reached out to embrace her.

She wasn't there.

She was in Merrick's arms, and being quite thoroughly kissed. His friend's mouth moved over hers with sure and certain purpose, one hand sliding slowly down her back to caress her rounded buttocks.

The wench not only responded willingly to Merrick's kiss, she ground her hips against him as if she wanted him to take her then and there.

Finally Merrick broke the kiss and removed the panting woman's clinging arms from around his body. As she staggered over to the nearest bench and sat heavily, fanning herself with her hand, he turned on his heel and marched out of the tavern without another word.

The moment he was gone, the Boar's Head taproom erupted with the noise of amused, drunken noblemen and laughing women.

"I don't think you should have implied that Merrick is second best when it comes to the bedchamber," Ranulf noted as he and Henry returned to their seats.

"Obviously not," Henry said with a good-natured smile. "But at least I got him to quit brooding for a bit, didn't I?"

"How can you be so calm? I'd be beside myself with excitement if I was going to see the man I was to marry, and after fifteen years!" sixteen-year-old Beatrice cried, her face aglow, her hands rapturously clasped, as she sat on the bed in Constance's bedchamber.

"I've been betrothed since I was five years old, so I've had plenty of time to get used to the idea of marriage," Constance replied without turning away from the polished silver plate that served as her mirror. She raised a gold necklace to drape it around her neck, then set it down before her cousin noticed that her hands were trembling. "Perhaps if my betrothed had come home once or twice in those fifteen years, I might be more excited. As it is, I hardly know what to expect. He may hate me on sight."

Indeed, she hoped he *did* hate her. For years her greatest hope had been that Merrick's long absence meant that he shared her aversion to their contracted marriage.

"I'm sure he'll like you," Beatrice assured her. "Everybody in Tregellas likes you. All the servants in the castle admire and respect you. Nobody else could handle the old lord the way you did, so Father says."

Constance tried to focus on adjusting her veil and not recall the shouting, the curses, the throwing of anything within reach, the blows aimed at everyone except her....

"I'm sure Merrick's a fine fellow," Beatrice went on. "He's won a lot of tournaments and he's been to court, too. Surely that means he can dance. I wonder if he sings? Maybe he'll sing a love song to you, Constance. Wouldn't that be delightful?"

Constance sent up a silent prayer for patience before she addressed her loquacious cousin. "I would rather he respect me."

Beatrice's brow furrowed. "Don't you want your husband to love you?"

"It's the dearest wish of my heart," Constance truthfully replied. Unfortunately, she feared any son of Wicked William would be incapable of that sincere emotion.

"At least you knew each other before," Beatrice offered.

"Yes, we did," Constance replied, keeping any animosity from her voice.

But Merrick had been a horrible boy who always demanded his own way and made sure he got it; who teased her until she cried, then derisively called her a baby; who never took the blame for any of the mischief he caused, but always found a way to turn it to a helpless servant.

Worse, if he was as vindictive as she remembered, he would surely demand compensation if she tried to break the betrothal agreement, leaving her with no dowry for another marriage, which was why she planned to induce Merrick to break the contract. That way, he couldn't claim that she'd wronged him.

Beatrice jumped up from the bed and threw open the large, carved oaken chest that held her cousin's clothes. "What are you going to wear to meet him?" she asked, surveying the few fine garments inside.

"The gown I have on."

Beatrice stared at her cousin as if she'd never heard anything so ludicrous in her life. "But your peacock blue bliaut with the silver threads looks so much better with your eyes and hair."

Constance was well aware that the long blue tunic

worn over a thinner gown of white or silver flattered her fair coloring and brought out the blue in her eyes. The yellowish green of the dress she was currently wearing made her look sickly—which was precisely why she'd chosen it.

"I don't have time to change," Constance replied, wondering if that was true, and praying that it was.

As if to confirm her reply, a sharp rap sounded on the door before it was immediately opened by Beatrice's father. Lord Carrell strode into the bedchamber, his long parti-colored robe swishing about his ankles. Ignoring his daughter, he ran a measuring gaze over his niece.

Her uncle had never loved her, of that Constance was quite certain. If he'd had any concern for her happiness, or any fear for her safety, he would have asked Lord William to release her from the betrothal years ago and taken her to his home. But he had not.

How different her life might have been if her mother hadn't died giving her birth, and her father from a fall not six months later.

"Merrick and his party are nearly here," Lord Carrell announced.

Constance felt as if a lead weight had settled in her stomach. "How many men did he bring with him?"

"Two."

"Only two?" she asked, dumbfounded. The Merrick she'd known would have delighted in a show of power and importance, so she'd expected him to have an escort of at least twenty. With that in mind, she'd ordered accommodations to be prepared for that number, with a warning to the servants that there might be more.

"That shouldn't be so surprising," her uncle replied. "No one in Cornwall would dare to attack the lord of Tregellas."

"No, I don't suppose they would," Constance agreed. They certainly wouldn't have dared to attack Merrick's father, whose retribution would have been swift and merciless.

"Smile, Constance," her uncle said with an expression she assumed was intended to be comforting, not condescending. "I doubt your life will be worse as Merrick's wife than when Lord William ruled here."

It couldn't get very much worse, she thought, except that as Merrick's wife, she'd share his bed—which might be terrible indeed. As for her uncle's attempt to console her, he wouldn't be the one living in hell if he was wrong.

"What do we really know of Merrick?" she asked, some of her genuine distress slipping into her voice.

Her uncle gave her a patronizing smile that set her teeth on edge. "What is there to know? He's your betrothed. And if you have any little difficulties, you should be able to deal with him. You're a beautiful, clever woman."

"What if doesn't want to marry me and is only doing so because of the contract?"

"Once he sees you again, Constance, I'm sure you'll please him."

As if she were a slave, or chattel to be bartered.

"Now come along. Lord Algernon has already gone to the courtyard to greet him."

If Merrick's paternal uncle was waiting in the courtyard, she had little choice but to follow at once.

Trailed by Beatrice, Constance and her uncle hurried down the curving stone steps and through the great hall, a huge chamber with a high beamed ceiling and corbels carved in the shapes of wolves' heads holding up great oaken beams. The raised dais sported a fireplace in the wall behind it—something only the most progressive nobles had added to their castles. The late Lord William had never denied himself any innovations that would add to his personal comfort.

In spite of her worries, Constance made a swift survey to ensure all was in readiness for the new overlord. Fresh rushes had been spread on the floor, with rosemary and fleabane sprinkled over them. The tapestries had been beaten as free of dust and soot as possible. The tables had been scrubbed and rubbed with wax, the chairs for the high tables had been cleaned, and their cushions repaired or replaced.

As they left the hall, Constance blinked in the sunlight. Lord Algernon, his portly body clad in rich garments of silk and velvet, bowed in greeting and gave her a slightly strained smile.

All of the garrison except those on guard stood in neat rows, their backs straight, their mail polished, their helmets gleaming. Groups of well-dressed folk from the village—merchants, tenants and vassals who owed

the lord tithes and service, as well as their families—
waited quietly, too.

Equally uneasy servants crowded the doors of the
buildings, and a few peered from the upper windows of
the keep, or the family bedchambers. Indeed, it seemed
as if the very stones of Tregellas were keeping a wary vigil.

And then her straining ears caught the sound she'd
been dreading: horses coming through the inner gate-
house.

Three knights appeared, riding side by side into the
courtyard. All three were tall and well built. All three
looked as if they could easily defeat ten men without
breaking a sweat.

The one to Constance's left wore a forest-green surcoat over his chain mail hauberk, and his horse's trap-
pings were likewise forest-green, with a worked-leather
breast collar and britchens. He reminded Constance of
a fox with his straight nose, pointed chin and reddish
hair. Merrick had been as clever as a fox, too, but there
was nothing in this man's features or coloring to make
her think he was Wicked William's son.

The smiling man on the right wore a surcoat of brilliant scarlet wonderfully embroidered with gold and
silver threads. The accoutrements of his destrier were
just as flamboyant and costly; they would be hard to
miss from a mile away. This merry, smiling fellow had
the easy confidence of a nobleman, but he seemed too
amiable and fair of face to be Merrick.

Therefore Merrick had to be the man in the middle,
wearing a surcoat of plain black. He didn't much resem-

ble the boy she remembered, either in form or feature. This man's eyes weren't impish slits, and as for his lips, they weren't thin now, or smirking, but full and well cut. He was also the tallest by half a head, lean and muscular, and his unexpectedly long black hair waved to his broad shoulders.

All three knights dismounted easily, swinging down from the saddle in perfect unison, as if their mail weighed next to nothing. The black-clad man's unblinking gaze swept over the yard and everyone in it until it finally settled, with unwavering directness, on her, dispelling any doubts as to which one was the son of Lord William. So had his father looked at her a hundred, nay, a thousand times, before he erupted into rage.

Disappointment, sharp and unexpected, stabbed at her. For a moment, her heart had leapt with an excitement she'd never felt before, but she could guess what it was. Merrick had become an impressive-looking warrior, and for that while, it had seemed she was looking at a man she could respect and possibly even admire— until those cold, dark eyes told her otherwise.

She glanced at the sober crowd watching. Did they see his brutal, lascivious father in his son's unwavering gaze and stern brow? Did they fear that he would be as harsh and greedy an overlord?

"Merrick, my boy…or I should say, my lord!" Lord Algernon cried, breaking the silence as he trotted down the steps, his stomach bouncing with every step. "Welcome! Welcome to Tregellas! How wonderful to see you again after all these years!"

Merrick stopped looking at Constance to regard his uncle with that same unwavering, unsmiling gaze.

Lord Algernon came to an embarrassed halt. "Surely you remember me, my boy…my lord. I'm your uncle, Algernon."

That brought the merest glimmer of a smile to the stony visage. "Yes, Uncle, I remember you."

Constance had never heard such a voice. It was husky and deep, and although he seemed to speak quietly, she didn't doubt that everyone in the courtyard had heard him.

Lord Carrell likewise hurried forward, albeit with more dignity. "I hope you remember me, my lord. I'm Lord Carrell de Marmont, your neighbor and Constance's uncle. Of course I would know you anywhere. You have the look of your father about you."

"Do I?"

Constance had had long practice studying a man's face for any hint of emotion, to better gauge what she should do. Never had she found a man more difficult to decipher, yet even Merrick's gaze wasn't impossible to read. Whatever else he was thinking upon his return, he was not flattered by the comparison to his late father.

Her uncle turned to Constance and held out his hand. "I trust you also remember your betrothed, Lady Constance, although of course she's changed."

"So I see," Merrick agreed as Constance approached, and in the depths of his eyes something seemed to kindle—a spark of recognition? Or a spark of…something else?

She knew she was a comely woman. She'd seen men watch her when she danced and leer at her when they thought she couldn't see. She knew what lust looked like. Was he his father's son *that* way, as well? If so, and betrothed or not, she would stay as far away from him as possible.

Yet his expression was different, too. The desire was tempered, restrained. Held in check, like the rest of his powerful body as he stood motionless in the yard.

Merrick put his hands on her shoulders and drew her close to exchange the kiss of peace. She steeled herself to feel nothing, and to betray nothing, either in look or word.

"I remember you, too, my lord," she said evenly as she moved back.

Surprise flared briefly. "You were very young when I left here."

"Not so young that I don't remember you and some of your... antics."

His brow furrowed slightly, as if he was trying to remember. "You must forgive me, my lady, if I have forgotten happier times. Much has happened to me since I last saw you."

She thought of the attack upon his cortege, and a tinge of guilt crept over her. Yet much had happened to her, too, and she would never forget Merrick's merciless teasing and pinches and the cruel tricks he'd played on the servants.

Merrick turned to the foxlike knight. "This is my friend and sworn comrade, Sir Ranulf." He nodded at the knight in scarlet. "This other fellow is also my friend and sworn comrade, Sir Henry."

"They are most welcome, too," Constance said with a bow.

Sir Henry stepped toward Beatrice, whose face turned nearly as red as his surcoat when he gave her one of the most disarming smiles Constance had ever seen. "And who is this lovely young lady?"

"That is my daughter, Lady Beatrice," Lord Carrell said stiffly.

"And she is *my* cousin," Constance added, a note of warning in her voice. Beatrice was young and had a head full of romance; Sir Henry was handsome and flattering.

"Then I am even more delighted to meet her," Sir Henry said.

Constance caught the look that passed between Merrick and his other friend—a sort of patient forbearance. So this Sir Henry *was* the sort who enjoyed charming women. She would warn Beatrice, and the maidservants, too. "I was expecting you to have more of an escort, my lord," she said, loud enough to draw the attention of everyone nearby, including Sir Henry.

"There was no need," Merrick replied. "I regret I neglected to inform you, but I had other things on my mind."

Although she wasn't sure if he was alluding to their marriage—and everything that went with it—Constance felt the heat of a blush steal up her face and tried to will it away. "What of your baggage, my lord?"

"A carter is bringing it."

"Shall we retire, nephew?" Lord Algernon asked, a bead of perspiration running down his plump cheek. "We have some fine Bordeaux wine awaiting in the hall."

"A most welcome suggestion," Merrick replied before turning to Constance. "I shall lead the way into my hall with my bride-to-be by my side, if she will allow me that honor."

Since she had no choice, Constance lifted her hand and lightly put it on Merrick's muscular forearm.

Which was as hard as iron.

An unexpected flutter of heat spread through her body, but she fought to ignore the sensation. So what if he was strong and well built? Had his father not been handsome in his day? Yet look how he had ended. She must not, she would not, tie herself to a man who might turn out the same.

When the group reached the dais, she immediately lifted her hand from her betrothed's arm.

Merrick didn't seem to notice. Instead, he addressed Lord Algernon. "Is there not somewhere more private? I prefer not to discuss my estate and my wedding where any servant or foot soldier may overhear."

His wedding. So he did plan to honor the betrothal agreement. So much for the hope that he would wish to be free of her. She would have to implement her scheme to win her freedom, and the sooner, the better.

"The solar, perhaps?" Lord Algernon suggested.

Merrick turned to his friends. "I leave you in Lady Constance's care."

She would have to be careful not to go too far, but

she wouldn't wait to begin her campaign for liberty. She would start now. "If you're going to talk about our wedding, I should come to the solar, too, should I not? After all, I *am* the bride."

At Constance's determined pronouncement, her uncle stared at her in amazement, while Lord Algernon gaped with undisguised disbelief.

In spite of their obvious surprise, the lord of Tregellas merely raised a coolly inquisitive brow. "As you wish. Lady Beatrice, will you be so good as to take charge of my friends?"

Beatrice blushed to the roots of her honey-blond hair. "Yes, o-of course, my lord," she whispered as if she were afraid to speak any louder, while Sir Henry smiled as if he'd just been given a present.

Yes, he would bear watching, and Beatrice, too. Constance loved her cousin, and didn't want Beatrice's heart broken—or worse, for Beatrice to be dishonored by a charming seducer her betrothed had brought into their midst.

Merrick paused in his progress toward the steps and glanced back over his shoulder. "Well, my lady, will you join us or not?"

Despite his imperious tone, she made no effort to rush as she followed the new lord of Tregellas.

Who seemed to be very much his father's son after all.

CHAPTER TWO

MAKING SURE NO PART OF HER came into contact with Merrick as he waited by the door, Constance followed the uncles into the solar, the small chamber Lord William had used for his private business.

As in the hall, expensive and colorful tapestries lined the walls to keep out the chill. A massive trestle table, pitted and scared from Lord William's blows and missiles, stood near the window. A wooden, bossed chest holding all the various parchments detailing the tenants and the tithes rested in the corner. There Merrick would also find a copy of his father's will, a document that had elicited many a raving tantrum before it had finally been completed to Lord William's satisfaction.

The lord's chair—a huge, heavy thing of carved oak with a cushioned seat—was behind the table. The only other seats were stools, set against the wall, and rarely used in Lord William's time. He preferred to have those brought before him standing like humble petitioners, no matter what their rank or worth.

"We hear you've been to court many times, my lord," Lord Carrell began as they arranged themselves like a

line of soldiers about to be inspected. "You must ha
met the king and queen, for which I envy you. Tell me
what do you think of our young ruler?"

Merrick didn't go around the table and take his seat,
as she expected. Instead, he stood in front of it and
crossed his muscular arms, regarding them steadily.
"King Henry is my sovereign lord."

"Your liege lord, the earl of Cornwall, often disagrees
with his brother the king," Lord Carrell replied. "Indeed,
we hear many barons fear King Henry is too much influenced by his French wife."

The corners of Merrick's full lips curved downward
in a frown. "Whatever the king does or does not do is
not for me to question, and how he comes to his decisions is not for me to ponder."

Merrick was obviously the sort of nobleman who
was loyal no matter what the king did, even if Henry and
his French queen were leading the country down the
road to rebellion.

And if Merrick, like most noblemen, believed a
woman's place was confined solely to the hearth and
home and children, her observations on the political situation, as well as her suggestions as to how he should
deal with the earl and the king, would surely be unwelcome. So she blithely began to tell her intended husband
exactly what she thought.

"From what I understand of the court, there's a great
deal of conflict between the English barons and the relatives of the queen. The king seems to be making a ter-

...he mistake giving Queen Eleanor's relatives so much ...ower. As for her insisting that her uncle be made Archbishop of Canterbury, is there a more ambitious, greedy candidate? If that man is holy, I'm a nun. Thank heavens he has yet to be confirmed because the pope is in such difficulty. Now we hear the earl of Cornwall might marry Eleanor's sister. No doubt the queen seeks to bind him closer to prevent him from leading a rebellion, since there are many who would prefer him to his brother when it comes to commanding the kingdom. After all, it's because of Richard's diplomacy that Henry is free after his failed campaign to win back lands in France. And then there's the matter of Simon de Montfort's marriage to the king's sister. Is it true de Montfort seduced her, or is that just gossip?"

She felt the uncles' gaze upon her, but she ignored them and continued to look at Merrick, her brows raised in query. "What if Henry does something stupid again and the earl doesn't rescue him? What if Richard finally turns against him?"

Merrick straightened, lowered his arms and regarded her sternly. "You speak of rebellion and treason, my lady. I will have no such talk, or even the suggestion of it, for any reason, in Tregellas while I command here. *If* the earl of Cornwall rebels against his brother, *if* this country is torn apart by civil war, *then* I shall choose which side to support, and not before."

A vein in his temple began to throb, just as his father's had before an enraged outburst. Having already endured enough fits of temper to last a lifetime, and realizing she'd achieved a certain measure of success, Constance changed the subject. "Perhaps we should discuss the wedding."

"Very well," Merrick said, nodding his agreement. His features relaxed a fraction, enough to tell her he preferred this subject to politics, or at least her political opinions. "I wish to be married within the week."

If he'd grabbed her and bitten her, she couldn't have been more shocked. How could she make him hate her enough to break the betrothal in that short a time? "That's impossible!"

Merrick merely arched his straight black brows. "Why? You knew we were betrothed, did you not? And that I was to marry you as soon as I inherited the title, if not before. I see no reason to delay."

"I do," she retorted, her dismay turning swiftly into indignation. "We need time to prepare food for the feast—"

"The larders are well stocked," her uncle interrupted. "Indeed, Constance, if Merrick is eager—"

She was anything but eager. "What about our guests? It will take at least a month to invite them, gather responses and prepare accommodations."

"The only guests I care to have at my wedding are already here."

"And then there are the wedding clothes..."

Merrick's dark gaze impaled her. "It wouldn't matter to me if you were married in your shift."

Her breath caught for an instant—but only that. "It would matter a great deal to *me,* my lord," she declared. "After being delayed for so long, I expect my wedding to be worth the wait."

"I hope to make it so, my lady."

Even though she was as incensed as she'd ever been, when he said those words in that low, husky voice, an unwelcome frisson of heated excitement flowed through her traitorous body. But she snuffed it out quickly. This whole discussion was proving that he was still the same selfish, spoiled brat, concerned only about his own needs and desires.

Therefore, she would give him a selfish need, if that was what he required. "Such celebrations are useful for creating alliances. Our wedding could be a valuable opportunity."

"I wasn't thinking of my marriage as a political opportunity."

Only a financial one, she supposed. Why else would he be in such a hurry? If he were truly chivalrous, if he cared at all about her feelings, he would have asked *her* when the ceremony should be.

"I believe she's right, nephew," Lord Algernon seconded, albeit warily. "Perhaps it would be best to move more slowly."

Constance could have kissed him. "Yes, my lord. I would rather not have our wedding marred by accusations of scandalous and undue haste."

Merrick's gaze flicked to the other noblemen. "If

you will excuse us, my lords, I would have some words with my betrothed. Alone."

Alone? Was he mad? Or that sure of his power?

Her uncle and Lord Algernon exchanged brief looks, then bowed a farewell and hurried out the door. So much for their help, she thought sourly. But she had stood alone before a powerful, arrogant man before, and she wouldn't give in now, not when her freedom was at stake.

"It isn't right for us to be alone together before we are married," she declared, heading after the noblemen. "This is most improper."

The lord of Tregellas moved to stand in her way with surprising, and surprisingly lithe, speed.

"My lord, you may not care about my reputation," Constance said through clenched teeth as she glared at the man in front of her, "but I do and—"

"I promise you nothing improper will occur, and unless *you* give me cause, any man or woman who dares imply that your reputation is less than spotless will have to answer to *me*."

The sheer forcefulness of Merrick's response stunned and silenced her.

He reached for one of the stools along the wall and swung it forward as if it weighed no more than a feather, placing it in front of the table. "Please sit down, my lady."

She crossed her arms. "I prefer to stand, my lord."

"Very well." Merrick mercifully stayed where he was. "Do you have some objections to the marriage itself, my lady? If so, I would hear them."

He spoke so coldly and so severely, she was absolutely certain he would demand her dowry in forfeit if she refused to marry him. "No, my lord," she lied. "But I would rather not marry so quickly. After all, it's been fifteen years. We barely know one another."

To her surprise, his features relaxed a little. "Forgive me, Constance. My suggestion came from my great joy at being home and here with you again. I left a pretty little girl, and I've come home to find a beautiful, intelligent woman."

Was she supposed to be flattered? "Perhaps if you'd come home even once in fifteen years, my appearance and the fact that I'm not a silly fool wouldn't be so unexpected."

He stiffened and the little vein in his temple started to throb again.

Good, but she must go carefully.

Yet instead of flying into a fury, Merrick merely shrugged his broad shoulders. "My father made no effort to see me, so I made none to see him."

What of his betrothed? Had he ever once thought of her until his father died? "He was still your father. As his son, your duty—"

"Don't!" Merrick snapped.

His dark eyes narrowed and his lips thinned. "Do not *ever* try to tell me about my duty, my lady," he warned, his voice low and rough. "Do you think my presence here would have made any difference? Do you honestly believe I could have influenced my father, or made his last days better? I more likely would have killed him."

Constance could only stare at him, aghast, as she realized he meant what he said. She'd known there was little love between father and son, but she hadn't expected so much naked hate.

Merrick raked his hand through his long dark hair. "I gather my vassals and tenants weren't eager to see my father's son return."

As it had so often, her concern for those under the lord of Tregellas's power arose within her and subdued any thoughts of her own troubles. "They're understandably wary, my lord. After all, they haven't seen you in years and have no idea what kind of overlord you'll be."

"As you, having known my father, are no doubt wondering what sort of husband I'll make, and likely fearing the worst. I shouldn't be surprised that you asked for more time before the ceremony."

She nearly choked. What was he, some kind of seer or mind reader? Or had she been too obvious?

"Did my father…" He hesitated for the briefest of moments before continuing. "Did my father ever lay hands on you?"

It would have been no thanks to her absent betrothed if he had. "My dowry was apparently worth more to him than my maidenhead."

Merrick winced at her blunt words.

"That was the sort of man your father was, my lord,"

she said without regret for causing him pain. She'd suffered often enough while he was God knew where.

Merrick regarded her steadily and spoke with what sounded like completely sincere conviction. "I know about my father's sinful nature. I vowed long ago that I would never treat any woman, whether high born or low, as he did. As long as I am lord here, no woman need fear death or dishonor at my hands, or be afraid of me." His voice dropped to a low, husky whisper. "As for my wife, I will be faithful to her until my death. I will honor, respect and cherish her. She need never fear violence or degradation at my hands."

Constance took a wary step back. Against his stern arrogance she was proof. Against his haughty orders, his firm commands, even his anger, she could defend herself, but this… She had no defense against such words, especially spoken by a man who looked at her thus, and whose voice was low and rough, but unexpectedly gentle, too.

And to speak of respect, the thing she craved most except for love…

She had to get away from him and his deep voice and intense dark eyes and the powerful body that made her remember things she'd heard the maids whisper about, concerning men and pleasure and secret delights shared in the dark.

"Since you wish to wait a month, so be it."

Constance came out of her reverie and told herself she was sorry she hadn't asked for six.

Merrick walked around the table and finally sat in the lord's chair. "There's an old man who lives at the edge of a village in a cottage that looks like a tumbled-down mess of stones. He spit at the ground when I rode by. Who is he?"

Despite her pleasure at the delay of their wedding, a shiver of dread went down her spine. Perhaps Merrick's concession was intended to soften her, to make her malleable and pliable, as if she were a simpleton easily duped. Maybe now he thought she'd tell him everything she knew, about everyone in Tregellas.

Being born and bred in Cornwall, he would be aware of the smuggling that had been taking place along this coast for centuries. Being a loyal follower of the king, he would probably seek to enforce the laws against it.

Well, kings and lords before him had tried to stop the smuggling, to no avail. Let him try—without her assistance.

She took her time as she lowered herself onto the stool and regarded him with calm rectitude. "I suppose you mean Peder, my lord."

She was fairly certain it was Peder he spoke of. The old man had been a tinner and smuggler since before Constance was born, and he hated the late lord of Tregellas passionately and with good reason, as she sought to make clear to Wicked William's son. "You may remember his daughter, Tamsyn, and the son she bore after she was beaten and raped, although likely the whispers that her attacker was your father were kept from you."

Was that a flicker of dismay in his eyes? Even if it was, she would feel no sympathy for him. She would make him understand why his people hated and feared his father, and why they were ready to hate and fear him, too.

"If that's true, I can see why Peder would loathe my father and be less than pleased by the return of his heir," he replied. "Is there proof that the child was my father's?"

"No one who knew your father and saw Bredon doubted it, my lord. The resemblance was too marked."

"Are the woman and her son still here?"

She wondered what Merrick would do if his sibling were still alive, but it didn't matter. "Bredon drowned in the river just after you left Tregellas. Sick with grief, Tamsyn hung herself. Peder found her in their cottage."

An emotion she couldn't quite decipher flashed quickly across Merrick's face, and was just as quickly gone. Was it sympathy, or relief?

Merrick rose and came around the table. "Did my father sire other bastards?"

"No, my lord," she replied, "despite his efforts. He had only two children, you and Tamsyn's son."

"I've never sired any bastards, at least none that their mothers have made known to me."

Was she supposed to be thrilled by that? "I didn't expect you to be a virgin." She got to her feet. "Now, my lord, I hope you'll give me leave to go. I'd rather not discuss your past liaisons, however fascinating they may be to you."

"There is just one thing more."

She opened her mouth, but whether to simply take a breath or ask a question, she could never recall, because before she knew what was happening, Merrick tugged her into his arms and captured her mouth with his.

For a moment she was too stunned to feel anything except surprise. Then she was simply, completely, overwhelmed.

Never, even in her most lustful daydreams, had she imagined *this*. The taste of him. The scent of man and leather, horse and salt air in her nostrils. The sensation of his strong arms about her, holding her close, steadying her when her own legs were suddenly without strength. Then his tongue lightly, insistently pushed against her lips, seeking entry.

This could not be right, because no matter how good it felt, this man kissing her was Merrick, Wicked William's son.

She struggled to break free. "I'm an honorable woman!"

"You're my betrothed," he replied as he let her go and stepped back. "There's no harm in a kiss."

There was if she didn't want to marry him "Betrothed or not, I didn't give you leave to kiss me!"

"Then I humbly beg your forgiveness, my lady," he calmly replied, bowing like the most chivalrous of knights.

He looked about to smile and his eyes seemed to glitter with…she didn't care what. "There is nothing *humble* about you, my lord, and I beg you not to touch me again unless I give you leave."

The little half smile melted away, and his expression settled into an impassive mask. "As you wish, my lady—*until* you give me leave."

Of all the vain, arrogant, impudent—! She turned on her heel and marched from the room, slamming the door behind her.

AFTER SHE WAS GONE, MERRICK ran his hand through his hair and walked to the window that overlooked the courtyard of Tregellas.

He wasn't that frightened little boy hiding in the woods anymore. He was the lord and master of this castle. He was the commander and overlord of Tregellas. His father was dead, and he had come home, back to where he used to know every path and field. Where he loved to stand on the shore, the rivulets of water running between his toes. When he was a boy, and things were so much simpler.

He shouldn't have kissed Constance, or suggested that they wed so quickly. He should have shown more restraint, acted with more fitting decorum.

But how could he, when the moment he'd seen her, that same ache of yearning had torn through him? Yes, he'd been but a boy when he'd left here, but he had never forgotten her. He had loved her then with all the affection of his boyish heart, and he loved her still, but not as a boy—as a man desires a woman, to cherish, to protect, to take to his bed. Yet he still felt like an awkward lad in her presence, not a knight of some fame who'd had women vying for his favors only a few short weeks ago.

He had never been a charming courtier like Henry. He could never think of the things that rolled so easily from Henry's tongue, and he was sure he would sound like a fool if he tried.

How did Constance really feel about him? Part of her desired him, of that he was certain. If she truly disliked or feared him, she would never have kissed him as she had, arousing such desire and hope.

Yet Constance's lust alone would not satisfy him. He wanted more from her—much more. He wanted her love. Without it, if she ever learned the truth about him, she might come to hate him—a thought that filled him with worse pain than any physical wound. It would be better to let her go rather than see hate and loathing appear in her eyes, the way it did when she spoke of his father.

But he'd discovered that he lacked the strength to give her liberty. He couldn't bear to abandon the hope that she could come to love him.

Deep in his heart, he knew it wasn't his natural reticence or his serious nature that was keeping him from proclaiming his feelings for her. It was the fear that by wedding her, he would be wronging her.

He kept trying to convince himself that if he ruled wisely and fairly, if he loved and treated her well, his past didn't matter. But his great misdeed was like a black shadow between them—a shadow of lies, of deceit, of death and pain and fear. His sin haunted him, except when his mind and body were fully occupied, such as when he fought in a tournament or played a game of foot ball. Or kissed his beloved Constance, who'd been the bright angel of even his darkest, loneliest days.

If he were truly a good and honorable man, he would confess his crime, and risk losing her.

Since he was not, he would keep his secret, as he had for fifteen years. He would tell no one, including Constance, what he'd done. Only he need know, and suffer for it.

As Constance was doing her best to discourage Merrick, Lord Carrell made his way to a secluded corner of the courtyard, followed by Lord Algernon. Algernon was so agitated, a private conversation seemed the best way to calm him down.

"What were you thinking, asking him about Henry and the queen as soon as we entered the solar?" Algernon whined as they came to a halt in the shadow of the wall walk.

Carrell pulled a small chunk off the nearest block of stone and rubbed it between his fingers as he shrugged. "Why wait to find out where he stands? Better to know before we say something to make him doubt our loyalty to the king. Now we know that we mustn't give him any reason to suspect we aren't as loyal as he is."

"And *I* say you should have waited. You could ruin our plans if you aren't patient."

"Patient?" Carrell sniffed, tossing the stone aside.

"God's blood, man, you don't have to tell *me* to be patient. I've been patient for fifteen years."

"I've been waiting for longer than that to get what I deserve," Algernon complained, "and I don't want to lose it because you have to push yourself forward and ask a lot of questions."

"If you'd taken the trouble to visit your nephew on occasion, I wouldn't have had to ask," Carrell retorted. "We'd have already known that he's loyal to the king."

"If I'd tried to see him, what do you think my detestable brother would have done?" Algernon grumbled. "He'd have assumed we were conspiring against him and had me killed."

"Not if you killed him first."

Algernon gave Carrell an incredulous look. "How could I have done it, with those guards of his? He didn't even leave his castle most of the time."

"Yes, it would have been very difficult," Carrell agreed, his tone appeasing.

It was a pity William's other brother had been sent north with Merrick and killed instead of this one. Egbert had been a far more ruthless fellow, especially where his own interests were concerned. Algernon was a greedy, weak, stupid man, although he had his uses, for now.

Algernon moved closer and, after surreptitiously ensuring that no one could overhear, lowered his voice and asked, "Have you had news from London? Any word of when the king or his brother will return to England?"

Carrell shook his head. "No news. The queen and her

husband are enjoying Bordeaux too much to be in any hurry to return to England and face their disgruntled nobles. I believe the earl of Cornwall has his reasons for staying with them."

"To keep Henry from making any more unwise decisions," Algernon agreed.

"To spend more time with the queen's sister," Carrell replied with a smirk. "Now that Richard's wife is dead, he needs another, and Eleanor's sister is a beauty, and pliable. You can be sure Eleanor will be doing all she can to promote a marriage between them. Richard's the only person who can influence her husband as much as she, and he's got the support of far more nobles. To her, he's a rival, and must be neutralized. How better than to have him wed her sister?"

"God save us from that woman," Algernon muttered. "She'll be the ruin of England."

"Which is why the king must be overthrown, and his brother, the earl of Cornwall, too, if it comes to that. But we'll let Merrick be lulled into believing all is well. Indeed, let's hope my niece can keep him so busy with lovemaking, he grows lazy and lax, and lowers his guard. Then it'll be easier to kill him."

"What about Constance? You assured me she was in favor of the marriage, but she certainly didn't sound like it today. I've never heard her speak in such an impudent manner."

Carrell fingered the jeweled hilt of the dagger stuck in his belt. "Of course she'll marry him."

"How can you be so certain? Have you ever before heard her speak to any man that way? I nearly swooned, she was so impertinent."

Carrell frowned. "Of course she'll marry him, for the people's sake if not her own. You've seen how she dotes on them. She was always like that, from a child. Any dead puppy or kitten would have her in tears for a day." His tone made it clear he considered this a great failing on her part, yet it was one he would happily exploit if it helped achieve his ends. "Leaving her here with your brother was one of my more clever moves. This is her home now, and these peasants are like her family. She'll never desert them, especially if she fears they'll come to harm under their overlord."

Carrell's frown became a smirk. "Even if she had any reservations, can you doubt that they were likely done away with the moment she saw him? What woman wouldn't be tempted to share your nephew's bed? If he didn't have the look of your brother in his face, I'd swear he'd been sired by Zeus. No wonder he's won all those tournaments. I was sure he'd paid off the other knights for the privilege until I saw him ride in."

"Constance is made of sterner stuff and not likely to be ruled by lust," Algernon said doubtfully.

A gleam of unhealthy curiosity sparkled in Carrell's blue eyes. "Knowing your brother for the lascivious scoundrel he was, do you think there was ever anything of *that* sort between them?"

"God's wounds, no," Algernon retorted, "and I would

have known if there was. William wouldn't have been able to keep from bragging about it." His features made no secret of his scorn. "I got to hear about every conquest he ever made, in disgusting detail, from the time he was twelve years old."

"I suppose that's just as well," Carrell said. "I don't think Merrick would care to wed his father's mistress."

"Not the Merrick we just met, anyway," Algernon agreed.

He looked away, out into the courtyard toward the stables. "Must we kill Constance?"

"If Constance is not dead, the king may decide to marry her to someone else, and Tregellas will be out of your reach. Merrick and his wife must both die if you're to inherit. And then you'll marry Beatrice, joining our families and our power as we've planned all these years. We're allies, Algernon. I don't forget that, and I hope you won't."

"No," his companion assured him. "I'll abide by our plans."

"Good. Now we should go back to the hall before our absence is noticed. And don't worry. Soon enough, you'll have Tregellas, and my daughter."

CHAPTER THREE

A FEW DAYS LATER, CONSTANCE and Alan de Vern stood in the buttery adjacent to the kitchen, looking over the wine that had arrived before a storm blew in from the ocean. Straw covered the floor of the chamber to catch any spills, and bits of chaff floated in the air. Over the years, spiders had created a vast array of cobwebs in the seams between the walls and the vaulted ceiling of the chilly chamber. At the moment, raindrops beat against the stone walls as if they were demanding entrance.

"Lord Merrick says we must have the best wine for your wedding feast," Alan said, his accent marking him as a native of Paris. "Wine from Bordeaux for the entire company in the hall, even those below the salt, and plenty of ale for the village."

"That will cost a small fortune!" Constance exclaimed, rubbing her hands together for warmth.

It would also make a very fine show of generosity, she added in her thoughts. Just as that kiss had surely been a demonstration of his vain belief that he could overwhelm her with his manly…masculinity. But he'd simply caught her by surprise; otherwise, she would have slapped his face.

She *should* have slapped his face.

"It is quite expensive," Alan agreed. "But he told me he had done well in his last tournament. He also said exactly how much I was to offer at first, and how much I was to spend altogether. Fortunately, the merchant settled for less than we expected." The steward grinned. "Lord Merrick has a head for figures. I doubt he'll ever spend as recklessly as his father."

"I hope not," Constance replied, thinking of all the times she'd heard Lord William screaming at Alan and the bailiff about money.

"Gaston is delighted with the menu for the wedding feast, too. A true chance to show his skill, he claims. Mind you, his first proposals were too extravagant by far, until Lord Merrick managed to get him to be reasonable. To hear Gaston tell it, they debated for hours."

"Lord Merrick *debated*?"

In answer to her incredulous response, Alan gave her a wry smile as he crooked his elbow and leaned against one of the large butts of ale. "I think we can both guess how it went. Gaston made his suggestions, Lord Merrick shook his head, Gaston made more suggestions, Lord Merrick shook his head, Gaston was finally reasonable, and Lord Merrick nodded his head."

Constance had to smile at that probably accurate description. "Yes, I daresay you're right."

Alan's gaze wandered to the shelf holding smaller

casks of English wine across the room. "A lady could do much worse for a husband than Lord Merrick," he reflected.

Although Alan was a trusted friend, and she'd often turned to him when there was trouble with the tenants, Constance wasn't about to share her innermost feelings with him. And a man who impressed a steward wouldn't necessarily be a good husband, even if he'd also apparently impressed the garrison commander, the soldiers and the servants in the time since he'd arrived.

"What of the fodder for the wedding guests' horses?" she asked, trying not to shiver.

"Well in hand, my lady," Alan said. "All we've invited have already sent notice they'll attend."

She hadn't expected their potential guests to respond so swiftly. "Including Sir Jowan and his son?"

"Yes, my lady. I believe they plan to visit before the wedding, too, to pay their respects to the new overlord of Tregellas."

"They haven't far to come," Constance replied, keeping any hint of dismay from her voice, although the last thing she needed or wanted was the distraction of Sir Jowan's son.

Beatrice burst into the buttery as if propelled by a gust of wind. She skittered to a halt in a most unladylike way, her face flushed and her eyes bright with excitement. "Demelza said I'd find you here. Have you heard? Lord Merrick has decided there should be a foot ball game as part of the celebrations for May Day.

The garrison against the men of the village. Sir Henry says the garrison is sure to win, but I told him not to be so confident. Some of the villagers are very good. He said Merrick was going to choose a Queen of the May, too."

He was going to—*what?*

As Constance and Alan exchanged shocked and dismayed looks, Beatrice frowned, her enthusiasm somewhat dimmed. "What's wrong?"

How was she going to tell Beatrice the reason for their horror at this news? Her cousin wasn't ignorant of some of Wicked William's abuses; nobody who lived within fifty miles of Tregellas could be. But she'd always tried to shield Beatrice from the worst.

"I'm sure he'll pick you for the Queen of the May, Constance," Beatrice ventured, as if Constance's silence was based on a worry far different from the one she was actually experiencing. "After all, he's going to marry you."

"It's not that," Constance replied. She searched for an explanation that wouldn't require her to go into sickening detail. "Being a new-made lord, Merrick probably doesn't appreciate all the complications that may arise from such events. I shall have to enlighten him. Right away. Good day, Alan. Until later, Beatrice," she finished as she hurried to the door.

She carried on quickly through the kitchen, nodding briefly to Gaston and the busy servants, then through the corridor to the hall, where she looked for Merrick. At least—since she wanted him to hate her—she need not couch her words with care. That held some danger, too, but she was on her guard now. Just let him try to kiss her!

Servants trimmed the torches and added wood to the hearth. Sir Henry and Sir Ranulf were playing chess, Sir Ranulf studying the board with care while Sir Henry laughed and said something about making a move before night fell. The uncles, deep in discussion, sat near the central hearth.

Merrick wasn't there.

She didn't want to ask anyone where Merrick was; Lord Algernon would smirk as he had lately taken to doing, her uncle would ask her why she wanted to know, and his friends would regard her with that unnerving curiosity.

The bailiff came scuttling down the steps from the solar. He looked even more pale than usual and licked his lips as if he wanted a drink.

"Ruan!"

He checked his steps and then, smiling in that obsequious way that he had, rushed toward her.

Everything about the man reminded her of a crawling, slimy thing—his pale skin, as if he'd just climbed out from under a rotting piece of wood; the way he stood with his head thrust forward as if he was either about to bow or just rising from one; his clasped hands that would have done credit to a shy maiden; the pleading tone of his voice, as if every utterance was made with regret and against his better judgment; and especially the shrewd gleam in his watery blue eyes that, in spite of his posture and manner, betrayed a clever and, she was sure, devious mind. "Is Lord Merrick in his solar?"

"Yes, my lady."

"Has he told you of his plans for May Day?"

Ruan's eyes shone with curiosity. "Yes, my lady. Didn't he tell you?"

A blush heated her face. "How do you think the villagers will take the news?" she asked, not answering his question.

Ruan frowned and ran his hand over his moist lips. "I think they'll be wondering if they've got to hide farther back in the woods when he chooses the Queen of the May."

That was what Constance was thinking, too.

"I'm sure he'll want to please you, my lady," Ruan said quietly, and in a way that seemed to imply all manner of unsavory things. "If you tell him—"

"Good day, Ruan," she interrupted, turning toward the stairs to the solar.

"Good day, my lady," he muttered under his breath as he watched the beautiful, haughty lady hurry on her way.

They thought themselves so fine and clever, all these lords and ladies.

Well, he was clever, too.

CONSTANCE RAPPED SHARPLY on the heavy wooden door to the solar, then entered without waiting for Merrick to answer. "I understand you have made certain plans for May Day."

The lord of Tregellas sat at the trestle table, which was now covered with scrolls. As the wind howled outside the walls, the tapestries swayed in the draught that made its way through the linen shutters that couldn't keep out the rain. Droplets ran along a jagged path across the sill, then trickled down the wall to puddle on the floor.

"I have," he said gruffly as he raised his head to look at her. The flame of the plump tallow candle on the table flickered, altering the shadows on his face. The planes of his cheeks. His brown eyes, so dark they were nearly black.

She took a step back, then berated herself for acting like an addlepated ninny. The lord of Tregellas was, after all, just a man.

He gestured at the stool in front of the table that Ruan had likely just vacated. "Will you sit, my lady?"

This might take some time, so perhaps she should. As gracefully as she could, Constance lowered herself onto the stool and arranged her skirts. "You should have consulted with Alan de Vern or me."

His hands resting on the table before him, Merrick leaned back in his chair and regarded her steadily. "Why? I remembered such activities from my boyhood here and assumed they still continued."

"There have been some changes since your boyhood, my lord."

He ran a swift gaze over her. "Yes, so I've noticed."

She frowned. "My lord, this is a very serious matter, and you'd do well to listen to me."

Furrows of concern appeared between his brows. "Very well, my lady. Explain what has changed."

How could she possibly make him understand? she wondered as a blast of wind sent another barrage of rain against the tower walls. The tapestry nearest her billowed, as if someone was hiding behind it, although that was impossible. There was no room; she'd supervised the hanging of it herself.

Nevertheless, she shivered and wrapped her arms about herself as she began to explain why there should be no competition between the villagers and the garrison, and especially why he should have nothing whatsoever to do with the Queen of the May. "The men of the garrison are hardened soldiers and they can be brutal when their blood is up. That may serve you well in battle, but can lead to trouble during such sport. The last time there was a foot ball game between the garrison and the villagers, the smith's son was nearly killed by one of your father's bodyguards."

Merrick wordlessly rose and brought the brazier full of glowing coals closer to her chair. She was grateful for the added warmth, and as he moved, she tried not to notice the lithe, athletic grace of his actions, or the power of those broad shoulders and the arms that lifted the heavy iron brazier as easily as another man would a slender branch.

When he went to the small side table that bore a silver carafe of wine and some goblets, her gaze traveled to his equally powerful thighs encased in snug woolen breeches, and his muscular calves.

"Wine, my lady?"

Blushing like a silly girl caught ogling a soldier or servant, she looked quickly up at his face, then away to hide her foolish reaction. "No, thank you."

He poured himself some wine before strolling back toward the table, bringing the goblet with him. "Such activity is good for my men. It encourages camaraderie between them, and given what I remember of the games in my boyhood, should ensure a healthy respect for the abilities of the villagers—whose blood, I believe, is just as swift to rise. I recall they were fierce competitors. Has that changed?"

She hesitated to answer, because he was right. If the young Eric hadn't been so keen to get the inflated pig's bladder through the sticks at the west end of the village, he wouldn't have collided with that mercenary and subsequently been struck so hard that he'd been knocked cold.

"Well?" Merrick prompted.

"I think they *will* give your men a battle—which is just what I'm afraid of. This 'sport' could turn into a riot."

"I won't allow that to happen."

If ever there was a man capable of holding off a riot single-handedly, she was looking at him. But she wouldn't grant him that concession. "If you're able."

Merrick gave her the closest thing to a genuine smile she had yet seen. "I think between Henry, Ranulf and myself, we can control my men, especially if they're tired from running after a ball. That's another reason I would have the game. It will weary my men and prevent them from expending their energy in more harmful ways during the festivities."

She hadn't considered that. But she wasn't willing to yield. "And it'll make them thirsty, too. We could have a gang of drunken soldiers wreaking havoc in the village."

"If that happens, they'll be severely punished. I also intend to provide meat for the villagers' feast, as well as ale. And I shall give my assurance that if any of my men cause serious harm or injury, or damage any property, the injured or aggrieved parties will be amply compensated."

This was more generous than most lords, and far, far more generous than his father had ever been.

Perhaps he was trying to buy the villagers' approval. If so, he was going to fail. The folk of the Cornish coast were far too independent to be purchased.

"I have another reason," he said, taking a sip of wine before setting the goblet on the table behind him. "Such competitions also keep the soldiers fit for battle or long marches."

She still wasn't willing to concede. "Whatever your reasons, my lord, this may create more trouble than you can foresee, and whoever wins, I doubt the villagers are going to be any more inclined to look on your soldiers favorably."

"If my people are honest, they'll never have anything to fear from my soldiers. If one of my men commits a crime, during May Day or any other time, he will be punished to the full extent of the law," Merrick said as he walked around the table.

As before, he sounded sincere...or else he was very good at pretending to be.

He made no move to sit. He stood tall and imposing, like a judge. Or a king.

"Although I hope to be merciful," Merrick continued, his expression stern and his voice grim, "I won't allow my people to flout the king's laws. Smuggling, for instance. I'll punish any smugglers I capture and confiscate their contraband for the king."

How like his father he sounded then! Except for the part about mercy. And the contraband. Wicked William had never made any pretense to be merciful, and he would have kept any contraband for himself.

"If they smuggle, my lord, it's because they feel justified in avoiding a harsh and unfair tax," she explained, taking the people's part as she had so many times before. "Cornish tinners are taxed at twice the rate of those from Devonshire, for the foolish reason that Cornishmen speak a different language. Therefore, according to the clever minds in Westminster, Cornwall must be a foreign country. But if it were a foreign country, the king would have no right to collect taxes at all. I ask you, is that fair? Is that just? Is it any wonder the men who dig the tin from the ground believe they have every right to hide some of their profits from the crown?"

Merrick was obviously unmoved. "The tinners pay no tithes, they are exempt from serving in my army, they have their own courts—far more rights than most. Would they agree to give up those rights, and cease smuggling, if the king reduced their taxes?"

She fidgeted on the stool. He had, unfortunately, hit upon a truth she couldn't deny. Smuggling had a long history in Cornwall, and unless taxes were abolished completely, it would likely continue forever. "You seem very well versed in the rights and privileges of the tinners."

"I did spend the first ten years of my life here. But as I'm also a knight sworn to the king's service, I'll enforce the king's laws."

She heard the implacable tone, saw the determination in his eyes. If she pushed him any more on this subject, he might finally lose his temper, and there was another important matter they had yet to resolve. "Very well, my lord. Have the foot ball game, and punish smugglers as the law allows. However, you must not choose the Queen of the May."

She had caught him off guard. "Why not?"

"Because, my lord, the last time the villagers allowed your father to choose the Queen of the May, he dragged her off, had his way with her and then passed her to his bodyguards to do with as they pleased."

She'd watched, terrified, as Wicked William had dragged the shrieking, crying, terrified young woman with a circlet of flowers in her hair toward the stairs leading to his bedchamber. His fiercest mercenaries who made up his bodyguard—frightening, vicious men she'd ordered from Tregellas the moment he'd died—had followed him, laughing and joking about the lord and his conquered queen.

"Oh, God," Merrick whispered. He splayed his hands on the table and bowed his head. "I should have guessed he would…"

His words trailed off as he stared down at the table. "My father left me quite a legacy," he muttered after a long moment of silence.

In spite of his bitter words, she would feel no sympathy for him, as he had none for his overtaxed people.

He raised his head and regarded her with that unwavering stare with which she was getting familiar. "I give you my word, Constance, that the women of Tregellas need never fear me. They need never hide from me. As lord of Tregellas, it's my duty to protect them, and that I will do, if it costs me my life."

His voice was strong, resolute, his gaze steady, and in his eyes, she saw complete honesty. Who would not believe him?

He straightened and started around the table toward her. "Perhaps choosing the Queen of the May will prove that I'm different from my father, and that they need not fear me." He reached down and, taking Constance's hands in his, pulled her to her feet. "If you stand by me when I go to the village on May Day and pick a queen, the village will see that the only woman I want is the woman I'm to wed."

God help her! Why did he have to touch her? Why did he have to say that, and in that deep, rough voice that sounded so intimate, as if he was whispering beside her in bed? Why did he have to look at her that way?

If he kissed her again, she would slap him. She would. She really would.

How far away was the door?

"Perhaps you can tell me who I should choose before the festivities," he suggested. "I'm not ignorant of the tensions and conflict inherent in the choosing of one woman over another, and your knowledge of the villagers can steer me to the least controversial choice."

If she refused, he might continue to try to convince her, to sound even more persuasive. "As you wish, my lord."

Although he didn't smile, she could tell he was pleased, and the resentment she felt at conceding began to melt away.

She thought a moment. "Annice," she suggested, "the chandler's daughter. She's very pretty and well liked, and already promised to the smith's son, Eric."

"The boy who was hurt in the foot ball game?"

"Yes. That was some years ago, my lord. He's certainly of an age to be wed now."

"Why haven't they married already?" Merrick asked. "Does her family object?"

"They haven't married because your father died, and as tenants of your estate, they require the lord's permission to wed. They will probably be seeking that permission at the next hall moot." She hesitated a moment, then asked, "Will you grant it?"

"Why would I not?" he answered. "If the families agree, I will not object."

Relief lessened her anxiety, and she grew more aware of his hands holding hers.

"I assume there'll also be a bonfire May Day eve," he said, "and the young people will go into the woods to collect flowers and branches, and that there'll be music and dancing around a Maypole." His eyes glittered and he gently squeezed her hands. "I would enjoy watching you dance, Constance."

Oh, heaven and all the saints help her! She should pull away and run out the door. Flee before it was too late.

But that would bring her no closer to freedom. Indeed, it might make him think he was gaining power over her, overwhelming her with desire, easily seducing her and bending her to his will.

Determination, fired by her pride, shot through her and as she tugged her hands from his, she gave him an insolent smile. "Do you intend to dance around the Maypole, too, my lord? *I* would enjoy seeing *that*."

Far from disturbing him, her question brought amusement to his eyes as his lips curved up into a devastatingly seductive smile. "I would far rather watch you."

He took hold of her shoulders and began to pull her to him. He was going to kiss her. She should get away. Turn and run. But when he touched her, she felt so…and he looked so…

He did kiss her, and the moment his mouth met hers, blatant, raw desire rose up within her, overwhelming her thoughts, washing away her protests.

Still kissing her, he pressed her closer, his body hard against her own. One arm wrapped about her, and his other hand traveled across her ribs and upward, to cup her breast.

This was…wrong. She should stop him…but it felt so…good. When his thumb stroked her pebbled nipple, her legs felt like water and she moaned into his mouth.

He slowly broke the kiss, although he continued to embrace her. She opened her eyes, to see him regarding her with desire-darkened eyes gleaming with need. "A month seems a long time to wait, my lady."

It was as if the storm outside had come into the room and thrown rain into her face. What did she really know of him, except that he was his father's son, and he'd made a host of promises and declarations that could all prove meaningless once she was his wife and he had her dowry?

What a fool she was! A weak, silly fool!

He made no effort to hold her as she pulled free of his grasp and stumbled backward. "I told you not to touch me unless I gave you leave."

"Did you not enjoy that, my lady? Do you find me so abhorrent?"

"Yes! No!" She fought to regain her self-control, to remember her plan to make him hate her. "When I marry you, my lord, you may kiss me all you like. Until then—"

"Until then, I am to ignore the yearning you inspire within me? I'm to pretend that I feel no desire? That I find you repellent?"

"I would have you treat me with respect!"

Merrick spread his arms wide. "I do respect you, and I admire you not just for your beauty, but for your competence and compassion. Alan de Vern, Ruan, the garrison commander, the servants—all speak most highly of their lady."

She swallowed hard and fought to retain her anger. "Then please respect my wishes and don't kiss me. Or is Sir Henry not the only practiced seducer in Tregellas?"

Merrick's dark brows lowered, and it was like seeing thunderclouds on the horizon. She told herself that was good. That was what she wanted. Needed.

"You think I have ulterior motives when I kiss you?" he demanded.

"I don't know what you want when you kiss me," she retorted. "I don't know *you*."

His hands on his hips, he glared at her, his dark eyes fiercely angry, his mouth a thin line of annoyance. "No, you do not, my lady, or you would never accuse me of selfish seduction. The women I've been with have all approached *me*, and they were made well aware that they should expect nothing more from me than a night's pleasure."

"How very generous of you, my lord."

"Would you prefer me to be like Henry? To speak flattery and honeyed, meaningless words? To murmur tender nothings?"

"I want you to stop kissing me! I'm not yet your wife."

His eyes widened for a brief instant, and then his expression changed. It was like seeing flames snuffed out, and she knew the storm raging within him had passed. "No, you're not," he muttered, running his hand through his long, thick hair.

She was so close to her liberty, she couldn't stop now. She must rouse his ire again. "I want you to order Sir Henry and Sir Ranulf to stay away from Beatrice."

Despite her irate tone, no answering spark ignited in his eyes. "They're both honorable knights and will never touch her or harm her in any way," he said coolly as he moved behind the table again, as if to put a barrier between them. "I trust them completely."

"I don't," she retorted. "Sir Henry seems the sort who cares only about his own desires, no matter what harm he may do. As for Sir Ranulf, he looks quite capable of doing anything to get what he wants. Woe betide your friends if they hurt those I love!"

"Let us understand each other, my lady," Merrick said, his voice still calm. Very calm, as he crossed his arms. "I trust my friends absolutely, or they wouldn't be my friends. I hope to be able to trust my wife in that same way."

"And if you cannot?"

His gaze was steady. Stern. Implacable. "Then she will not be my wife."

Outside, the rain slashed against the stones and the wind moaned; inside the solar, the very air seemed to quiver with expectation.

Her freedom was within her grasp. All she had to do was tell him that she would not be faithful. That she would break her marriage vows, or even that she was no longer a virgin. All she had to do was lie, and say she would bring shame to him. And to herself.

So why did she hesitate? Her honor or her freedom. Why not choose and be done?

Because she simply couldn't tell this man she was, or would be, no better than a whore.

"I will have no unwilling wife, Constance," he said softly, coming around the table toward her. "If I've offended you by my decisions, or if you care more for another, tell me now and I'll release you."

Perhaps he would—but at what price? "What penalty would you seek if I refused? My dowry?"

Surprise flashed across his face. "Nothing. I would want nothing at all from you, my lady."

She couldn't believe that he would be so generous, so willing to let her go free without some compensation. "If that's so, you're not the same boy who left here fifteen years ago."

"No, I am not."

Tell him to let you go, her mind urged.

The words wouldn't come.

She'd been so sure of what she wanted for so long, yet he seemed so different from that spoiled boy. He might be a chivalrous knight, a just overlord, a man she could respect, perhaps even, in time, to love. He certainly aroused her desire as no other man ever had.

But could she trust him? Despite his apparent sincerity, could she truly believe he would let her—and her dowry and the connection to her family—go so easily?

No, she couldn't. At least, not yet.

"Yes or no, Constance? Will you be my wife or not? I would have an answer one way or the other, my lady."

If an answer was what he wanted, she'd give him one. "In spite of your seductive skill, my lord," she said, "I require more time to make up my mind."

Then she strode out of the chamber, and did everything she could to avoid being near him until the first of May.

CHAPTER FOUR

ON MAY DAY MORNING, CONSTANCE stood beside Merrick on a raised platform that had been erected at the edge of the village green.

In the center of the green was the Maypole, with its bright ribbons and wildflowers and, gathered around it, the villagers and tenants of Tregellas, as well as the garrison soldiers not on duty. Tumblers and other entertainers were at the far end of the green, stretching and preparing as they waited for the lord to select the Queen of the May.

The uncles, Henry, Ranulf and Beatrice were on the dais with Merrick and Constance, and it seemed the excitement of the crowd had transferred itself to Beatrice and Henry, at least. Beatrice's eyes glowed with delight, and Henry had been making jokes the whole way from the castle. The uncles stood with appropriately serious lordly dignity, while Ranulf regarded the celebrations with cynical amusement.

"Which one is Annice?"

Fanning herself with her hand, for the day was sunny and warm for May, Constance answered Merrick's query. "She's beside the chandler's stall."

"And that young man holding her hand is Eric?"

"Yes."

"Merrick, why don't you get this moving along and declare Lady Constance the Queen of the May?" Henry suggested, moving closer. "I'm parched from the heat already."

"As much as I would like to give my bride that honor, I've been informed I should choose another, for the sake of peace," Merrick said to his friend.

Henry's eyes widened with surprise for an instant, then he shrugged and said, "What about Beatrice then? She's very pretty."

Beatrice reddened and started to giggle.

"No," Merrick brusquely replied.

Beatrice's face fell.

"A choice from the village will please the people of Tregellas," Constance explained to the disappointed Beatrice and her champion.

She gave Beatrice a comforting smile. "You shouldn't begrudge one of the village girls the chance to be the center of attention. One day, you'll have a great wedding, with feasting and dancing and music and guests from all over England. You'll be far more important than a Queen of the May that day."

Beatrice brightened. "Like you, on your wedding day."

Fortunately, Merrick spoke, sparing Constance the necessity of answering. "Constance thinks Annice would be best, so Annice it will be," he said with quiet force.

Then he unexpectedly reached for Constance's hand,

an act that would surely be interpreted by all in the village as a confirmation that she was eager to have him for her husband.

Unfortunately, he held her tight, and short of yanking her hand from his firm grasp, she had no recourse but to let him continue holding it.

"Good people of Tregellas," Merrick called out, his gruff, strong voice carrying easily in the warm spring air, "it is my honor today to choose the Queen of the May. After consulting with Lady Constance, I have made my decision. This year, your queen shall be Annice, the chandler's daughter."

A cacophony of cheers and happy murmurings went up from the gathering, enabling Constance to relax a little. Her choice had been as well received as she'd hoped.

Merrick, too, seemed pleased as he looked at Constance and squeezed her hand. Given what holding her hand might signify, she should be annoyed. But she wasn't, until she wondered if that firm grasp signified possession, too.

Looking both wary and proud enough to burst his tunic lacings, Eric led a blushing Annice to the dais. When they arrived, Merrick gravely held out a plain silver ring as her prize—something Constance hadn't expected. She wasn't sure what to make of the gift as Annice hesitantly reached for it, her big green eyes staring up into Merrick's dark brown ones.

"Go ahead, my girl," Henry said jovially. "He won't bite—unless you want him to."

Appalled, Constance gasped. Annice turned pale and Eric glared, while Merrick glowered at his friend.

Henry smiled sheepishly. "Forgive me. I, um, forgot that I'm, um…"

"A fool?" Merrick snapped. He quickly turned back and addressed the young woman. "Don't be afraid, Annice," he said, his deep voice appeasing. "Your virtue is safe from me and—" he darted another sharp glance at Henry "—my men."

He raised his voice. "I would have all in Tregellas know that your women have nothing to fear from me. As your overlord, their honor is mine to protect, not destroy. If any of my men ever harm you or your wives or children, you are to come and tell me, without fear that further trouble will befall you. As long as you obey the law, I promise to do my utmost to fulfill my duty to you, as I hope you will fulfill yours to me."

He again took hold of Constance's hand. "With my gentle lady wife to guide me, I hope to rule you well, with justice and clemency, as my father did not."

As the assembly burst out cheering, Constance pulled her hand from his. He spoke as if she'd consented, or as if his offer of freedom had been bogus all along.

Seething with anger and indignation, she cursed herself for a weak-willed, lust-addled fool. Just because his touch and his kisses aroused her desire, she mustn't forget what she feared—that he would prove to be a second version of his hated father.

Merrick turned to Henry, who was whispering something to Beatrice that made her giggle.

"I would speak with you, Henry," he said in a tone that, even in the midst of her own concerns, made Constance shiver.

Henry, however, merely rolled his eyes. "God's wounds, Merrick, it was a slip of the tongue."

"So you said. Will you never learn to think before you speak? Your stupid jest could have cost me dear."

"Well, obviously it didn't," Henry said, nodding at the crowd.

Several villagers clustered around Annice and Eric, admiring her ring. Two girls were trying to get a circlet of flowers to stay on the queen's glossy tresses, laughing as it fell first to one side, then another. Others had already retired to the alehouse and tavern, where the innkeeper had set up tables and benches outside so his customers could observe the entertainers. Several couples were beginning a round dance near the Maypole, and children were anxiously and eagerly gathered there, waiting for that part of the festivities to begin. Many were already eating sweetmeats and other treats, to judge by the remainders around their mouths.

Henry turned to Beatrice and Constance for support. "It wasn't so terrible, was it?"

Not unexpectedly, Beatrice smiled and shook her head. Constance, however, was not so inclined to agree. "The women here have had good cause to fear their

overlord in the past. Your jest might have made them
think their days of dread were not yet over."

"I must have these people's trust, Henry," Merrick
said. "I can't allow *anyone* to undermine it."

"Of course I understand that —"

"No, I don't think you do, or the magnitude of the
mistrust and hatred I have to overcome here if I'm to
rule and my family be safe."

"He's right, you know," Ranulf remarked before
Henry could reply. "It wouldn't be the first time a war
got started over a few ill-chosen words."

"Then maybe I ought to leave," Henry said with obvious annoyance.

"Oh, surely not!" Beatrice cried, looking beseechingly from Constance to Merrick. "He didn't mean any
harm, my lord, and you've been such friends in the past,
it would be terrible to break it off over such a little
thing." She gestured toward the green. "See? Nothing's
amiss. Everyone seems happy and content. Surely as
long as Henry behaves honorably—which I'm certain
he will—there's no cause to banish him. Sir Henry will
be more careful in the future, won't you, Sir Henry?"

A swift glance at Lord Carrell told Constance her
uncle was also suspicious of Beatrice's defense of the
roguish and handsome young knight.

"Forgive me, my lord," Henry said with genial remorse. "I promise I'll be as serious as a monk after a
two-day fast from here on."

"Then you may stay—provided you curb your tongue."

Henry put his hand on his heart and bowed. "If I ever speak in a way that leads to trouble for you, you may cut it out."

"I'll remember that."

Henry reddened, then smiled, although his eyes were not so merry.

Ranulf clapped a hand on Henry's shoulder. "Let's go get some ale and watch the dancers, my swift-tongued friend."

"Come, Beatrice," Lord Carrell ordered as the two knights walked away.

Whatever Beatrice was thinking, she meekly followed her father from the dais. Lord Algernon bowed and hurried after them, leaving Constance alone with Merrick.

"I want to meet Peder," he announced, to both her surprise and chagrin. She'd been hoping to abandon him.

"I don't see him in the crowd, my lord," she replied.

Merrick nodded toward the smithy. "Isn't that Peder sitting outside the blacksmith's?"

Since Merrick was, unfortunately, right, Constance had to agree. "Yes, but I don't think you need me to "

"I would prefer it."

His words didn't offer the possibility of refusal, so she silently led him toward the smithy, making easy progress because anyone who was in their path quickly got out of it.

Peder, whose eyesight was remarkably good for a man of his years, soon realized they were headed toward him, yet he made no move to stand until they reached him. Then he got to his feet, smiled and bowed to Constance. "My lady." His expression hardened as he bowed to Merrick. "My lord."

"Please, sit," Merrick said in Cornish after Constance had made the introductions.

Peder and Constance exchanged surprised looks as Peder obeyed.

"I did spend the first ten years of my life here," Merrick said in answer to their silent query, "so it shouldn't come as a shock that I can speak the native tongue."

"It's been fifteen years," Peder said, as if he suspected this was some kind of trick.

"I kept in practice by saying my prayers in Cornish," Merrick explained. "But that's not what I wish to discuss with you, Peder. I gather Lady Constance relies on you for information about the villagers."

Constance stared at him with offended dismay. How had he come to that outrageous conclusion? She had never said that, nor would she ever betray the villagers' trust.

"Lady Constance and me are friends, from when she was a girl," Peder replied with scorn. "And neither of us are the sort to carry tales."

"I meant no insult," Merrick replied, glancing at Constance before again addressing Peder.

She wondered if he realized that he'd affronted her, too. Or cared if he had.

"I'd appreciate any guidance as to how I can best

govern my people," he said, "from a man who's lived here all his life and has the respect of everyone."

Was this a genuine request, or did he seek to flatter Peder into cooperation? Yet there was a tension in Merrick's shoulders, as if he cared what Peder would do, or say, that seemed to belie that motive.

Peder regarded the nobleman steadily, without a hint of fear or favor, and Constance detected a note of pride in his voice when he answered. "It's hard to tell what folks really think when you're a great lord, I suppose. Too many tells 'em only what they want to hear."

"A man in power needs trustworthy advisers," Merrick agreed, his body still tense.

Would he heed a wife's advice? Or would he pay attention to his betrothed's views only until they were wed?

"You'd have me advise you, eh?" Peder asked, making no secret of his skepticism.

Merrick frowned, but she thought she saw disappointment lurking in his eyes, not anger. "I remember you from when I was a boy," he said. "You were considered a good man. I could use the help of a good man."

Constance hoped he never found out Peder had been smuggling out a significant portion of his tin for years.

"Please God, I'll always be a good man, as much as one can be in these troubled times," Peder said. His expression darkened. "But I'll not spy on my friends."

Merrick looked genuinely surprised. "Have I asked you to do so?"

What *did* he want, then?

"As I said, I remember you from before I left Tregellas," Merrick continued. "I seek your help, if you'll give it. Whether or not you do, I want to help you." He went down on one knee so that he was looking directly into Peder's face, his gaze searching for…what? Understanding? Agreement? "My father sinned greatly against your daughter, Peder, and caused your family much harm. I'm truly sorry for your loss. Although nothing can replace your daughter and her son, if there's anything you ever need to make your days comfortable, you are to tell Constance or me, and I will see that you get it."

Forgiveness? Was that what he was looking for in Peder's aged face?

He didn't get it.

Peder glared at him, anger furrowing his brow. "That can't make up for what your father done."

Disappointment flashed across Merrick's face before he rose. "My offer stands, regardless," he said before a loud, joyous cry coming from from the green made all three look that way.

"Unless I'm mistaken, my lady," Merrick said, turning toward her, "they're about to start the dance around the Maypole. I recall you were going to participate."

"Can she still visit with me?" Peder demanded.

Merrick inclined his head. "Of course. I see no reason to forbid it. I'm grateful Lady Constance had such a friend while my father was alive."

Peder got to his feet. "Then I'll take her to the dancing, my lord."

Merrick inclined his head. "Very well. I should discuss the boundary for the playing field with Sir Ranulf."

Peder winked at Constance, although the look he gave Merrick when he addressed the lord of Tregellas was one of respect due to a nobleman. "Then good day to you, my lord."

"Good day to you, Peder," Merrick replied before heading toward the tavern where Sir Ranulf and Sir Henry were deep in discussion, and their ale.

"Look at 'im, the devil's own spawn," Peder muttered as he watched Merrick stride away. "Arrogant bastard. Handsome, like his father, and probably as sinful as his sire, too." He slid Constance a sudden, piercing glance. "Maybe I shouldn't be so free with my opinions."

Constance couldn't blame Peder for his hatred of the son of Wicked William, or the vices he believed Merrick would possess. She had been suspicious of him, too. How could she not be, remembering his father and all that he had done? Yet Merrick hadn't acted the lascivious scoundrel since his arrival. The only woman he'd attempted to be intimate with, as far as she knew—and she would have heard—was herself. "Lord Merrick has given me his word that women will be safe from him."

Peder scowled. "You think that means anything?"

Constance thought of Merrick's tone and the look in his eyes when he vowed to respect her and to protect the women of Tregellas. "Yes, I do. At least, I hope so, and so far, he's done nothing to make me believe otherwise. Maybe it's because he was sent away from here so young. Perhaps Sir Leonard taught him to be a better man than his father ever could."

"The boy decrees the man, my lady, and I'm old enough to know," Peder declared as they walked toward the Maypole. "If that's the Merrick who left Tregellas fifteen years ago, that's a man you shouldn't marry, or he'll make you miserable, as his father did his poor mother. She was a gentle soul, and she thought she could change her husband. She found out quick enough she couldn't, and many of us thought it a mercy she died giving birth to the boy." Peder paused, and when he began again, his voice was thick with emotion. "You know what his father did to my daughter, my lady, and what became of her. Despair and disgrace and then…"

"Yes, Peder, I remember," she said softly, squeezing his arm. "I will be wary. I promise. And there is something else I must tell you, while I have this chance. Merrick is determined to uphold the king's laws against smuggling. You should cease for the time being, and pay taxes accordingly."

"What, give all that money to the Norman king?"

"Lord Merrick may not prove to be as cruel and vindictive as his father, but until we know for certain, I think it would be best to be cautious. I appreciate that means less money for you, but that's better than death, isn't it?"

"That tax isn't fair."

"That's why Alan de Vern and I were willing to turn a blind eye. Perhaps in time, Lord Merrick will come to appreciate that, but until then, I fear for your safety if you continue. Please, Peder, for my sake. You are like a grandfather to me and if anything happened to you…"

Peder looked at her with love in his steadfast brown eyes. "And you're as dear to me as any granddaughter could be." His gaze turned intense and he lowered his voice so she had to strain to hear him. "I think you should run, my lady. Run as far and as fast as you can from that Merrick."

"I have thought of that, Peder," she answered just as quietly. "But what would I do? Where would I go? How would I live?"

"I'm not the only one in the village who loves you like family, my lady. We know how many times you calmed the old lord when he was in one of his rages, and spared many a man's life and a woman's honor when you did. If you want to run away, come to me. We'll help you get away and keep you safe."

Although she was grateful for this offer, Constance felt no real relief or joy. If she got away, she would have to travel far before she could feel safe. She would be alone, in a strange land, among foreigners. She would be poor, for she wouldn't take much from the villagers, who had little enough as it was.

Right now, that fate seemed far more lonely and frightening than…staying here.

Yet when she saw how anxious Peder was, she gave him a thankful smile. "I promise you, Peder, that if I decide to flee, I'll come straight to you."

"Hurry, Constance, hurry, or the game's going to be over!" Beatrice chided with bubbling enthusiasm as she led her cousin toward the river meadow a short while later.

"I think there's plenty of time left," Constance said, reluctantly following. She had no desire to lend her support to something she feared would end in disaster.

As they approached the mill, she was sure it had, for it sounded like a riot was already under way. Gathering up her skirts, she started to run.

"Wait! Wait for me!" Beatrice cried, hurrying after her.

"Go back to the castle," Constance ordered over her shoulder. The last thing she wanted was for Beatrice to be involved in—

A cheering, extremely excited crowd?

That was what met her eyes as she rounded the mill and discovered groups of villagers gathered at the north edge of the meadow, shouting encouragement to the village men dashing about the field. Off-duty soldiers not involved in the game were gathered at the other end of the field, likewise shouting praise and suggestions to their fellows.

She came to a halt, panting. She was thrilled she was wrong, of course, but even so, one hard hit could still lead to trouble.

Beatrice stopped beside her. "I didn't mean we had to run," she said, trying to catch her breath.

"I misjudged the cheers," Constance admitted. "I thought the men were fighting."

"Oh," Beatrice murmured, her attention now fully on the game.

Or at least the half-naked players, Constance realized with a bit of a jolt. For half-naked and sweating they certainly were.

She was no sheltered child, and neither was Beatrice. They'd seen half-naked men before, and men wearing even less working in the fields on a hot summer's day. Nevertheless, the sight was certainly…disconcerting.

"I just hope nobody gets hurt," she said, trying to pay attention to the game.

Beatrice gave her a confident smile. "They'll all be careful, I'm sure. The garrison won't want Merrick to be angry with them—which he would be if someone got hurt and he had to pay—and the villagers will be afraid to hurt the soldiers because they won't want to anger Merrick, either."

That was very likely true, Constance thought with some relief. Then she wondered why that hadn't occurred to her. She'd obviously been too distracted by…other things.

"Isn't that Lord Merrick on the field?" Beatrice asked, pointing.

Surely not, Constance thought as she followed her cousin's gaze. But unless she was going blind, the man in the front of the pack chasing after the ball, with his dark hair streaming behind him like a pennant, was the lord of Tregellas himself. His powerful arms churned and his long and graceful strides reminded her of a stag bounding over the moor.

Constance could hardly believe the evidence of her own eyes. Yet wasn't that Sir Henry and Sir Ranulf running neck and neck behind him? "By the saints," she murmured, aghast at both a lord engaging in such play and the sight of her betrothed's undoubtedly fine body.

"Oh, look! There's Sir Henry!" Beatrice cried, jumping up and down in her excitement. "He's got the ball!"

Henry deftly passed it back to Merrick, who charged up the field, keeping the ball just ahead of his rapid feet.

Who was winning? It was hard to tell, for both the villagers and the soldiers were cheering wildly. Constance spotted Talek, the garrison commander, among the soldiers and, taking hold of Beatrice by the sleeve, pushed her way through the crowd of men surrounding him. They were so intent on the game, they didn't realize who was shoving them aside until after she'd gone past.

She tapped Talek on the arm to get his attention. "Who's winning?" she shouted over the din.

"It's a tie," the middle-aged soldier answered just as loudly. "But we've got his lordship, so it's going to be us who win. I've never seen such a fine—"

His words were drowned out by a great roar from the spectators. Merrick had stumbled and nearly fallen, but in the next moment he recovered with a fluid twist of his body. Then he ran even faster, as if that brief setback only spurred him on.

He was nearly at the two posts stuck in the ground marking the goal. The soldiers shouted themselves hoarse. The villagers screamed at their men, and some groaned with dismay.

Constance tried not to get caught up in the excitement. She was a lady, after all, and thus should behave with decorum and dignity. Besides, it was only a game. It didn't matter who won, as long as fighting didn't break out.

Merrick was almost at the goal....

The smith's son charged forward and got the ball away from Merrick. The villagers shouted, loudly urging on their men; the soldiers cursed with astonishing variety and fluency.

Eric passed the ball to his father, who passed it to—

Ranulf intercepted it and, with a quick move, kicked it back to Merrick. His mighty chest heaving, Merrick again started up the field, this time with Henry and Ranulf guarding him on either side.

Perspiration made Merrick's chest shine in the sun as if it'd been oiled. His breeches were soaked with sweat at the waist and clung to his strong thighs.

More cheering, more cursing—Merrick scored!

"Well done!" Constance cried as she leapt into the air. Then she slapped her hand over her mouth. Could she possibly be more undignified?

Beatrice, whom she'd quite forgotten, had no concern about her appearance as she danced with delight. "I knew we'd win! I knew it!" she declared, clapping.

As the soldiers, led by Talek, surged into the field past them, Constance tried to compose herself. "Yes, well, that was certainly interesting," she said, keeping her eyes—and attention—on the crowd as the villagers surrounded Eric and the others. There could yet be trouble.

Beatrice stopped prancing. "Interesting? It was wonderful! Merrick was so fast. Whoever would have thought he could run like that?"

"Indeed," Constance murmured as the foot soldiers surrounded their overlord, who gulped down what seemed an enormous mug of ale that a grinning soldier handed him.

Lord William wouldn't have deigned to let one of his men get within ten feet of him.

And then Merrick did something more surprising still: he went to the villagers and praised them for their efforts. He was followed by his men, who were laughing and bragging good-naturedly, as were the equally happy and proud villagers.

Obviously Merrick knew men and their reactions better than she did, and he was certainly far more willing to mix with his people than his father had ever been.

What kind of man *was* the new lord of Tregellas? Could he truly be so different from his father, and the brat she'd loathed for so long?

"Come along, Beatrice," she said, moving away before the excited soldiers and villagers engulfed them. "I don't think there's any need to linger."

"Don't you want to congratulate Merrick?" Beatrice asked.

"I don't think that will be necessary."

Beatrice frowned. "You do *like* Merrick, don't you?"

"Yes," she replied, not quite sure if that was a lie or not.

Beatrice leaned closer and dropped her voice to a whisper, as if she feared she was about to impart something scandalous. "I know age and looks aren't supposed to be as important as family or wealth when it comes to a husband, but you're so lucky he's handsome. Really, Constance, would you want to make love with someone who looks like…like Ruan, for instance? Thank the blessed Virgin you can look forward to your wedding night."

Merrick's voice rose stern and commanding from the midst of the mob of soldiers. "Let me pass."

Now *that* could have been his father, Constance thought with a stab of disappointment.

Then she realized that Merrick—still blatantly half-naked, although he held a shirt in his hand—was walking toward her, while the men made way for him as if he was a king.

CHAPTER FIVE

FOR ONE BRIEF INSTANT Constance thought of running away. But how would that look to the men, and Beatrice, too? And hadn't she faced down the infamous Wicked William of Tregellas more than once?

Beatrice, however, started to sidle away. "I believe I'll change my gown before the feast," she murmured.

Then she was gone, leaving Constance feeling like the lone soldier on a bloody battlefield awaiting the enemy's army.

Except that it was no horde of soldiers who walked toward her, but the handsome, young and unabashedly virile man to whom she was betrothed—the same man who had a satisfied grin playing about the corners of his lips.

So he was pleased he and his men had won—why didn't he put his shirt on? Was he trying to make her feel uncomfortable? Was this some sort of attempt to intimidate or embarrass her? If so, he'd drastically underestimated her. She straightened her shoulders and prepared to show him how wrong he was.

"So, my lady," he said when he reached her, "all your worrying was for naught. No death, no injuries beyond a twisted ankle, no riots. My soldiers are happy—except those who wagered against us—and the villagers put up enough of a challenge that they can retire with pride to play another day."

She wasn't about to let him gloat, either. "I know you're the commander of Tregellas, but isn't running around after a pig's bladder taking things a bit too far?" she asked as Henry and Ranulf, Talek and a few of the other soldiers walked past them toward the mill. "I suppose it was Sir Henry's idea. He seems just the sort to try to get his friends to behave in a wanton and undignified way."

The smug grin faded as Merrick's brow furrowed with a frown. "You think Henry capable of leading me astray?"

It suddenly seemed foolish to suggest that anybody could lead this man anywhere; however, having started, she would continue. "I think he tries, and likely sometimes succeeds."

The telltale vein in Merrick's temple started to pulse. "When you know me better, you'll appreciate the folly of that opinion. Would you accuse Ranulf of trying to lead me astray, as well?"

"I have no idea what Sir Ranulf is capable of."

Merrick's fierce gaze impaled her. "I see no indignity in doing what the men who may die for me are asked to do."

She was treading on thin ice, and she knew it. So she said nothing.

"Whatever *you're* trying to do, my lady," Merrick said, stepping closer, "understand this. Never again presume to question my actions or my decisions in front of my men. I am the lord here, my lady, not you, and I will not be criticized in public."

As she flushed hotly and told herself her indignant anger was necessary, he finally put on his shirt. It hung loose from his broad shoulders, the hem at his muscular thighs. The unlaced neck gaped, revealing enough of his chest to make this seem a tease.

Rolling the sleeves up over his forearms, he gazed at her steadily, and his voice dropped to a low growl, like the purring of a large and not-quite-tamed cat. "However, when we're alone, you may criticize me all you like."

He couldn't be sincere. "You don't mean that."

"If I didn't, I wouldn't say it."

She couldn't believe any nobleman could truly be so acquiescent, let alone this one. "And you won't take offense?"

"I may very well take offense, but I won't punish you for it."

She sniffed derisively. "How can I believe that?"

"Because I give you my word."

"And if I should refuse you your rights in the bed-chamber?" she challenged, certain she had found one thing he would insist upon.

"I would expect you to tell me why, so that I may remedy the situation."

She backed away from him. She didn't dare stay close, not when he was looking so incredibly virile, and making such astonishing, seemingly sincere concessions. "If you'll excuse me, my lord, I...I have things to do."

It was a pathetic excuse and she felt like a coward, but it was that...or kiss him.

THE WINE FOR THE MAY DAY feast was the best Constance had ever tasted, and Gaston had outdone himself with the food. Dish after dish of soup, stew, meat with rich sauces, pasties, greens and bread came and went, ending with sweetmeats and fruit both cooked and fresh. Afterward, a minstrel entertained with songs of Arthur and his knights, making references to Tintagel, home of Arthur's mother and now one of Richard of Cornwall's strongholds. Other musicians played tunes for dancing on lute and tabor, and of course there'd been more wine. After one particularly lively round dance with Henry as her partner, Constance had removed her veil because she was too warm and taken out the pins that held her coiled braids tight against her head.

Henry was really a very amusing fellow, and as he and Ranulf bantered about the relationship between Arthur, Guinevere and Lancelot—Henry maintaining Arthur must have been so busy looking for grails and otherwise "dashing about" that he'd neglected his wife, and Ranulf claiming Lancelot was an immoral fellow whose battle prowess had gone to his head—she laughed so hard, she could scarcely draw breath. Even Merrick had chuckled, a surprisingly pleasant rumble of amusement. Beatrice giggled until the tears ran down her cheeks and her father, with a look of disapproval, sent her off to bed.

Constance smiled indulgently as Beatrice wove her way toward the stairs, helped by Demelza. Her father wasn't paying much attention to her progress; he had returned to a lively discussion about hounds and their merits with Lord Algernon.

She felt free and delightfully happy, even with Merrick beside her, looking handsome in his black clothing and his long, thick, waving dark hair. And splendid features. And well-cut lips. If he were to take her hand now, she might even welcome that attention.

"God save me, it's warm in here!" she murmured to no one in particular as she held out her goblet for more of the rich red wine.

Merrick plucked her goblet from her hand.

Since she was in a good humor, instead of being angry, she gave him a saucy smile as she tried to get it back. "I'm thirsty, my lord."

He held it up just out of her reach. "Have you not had enough wine to slake your thirst, or is your throat still dry from all the cheering you did today?" he asked, one brow raised in query.

"I was cheering for you, my lord," she protested, recalling the sight of the lord of Tregellas, half-naked, his long hair flying, running after the inflated pig's bladder with the grace of a deer. He had, without a doubt, the finest body in Cornwall, perhaps even England. "You were really quite magnificent. No doubt the garrison would have lost without you. I never thought you'd play, though. I could more easily imagine you commanding the bladder as if it were one of your men." She lowered her voice to an imitation of Merrick's deep growl and pointed an imperious, if slightly wobbly, finger at an imaginary ball on the floor. "Bladder, come here! Bladder, I command you to cease rolling! Bladder, obey me or I shall pierce you with my trusty blade!"

Amused by her jest, she started to giggle. "And your good friend Sir Ranulf would say, 'Bladder, my friend, what the devil are you doing? You weary me with all this rolling,' while Sir Henry would no doubt try to charm it into stopping with smiles and gentle pleading. 'Please, pretty bladder, come back to me….' And it probably would, too. He's a very charming fellow, your friend." She waggled a warning finger at Merrick. "I shall have to keep my eye on him."

Merrick didn't seem the least bit amused. "I think it's time you retired, my lady."

She opened her eyes wide, both to display her surprise and the better to focus on his somewhat blurry face. "The night is young, my lord." She gave him her very best smile. "And there may be more dancing."

"Not for you, I think."

Constance leaned over him to address her uncle, her breasts pressing against Merrick's forearm. The sensation was quite pleasant. Exhilarating, even.

"He says I must retire, Uncle," she complained, interrupting their debate about the bloodlines of their respective hunting hounds. "Tell him I'm old enough to decide for myself when I go to bed."

To her chagrin, her startled uncle looked to Merrick before he answered. "I believe, my dear, that you've had quite enough excitement for one day."

"I have not." Determined not to be sent from the hall like an errant child, she again smiled at Merrick. "Don't you want to dance with me, my lord?"

She couldn't quite read the expression on his face, but he might have been amused. "Not when you're in this condition. Come, my lady, retire before you make a fool of yourself."

She bristled at both his words and the laughter lurking in his eyes and the corners of his shapely lips. "I never make a fool of myself."

"There's always a first time."

Affronted, Constance rose to her feet with all the dignity she could muster, in spite of the wine. "Very well, my lord, since heaven forbid you should be ashamed of me, I'll retire."

Unfortunately, the floor seemed to have become somewhat unstable during the meal. She reached for the back of her chair to steady herself—and instead found herself swept up into Merrick's arms. She gave a little screech of protest and clamped her arms around his neck so she wouldn't fall.

"Gentlemen, if you'll excuse us," he said to the uncles and his friends at the high table.

She was not so far gone with drink that she thought

this acceptable, even if it was rather…delightful. "Put me down!"

"I wouldn't want you to fall and break a limb before our wedding," Merrick replied as he leapt lightly down from the dais and proceeded through the hall.

Alan de Vern, who should have come to her aid, started to chuckle. So did his pleasant, plump wife and those around them, and soon the hall rang with laughter. A swift glance showed that her uncle and Lord Algernon were also amused, and Henry grinned like a gargoyle. Ranulf was apparently more intent on the fruit pie before him.

"Let me down, you big ox!" she hissed in Merrick's ear as he wove his way through the tables. "What will people say?"

"I believe, my lady, they already have plenty to discuss about you and me," he said as he reached the stairs. "If you were afraid of scandal, you should have watched how much wine you imbibed. You were gulping it like a sot."

"Put me down!" she insisted. This had gone far enough.

"Put me down!" she repeated when he didn't. She was no piece of baggage. She wasn't yet his chattel. To rule as he would. Or ignore as he would.

When he still didn't release her, she slapped him.

The whole hall seemed to gasp with one breath and she instantly realized the enormity of what she'd done. Although he didn't so much as flinch, she could see the red mark of her palm on his cheek. "My lord, I—I'm—!"

Without a word, he tightened his hold. Grimly silent, he began to take the stairs two at a time. She clung to his neck, afraid he would drop her, and more afraid of what he'd do when they reached her bedchamber. "My lord, forgive me!"

"Say nothing, Constance," he growled. "Nothing until we're alone."

She'd be lucky if he only slapped her in return.

A tear slid down her cheek. Then another. If he beat her, that would be the proof she needed that he was his father's son.

She didn't want him to be his father's son. She wanted him to be the man she'd come to respect. To admire. To…

He reached her chamber and shoved open the door with his shoulder. A rushlight burned on her dressing table, the weak flame leaving most of the room in shadow as he set her down. Distraught, dismayed, still a little drunk, she felt her knees give way and she slid to the floor.

"Get up," he ordered.

"I…I can't."

He reached down and pulled her to her feet. Holding her steady by the shoulders, he glared at her. Then his dark eyes widened with shock. "Are you crying?"

"Are you going to beat me?"

"I've never struck a woman in my life!"

A sob of relief broke from her lips.

"I could never hurt you, Constance—never!" he whispered as he pulled her into his arms.

She heard the sincerity in his voice, felt it in his tense body, and believed him. He would never hurt her.

She relaxed into his embrace and wrapped her arms around him. Closing her eyes, she drew in a shuddering breath, leaning her cheek against his chest. She was safe in his arms. Protected.

He drew back and she hoped to see some affection in his eyes, but while there was concern, there was reserve also. "I will leave you now."

She didn't want him to go, so she kept her arms around him. "I *did* have too much wine. It's a different thing when men get drunk. Nobody thinks anything of that."

His little smile warmed her entire body. "I've never been drunk."

"What, never?"

"No," he replied as he stroked her cheek with his calloused palm. It was a man's touch. A warrior's gentle caress. "Constance," he asked softly, "do you want to marry me?"

"I…I beg your pardon?" she stammered, trying to focus on what he was saying, and not just his moving lips.

"I am asking you if you *want* to be my wife."

She didn't answer. She couldn't. It was too hard to think right now, to know what to say.

His expression darkened as his hand left her cheek. "Clearly you're reluctant. Perhaps I should take that as a refusal."

"Yes—no!"

His brows rose.

The anguished truth broke from her lips. "I don't know what I want!"

"You require more time to come to a decision?"

She grabbed at that suggestion like a miser after gold. "Yes!"

"Then you shall have it," he said, as calm as a placid pond on a windless day as he stepped back, while she felt as if she'd been caught in storm-tossed waves.

Yet, as he looked into her eyes, she saw a longing, an almost desperate hope. Did her answer mean so much to him? Could he truly care for her?

What of the little boy he'd been? Had she remembered only the worst of his childish behavior? Had the years that he'd been gone truly writ a change in him?

Her speculation didn't last. It couldn't, when he gathered her into his arms and kissed her. His mouth captured hers with heated, powerful longing.

The fervor of his passion destroyed what remained of her wine-induced languor. Her body leapt to life with his kiss, and responded with its own ardent need. Eagerly, boldly, she gathered him to her, reveling in the sensation of his strong body against hers.

His lips left her mouth, to trail along her cheek toward her ear. "I've thought of you every day, Constance, no matter where I was or what I was doing," he whispered. "I remembered you sitting cross-legged in a field after the haying, with two sheaves on either side of you, like sentinels. Your hair was long and loose, and you were watching a bug in the chaff so intently, you were lost to everything around you. You reached up to brush a strand of hair from your cheek with the most graceful gesture I've ever seen."

He cupped her chin gently in his calloused palm. "You were but a child then, yet I knew in my heart that you would grow up to be a beautiful, graceful woman. And finding you again, discovering you've become so much more than that… Even if there'd been no contract, no betrothal, I would have sought you out to be my bride. I want you for my wife, Constance, more than I can ever say. I promise to do all in my power to make you happy. Will you, Constance? Will you marry me?"

Did he love her? Could he?

"I don't want to make the wrong decision and live to regret it," she answered honestly, her gaze searching his face. "Can you understand that, my lord?"

"I respect your honesty," he said, turning his head as if she'd struck him. "And I'll continue to hope you decide in my favor."

"If you're always fair and generous, I believe I might" was all she trusted herself to say as she guided his head toward her. Then she went up on her toes, and brought her lips to his.

As she kissed and caressed him, as he eagerly kissed and explored her body with his hands, the last of her old hatred and bitter resentment drifted away. The tormentor of her past was gone. She could believe the days of fear and worry and having to watch every word, every look, of anticipating every shift of mood and humor, were over.

That she was free.

Excited, light-headed with joy, emboldened, she reached down to stroke the hardened evidence of his desire. Still kissing her, he groaned.

His hand found her breast and kneaded it gently as the other cupped her buttock and held her tight. Leaving his erection, she reached under his tunic, running her hand up his hot, bare skin. She encountered his nipple and brushed her fingers across it.

He broke the kiss and grabbed her hand. "Constance!"

"What?" she cried, wondering what she'd done wrong. "Don't you like—?"

His dark eyes glittered in the dim light. "Too much, I fear. Unless you want to lose your maidenhead tonight—"

Someone's knuckles rapped sharply on the chamber door. Constance started and jumped away from Merrick, who looked just as surprised.

"Constance? Merrick?" Lord Carrell called.

Blushing as red as holly berries, Constance adjusted her slightly disheveled clothing while Merrick strode to the door and yanked it open.

Standing on the threshold, Lord Carrell looked past Merrick. "Constance, are you all right?" he asked, running a searching gaze over her.

"She's quite unharmed, if that's what brought you here," Merrick said, making no effort—or unable—to hide his frustration.

Lord Carrell stopped looking at Constance. He

glanced down below Merrick's belt and flushed. Lord Algernon followed his gaze, then immediately disappeared from view.

"I, um, that is, my lord," her uncle began, "until you marry her, Constance is under my care and I—"

"I understand, my lord," he replied, his voice once more calm. "I give you good evening." He turned to Constance, and the look in his dark eyes set her heart racing. "Good night, my lady."

She could only bow her head in response as Merrick strode from the room.

Lord Carrell smiled at his flustered niece. "Since you're betrothed, there's no harm done." He gave her a wink. "Good night, my dear."

Then he, too, left her chamber.

Alone, Constance staggered to her bed and sat heavily. God help her, what was she going to do? Should she wed Merrick or not? Obey her head, which urged her to take the way of caution and refuse, or follow her desire...and accept?

CHAPTER SIX

THREE DAYS LATER, MERRICK strode into the courtyard, followed by Ranulf and Henry. He'd been summoned from the outer ward where the men were training with quintains and swords, despite the drizzling rain, because Sir Jowan, who held the manor of Penderston to the west of Tregellas, and his son, Kiernan, had arrived.

Sir Jowan was obviously the stout, apple-cheeked, white-haired man sitting on a very fine gelding. His son, a slender young man, fair-haired, fair skinned and with a pleasant, if not overly handsome face, rode another excellent horse. They were accompanied by a troop of twenty, who were clearly waiting for their lord's signal before dismounting.

"Welcome to Tregellas," Merrick said, ignoring both the older man's steadfast, measuring gaze and his son's haughty glare. He had encountered both reactions often enough before, so he attached no particular significance to either. "I assume I have the honor of addressing Sir Jowan of Penderston and his son?"

"Indeed, you do, my lord, indeed you do," Sir Jowan said, his deep voice hale and hearty.

Merrick didn't recognize it, or the man himself.

Sir Jowan called for his soldiers to dismount, and the noblemen did likewise. Watching the younger man out of the corner of his eye, Merrick noted that he had come fully mailed and armed. Interesting, especially as his father had not.

"Welcome back to Tregellas, my lord. I hope you remember me," Sir Jowan said.

"I do," Merrick lied. If he'd seen Sir Jowan before, he had no recollection of it. But he saw no reason to create any ill will—or increase any that existed between his neighbors and himself. "These are my friends, Sir Henry and Sir Ranulf, who trained with me under Sir Leonard de Brissy."

"I remember *you,* my lord," Kiernan said, and it was clear Merrick was not supposed to be flattered.

He didn't remember Kiernan, either, but that wasn't so surprising. He wondered how many times they'd visited Tregellas both before and after he was gone. Not many, he suspected.

On the other hand, Kiernan looked to be near in age to Constance, and she was attractive enough to make men risk much for her company. Kiernan was also young, from a prosperous family and clearly beloved by his father. No lines of worry or hint of past sins darkened his brow. He likely had no secrets to stand between him and the woman he yearned for.

Where was Constance now, he wondered. The kitchen? The storerooms? How would she greet these visitors?

Reminding himself that he, not Kiernan, was betrothed to Constance, and that she had not yet refused him, Merrick buried his jealousy deep and betrayed nothing on his face.

"Please join me in my hall," he said, leading the way.

Once they were inside, Demelza hurried to bring wine, bread and cheese without having to be told. Constance had trained the servants well.

There was a long, awkward moment of silence while they waited for the wine, which Henry eventually broke. "So, Sir Jowan, has your family held land in Cornwall a long time?"

"Since before the Conquest," the older man said, his bass voice full of pride.

"Really? And it wasn't taken from your family by William? I wonder how that came to pass."

"By marriage, sir," Sir Jowan replied with a frown. "A Norman married into the family, and the land passed down that way. How did *your* family get their land in England?"

"Forgive me if I've offended you, my lord," Henry said while Merrick silently took note of Sir Jowan's easily roused pride. "Merely my natural curiosity, as my friends will avow."

Ranulf nodded. "He's always asking noblemen how their family came into their estates because he has none himself," he explained.

Henry grinned. "Alas, Sir Jowan, 'tis true. My family has no land in England at all. We did have some in Normandy, but my father lost it all through a series of injudicious alliances and a tendency to gamble. My brother has a fine estate in Scotland—not that it does *me* any good." He gave the older man a hopeful look. "You wouldn't happen to know any well-landed Cornish maidens or widows who might be in need of a husband?"

Sir Jowan stopped frowning, and chuckled good-naturedly. "No, I don't, but if I did, I'd surely introduce you."

So he was proud, but didn't seem to hold a grudge.

The younger Cornishman, however, shot his father a condemning look. The fierce pride of youth, which is not so quick to recede, or a hatred for Normans? Merrick wondered. Or perhaps he didn't approve of Henry and his easy charm.

"With your manners, you won't be landless and unmarried for long," Sir Jowan assured Henry, apparently not noticing his son's reaction. "I'm surprised no woman's caught you yet."

"I'm waiting to fall in love," Henry said with a smile. "My brother and sister recommend it as a prerequisite to marriage."

"And you, my lord?" Kiernan demanded of Merrick. "Do you agree that love should be a prerequisite to marriage?"

Merrick gave him an honest answer. "No."

His brusque response caused another momentary silence to descend, until it was broken by Kiernan. "Where is Lady Constance?"

"I don't know," the lord of Tregellas replied.

Kiernan got to his feet. "Then if you'll excuse me, I'll see if I can find her. We're friends of long acquaintance and I should wish her joy on her marriage after all these years of waiting."

As Henry and Ranulf exchanged glances, Merrick's lips curved up in what was a sort of smile. "You have my leave to go."

Henry and Ranulf realized the gleam in his eyes did not bode well, but Kiernan was too ignorant of his enemy to notice, or too upset about Constance's marriage to care even if he did.

"Thank you, my lord," the young man said before he bowed and strode out of the hall.

"You'll stay until the wedding?" Merrick asked Sir Jowan as the heavy door closed behind his son. "I should get to know my neighbors."

"We'd be delighted to stay, except that we brought nothing with us," Sir Jowan replied, a trifle uneasily. "To speak truth, my lord, we hadn't expected such a kind invitation."

"Servants can be sent to bring what you require from home."

Sir Jowan looked as if he wasn't sure he should be pleased or wary, then decided to be pleased. "We'll stay, my lord, and gladly."

"CONSTANCE!"

Startled and annoyed, Constance shoved back her embroidery frame and quickly got to her feet. Knowing that the priest was visiting some of the poor and sick in the village, she'd brought her embroidery to the small chapel after she heard Sir Jowan and his son were at the outermost gate. She'd been determined to avoid Kiernan and his sighs and lovesick looks until she was forced into his company at the evening meal.

"What are you doing here?" she demanded as he hurried forward. "You must go at once!"

"I had to speak to you. Nobody saw me. I made sure of it."

"You mustn't stay. If you're caught here—"

"I love you!" he cried, rushing toward her as if he would embrace her.

She pushed the frame so that it was between them. This wasn't love. This was madness, or the act of an upset, selfish boy. A man who loved her wouldn't put her, and her reputation, at risk by seeking her out when she was already betrothed to another, and alone.

"If you truly care for me, you'll go at once," she said. "What would Lord Merrick make of this? Or my uncle? They'll think I invited you here."

Kiernan regarded her with bright-eyed hope. "What if they did? We would have to marry, that's all."

"I don't want to be forced to marry anyone, and I'd prefer not to have my honor besmirched," she forcefully replied. "And you may be lucky to escape with your life if Merrick finds you here."

"I don't care!"

"*I* do! And have you no thought of what might happen to *me?* Scandal or not, Merrick might still marry me, but always believe me capable of deception. What kind of life would I lead then?"

"You could refuse him." Kiernan took hold of the frame and pushed it aside. "Why haven't you refused him? You mustn't feel bound by a contract made when you were a child and had no voice to protest."

His action reminded her of another man who raged, and she backed toward the altar. "Leave me, Kiernan."

"Can't you see, Constance? He only wants your dowry, and the power that goes with the alliance to your family. He'll treat you badly and make you miserable. I could never do that. Never!" He grabbed her shoulders and pulled her toward him. "I love you, Constance, and I know you love me."

Anger, disgust, outraged pride and revulsion filled her as she twisted free of Kiernan's grasp. "I *don't* love you and I never have. Now go, and don't try to speak to me alone again."

Kiernan stared at her, aghast, and his eyes filled with tears. "What were all those smiles, those happy hours we spent sitting together, your joy when I came to visit?"

"I was glad of your company, as I was for any friendly face. Now please go."

"You can't *want* to marry him," Kiernan charged. "You feel bound by your father's word and the need to protect the people of Tregellas."

"Don't presume to tell me what I feel. All you need know is that even if I were free, I wouldn't marry you."

When Kiernan's shoulders finally slumped as if in defeat, her anger softened into sympathy. They had enjoyed some pleasant times together, although to her they were no more than a brief respite from anxiety and fear. Yet for the sake of those happier times, and his friendship, she spoke gently. "I want you to be happy, Kiernan. I want you to have a wife who loves you with all her heart. I'm not that woman."

"You're wrong," he whispered, raising his head, his gray eyes flashing with what could be passionate devotion—or passionate hate. "You'll see."

She put out her hand to touch his arm. "Kiernan, don't do anything foolish. Merrick is a proven warrior and..."

Kiernan stepped back as if he feared contact with her would scald him. "I'm not a child, Constance. I grant that I made a mistake coming here like this, but I can't believe you want to marry that man I met in the hall. You're a warm, loving woman and he's as cold as snow."

"Snow can melt."

"Or freeze what it covers. He'll destroy you, Constance, as his father destroyed his mother. Love me or not as you will, but I won't let that bastard have you."

His words chilled her. "I'm not a thing for you to wrest from his grasp."

"But you're not free, either." He took hold of her hands. "Let me set you free."

She pulled away. "Kiernan, please leave me and let me look after myself."

"You're only a woman—"

"Who kept Wicked William from laying waste to Tregellas, or making the people rise up in rebellion to protect themselves. If you have no faith in my ability to make my way, *I* do." She put her hand on his chest and started propelling him down the nave. "Now go, before you're discovered here and our lives are ruined."

"Am I to have no hope of you, Constance?" he pleaded.

"No," she answered firmly, but not unkindly, as she looked out the door to make sure no one would see him.

His expression hardened. "Someday you'll be glad of my company again," he said before he hurried swiftly from the building.

Sighing, Constance gathered up her sewing, since there was no longer any need to stay here. How she wished Kiernan and his father had not come! It would be better if they were in London. Or on a pilgrimage to Rome.

She left the chapel and was nearly past the lady's garden beside the family apartments when she spotted Beatrice seated on the small stone bench inside.

Her cousin's shoulders were slumped and she rested her cheek on one hand, the very picture of despondent despair. That was so unlike Beatrice, Constance immediately opened the gate and hurried toward her along the narrow, pebbled pathway.

It wasn't much of a garden, Lord William considering it a waste of money. Three rosebushes made a brave attempt to climb the wall, and a few small groups of hardy flowers had begun to sprout.

Her worries increased when Beatrice didn't seem to hear her approach. "Beatrice?" Constance said softly, sitting beside her and setting her workbasket on the ground. "What's wrong? Are you ill?"

Beatrice looked up at her and woefully shook her head. "I'm not sick. I'm…" She shrugged and sighed, then fixed an anxious gaze on Constance's face. "Has my father ever said anything to you about when I'm to be married?"

"No," Constance admitted.

"He hasn't once spoken to me about it, either, and I'm nearly sixteen. You were betrothed when you were five."

Constance had wondered about this more than once, and the conclusion she'd reached had been a painful one for her. "He must intend to consult with you when it comes time to pick your husband."

Beatrice stared sullenly at the path. "I fear he simply hasn't found anybody he believes has the right qualifications—lots of money and a powerful family."

"Many noblemen seek such husbands for their daughters," Constance soothed, hoping she was right and that her uncle had Beatrice's best interests at heart. "He'd be remiss if he didn't."

Frowning, Beatrice looked at her. "But what about my happiness? Surely that should be important, too."

"I'm sure it is," Constance replied, "or he would have betrothed you long ago."

As he did me.

Beatrice's eyes filled with remorse. "Oh, Constance, I'm so sorry. I never thought…it never occurred to me that you might resent…"

Constance hurried to assuage her fears. "It's all right, Beatrice. He's not my father, after all. I can't expect him to care for me as he does for you."

Beatrice shifted, and her expression grew even more worried. "Constance, since you *are* betrothed, I've been wondering…do you…do you think Lord Merrick will make you happy?"

"I believe he could," she answered, uncertain if this was a lie to assuage Beatrice's fears, or the truth.

"Is he different when he's alone with you? Does he talk more, or less?"

That was an odd question. It would have been difficult for Merrick to talk any less than he did when he was in company. "Yes, he talks more."

"I'm so relieved! I'd hate to think he was cold and aloof when you were alone."

"No, he's not cold then," Constance confirmed, thinking Merrick was anything *but* cold when they were alone.

"How can I be sure about the man I'm to marry?" Beatrice asked piteously. "How will I know that he won't make me miserable?"

"How can any bride be sure?" Constance mused aloud. "We must all hope for the best, I suppose."

She thought of Beatrice being forced into an unhappy marriage. Given her uncle's disregard for his niece's feelings, it was possible. Although she hoped she was wrong, she decided to offer a suggestion to her cousin, in case that came to pass. "If I was convinced my husband would make my life a misery, I'd find a way to break the contract or, if there was no other way, I'd flee."

"By yourself?" Beatrice asked, her eyes wide with wonder.

"Only as a last resort," Constance clarified, hoping Beatrice appreciated that she would be truly desperate to do that. "You have friends who would gladly offer you sanctuary, and there is always the church."

"I could come to you here, couldn't I?"

"Of course." If she was still there.

Beatrice regarded Constance with unexpected and fervent intensity. "Constance, do you think I could stay here for a little while after your wedding and not go home with Father?"

Before Constance could answer, Beatrice hurried on. "I have no one to keep me company there except Maloren, and she chatters on so, she's like to drive me to lunacy."

Maloren had looked after Beatrice since she was an infant, and while Beatrice was talkative, Maloren was ten times worse. Yet although she could sympathize with Beatrice's complaint, Constance wasn't sure what answer to give her cousin. "I thought you liked Maloren."

"Oh, I love her dearly!" Beatrice cried. "But I want

to learn how to be a good chatelaine like you, for when I'm married. Would you mind?"

"It wouldn't be up to me, I'm afraid," Constance said slowly. "It would be up to Merrick."

Beatrice clasped her hands together. "Will you ask him? Please? For me? If *you* ask him, I'm sure he'll say yes!"

She was so keenly hopeful, Constance couldn't bear to say no. "I'll ask."

"Oh, thank you!" Beatrice cried, sighing rapturously. Then she gave Constance a sheepish smile. "I have to confess that before Merrick came, I thought that you might…that you and Sir Jowan's son…I thought you might run away with Kiernan."

"I've never cared for Kiernan that way," Constance answered honestly. "He's like a brother to me."

A much younger one at that, even though Kiernan was nearly a year older than she. And as for what Kiernan wanted…

Beatrice frowned. "Does Kiernan know how you feel?"

He certainly does now, she thought. "I've never given him any reason to think I cared for him in any other way."

Suddenly a terrible dread filled her. Had Beatrice seen Kiernan coming in or going out of the chapel? "He and his father have arrived. Have you greeted them yet?"

"No. I've been here since the noon meal." She gave Constance a wistful smile. "I feel so much better having talked to you."

Constance felt much better knowing Beatrice hadn't yet seen Kiernan.

"I wish I'd spoken to you sooner," Beatrice continued. "I can't tell you how much sleep I've lost worrying."

"Then I wish you'd talked to me sooner, too," Constance said sincerely.

Beatrice sighed again. "I do so want to love the man I marry."

With a sudden sick feeling in the pit of her stomach, Constance wondered if Sir Henry had something to do with Beatrice's unusually melancholy ruminations.

She shouldn't have been so wrapped up in her own troubles that she neglected the young and impressionable Beatrice. It would truly break her heart if Henry, or anyone else, dishonored or deceived her cousin. "Is there any young man who's come close to winning your affections?" she ventured.

Beatrice blushed and didn't answer a reaction that made Constance silently curse her selfish lapse. "Henry and Ranulf certainly seem to enjoy your company," she noted, trying not to sound overly concerned.

"I enjoy theirs, too," Beatrice readily admitted. "They're both very entertaining, in different ways, of course. Henry's been all over England, and much of Scotland with his brother, and into Wales, too. And he's spent many days at court, meeting all sorts of important people." This time, Beatrice's sigh seemed to come up all the way from her toes. "I must seem dreadfully ignorant to him."

Constance was well aware some men of the world liked ignorant girls, precisely because they were ignorant. "He *is* some years older than you," she said, "and very pleasant and charming. Unfortunately, I fear Sir Henry is also quite capable of seducing a woman merely for his own amusement."

Beatrice stared at Constance, amazed. "Me? You think he might try to seduce *me*?" she asked as a smile bloomed on her face.

This was not the reaction Constance wanted to see. "That's not a *good* thing."

Beatrice looked away. Constance couldn't tell for certain, but she thought Beatrice was blushing as she stammered, "No, no, of course not. I just never thought…imagined…" She drew in a quavering breath. "You think that he was being nice to me only because he was trying to seduce me?"

Constance put her arm around her cousin's slender shoulders. "I didn't mean to upset you, and I could be wrong about him, but you're not a little girl anymore. You're a pretty young woman, and we don't know much about Sir Henry—or Sir Ranulf."

"But they're Lord Merrick's friends."

"Even so, we can't be sure of their morality, especially when you're here to tempt them. It would be terrible if some charming, smooth-talking man dishonored you."

"Yes, I see," Beatrice answered softly. She threw her arms around Constance and hugged her tightly. "You are so good to me—like another mother. When you're married and busy with your children, I'm going to miss you so much!"

Constance gently extricated herself from Beatrice's embrace. "I'll be married, not dead," she said, hoping that she wouldn't be either any time soon. "Now, come, let's go inside. I'm sure Sir Jowan has been wondering where you are. You've always been a great favorite of his."

Beatrice laughed, and merriment once more danced in her eyes. "I like him, too. He always listens to everything I say—even when it's nonsense."

"THIS KIERNAN FELLOW," Henry mused aloud later that evening as he sat on his cot across the small chamber he shared with Ranulf and pulled off his boots. "What do you make of him?"

Seated on a stool with one ankle resting on his knee, Ranulf looked up from cleaning his fingernails and shrugged. "Not much. His father seems a pleasant sort, and more inclined to be Merrick's ally than not, which is good."

Henry tossed his boot into the corner. "I tell you what I think. The lad's in love with Lady Constance— or thinks he is."

Ranulf snorted as he put away his dagger. "Upon what evidence do you base this startling conclusion?"

Henry's second boot hit the floor. "The way he looks at her. He might as well wear a placard declaring his eternal devotion."

This was unwelcome news, but Henry was usually right about such things. He could always tell which knights and ladies were engaged in love affairs, with unfailing accuracy. "Supposing you're right," Ranulf said warily, "do you think she returns his affection?"

"That's the trouble. I can't tell. But if she does, then obviously Merrick shouldn't marry her, dowry or not. I won't have him wed to an adulterous wife."

"And Lord knows you've had plenty of experience with them."

Henry made a sour face as he lay back on his cot, cushioning his head with his hands. "It's because I have that I don't want Merrick wed to a woman who's going to betray him. Honor and duty are all in all to him, and if he's disgraced…"

"It would be a disaster," Ranulf finished, nodding his head in agreement. "But you may be making trouble where none exists. What woman of any sense and taste would prefer young Kiernan over Merrick? And I see no sign that she reciprocates that young man's infatuation, if it exists. We should give her the benefit of the doubt. She's a beautiful woman—she can't help it if some lovesick milksop swoons over her."

Henry turned on his side, levering himself up on his elbow to look at Ranulf. "I don't trust her, and I certainly don't trust that Kiernan, either."

Neither did Ranulf, but should they tell Merrick Henry's suspicions? Was it worth causing yet more fric-

tion between his friend and his bride? For friction there
certainly was. After all, what proof did they have to accuse her? What if Henry was wrong, for once?

"If we find evidence that Lady Constance does indeed reciprocate the Cornish Kiernan's feelings, we
should warn Merrick," he said after considering the situation. "Otherwise, I think we should keep your suspicions to ourselves."

Henry wasn't pleased. "I don't want Merrick to make
a mistake and marry a woman who'll ruin his life."

"Neither do I, but I don't want to plant suspicion
when there's no cause."

"Because he loves her," Henry agreed.

Ranulf made no secret of his surprise. "Has he said
that to you?"

"No, not a word. But I've known the man for fifteen
years and I've seen him around other women. He's never
been more attentive—for him. Nor has he offered to release Lady Constance from their betrothal. If he didn't
care for her, he would have."

Ranulf let out his breath in a low whistle. "God's
blood, Henry, I think you're right."

Unfortunately, this made the situation even more
complicated.

"You may be clever in matters of war and politics,
my friend, but when it comes to men and women..."
Henry gave a shrug that wasn't entirely modest.

"I could keep a watch on her," he suggested as Ranulf tried to decide what to do. "See if she meets Kier-

nan secretly or if there's any other sign she reciprocates the lovesick lad's adoration."

Ranulf tensed ever so slightly. Merrick seemed to trust Henry, but Henry's reputation when it came to women was well deserved. "I don't think that would be wise."

Henry frowned. "Oh, for the love of God! She's betrothed to Merrick, so even if I was tempted to try to get her into my bed, which I confess I would be if she wasn't his betrothed, I'd never…" His frown deepened. "I swore an oath of brotherhood with both of you, and I would die rather than dishonor it."

"I trust you, and I'm sure Merrick does, too," Ranulf replied, "but what do you think Lord Algernon or Lord Carrell or the servants will say if they see you skulking around Lady Constance? *I* should watch her."

"You're not exactly a dog's breakfast yourself," Henry observed, clearly a little peeved.

"Thank you," Ranulf said, acknowledging the compliment and trying to defuse the tension that had arisen. "But as you're forever telling me, I'm not nearly so charming, and thus less suspicious. Plus, I'm more subtle."

"I can be subtle."

"When you're trying to seduce a woman," Ranulf agreed. "We don't want anyone to think that's what you're doing with Lady Constance—or Lady Beatrice."

Henry gave him a look that was genuinely astonished. "I have no interest of that sort in little Lady Bea."

"If you say so," Ranulf replied, masking his relief. "But I would take care, Henry. Beatrice is young and not like the more worldly ladies of the court. She might interpret your chivalrous nonsense as meaning more than it does. You wouldn't want to find yourself roped into marriage because of a girl's misunderstanding, would you? And Merrick has enough to think about without having to defend his friend's actions."

Henry scowled for a moment, then his eyes brightened with merry jubilation. "I tell you what—we can set Beatrice on Kiernan."

Ranulf stiffened. "What?"

"She can keep him company and away from Lady Constance. And he's so besotted with my lady, there's no danger to the little chatterer's honor."

"I wish you wouldn't call her that," Ranulf said, annoyed. "Beatrice *is* a noblewoman."

Henry laughed and bowed his head. "Forgive my impertinence. But what do you think of my plan?"

"You wouldn't tell Beatrice why you were encouraging that, would you?"

"Do I look a complete dolt?" Henry demanded with a grin.

That grin did nothing to improve Ranulf's mood. "You look like a man quite capable of getting a young woman to do whatever he likes for his own purpose. Maybe we should find another way to keep the Cornishman away from Lady Constance."

"I tell you, this is perfect," Henry declared, too enthused with his plan to see any problems. "I'll become much too busy to spend time with little Lady Bea and suggest Kiernan play chess with her, or go riding. That way, we can see if Lady Constance turns peevish, or welcomes his absence."

"I'm not convinced this is a good idea," Ranulf said slowly.

"Of course it is," Henry insisted. "You want Merrick to be happy, don't you?"

"Yes."

"Then we've got to be sure Lady Constance won't break his heart."

Ranulf didn't disagree, or voice any further objections to Henry's plan. But he was no more thrilled to think of Beatrice spending time with the not unattractive young Kiernan than he had been to see her with Henry.

AT THE SAME TIME THAT HENRY was voicing his concerns to Ranulf, Sir Jowan was confronting his son in the wall chamber given over to their use while they were in Tregellas.

"For God's sake, show some sense!" he cried, looking at his son with both annoyance and concern. "God help us, boy, keep your feelings to yourself or the man'll kill you."

An oil lamp filled with sheep tallow hung from the ceiling by a slender chain, and its flickering flame illuminated Kiernan's baleful face as he looked up at his father from where he sat on one of the two beds made with fresh linen and wool blankets. "Can I help it if I love her?"

"You'd better help it," Sir Jowan declared, sitting heavily on the cot opposite his son. "They're going to be married, and there's not a damn thing you can do about it."

Kiernan rose and started to pace in the center of the narrow room. "He doesn't even pay attention to her," he grumbled, rubbing his fist into his palm. "You saw him tonight—he barely spoke to her."

"He barely spoke to anybody."

"I don't care what agreements have been signed—he doesn't deserve her."

Sir Jowan reached out to stop his son in his agitated tracks. "Whatever we think of him, agreements have been signed, and the only people who can break them are Lord Merrick and Lady Constance."

"You know she won't," Kiernan muttered as he threw himself down on the cot. "Her family honor means too much to her, and she's anxious to ensure that the tenants don't suffer. Look what she endured with his father."

"But who are you to interfere? Has Constance ever given you any reason to think she wants to be free of the agreement? Has she ever told you, or given any sign, that she cares enough to marry you? That she loves you?"

Kiernan couldn't meet his father's gaze. "She may not love me yet, but I love her, and in time—"

"In time is not now," his father declared. "If she doesn't want you, you shouldn't try to come between her and Lord Merrick."

Kiernan raised his head, his eyes blazing with righteous passion. "I'd rather die than see her married to that grim brute."

Real fear lodged in Sir Jowan's heart as he pleaded with his beloved, headstrong son. "If you challenge him, you *will* die. He's been trained by the best and he's won tournaments all over England. He outweighs you by at least five stone. You'd have to train for a year to come close to beating him, and even then, he'd still be bigger than you."

"Big doesn't mean he'll beat me."

Sir Jowan grabbed his son by the shoulders and forced him to meet his gaze. "Listen to me, Kiernan. If you interfere with this marriage, if you challenge Merrick, he'll surely kill you without a moment's remorse. How would that help Constance? How will he treat her if he thinks there was something between you, *when there was not?* Is that fair or just to her?"

His fierceness softened. "My son, it's her right to refuse, if she so wishes, and you know as well as I that Constance is not a woman to be bullied into marriage. If she marries this man, it will be because she wants to."

"It will be because she's worried about the tenants and villagers," his son stubbornly persisted.

"Whatever reason she has for marrying him, if you do love her, if you respect her and want her to be happy, you won't make things worse, even with the best of intentions," his father pleaded.

Kiernan wrenched himself free, then stood with his shoulders slumped, his head hanging, the very image of despair. "I can't stand to think of her married to that Norman lout."

"I know, I know, my son," his father said softly, his heart aching for his unhappy child. "But if you truly love her, you must let her choose her fate. All you can do is let her know that if things go awry, she has friends, and we will help her all we can. Do you hear me, my son?"

Kiernan nodded.

"Will you give me your word that you'll not interfere?"

Again Kiernan nodded.

"Then leave them be and go to sleep." He patted his son on the shoulder, wishing he could always keep him safe. "If Constance wants our help, I'm sure she'll ask for it."

Kiernan dutifully disrobed, washed and got into bed. But he did not sleep.

CHAPTER SEVEN

CONSTANCE GLANCED UP FROM HER embroidery at Beatrice seated across from her, working on an altar cloth in a most desultory manner. At the rate she was going, it wouldn't be finished before the Second Coming, even though she'd been silent since sitting down.

"I know you're disappointed that we couldn't join the hunt, Beatrice," Constance said, trying to sound sympathetic although she was, in truth, relived. It had been very difficult avoiding Kiernan since that disastrous encounter in the chapel, but avoid him she must. Did he think Merrick was blind or stupid? Did he truly not appreciate the trouble he could cause her if Merrick suspected his aim, or did he simply, selfishly, not care? "It really is far too muddy for us to ride out. You'll have other opportunities, I'm sure. We'll need plenty of game for the wedding feast."

Which would be in a se'nnight.

A se'ennight, and she would have to choose if she would marry the lord of Tregellas or refuse him. To think that decision had once seemed so easy, it could hardly be called a decision at all.

Beatrice sighed as if life were really too tragic and regarded her cousin with a melancholy expression. "If only it hadn't rained last night."

"It's Cornwall," Constance replied with a rueful smile. "And it's cleared up. If it stays nice, perhaps we can ride out later in the afternoon. Now come, tell me a story while we work. Or is there some news you've heard from the servants?"

Constance wasn't above listening to gossip. For one thing, it was part of her responsibility to know what was going on among the servants and their guests. For another, it was entertaining, even if she had to try to separate fact from fancy, especially when Beatrice was the source.

Beatrice put down her needle and thought a moment. "Well, Eric is determined to ask Merrick for permission to marry Annice at the next hall moot."

"There's nothing new in that, is there?"

Beatrice's eyes began to sparkle. "Some of the women think he was going to wait a bit longer. There's been talk of another girl in Touro who's caught his eye. But then Annice was made Queen of the May. Apparently that encouraged Eric not to delay."

Constance frowned.

"Oh, not that he's worried about Merrick. No, no, the women are all much more confident he's not going to be like *that*. It's just that some of them think Eric was, well, taking his own sweet time about it and now he's realized he'd better not delay, or someone else may come a-wooing."

"Annice must be pleased."

Beatrice picked up her needle and threaded it with a piece of emerald-green silk. "I suppose so, although I heard that she's been acting quite aloof lately. Some wonder if being Queen of the May has gone to her head."

Constance was surprised to hear that. "I didn't think she was particularly vain."

"Neither did I, so it's probably just jealous tongues wagging." Beatrice stuck her needle in her work again and leaned closer. "There's something else, about Sir Henry. I think he's got a mistress in London."

Constance stared at her incredulously. "Did he *tell* you that?"

"Of course not!" Beatrice grinned with pride. "I figured it out myself, from things he's said."

This being Beatrice, that could mean Henry had merely mentioned a woman who lived in London.

"I think you were absolutely right about him, Constance. He's just a charming cad, and no woman should trust a word he says. *I* could never care for a man who kept a mistress."

Whether Sir Henry had a mistress or not, Constance didn't care. She was simply relieved Beatrice suspected such a person's existence. That should prevent her from making a mistake that could end in shame and ruin.

"I don't think Sir Ranulf has a mistress," Beatrice mused aloud. "I'm sure he's suffering from a broken heart."

Constance thought it unlikely that the sardonic Ranulf would admit that, if it were true. "What makes you say that?"

Beatrice shrugged, but her eyes shone with certainty. "What else could make a man so cynical about love? He actually said he thinks the tales of King Arthur and his knights are ridiculous!"

Beatrice was surely safe from Sir Ranulf, too. Even if he had nefarious designs on her—which Constance doubted—any man who disparaged the tales of the Round Table would never get far with her cousin.

Constance wondered if Merrick had ever had a mistress, but surely if Beatrice knew, she would have told her already. She would consider that information Constance should know. Since she hadn't, she either didn't know or thought he must not.

A clatter of hooves and shouting male voices arose from the courtyard. Beatrice immediately jumped to her feet, smiling with delight. "They're back!"

Constance pushed her embroidery frame to one side and likewise rose, albeit a bit more sedately. "They weren't gone very long. I hope nothing—"

The doors to the hall burst open and Merrick, his hair disheveled, his face a mask of stern annoyance, came striding into the hall, his right sleeve covered in blood, with more dripping onto the rushes as he passed.

"What happened?" Constance cried as she ran toward him while the rest of the hunting party came into the hall. "Were you attacked?"

"No," Merrick snapped as he continued past her without so much as a pause or a glance in her direction.

A hunting accident, then—perhaps from the tusks of an enraged boar. "I'll fetch my medicines to tend to your wound."

That brought him to an abrupt halt. "No." He turned eyes as fierce as any angry beast's onto her. "I'll tend to my wound myself," he growled before going on his way.

As Constance stood motionless, stunned by his harsh reply, Henry appeared at her side. "We cornered a boar, and in the excitement, Talek struck Merrick's arm with his spear. I don't think the wound's serious. You wouldn't, either, if you'd heard Merrick shouting for his horse and cursing Talek and anybody else who got within five feet of him."

Even while she told herself that men like Henry had been in enough tournaments to know when a wound was serious or not, she closed her eyes and remembered another man's shouts and curses.

Henry lightly touched her arm. "Don't be upset, my lady. I assure you, he's not badly hurt and he's always like this when he's sick or injured. He hates having people fuss over him."

"Henry's quite right," Ranulf confirmed. "That's his way. But he's no fool. If he thought himself seriously hurt, he would seek a leech."

Beatrice stepped forward shakily. "You're bleeding, too," she said, pointing at Sir Ranulf's blood-spattered tunic.

"That's the boar's blood," he replied dismissively before addressing Constance again. "My lady, if there's a leech in the castle, you could try summoning him, although that would be more for your comfort than for any good it might do Merrick. He'll likely just send the fellow away."

Constance was too aware of her duty as chatelaine to leave the care of a wounded man—any wounded man—to fate or the dubious skill of a leech.

And there was another reason she wouldn't leave Merrick to nurse his wound alone. She'd spent most of her life tiptoeing around one man's moods. She wasn't going to do so again.

"I'll tend to Lord Merrick's injury," she said, her tone implying that she would whether he liked it or not, which was precisely what she meant.

"He's very angry, Constance," Lord Algernon said warily, "and if his friends think he's better left alone—"

"It's my duty to see that my guests receive the best care possible."

The garrison commander, paler than she'd ever seen him, hurried up to her. "Please make sure he understands it was an accident, my lady," Talek pleaded. "I was aiming for the boar and he moved and got in my way."

Constance put a comforting hand on the faithful soldier's shoulder. "I will. I'm sure he'll understand."

In time, and if he truly wasn't like his father, who held a grudge over the smallest thing for months.

Out of the corner of her eye she saw Kiernan and his

father enter the hall. Kiernan immediately started toward her, but she ignored him.

At least he hadn't been the one to wound Merrick, although that kind of underhanded attack wouldn't be Kiernan's way. If she gave him the slightest encouragement, he'd probably challenge Merrick to combat. He would surely consider anything less the act of a coward.

Leaving the hall before Kiernan reached her, Constance hurried to her bedchamber to fetch her medicines, including fine needles and thread for stitching wounds. From a chest near her bed she filled a basket with clean linen, some already in strips for bandaging, as well as a sicklewort ointment that helped stop bleeding and took away pain.

An anxious Beatrice hovered in the doorway. "Is there anything I can do?"

This might be a good chance for her cousin to learn a little about caring for wounded men. "Have a servant fetch some hot water from the kitchen and bring it to Lord Merrick's chamber right away."

With a nod, Beatrice ran off.

When Constance strode back through the hall, she noted that Henry, Ranulf and Lord Algernon were already enjoying wine by the hearth, even though they were still in their dirty, bloody and mud-bespattered clothes. Sir Jowan was in the courtyard, shouting something about his horse; Kiernan was nowhere to be seen.

She forgot about Kiernan when her uncle detained

her with a hand on her arm. "If he dies," Lord Carrell said with quiet urgency, "the king may decide to give you to one of his French relatives."

That was not a fate she cared to contemplate. "I'll tend to Merrick's wound as best I can, Uncle. Fortunately, Sir Henry says it's not serious. Now I had better get on my way," she finished as she continued to the stairs leading to the bedchambers.

"Good luck, my lady!" Henry called out, saluting her with his wine goblet. "You'll need it!"

If they were expecting her to come running back, upset and in tears because Merrick wouldn't admit her to his presence, they should have been here when Lord William was in his foulest humors, calling her terrible names, throwing anything he could lay his hands on at her—including his chamber pot.

Yet in spite of her determination to do her duty, once outside the door to Merrick's chamber, Constance hesitated. What if he was like his father in his injured rage?

If he was, the sooner she found out, the better.

Taking a deep breath, she rapped smartly on the door.

"Who is it?" Merrick demanded from the other side.

"Constance. I've come to see to your wound."

The door flew open. A half-naked Merrick stood there, his hair a mess, his eyes blazing, the long cut in his right arm still dripping blood. "I don't need any help," he growled.

At least he didn't shout. "I don't care," she said with

equally determined calm. "I'm going to sew up that wound before you bleed to death."

"I've had worse wounds and tended them myself," he said, starting to close the door.

She stuck her foot in the opening. "You're handy with a needle and thread?"

Glancing down at her foot, he frowned, but he stopped trying to close the door. "It will heal without it."

"Perhaps. Perhaps not," she said as she pushed through the door and into the room.

The last time she had been in this chamber, she'd been ensuring that all was in readiness for Merrick's arrival—the linens clean; the feather bed plump with goose down and the curtains surrounding the large bed free of dust; the thick carpet that had cost more than most tinners earned in two years, even avoiding the tax, shaken and replaced; the silver ewer and basin ready on the stand near the window; the thick beeswax candle on the table beside the bed; and the brazier prepared in the corner.

As she set her basket on the wash table, she took in the bloody water in the basin, the stained shirt in a heap on the floor, the spilled wine on the side table that he must have tried to pour, and the ragged strips of torn linen. She ignored the huge curtained bed.

"How did you do that?" she asked, nodding at the strips. "With your teeth?"

"I told you, I can tend to my wound myself."

She started to drag a chair beside the wash table.

"I'm not leaving here until I've done my best to help you. You can't sew that wound up yourself, so you'd best sit down and let me get at it."

"The cut's not that deep."

She put her hands on her hips. "I suppose you don't want the ointment I brought, which stops the bleeding, speeds healing and takes away pain, either. Just how stubborn a man are you?"

After a long moment of mutual glaring, he finally—much to her relief—threw himself into the chair and held out his arm. "I give you leave to touch me."

Such arrogance!

His dark-eyed gaze mocked her. "You told me I must have your leave to touch you, so I think it's only fair that you require *my* leave to touch *me*."

Her lip curled with scorn as she took hold of his hand and held his arm still while she examined the cut. Mercifully, it wasn't deep. The use of his hand and arm should be unaffected. "Talek keeps his spear sharp, I see. That's good."

"Good? The man could have killed me."

"A ragged-edged wound is worse than a clean-edged one," she replied. She lifted her eyes to his face, noting that he was a little pale. "But then, if you've tended to your wounds yourself, you'd know that."

"Constance?" Biting her lip, Beatrice stood on the threshold of the bedchamber, an ewer in her hands and more clean linen hanging over her arm.

"Ah, excellent," Constance said, moving briskly to

take the ewer and linen from her cousin, who didn't stir a step as she stared at Merrick.

"God's blood, am I to have an audience?" he demanded.

Perhaps this was not the best time for Beatrice to learn about tending to a man's wounds. "Thank you, Beatrice. You can go."

Beatrice nodded and quickly disappeared.

"There was no need for you to be so rude, even if you're in pain," Constance admonished as she poured the bloody water from the ewer into the empty chamber pot. "She was only trying to help."

Merrick flinched as she started to wash his wound. "Would you enjoy having some soldier watch as I tended to a wound on *your* arm?"

"It's Beatrice's duty to learn to care for wounded men. How else can she take care of her husband or sons, or the knights in their command, if they're hurt?"

"Let her learn by watching somebody else."

Constance pursed her lips as she concentrated on cleaning the wound. Merrick sat perfectly still, without so much as a grimace, when she began to sew it shut. At least his stoicism wasn't feigned.

"I've noticed, my lady, that your steward holds you in high esteem," he said as she gently pushed the needle through his skin.

"He's a trusted friend, my lord," she replied, biting her lip as she pulled the thread to make the first stitch.

"I can see why. He seems a most reliable and honest man."

"He is," she confirmed. Her brow furrowed as she worked, and she considered asking him to be quiet, until she realized Merrick might be trying to take his mind off his pain.

"I've noticed a house in the village," he said, "one that wasn't there before I left when I was a boy—a rather large building made of stone and with an upper floor of wattle and daub."

"That belongs Ruan, your bailiff. He had it built three years ago."

"You don't like him. Why not?"

She thought she'd kept her voice carefully neutral as she replied but, obviously, she hadn't.

She shrugged as she took another stitch. "Although there's never been any evidence that he's dishonest, there's something underhanded in his manner, in the way he speaks, as if he's cheating you, and you know he's cheating you, but you can't quite figure out how."

"So your animosity toward the bailiff is based solely on a feeling?"

How she wished she had some proof of Ruan's dishonesty! "Yes, my lord, it is."

"I won't dismiss a man based on a feeling, especially when I've seen nothing that would condemn him as a thief."

"You asked me what I thought, and I told you," she replied, disappointed that he was disregarding her answer.

"Sometimes a feeling is a warning, and one worth heeding. Because of your apparent mistrust, I've gone over the accounts very carefully. I've found nothing wrong."

Despite her task, a little thrill of pleasure went through her at Merrick's measured words. Lord William had openly scorned most of what she said. Her uncle ostensibly listened, but she knew that he held her observations in low esteem. "Perhaps," she suggested, "he's been too afraid of being caught to do anything dishonest. That's not the best reason to trust a man, but…"

"But it would explain why I find nothing amiss even though he appears untrustworthy."

"And perhaps I shouldn't condemn a man because of his outward appearance."

Merrick flinched and she glanced swiftly up at his pale face, so close to hers. "I'm sorry."

He shook his head. "I have had worse hurts before, without so lovely and gentle a nursemaid to attend me."

She blushed as she tightened the last stitch, and tried not to think about his proximity. Or note his disheveled dark hair, as if it was tousled from sleep. Or be excited by the low, husky rasp of his voice so close to her ear. Or be distracted by his lips, mere inches away.

"Very neatly done," he observed as she finished the stitches. "I won't refuse your aid again."

"How kind of you, my lord, but I point out, I didn't let you refuse this time," she said as she smoothed the sicklewort ointment over the stitches. "Fortunately, it takes more than a foul temper and harsh words to prevent me from doing what I believe to be right."

"So I gather. I shall remember."

As the slightly minty fragrance of the salve infused the chamber, she started to wrap his arm in a clean bandage with swift efficiency, thinking it would be best if she finished quickly. "The binding should be changed and the ointment reapplied before you sleep, and again in the morning."

After she knotted the bandage, he rose without speaking and went to his wooden chest. He lifted the lid and as he reached down for a clean shirt, he wobbled a bit as if he was dizzy.

Proud, stubborn fool, she thought indulgently as she hurried to his side, regardless of his attempts to wave her away. In some ways, men could be such children.

"Sit down before you fall down," she commanded. "There's nobody here to impress with your manly fortitude."

"Except you."

"I'm duly impressed. Now sit down."

He did, but not before he grabbed a shirt. Then he sat on the end of his bed. "Are you always this obstinate?"

She returned to the table and started to put the unused linen bandages back inside the basket. "When I'm dealing with a stubborn man, yes."

"I'm not stubborn."

She gave him a very skeptical look.

"I don't like to be fussed over."

"So I hear."

She went to help him put on his shirt, which he was holding in his left hand.

"I can do it myself."

"I don't care," she retorted, her patience wearing thin. She took the shirt from him, found the neck and put it over his head.

This brought her breasts very close to his face.

As she attempted to concentrate and ease his right arm through the sleeve, she reminded herself that she'd helped men dress before. Sick men. Injured men. None of them handsome, and none of them her betrothed.

Despite her efforts to ignore his proximity, sweat started to trickle down her back. She got an itch between her shoulder blades.

Determined to overcome her foolish reaction and to explain what might seem to be a preoccupation with the muscular male body so close to her own, she said, "I see by your scars that this isn't your first wound that required sewing. Is it true you've won over twenty tournaments?"

He nodded.

"Even though they're illegal?"

He inclined his head.

"And this in spite of all your talk about upholding the king's laws?"

"The king knows he can't abolish tournaments completely. The barons would never stand for it."

"So if the king winks his eye at his own decree, then it can be ignored?" she asked with a hint of scorn.

"If the king winks his eye at his own decree, so do I," Merrick matter-of-factly replied. "If he does not, I don't."

She probably shouldn't be surprised he would subscribe to that convenient excuse. Most noblemen would. But that didn't mean there was no risk. "Yet surely you've heard of all the trouble Walter Marshall's had getting the king to confirm his inheritance after his brother died in a tournament. What if you'd been killed doing the same thing? Your family's land might have been forfeit to the crown."

"If I'd been killed, I don't think I would have much cared what happened to my family's land."

Not at all amused by his answer, she frowned and let some of her disgust slip into her voice as she tied the laces of his shirt at the neck, which also closed that gaping opening that revealed his chest. "Are you really so irresponsible, my lord? Or are you so sure of the king's favor that you saw no danger?"

"Henry's a capricious man," he answered with a shrug. "One can be in the king's favor one day, and out the next."

"Then why court his displeasure?"

"Because it was *my* pleasure."

God help her! Between that slight grin, the proximity of his body and his low, deep voice, shivers of…not dread…ran down her spine.

She quickly went back to cleaning up. She drained the newly bloodied water into the chamber pot and put the cloths used to wash his wound into the empty basin. "I hope you won't hold what happened today against

Talek," she said, speaking of another serious matter, and one that would surely not lead to any unwelcome thoughts or images. "He's a good soldier and very loyal."

"I'll deal with Talek in due course."

Merrick's deep voice was so stern and unyielding, her formerly heated blood ran cold. "What are you going to do?"

"He must leave Tregellas before nightfall and never return."

She stared at him, aghast at the severity of his reaction. "But why? Because he missed his aim and struck you instead? I assure you, my lord, Talek is a good man."

Merrick rose and regarded her with frustrating impassivity. "A fine soldier Talek may be, but as garrison commander, he has control of the soldiers, as well as the arms and weapons, and the defense of this castle. If I have even the slightest doubt as to his abilities, his loyalty or his desire to protect me and mine, he cannot remain here."

"What cause would he have to harm you?" she protested.

"I don't know."

"Then why…?"

"Because he *did* harm me. Whether he meant to or not, I can't let such a thing pass."

"But to send him away, to shame such a loyal man—"

"What would you rather I do? Demote him? Have him become a common soldier? Would that not shame him more?"

Constance had to admit—to herself—that was true. But even so… "He wasn't trying to kill you. I'm sure of it."

"Enough to risk your life, and mine, and everyone else's in Tregellas? Alas for you, my lady, I have no such faith. He must go."

Obviously Merrick had no real regard for her opinion, and Talek's years of service meant nothing.

The hard line of Merrick's mouth softened a little. "I have reasons for my decisions, Constance. You may not understand them, or agree, but I don't act on whims, or without good cause. I will protect what is mine, whether it is my life or my castle or my wife. I will guard what I hold dear."

Did that mean he cared for her, or only that he would fight to keep what he considered his possessions, including his wife?

Yet as he looked at her, and she at him, the fiery gleam in his eyes altered to another kind of fire. She tried to ignore it, and the answering flame kindling within her, but her desire was stronger than her will. Her breathing quickened. Her heartbeat pulsed with excitement. His face was inches away, his body close enough to touch. She felt her resolve slipping, melting away under the heat of his gaze.

His steady stare still holding hers, Merrick reached out and drew her to him.

If he kissed her again, the last of her resistance would disappear like so much mist in the summer sun. She would be surrendering, perhaps forever. Accepting her role as his property.

She backed away.

Merrick's expression hardened, and once more the stone-faced commander of Tregellas stood before her. "Go and find Talek. Tell him I will speak to him in the solar. At once."

"I will do as you ask because you rule here, my lord," she answered. "But I still think you're wrong."

A SHORT WHILE LATER, Merrick regarded Talek with such stern, merciless eyes, the garrison commander—who was no coward—began to tremble. "Forgive me, my lord! It was an accident."

"Did I ask you for an explanation?"

The lord of Tregellas didn't shout, or even raise his voice, but the cold steadiness of his deep voice terrified Talek even more.

Merrick walked up to the quivering commander until he was nearly nose-to-nose with him. "You didn't want to hurt me?"

"No, my lord!"

"You didn't see me?"

Talek's throat was as dry as if he'd marched through a desert. "No, my lord."

"Am I a small man, Talek?"

"No, my lord." The garrison commander swallowed hard. "But it was crowded around the boar, my lord, and accidents sometimes happen on hunts." Talek dropped to his knees. "My lord," he pleaded, "why would I try to kill you?"

Merrick crossed his arms and raised a brow in silent query.

"I'm your loyal servant, my lord! Remember when you was a boy? I was loyal to your father, too. Ask Lady Constance. She'll vouch for me, my lord."

"She's already assured me of your faithfulness."

Hope rekindled and Talek spoke with frantic enthusiasm. "I knew she would, my lord. I've served in Tregellas for twenty years and—"

"I know. I remember you, Talek."

Talek was chilled anew, but he clung to his hope, and his history with Wicked William's son. "I was a good friend to you when you was a lad, wasn't I, my lord? I never questioned what you wanted, did I?"

"Yes, you were a good friend to your lord's son," Merrick confirmed, but in such a way that it seemed a condemnation.

"I'll follow any orders you give me now without question, too," Talek vowed.

Merrick continued to regard the man with a stony gaze. "*Any* orders?"

Talek blanched, but he answered eagerly nonetheless. "Aye, my lord, any orders."

"Good. Go back to the hall and tell Sir Ranulf I wish to speak with him. Then leave Tregellas immediately and never come back." Merrick splayed his hands on the table, leaning forward and regarding Talek as he might a loathsome creature he was about to destroy. "And know you this, Talek—if any man ever tries to hurt me or my family, I'll hunt him down and kill him even more slowly than my father would have."

"My lord!" Talek gasped, his pale face flushing. "Today was an accident. I swear on my life!"

Merrick's eyes held no pity. "Be glad I don't have you executed for attempting to assassinate me. Now go, before I change my mind."

Talek obeyed, hate replacing fear as he left the solar.

Chapter Eight

"HERE I AM, MERRICK, in answer to your summons," Ranulf said when he entered the solar. His friend stood at the window, his back to the door and his wounded arm cradled in the uninjured one. "I couldn't find Henry."

The lord of Tregellas turned away from the window and faced him. "Did Talek say I wanted to speak to Henry?"

"No," Ranulf admitted, his brow furrowing at his friend's brusque tone. "So what did you decide to do with the garrison commander? When he spoke to me he didn't look happy, but he wasn't surrounded by armed guards, either."

"Talek is leaving Tregellas and won't be returning."

Ranulf sat without waiting for an invitation to do so. "You're letting him go free?"

Merrick took his seat opposite Ranulf, with the wide table between them, and explained as he had to Constance. "I have no proof that he was trying to kill me, but I won't run the risk that he wasn't."

"I understand, of course," Ranulf replied. "Unfortunately, it seems your bride doesn't appreciate your reasoning. She looked very upset when she left the hall. From what I can gather, Talek's been one of the few men truly loyal to her. Perhaps she even looked upon him as a friend."

Although Ranulf was his boon companion, Merrick had no intention of revealing how Constance's reaction had upset him. Given her concern for others, he had thought she would understand the necessity of his decision, and had been disappointed to encounter her anger instead. Surely she would realize he was right…eventually. "Whether I upset Constance or not, the man has to go."

"I'm not disputing that," Ranulf said. "The question is, will you speak to her and try to explain, or will you let this lie between you like a different sort of wound?"

Merrick couldn't see that reiterating his opinion would make much difference. Nor did he appreciate Ranulf's unwelcome advice. The quarrel with Constance had not been his fault. He was right to do what he must to protect Tregellas, and those who lived here.

Yet even as his temper flared again, he tried to keep from betraying his annoyance in either his manner, his expression or his voice. "Are you offering me advice about women? I thought that was Henry's province."

Ranulf colored and his mask of placid neutrality slipped a little. "I'm trying to help."

"Good, because I have a request to make of you," Merrick replied, gladly moving the discussion away from Constance.

Ranulf raised an inquisitive brow. "This should be…interesting. I don't recall you ever asking a favor of me before."

No, he hadn't, because like Ranulf and Henry, he had his pride. But there was no one else of whom he could make this request, except Henry. While Henry was a loyal and amusing friend, and Merrick trusted him as much as he did Ranulf, Ranulf would be the better choice. "Since Talek is leaving, I require a new garrison commander. I would like you to take that place."

Ranulf flushed, and Merrick knew it wasn't from modesty. "I'm not a soldier or hireling," his friend frostily replied.

"I meant no disrespect," Merrick said. Nor had he, but he had need of his friend's help now, and he wasn't too proud to ask for it. "Until I can decide who among the soldiers here deserves that responsibility, I need someone I can trust in that position."

"I see," Ranulf replied noncommittally.

"If you'd rather not, so be it, of course."

Merrick watched Ranulf as he waited for his friend to answer, hoping Ranulf would comprehend the situation better than Constance had.

After what seemed a very long time, Ranulf gave him a sardonic smile and shrugged. "Very well, my friend. I'll act as your garrison commander—but only until you find another, and I hope that will be soon."

Merrick subdued a sigh of relief, and so pleased was

he, he came around the table and clapped his hand on his friend's shoulder in a rare gesture of camaraderie. "Thank you, Ranulf. I won't forget this."

"Brothers to death," Ranulf gravely replied.

"Brothers to death," Merrick repeated.

"So, my lord, what orders do you have for me?"

"I'll tell the men myself of my decision about Talek and that you're taking his place. I'll leave it to you to tell Henry."

"As you wish, my lord. Is there anything more?"

"No."

"Then I'm free to leave?"

"Yes, Ranulf, of course, if there's nothing more you think we need to discuss."

"No, my lord, there isn't," Ranulf replied. He strolled to the door with his usual easy, athletic stride, showing no sign that he was offended, yet Merrick realized he'd upset his friend. He'd known Ranulf too long to be fooled by his air of dispassionate detachment.

After he was gone, Merrick threw himself into his chair and bit back an oath. Why could no one else see the necessity of his decisions? Why did they think he was being unreasonable? Someone had tried to kill the heir of Tregellas before and they might try again. If they succeeded, what fate might then befall his wife, his friends and everyone else here?

It was his duty to protect them all, and by God, he would—whether anyone else approved of his methods or not.

BACK AND FORTH CONSTANCE strode in the garden, too agitated to sit, her mind full of tumultuous thoughts about everything that had just happened, with one exception: she refused to examine the fear that had arisen, strong and searing, when she saw the blood dripping from Merrick's arm.

Why had he not listened to her this time, as he had about Annice? Was that to be his way—to agree in some things, but not all, and to refuse to listen to reason when he believed he was right?

But she had lived here for years; she knew these people as he did not. Merrick was an intelligent man—why could he not see this and pay heed to her opinion? Why was he so certain Talek posed a threat?

She thought of his sire's fears, and the extreme precautions he'd taken for his own protection. There was one important difference, though. Lord William had never once mentioned any concern for the safety of anyone except himself, even when his son lay wounded far away in the north.

"My lady?"

God help her, she didn't want to be bothered with Henry now.

Unfortunately, and despite the look she gave him that would have told a less selfish, more perceptive man that she wished to be alone, he opened the gate and sauntered into the garden.

"I've come to talk to you about Merrick," he said.

It was on the tip of her tongue to ask him to leave, but she reconsidered. Merrick was still very much a mystery to her. Surely Henry could provide some answers.

"I assume you quarreled, and you took the garrison commander's part," he continued, studying her.

"With just cause," she replied, her anger again rising as she thought of Merrick's harsh decision. "Talek's been a loyal soldier here for twenty years. Merrick has no reason to think he would deliberately harm him."

Henry regarded her gravely, and for once, there was no hint of merriment in his eyes. "I fear, my lady, that your betrothed has a suspicious nature. I'm not sure he even trusts Ranulf and me, although we've been friends for fifteen years and sworn an oath of loyalty to each other."

She sat on the edge of the stone bench and gestured for him to join her. "Fifteen years? You must have met him at Sir Leonard's castle shortly after his cortege was attacked."

Henry nodded. "I had just arrived myself."

"Sir Leonard wrote to tell us what had happened and to assure us that Merrick was in no danger of dying. Then he wrote asking why Lord William didn't come. Lord William said his son was no baby to need coddling. Let Sir Leonard take care of him, as was his duty."

How hard-hearted Lord William had been. How selfish. How cruel. Even though his son had nearly been killed, he wouldn't bestir himself a step.

"Perhaps because Merrick had no life-threatening

wounds," Henry suggested. "Even so, he didn't talk to anyone, including Sir Leonard, for weeks. There was some fear his wits had been damaged since there was no wound to his throat. The physician thought it might be a result of the panic and fear from the attack. He had seen such things before in children. They didn't find Merrick until the day after the attack, you see. He spent hours alone in the dark hiding from the men who'd slaughtered his uncle and the escort."

"I didn't know that," she confessed. He must have been terrified, all alone and lost in the dark, with the bodies of those sent to protect him nearby. Was it any wonder, then, that he feared assassination?

"What made him finally speak?" she asked after a moment.

"Me," Henry replied with a sheepish grin. "He told me to shut my mouth."

In spite of her distress, Constance had to smile as she imagined a young and annoyed Merrick losing his patience with an equally young and lively Henry.

"After he was well enough to train with the other fostered boys I pestered him unmercifully. I kept asking him to help me." Henry's grin became a wistful smile. "It was obvious even then that he was the best of us all."

That came as no surprise. Yet when Henry's admission was accompanied by a sigh, she realized how distressing it must have been to always be surpassed by Merrick. "I'm sure you're an excellent knight, too," she said, using the same tone of voice with which she comforted Beatrice.

Henry's eyes lit with pleasure. "How delightful of you to say so, my lady." His expression softened. "But then, you are ever kindhearted and generous."

She suddenly felt a little uncomfortable. Henry hadn't said or done anything to make her fear that his motives were anything but genial and honorable, and yet…

"Ah, here you are, Henry," Ranulf declared as he sauntered along the path toward them.

Constance shot to her feet. She could guess how this might look, especially to the cynical Ranulf.

Henry likewise scrambled to his feet, while Constance attempted to regain her composure. After all, she had done nothing wrong and she shouldn't act as if she had.

"There's no need to worry, my lady," Henry said with a smile that was no doubt intended to be comforting. "Ranulf knows I have no seductive designs on you."

She was not a young girl in need of reassurance. "That is well, sir," she said sharply. "For if you did, you would be wasting your time."

Ranulf's brows rose. She didn't see Henry's reaction, because she didn't look at him.

"You see, Ranulf?" Henry replied, sounding as merry as ever. "Even if I were the most practiced seducer in England, I stand no chance with her."

She glanced at him and he laid his hand over his heart. "Although it wounds my pride to hear such a denunciation from those lovely lips."

Constance frowned. Had the man no sense at all? "Sir, I'm in no humor for your jests."

"Alas!" he cried in mock anguish. "A blow from your slender hands would pain me less!"

Constance had had quite enough of Henry. "If you'll excuse me, gentlemen, I have duties that require my supervision," she said, and she headed for the gate.

AFTER LADY CONSTANCE HAD departed in high dudgeon, Ranulf turned to Henry. "What the devil were you doing?" he demanded, his eyes glittering like cold, hard stones.

"No need to get your breeches in a bunch," Henry lightly replied. "I wanted to talk to her about Merrick, to try to see if I could broker a peace between them after their quarrel. I believe, my friend, that I may have succeeded."

Ranulf relaxed. "Well, for God's sake, take care. If somebody else had seen you alone with her here, who knows what mischief you might have made."

"What about you? Did you have any better luck with Merrick?"

"I don't think so. I tried, but he had something else he wanted to talk about." With a rueful expression, Ranulf spread his arms. "Congratulate me, my friend. You're in the presence of the new garrison commander of Tregellas."

Henry stared at him in stunned disbelief. "What?"

"Since Merrick no longer has a garrison commander, he's asked me to take that place until he can find another," Ranulf replied.

"As if you're some soldier for hire?" Henry demanded.

"As if I'm a man he can trust."

"In that case, why not me?"

"Because he needs somebody who can command the

garrison, not go drinking and wenching with them," Ranulf replied with a sardonic grin.

"I wouldn't…well, all right, maybe I would," Henry genially acknowledged. He clapped a hand on his friend's shoulder. "So what say we visit the village tavern and do a little of both to celebrate?"

"You, Henry, are completely incorrigible."

"And that's why you like me," Henry agreed with a merry smile.

That didn't quite reach his eyes.

LATER THAT NIGHT, LORD Algernon grabbed Lord Carrell's arm and pulled him into the alley between the armory and the stables.

Carrell coolly regarded his confederate in the dim moonlight. "God's blood, Algernon, whatever is the matter?"

"You didn't pay him to do it, did you?"

"Pay who to do what?"

"Don't play the fool, Carrell!" Algernon charged in a heated whisper. "Talek. Did you pay him to try to kill Merrick?"

"If there's a fool here, it isn't me." Carrell retorted, going deeper into the narrow alleyway. "I'm not the one asking questions where any servant might overhear."

"This is safe enough. Did you have a hand in it?" Algernon persisted.

"Certainly not. I'm sure it was an accident, as Talek claims. He has no reason to kill Merrick."

"That we know of."

Carrell frowned. "Why would he want his patron dead? You know as well as I that Talek was Merrick's strong right arm when he was a boy. Talek surely had every reason to think Merrick would believe him. I must say, so did I—unless Merrick has another reason to wish the man gone. I wonder…"

"What?" Algernon asked eagerly. "What are you thinking?"

"Your brother's son was a brat of a boy. Who can say what mischief he got up to, or what schemes he involved Talek in." Lord Carrell stroked his chin. "It could be that Talek, not being overly shrewd, said the wrong thing to the new lord of Tregellas, reminded him of something Merrick would prefer to forget. I doubt it was anything serious, though, or Merrick would likely have killed the fellow."

Carrell sighed with regret. "No, it must be some minor indiscretion. What a pity. We could have used it against Merrick, perhaps. However, since Talek has already gone, our plan must remain as it is. Merrick marries Constance, they both die, you inherit Tregellas and my daughter becomes your wife. That's more money and land for you, and a richer, more powerful husband for my daughter."

"You make it sound like a simple thing."

"Nothing will go wrong as long as we keep our heads and stick to our plan."

"And if Constance doesn't prove a problem. I'm not convinced—"

"You leave my niece to me. If she wasn't such a beauty and didn't have a considerable dowry, I'd be more worried. But as it is, I think we have little reason to fear."

Algernon nodded, but he continued to look anxious. "What of our allies in the north?"

"They grow impatient, as such men do. I've told them we must wait until all is well in hand here. I've assured them things are progressing as they should, but no doubt more letters will have to be sent. They're like children who need to be told again and again that nothing can be achieved by haste. Now you'd best go back to the hall before we're seen here. I'll join you in a moment."

Algernon put his hand on Carrell's arm. "I'll never forget what you're risking for me."

"And my daughter," Carrell reminded him in case the stupid fool remembered that Carrell's family stood to gain, as well.

Algernon checked to make sure no one was watching, then crept out of the alley and headed for the hall.

As Lord Carrell watched him go, his lip curled with scorn and he thought, with great satisfaction, of the lands he would rule in his daughter's name when her envious, self-pitying idiot of a husband was dead.

EVEN LATER THAT NIGHT, TALEK stared into the fire in Peder's stone cottage. He was dressed as any traveler might be, in cloak, tunic, breeches and boots, with a full purse tucked inside his wide belt, and a sword dangling at his side.

"Twenty years I've served the lords of Tregellas—

twenty years!—and he dismisses me as easily as if I'd come yesterday," he muttered, kicking the bundle that held his clothes and everything else he possessed. "Wasn't I a good servant to him when he was a boy? Didn't I follow him about like a dog, just as I was ordered, and him the most spiteful, vicious brat in Christendom? I only wish I *had* stuck him with my boar spear!"

"Then you'd be dead for sure," Peder replied.

Talek took another swig of ale.

Peder leaned forward, trying to see Talek better in the dim light. "So it *was* an accident, then?"

"Aye," Talek muttered, running his hand over his close-cropped hair. "Why would I want to kill him?"

"Because he wants to put a stop to the smuggling?" Peder suggested.

Talek snorted. "That's not likely to work, no matter how hard he tries. This coast is too tricky to patrol, even with the army he's got at Tregellas. He'd be no more of a nuisance than his father."

"Maybe you wanted to help Lady Constance be free of him."

"Me and my men would have backed her if she'd asked us."

"Could be she's afraid to refuse him," Peder proposed.

"Her? Afraid?" Talek scoffed. "If she wasn't afraid of the old lord, why'd she be afraid of the new one?"

"She wasn't betrothed to the old one. Now she's lost a man who'd protect her."

Talek whistled softly. "That bloody bastard."

Peder poured them both more ale from the pitcher at

his elbow, then stretched out his legs and shifted, trying to find a comfortable way to rest his aching hip. "Where'll you go now?"

Talek's wide mouth turned up in a smile and his eyes blazed with determination. "Not far."

IT BEGAN IN THE HOUR JUST before dawn two nights later, with a small spark set to an oiled rag tucked into a pile of straw in the shed beside the mill. From there, the fire spread to the barrels of tallow used to grease the gears in the wheel pit of the mill. Then to the old, dry timbers supporting the roof. Squeaking in panic, mice and rats scurried from their holes, seeking escape as smoke filled the building.

When the timbers were well ablaze, the wind picked up more sparks and sent them spinning in the air toward the mill and the sluice channeling the water from the leat to the wheel. The great wooden wheel itself and the main shaft of white oak were too wet to catch fire, but the cinders blew into the wheel pit. There the fire found more to feed on—tallow around the lantern gear, and the dry wood of the inner shaft and spindle.

Like capering children the flames raced up the spindle to the rap, the shoe and the hopper, onward to the floor above. The millstone casing caught fire. And the garners storing the grain to be ground. Eventually the entire inner workings of the mill, the beams and the floors were all aflame.

CHAPTER NINE

THE BEDCHAMBER OF THE LORD of Tregellas was dark, save for the flickering light of a single candle on the table beside the large bed, its heavy dark blue curtains drawn.

How or why Constance had come there, she didn't know…but she knew she shouldn't linger. She had no business here. She should go…except that her feet wouldn't—couldn't—move.

The curtains were slowly parted by a strong male hand.

Merrick's hand. He was there, in the bed, covered to his waist by a sheet, the rest of him naked and exposed, his long hair unbound. He sat up and smiled slowly, seductively. "Come to me, Constance," he whispered as she stood rooted to the spot. "You know it's what you want."

She didn't dare move. If she went to him, if she let him enfold her in his arms and take her to his bed, she would never be free of him.

But did she want to be free of Merrick? If she were his wife, he would protect her. He would treat her kindly and with respect, as his father and her uncle never had. She would be cherished, for she'd seen more than lust in his eyes when he looked at her.

Why not surrender? Why not take what he offered and what, deep in her heart, she truly wanted?

She took a hesitant step forward. Then another. His smile grew and his passionate eyes gleamed in the candlelight. He raised his hand, reaching out for her.

Sounds from outside interrupted. Far-off, distant, but persistent, and her dream dissolved.

Struggling awake, Constance stumbled out of bed and went to the window, sucking in her breath when her feet touched the cold stone floor.

The wall walks were deserted. No guards were at the gates. Where were the soldiers? Where was Merrick?

A group of men went running through the courtyard, half dressed and unarmed. Were they under attack? Had it come to civil war at last?

Smoke. Smoke was in the air. Where did it come from? She scanned the yard and buildings around it. Not the kitchen or the stables. Not anywhere in the castle.

Then she saw the illumination against the dark night sky and realized what it meant. The mill was on fire!

Pulling on her shoes, Constance hopped to the chest where she kept her basket of medicines. They might be needed. Then she threw a gown over her shift, tied the laces as best she could, grabbed her basket and rushed to Merrick's bedchamber. She opened the door without pausing to knock.

Merrick was already gone. He must have heard the commotion. She pulled the door shut as Beatrice, rubbing her eyes, appeared on the threshold of her bedchamber, a bedrobe over her shift. "What is it?" she asked sleepily.

"The mill's on fire. I must go and see if I can help."

Beatrice's eyes widened in alarm. "What can I—?"

"Go to the kitchen. Tell Gaston to make soup and stew—lots of it."

"Why would—?"

Constance didn't stay to answer. Nor did she seek out the uncles or their guests. All she could think about now was the horrible possibility that someone might be hurt, perhaps even dead.

Holding her basket, she ran down the stairs to the hall. A group of frightened servants huddled near the kitchen. They gave a cry when they saw her and hurried to her.

"Oh, my lady, what can we do?" Demelza asked, tears in her eyes as she wrung her hands. "It's the mill. It's on fire. Oh, what'll we do?"

"You women go to the kitchen. Prepare food, and do as Lady Beatrice commands. She's in charge while I'm at the mill. You men, follow me," Constance ordered.

Her basket over her arm, she gathered up her skirts and ran to the mill as fast as she could. The servants following her were joined by the village women who had no young children to tend.

As Constance got closer to the river, the sight that met her eyes confirmed her worst fears. The wooden parts of the mill were completely ablaze. Flames shot out of the wheel pit and the open door, and flickered around the edges of the slate roof, telling her the beams were alight. Smoke billowed into the sky, obscuring the moon and stars.

A clear night—heaven help them, for never had they needed rain more.

Around the mill, illuminated by the flames, coughing from the smoke, choked by the chaff thick in the air, several men and women stood motionless, stunned by the disaster unfolding before them.

Others—thank God!—had formed a line from the leat to the mill. They dipped leather or wooden buckets into the water and passed them on to those who flung the contents onto the nearest flames. Children took the empty buckets and ran them back to those at the leat.

Was that Ranulf bending and handing off buckets, grabbing more with frantic haste? Where was Merrick? And Henry?

She ordered the men from the castle to join those fetching water.

A cry went up as the roof of the mill collapsed, flames shooting into the dark sky. For a moment nobody moved, until Merrick's deep, commanding voice rang out. "More water! Don't stop!"

He was to the west, naked to the waist, helping to tear down the slate roof of the shed where the tallow was stored. It, too, was aflame, sparks flying from it toward the miller's house. If they could bring down the roof, it would smother most of the flames before the miller's house was in serious danger.

She couldn't see Henry in the crowd as more people came to lend a hand and bewail the disaster.

She spied the miller's wife, her arms about her crying children. The flames made the tears on her cheeks shimmer and she was silently mouthing prayers.

Constance hurried to her. "Has anyone been hurt?"

The miller's wife stared at her as if she didn't recognize her. "What's to become of us?" she moaned. "What's to become of us?"

Constance took hold of the woman's face to get her undivided attention. "Has anyone been hurt?" she repeated with slow deliberation.

The woman's eyes focused. "No, my lady," she murmured. "I don't think so."

"Where are your maidservants?"

The miller's wife nodded at the line of people passing the buckets and a few wandering aimlessly.

"Fetch your maids. Set one to watch your children and keep them out of danger. Have the others help you take what valuables you can from your house."

The woman gasped as she understood what Constance was implying.

"Only as a precaution," Constance assured her. "If the wind holds as it is, and the shed comes down, your house should be spared."

But if it shifted…

"If the house catches, you must get out at once. Your lives are worth more than anything you possess."

"Yes, my lady," the woman said, choking back a sob. "Oh, my lady, what'll we do if the house burns down?"

"Lord Merrick will build you another," Constance staunchly replied. "Have no fear that you'll be left homeless."

Another cry went up from the line. Someone had fallen.

Coughing when a gust of wind blew smoke into her face, Constance ran to help, pushing her way through the people gathered around the man lying on the ground.

"Peder!" she cried, her heart sinking when she saw who it was. She knelt beside the old man, whose face was drawn and gray.

She pointed at a younger servant from the castle. "You, there, take his place. Someone help me carry—"

Two strong, familiar hands appeared and pulled Peder up. Constance raised her eyes to see Merrick cradling Peder in his arms as if he were a child and, without a word, he carried the elderly man away from the fire and smoke.

She ran after them. "Here. Set him here," she said when they reached a small embankment where Peder's head could be elevated.

Merrick set the old man down as gently as if he were a slumbering infant. Once Peder was on the ground, she used the corner of her sleeve to wipe the soot from his face.

"Is he dead?" Merrick asked, his voice as cold as the north wind.

"No. He's breathing. I think...I hope...he swooned

from the effort of hauling buckets," she said as she examined Peder's face.

When she looked up, Merrick was gone. Soon she could hear him calling out for the men to pull harder.

As the shed's roof came down, she gave Peder a sip of a restorative made from foxglove. He coughed and spluttered, then opened his eyes. "What—?"

"You swooned."

He struggled to sit up. "The hell I did."

"You fell to the ground unconscious, and I call that a swoon," she said more firmly, forcing him back down. "Do you have any pain in your chest or arms?"

"No."

"Truly, Peder?"

"Just my back, a bit."

"You must rest and stay out of the smoke "

"I tell you, I'm all right," he insisted.

"I tell you, you're not. Do I have to summon Lord Merrick again to keep you here?"

"Lord Merrick? What's he—?"

"He carried you from where you fell."

Peder's brow furrowed. "He never."

"He did, and unless you want him demanding an explanation for why you're risking another fainting spell, you'll stay here and rest."

Before he could answer, two more men came toward her, with a third hobbling between them, holding on to their shoulders.

"One of the slates from the roof fell on me foot," the

middle man said, grimacing as his friends set him down. "I think it's broke, my lady."

After she tended to that man's injury, another came with a burned arm from a falling piece of timber. Then another with a strained arm. It was only when the sun was nearing its high point in the day and the mill was a smoking hulk of masonry that she realized the fire was out, and the miller's house was still standing.

Beyond the small circle of the injured, the men and women who'd carried the buckets and otherwise fought the fire lay or sat on the ground, too exhausted to move, including Ranulf and Henry, who was, it seemed, too tired even to talk.

Demelza and other servants from the castle went among them, serving them water, ale, soup or stew in wooden bowls. Beatrice had done her job well.

She should tell Merrick about the injuries she'd tended, and what must be done next for those who'd been hurt.

"Have you seen Lord Merrick?" she asked Ranulf.

"He's in the mill," the knight answered, nodding at the smoking, soot-blackened building.

"Probably trying to figure out how it started," Henry said, wiping his sooty brow with the back of his hand. "Thank God no one was killed."

"Yes, thank God," Constance seconded as she left them to go to what was left of the mill, wondering who could be so evil as to fire a building whose destruction would affect everyone in Tregellas.

"My lord?" she ventured as she gingerly picked her

way through the open door that was hanging off one twisted leather hinge. The sunlight shone in where the roof had been, illuminating the charred wood and smoke-stained walls. She wrinkled her nose at the heavy smell of scorched, damp wood and burnt grain.

"Here."

He stood near the huge millstones that had fallen to the ground and cracked in two. His hands on his hips, he was black with soot from head to toe, his chest and arms and face streaked where the sweat had run down in rivulets.

He looked the way Vulcan might have, before he'd been thrown from Olympus—a powerful, dark god, and one burning with a righteous wrath she shared.

"Some of your soldiers will need assistance to get back to the castle," she said, moving closer. "And they'll have to rest for a few days. Fortunately, their injuries are minor."

"I wish the damage to the mill was minor," he muttered.

The walls still looked sound to her. "Can it not be repaired?"

"I'm no mason, but I fear the heat has ruined the mortar and cracked some of the stones." He nudged the fallen millstones with his foot. "These will have to be replaced."

Constance thought a moment. "Sir Jowan has been praising the mason leading the work on the rebuilding of his northern wall. Perhaps he could come and tell us if we can make repairs to the walls, or must rebuild entirely."

"I'll ask Sir Jowan if he can spare his mason for a few days," Merrick agreed.

It occurred to her that she hadn't seen Sir Jowan anywhere, or Kiernan. Or Lord Algernon or her uncle. They must have stayed at the castle. "If we have to rebuild, how long do you think it will take?"

Merrick shrugged his powerful shoulders as he picked his way through the debris toward her. "As I said, I'm no mason," he answered, running his hand over his eyes, smearing the sweat and soot more.

"You should go back to the castle, my lord. You need to eat and rest."

"And wash," he muttered, looking down at his smutty chest.

He ran his gaze over her. She had no girdle to cinch her waist, so it hung loose about her, nor had she covered her hair, which had to be a mess. "You must be very tired, too," he observed.

She didn't disagree. With a nod, she turned to go back, then stepped on a piece of wood and nearly fell. His strong hand gripped her arm to steady her, his touch warm and, this time, welcome.

"How is Peder?" he asked, letting go.

"Much better. I think he simply overtaxed his strength. Although he's a strong man, he sometimes forgets he's no longer young."

Merrick nodded, but her news didn't seem to please him. "When you were tending to the injured, did you hear anything about how this fire may have started?"

She shook her head.

"I believe the shed caught fire first and it spread from there," he said. "But a fire should *not* have started there."

"You think it was set deliberately?" she asked, hoping he'd have some other explanation.

"Yes. To hurt Tregellas. To hurt *me*."

That had a familiar, horrible ring to it. His father had often cried that the whole world was out to destroy him, and all men wanted him dead. Yet Merrick did have some cause for his fears. When he was younger, someone had set upon his cortege and murdered everyone else in it. Perhaps they were thieves, but perhaps they were assassins. She wondered, and not for the first time, who might have sought his death and how Merrick had managed to escape.

"Perhaps the fire was an accident," she proposed with more hope than faith. "A stray spark from the miller's chimney landing on a bit of chaff."

"The shed had no windows and the roof was made of slate."

"Under the door, perhaps?" she suggested, knowing she was grasping at straws, but still reluctant to consider the alternative.

Merrick's expression told her he didn't think that likely, either. "Angry or evil men will do anything to have revenge or advantage, and don't care that innocents suffer," he said grimly.

"How could burning down the mill be to anyone's advantage?"

"It would weaken Tregellas. We'll have to grind our grain elsewhere until the mill can be repaired or rebuilt, and that will cost money that could be spent on men or arms. I'll have to pay for the repairs, again taking money that could be spent on defense or men or horses."

"Is there anyone you suspect?" she asked, almost afraid to hear his answer.

"There are those who believe I'll be as bad an overlord as my father. There are those who fear I'll join in a conspiracy against the king, or others who fear I won't. There could be others who would simply have me vulnerable. There may be more, with more personal reasons. Talek, for one."

"He's gone. You banished him." Yet even as she protested, a sickening wave of dizziness and nausea overcame her when she thought of the garrison commander's wounded pride.

"It's possible he didn't go far."

Putting her hand to her head, she reached out toward a charred strut to keep herself from falling. Merrick's powerful arm encircled her waist and held her close.

"I shouldn't have kept you here," he said, starting for the door and all but carrying her.

For a moment, as in her dream, she wanted to surrender. To lean against him and let him take full command. To go to the castle, where she could be safe and secure as his wife-to-be and let him deal with the aftermath of the fire, including finding out who might be responsible. But she weakened only for a moment, because she'd felt responsible for the people of Tregellas for too long to stop now.

She gently extricated herself from his grasp. "I must

see that the injured get to their homes or the castle, as need be."

When she saw Merrick wince, she suddenly remembered the cut from Talek's spear. She looked at his arm. "What happened to your stitches?" she cried, staring at the welt.

"I took them out."

She looked up, aghast, at his impassive face. "By *yourself*?"

He shrugged as if what he had done was not something worth mentioning. "I told you I'm used to taking care of my wounds."

But to pull out stitches! She went to take hold of his arm to examine it, but he held her off with an upraised hand. "You tend to the injured first. You can look at my arm later."

There was no room for dissent in his tone. "Very well," she reluctantly agreed, "as long as you'll give me your word I can do so and you won't try to stop me."

His lips curved up, revealing teeth that looked very white against his soot-darkened skin and he bowed as if they were in the king's court. "I give you my word, my lady."

AFTER LEAVING HIM, CONSTANCE made straight for Peder, who was sitting on a blanket the miller's wife had brought him. Fortunately, no one was near him, so no one would hear their conversation. He smiled when he saw her, but she was in no mood to smile back.

"Has Talek left Tregellas?" she asked in a whisper as she crouched beside him.

She was well aware that not only were Talek and Peder friends, they shared some of the profits from the smuggling of Peder's tin. Peder dug the metal out of the ground and prepared it for transport to France; Talek ensured Peder's cache was never discovered and the French seamen never caught when they came ashore to collect their contraband cargo.

The old man's eyes widened with surprise. "What makes you ask that, my lady?"

"Do you think he was angry enough to set fire to the mill?"

"God help us, no!" Peder cried. "I'd wager all the profit I've ever made that it wasn't Talek."

"Then who do you think could have done it?"

Peder scratched his grizzled chin. "I don't know anybody who'd do something so terrible—except a Norman. That's the sort of game those bastards play. Beggin' your pardon, my lady."

"In retaliation or during a siege perhaps, but Merrick's not made war on anyone hereabouts."

"Not yet," Peder said significantly. "And there's been plenty of talk about what he'll do if the earl moves against the king. Maybe some want to prevent him from helping one side or the other."

"That's what—" She hesitated. Perhaps it was wiser not to say what Merrick suspected. "That's what I was thinking."

Since Peder knew no more than she, she rose. "I've

arranged for Elowen to take you in until you're well. I think she's already missing Eric."

"The lad's not married yet," Peder said, wheezing a laugh. "What'll she do when he's off on his own, with a wife to boot?"

"Take in stray dogs, I expect."

"Or help old men with no one else, eh?"

Constance regretted making that flippant remark and bent to kiss Peder's forehead. "You've got me, Peder. And didn't Lord Merrick say you could ask for his help? I'm sure he meant it."

Peder frowned. "Aye, I think he did, too," he muttered.

And for once he didn't hawk and spit when speaking of the lord of Tregellas.

BY THE TIME CONSTANCE HAD ensured that all the injured were taken care of, she was desperately in need of washing herself. A little embarrassed by her filthy, untidy appearance, she tried not to be noticed as she made her way to the stairs leading to her bedchamber.

That wasn't as difficult as it might have been. Henry and Ranulf had already washed and changed their clothes, and Henry was now seated on the dais, goblet in hand, describing the fire and their attempts to stop it to his rapt audience that consisted of a gaping Beatrice—who was too entranced to ask questions—as well as her father, Lord Algernon, Sir Jowan and Kiernan, who likewise seemed too spellbound to pay attention to anything else. She gathered from a comment Sir Jowan made that the nobles had watched the fire from the wall walk of the castle.

She wondered if Kiernan had been there, too. *He* wouldn't have set fire to the mill, no matter how upset he was. He would plead, cajole, beg and complain, even issue a challenge to combat, but he'd surely consider firing a building beneath his dignity.

She paused to speak in a hushed whisper to Demelza, who assured her that there was clean, warm water waiting in her chamber. Lady Beatrice had ordered it the moment Sir Henry and the others had returned, and she'd ensured that it was kept warm.

Beatrice was proving herself very capable indeed. "And Lord Merrick? Is there hot water for him, as well?"

"Yes, my lady. He ordered a whole bath."

Considering how dirty he was, she could see why.

After dismissing Demelza, she hurried to her chamber to fix her hair, and wash and put on some clean clothes. Then she would examine Merrick's arm and make sure he'd done no further damage.

When she was ready, and wearing a soft, plum woolen gown with a gilded leather girdle about her hips, she took her basket of medicines and went to Merrick's bedchamber. She wondered if he'd be asleep. He had to be utterly exhausted after his efforts last night. Not wanting to disturb him if he was sleeping, she didn't knock, but quietly eased the door open.

To find Merrick immersed in a large wooden tub full of dirty water, his muscular arms draped over the sides, his head lying back against the linen cushioning the edge, his hair wet and damply curling, and his eyes closed, the dark lashes resting on his sun-browned cheeks.

CHAPTER TEN

SHE COULD EXAMINE THE CUT ON his arm as long as he stayed asleep, Constance reasoned as she crept into Merrick's bedchamber, averting her eyes from the water and what lay beneath.

When she reached the tub, she picked up the lump of soap from the stool beside it and inhaled its scent. She recognized the spicy smell from when he'd held her and kissed her.

Her gaze wandered to the bed, and the memory of her dream and Merrick's invitation. Her heartbeat quickened, and so did her breathing as warmth suffused her body. If they wed, she would share that bed. With him. And do more than sleep

She looked back at Merrick—whose eyes snapped open.

She dropped the soap. Trying to collect her scattered wits, she bent to retrieve it. "You'll fall ill if you stay in that water," she said, her embarrassment making her peevish.

"Then I won't," he agreed, starting to rise.

God help her, he was as naked as a newborn babe—but very much a man.

She quickly turned away. "I came to examine your arm and make sure you have no other hurts," she explained as she heard him step from the tub, water dripping.

"I'm uninjured."

"Your notion of uninjured and mine may differ."

"Then examine me, if there's nothing else that will content you."

She'd made this stew, so she had to eat it, she told herself as she turned to face him. In spite of her efforts, she couldn't prevent the heated blush that flooded her skin when she saw him rubbing himself dry with a small piece of linen while making absolutely no effort to hide any part of his body.

She commanded herself not to be so foolish, and approached him. "Let me see your arm."

His face expressionless, he held it out to her.

"You didn't do any more damage, thank God," she noted. She ran a studious gaze over his magnificent body, trying not to focus more attention than strictly necessary on certain parts.

"Do you see anything that displeases you?"

She glanced sharply up at his face, but he seemed perfectly serious. "You look otherwise unharmed," she replied.

He went to his chest and threw open the lid. Since she was obviously not needed here, there was no reason to stay....

"What of my men and those who helped? Were they all fed?" he asked as he pulled out some dark woolen breeches and started to dress.

"Yes. Beatrice did an excellent job. I left her to organize the food."

"She seems a clever girl, when she stops talking," he remarked as he tied the drawstring.

Constance bristled in defense of her cousin. "We cannot all be as quiet as you."

"I speak when I have something to say," he answered, and she had the feeling he'd given that response before.

However, she had no particular wish to get into a discussion about his conversational skills, or lack thereof. "Have you asked Sir Jowan about his mason?"

"Yes. He's agreed to send the man over to give his opinion. Sir Jowan's son didn't seem pleased by his father's generosity," he remarked as he put on a shirt and a pair of scuffed black boots. "I gather young Kiernan doesn't like me."

His voice betrayed no particular interest or concern— but his eyes were something else. "I suspect he wouldn't like any man who was betrothed to you."

A jolt of fear stabbed her. What if someone had seen Kiernan enter the chapel while she was there, and told Merrick? Yet if that had happened, surely he would have said something before now. Relief came, and then annoyance. How she wished Kiernan had stayed at home!

Given how she felt, she had no qualms about making her feelings for Kiernan—or lack of them—quite plain. "Whatever Kiernan feels, I've never encouraged him to see me as anything other than a friend. I don't love him, and I never have. All I harbor for Kiernan is affection for a friend."

"He can't be your only admirer."

"There have been others," she readily and honestly admitted. "A few bold young men who thought it would be an easy matter for me to break my uncle's word, and others who thought my uncle could be persuaded to do so. After they met your father, they realized that his vengeance would be swift if they were successful, and thought better of their plans."

"So they were cowards?"

"I would say they were wise."

He came toward her, his gaze intense—and doubtful? "I don't want you to accept me out of some sense of obligation or duty, Constance."

She yearned to tell him the truth—her hopes and fears, and what she wanted most of all: a husband she could love, who would treat her as a trusted friend and not a child to be commanded and patronized. She studied his face, his eyes. Could he be such a husband?

His gaze faltered and he turned away to put on a gray woolen tunic. "I hope you won't continue to hold my decision about Talek against me."

After her conversation with Henry, which she wouldn't mention now, she could no longer blame him for his suspicions. "Although I still think your decision was wrong, I was too upset to remember the attack upon your cortege fifteen years ago, and why you might fear assassination."

His dark brows furrowed. "You understand me, do you?" he queried as he approached her.

She shook her head. "No," she admitted, wondering if she'd ever truly comprehend a man seemingly so full of contradictions, "but I can appreciate why you felt you had to send Talek away."

"Then is there some other reason you dislike me?" he asked, his voice a husky whisper.

"I...I don't dislike you," she answered, compelled to be honest by his voice and unexpectedly vulnerable expression.

"Yet you either quarrel with me or avoid me," he replied. "I could believe you want to break the betrothal, except that you didn't take the chance I offered, and your kisses tell me you want me, at least in your bed.

"Do you regret our betrothal, Constance?" he continued softly, taking hold of her chin and gently forcing her to look up into his questioning face. "Do you wish to be free of me? If you do, I beg of you, tell me."

Doubt flickered in his eyes as he spoke to her with hushed but fervent resolve. "If you do want to be my wife, I would hear you say it. Or do you still fear that I'll be like my father? That you'll become nothing more to me than a broodmare? That in spite of my vows of fidelity, I'll take other women into my bed when they're willing, and force myself upon them when they're not? I give you my word I will not. I assure you, I did vow long ago that I would never take a woman against her will, and that includes my wife. Nor will I ever strike you, or mistreat you. I will be faithful to you, as I honor every vow and promise I make. So I will ask you this one last time—will you marry me or not?"

All the reasons she should refuse him flashed through her mind.

The younger Merrick had been a spoiled, cruel little brat. His father had been a lascivious, brutal tyrant given to fits of rage, living in constant fear of betrayal and assassination. She couldn't face a future where she might have to endure living in dread and terror again.

What did she really know of Merrick? He was an enigma, a mystery, a man who betrayed almost nothing of his feelings...but he had shown her something she was sure he rarely revealed to another: a hint of doubt, a shadow of vulnerability, a notion that she could hurt him profoundly if she refused. And make him happier than he would ever say if she agreed.

Could she be happy married to him? She didn't know. She couldn't be sure. She had no compass, no guide to tell her what to do.

Except her heart, and the defeated, disappointed look lurking in Merrick's eyes as the silence stretched between them.

If she denied that silent plea, and the urging of her own heart, she might regret it for the rest of her life.

And had he not treated her with respect? Had he not listened to her opinions and done as she suggested, or offered a reasonable explanation when he had not? What more could she really expect from a husband?

No other man had ever aroused such desire within her. No other man made her feel as wanted and needed as he did. "Yes, my lord, I'll marry you."

With a gasp and a look of astonishment, he pulled her into his arms. He was going to kiss her, and, oh, how different was this anticipation from the dread of Kiernan's embrace, or the worry that Henry's kindness was not completely honorable.

When Merrick took her in his arms this time, his lips met hers not with fiery desire, but with tenderness, asking that she respond.

She did, willingly. At the first touch of his mouth on hers, her body ignited, the flames of desire licking along her limbs until she was alight with it. He was simply too much to resist. The need, the hunger he inspired, was too overwhelming. And wonderful.

As he continued to kiss and stroke her, her knees grew weak and her whole body relaxed against him. With no conscious effort, an encouraging moan sounded deep in her throat, while his fingers lightly brushed the pebbled tip of her nipple pushing against the fabric of her gown.

His mouth left hers to slide in slow torment down her neck. Gripping his shoulders, she leaned back, offering her body to him.

His chin nuzzled her bodice lower, exposing the rounded tops of her breasts to his lips and tongue. Then, suddenly, he raised his head to give her an intensely ardent kiss.

As she eagerly responded, his hands continued their slow exploration of her body. Every inch of her skin felt alive to his touch, every caress a new call to desire.

Still kissing her, he swept her into his arms and carried her to the bed. She had one moment's thought that she should stop him, but in the next, he was beside her.

She wrapped her arms about him, pulling him closer. She vaguely guessed where this might end—and did not care. He was not the Merrick she had known, and were they not betrothed, as good as married except for the blessing and consummation?

One hand left her breast to travel lower, cupping her between her parted limbs. Kneading her there. Making her cleft throb and moisten.

Ready for him.

A finger pressed against her through the fabric. His mouth took hers again with hot intensity. She lifted her hips, seeking more. Wanting more. Needing more.

His tongue swirled and danced with hers, gliding over her teeth, plunging into her warm mouth. A prelude to that other thrust.

His hand, his fingers, that glorious pressure provoked more yearning within her.

And then…the tension snapped. Crying out, she dug her fingernails into his shoulder, bucked and groaned as wave after wave of unimagined release tore through her, blinding her to everything except that incredible sensation.

Afterward, she leaned against him, panting, spent. "What…what *was* that?" she murmured.

"Your pleasure," he whispered, his voice a husky rasp, his breathing heavy as if he'd run a long distance.

"Only mine?"

"For now. I can wait."

She imagined her wedding night, realized he would love her, that his body would join with hers…

He reached out and tucked a lock of hair behind her ear, for her braids were undone and fallen into disarray. "This was but a taste of what's to come, Constance."

A taste? She wanted a meal. "As I seem to recall you saying once, we're already betrothed."

Desire flared in his eyes, but he shook his head. "I will have no one say I took you too soon, that you had no choice except to marry me because I'd taken your maidenhead."

She had made her decision. There was no need now to pretend she didn't want his kisses, his caresses, his body loving hers. No reason to deny what they both so obviously craved. She pressed her body closer. "No one need know."

"I will know, and so will you," he grimly replied. "I will have no shadow of doubt, no cause at all for you to suspect me of other motives."

She couldn't fault him for wanting to be honorable, and yet surely there was some way…

She remembered something she'd overheard, a giggled conversation between Demelza and another maid, about what Demelza had done one May Day eve. At the time, she'd been shocked—and then ashamed for listening. But now...now she was glad she'd eavesdropped.

Emboldened, she stroked his hardened shaft through his clothing. "I don't think it's right that I should be pleasured but you must go lacking, even if we aren't yet wed. I've heard there are other ways for men to seek release," she offered.

"It's a sin for a man to waste his seed," he muttered thickly, his eyes pleading as he reached for her hand. "Constance, you should stop that."

"I would feel it a greater sin that I should leave you without ease when I've been satisfied," she replied, ignoring his halfhearted protest. "We can confess and seek absolution later."

His only answer to that suggestion was a low groan as she untied his breeches. Making no more attempts to stop her, his eyes closed, he leaned back and braced himself as she straddled him and slipped her hand inside his breeches.

She'd never touched a man's naked shaft before. It was softer than she'd expected, and he, this powerful knight who'd defeated so many men, shivered and gasped when she encircled him with her fingers.

Leaning close, she kissed his mouth, and in spite of whatever reservations he harbored, he returned her kiss fiercely as she continued to stroke him.

Her lips left his to trail down his chin. She kissed his collarbone and the little hollow in the middle, where she could feel his rapid breathing like the beating of a bird's wings.

His shirt was a hindrance, and she stopped her ministrations for a moment. "Sit up," she ordered.

His eyes flew open, surprised and wary.

She tugged at his clothing. "I want this off."

Doubt dimmed the desire in his eyes. "Perhaps we should—"

"Now," she ordered, yanking up his shirt.

His lips began to turn down until she merrily murmured, "Please?"

He laughed softly and obeyed, pulling his shirt over his head in one swift motion. "I fear I can refuse you nothing."

"Good," she murmured as she bent forward. While her hand returned to his erection, her tongue circled his areola, then licked the tip of his nipple.

He groaned and squirmed, the motion increasing her desire, too. When she sucked his nipple into her mouth, it sent him over the edge. He groaned and bent forward, jerking like a landed fish as he spilled over her fingers.

Panting, he fell back against the feather bed as she withdrew her hand. "There's linen—" he gasped.

"I know," she said, climbing off him to fetch it. Her legs were a little shaky as she washed, then brought him a clean, damp square.

"God help me, if that's a sin, I may not want to go to heaven," he murmured as he washed himself. Then he looked up at her and smiled in a way that made her wish she'd done more than pleasure him with her hand and lips. "Thank you," he said, his voice low and so seductive, she nearly climaxed from that alone.

"You're most welcome, my lord," she said, her body hot and yearning for more.

He stood up and tied his breeches. "Although nothing would make me happier than to linger here with you, I fear I've already stayed too long. It smells like rain, and while that might prevent any smoldering sparks from flaring and setting fire to what's left of the mill, it might also destroy any evidence we might find."

Constance was disappointed, but she couldn't fault him for wanting to find out who'd set the fire. So she gave Merrick a wry little smile. "Go about your business, my lord, and I'll go about mine. We'll meet at the evening meal, and I hope you'll share any discoveries with me, whether for good or ill."

"I will."

He grabbed her hand and tugged her close for one more quick kiss, then together they went down the stairs.

Although he tried to focus on what he must do next, Merrick's heart swelled with happiness. Constance was his, of her own free will, and not because of a legal contract signed years ago when she was a child. She would be his wife, not the promised bride of the heir of Tregellas. He had given her every chance to refuse, yet she had not. Surely that was a sign from God that he was forgiven. That he was worthy of her after all, in spite of what he'd done.

BEATRICE MIGHT HAVE BEEN exhausted, but she wasn't too tired to talk.

"I'm so glad no one was seriously hurt," she exclaimed to Constance as they stood in the kitchen, which looked as if a small army had gone through and stripped it clean. Gaston was nodding off in the corner, and the servants seemed to be slumbering wherever they could lie down.

"What a terrible, terrible thing!" she continued. "How could it happen? I've heard of mills being struck by lightning, but the sky was clear last night. And of course they're often set on fire during wars, but we're at peace—mostly. It must have been an accident, or a drunken man going home with a torch."

As improbable as Beatrice's last suggestion sounded, and despite Merrick's certainty the fire was no accident, Constance wondered if Beatrice might be right. She should tell Merrick Beatrice's idea the next time they were alone, before they kissed and she got…distracted.

"You did very well in the kitchen," she said to Beatrice, deciding it was better not to share Merrick's suspicions with her loquacious cousin. "I'm most impressed, and so is Merrick."

"Really?" Beatrice cried happily. "I did what I thought you'd do."

"No wonder I don't see any mistakes," Constance replied with a smile.

"Henry said I'd make some lucky man an excellent wife," Beatrice boasted. Then she giggled. "He nearly fell asleep before he finished his stew, right there at the table. He put his head down and if Ranulf hadn't nudged him, all I would have heard is that I would have made some lucky man, as if I should start wearing breeches!"

Her expression changed as she looked around surreptitiously, then whispered, "I know you're tired and it's been a terrible night, but I was wondering if you'd had a chance to ask Merrick if I might stay in Tregellas after you're married."

"To be honest, Beatrice," Constance admitted as she stifled a yawn, "I'd forgotten. I'll do so the next time I speak with him."

"If he isn't pleased by the idea, you needn't insist. Sir Jowan has invited me to Penderston. I told him that I had asked to stay here, but Kiernan was kind enough to say I could go there after the wedding instead."

"Kiernan wants you to visit?" Constance asked, trying not to sound overly surprised—or to *be* overly surprised. Sir Jowan had been a friend of Lord Carrell's for many years, if not a very close one.

Beatrice tossed her head, like a colt let loose in a large field on a spring day. "Since you don't want him, maybe I should see if he'll suit *me*."

Constance *didn't* want Kiernan, yet she didn't think he'd be suitable for Beatrice, either. Or any woman she cared about. He was nice enough in his way, but there was something…lacking…somehow. However, there was no point voicing any reservations. After all, Kiernan might not "suit" Beatrice, either.

Beatrice covered her mouth to hide a prodigious yawn. "God's rood, I *am* tired. I suppose everybody is. Ranulf barely spoke two words when he came back to the hall and had some stew. I wonder how long he's going to stay. Has Merrick said anything about a new garrison commander?"

"No." Constance suddenly felt utterly exhausted. "Come, Beatrice, we should both have a nap. It was a long and busy night."

"I suppose that would be wise," Beatrice agreed, albeit reluctantly, as she followed Constance from the kitchen. "And I suppose I should be more upset about the fire, but it was rather exciting, too. That must be a little like being in battle, don't you think? I felt like the leader of an army, although of course, servants aren't soldiers. I had no time to worry if what I was doing was exactly right or not."

"I suspect battles are much worse," Constance said as she slowly made her way up the steps toward their bedchambers, gripping the handrail carved in the side of the wall and worn smooth over the years. "Either way, both are terrible things."

Beatrice flushed. "I know. That is, I'm sure battles are horrid. So many people die! I didn't mean to imply—"

"It's all right, Beatrice," Constance said as she stifled another yawn. "I know what you meant."

At least Beatrice would be quiet once she was asleep.

THE NEXT MORNING AFTER compline, Constance took herself to Merrick's solar. He'd gone with some soldiers to search the area around the mill, and ordered more patrols of the estate. He shouldn't be absent from the castle for much longer, though, and even if he was, she wanted to get away from Beatrice, who was still going on about the fire and speculating as to its cause until Constance thought she was going to scream at her to be quiet.

Strolling toward the table, she looked over the parchments open there. That must be his writing, she thought as she studied a few notations beside some figures Alan de Vern had written. It was a strong, firm hand—like the man himself.

She sat in his cushioned chair. How many times had she stood on the other side of this table and waited for Lord William to start shouting or throw something at her? How often had he screamed at her, shrieking his anger, claiming that everyone was out to destroy him? Accusing his brother Algernon of coveting his possessions, and crying out that he had legions of enemies plotting to assassinate him. Toward the end, the shouts had become feeble cries that ended, more often than not, in self-pitying sobs.

She closed her eyes and drew in a deep breath. Those days were over now. Really over…

A kiss on her forehead brought her awake with a start, to find Merrick bending over her, his expression as grave as she'd ever seen it.

Constance gripped the arms of the chair. "What is it? What's wrong?"

His lips curved upward, and his eyes shone with affection. "Nothing. I simply couldn't resist the urge to kiss you."

Constance put her hand to her breast. "You frightened me." She realized where she was sitting and hurried to stand. "I didn't realize I'd fallen asleep."

He went to the small side table and poured some wine. "There's no need for you to vacate my chair," he said as he came toward her and held out a goblet.

Since she was thirsty, she didn't decline the offer, and since she was tired, she sat.

"Did you discover any sign of who might have set the fire?" she asked.

Merrick shook his head as he got himself a drink. "The ground was trampled and muddy from the rain yesterday evening, and if there was evidence in the shed, it was destroyed."

"Did anybody in the village see anyone skulking about the mill before the fire started?"

"No. Whoever set it, they weren't seen—or if they were, somebody's protecting them, the same way they protect smugglers."

Constance tensed, then answered with firm conviction. "This is different, Merrick. Setting fire to the mill hurts everyone who eats bread. The smugglers believe the only person they're robbing is a king who regards them as foreigners and taxes them unfairly." She remembered Beatrice's suggestions. "Beatrice wondered if it might have been caused by a drunken man on his way home."

"The miller says the shed was kept locked, and we found what was left of the heavy iron lock outside the door. It was broken in two pieces, but whether before or from the heat of the fire, we can't tell. If it was done before, to gain entry to the shed, I doubt it was done by a man sodden with drink, although it's possible, I suppose. But the night was clear. What reason would a man have to seek shelter in the shed?"

"Perhaps he didn't want anyone at his home to know he was drunk," she proposed.

"Do you have anyone in mind?"

She shook her head. "Alas, no."

He sighed. "I fear it's as I suspect. The fire was deliberately set. Is there no one in or near Tregellas you think might be capable of such a crime or believe he has cause for such an act? Perhaps a disgruntled soldier or a disappointed lover? I can believe a man who feels the sting of rejection could be driven to some mad form of revenge."

She guessed what he was implying and hastened to clear his mind of that suspicion. "Not Kiernan. He wouldn't be so evil…or so furtive."

"I agree that he's the least likely. He's the sort to challenge me directly."

"Has he?"

Merrick shook his head.

"Good," she replied with genuine relief. She might be upset with Kiernan for causing her some trouble, but she wouldn't want him seriously injured. And anyway… "He would have to be mad to think he could beat you."

Merrick gave her a little smile that warmed her from within. "I shall take that as a compliment." His smile disappeared. "What about Talek?"

Constance shifted in her chair. "I'd like to think he wouldn't, but…"

"I agree. I should have had him escorted far away before I let him go."

"Constance, I—oh, I'm sorry!" Beatrice halted awkwardly on the threshold and blushed bright red. "I didn't realize you'd come back, my lord, or that you were here."

As Merrick faced her, her expression became surprisingly resolute. Before Constance could figure out what that meant, Beatrice pressed her hands together as if she were praying and addressed Merrick as she entered the room. "Since you *are* here, my lord, I have a boon to beg of you. I would dearly like to remain here for a little while after your wedding. I realize it's an imposition, but we *are* going to be related. Otherwise, when I go home, I'll just have my maidservant, Maloren, for company and I'll be utterly miserable. You can't think how she goes on and on, and she'll pester me for details about the wedding and the feast and who was here or not here until I'm like to go mad. My father won't miss me for a moment, either. His leman can run the castle better than I can anyway and—"

Her eyes widened and she clapped a hand over her open mouth. "I didn't mean... I shouldn't have said... Oh, he'll be so angry I told you!"

Constance rose and hurried to assuage her cousin's discomfort. "I figured out what Eloise's position was long ago, and many men have mistresses," she assured Beatrice before glancing at a stone-faced Merrick. "Isn't that right, my lord?"

As he nodded, she tried not to wonder if he'd ever had a mistress. He'd told her he'd be faithful once they wed; surely that was more important than any liaison he'd had in the past.

"You are welcome to stay, Beatrice," he said.

Her cousin ran to Merrick and threw her arms around him, laying her head on his chest. "Oh, thank you, thank you!"

He was completely, utterly astounded, and Constance rushed to disengage her impetuous cousin.

Aghast at what she'd just done and to whom, Beatrice stared at Merrick with a horrified expression. "Oh, I'm sorry! I'm just so happy. And grateful." She made her flustered way to the door. "I'll go tell—ask— my father. Thank you, my lord, thank you!"

After she went out, Merrick raised a sardonic brow that would have done credit to Ranulf, although Constance could see laughter lurking in his dark eyes. "I fear I may regret that moment of generosity, but I can't refuse a woman who begs."

"She's young, my lord."

"In some ways, very young." The merriment in his eyes disappeared. "As you and I were not allowed to be."

His quiet words touched something deep within Constance, like a low note on a harp. No, she'd never been as carefree as Beatrice, and it had been a very long time since she'd been as innocent. But now she realized the burden Merrick had borne had been no lighter. "I add my gratitude to hers, my lord," she said softly.

He came toward her and his voice fell to a deep, intimate whisper that set her blood tingling. "Perhaps I shouldn't have revealed my inability to resist pleading women. You may use it against me."

"On the contrary, it pleases me to know you have a weakness."

"I assure you, I do," he said as he took her into his arms. "And her name is Constance."

Whatever liaisons he'd had with women in the past, they were in the past, or he wouldn't look at her the way he did. Hold her as he did. Kiss her as he did.

With a sigh of surrender, she relaxed into him as his lips brushed gently over hers.

Regrettably, his kiss did not last long before he drew back with a heavy sigh. "I have to go back to the mill and see what can be salvaged."

He kissed her again on the forehead, light as a moth's wing, and then he was gone.

She leaned back against the table. To think that once she had considered him as cold as ice....

MERRICK AND HIS MEN FOUND no clues as to who had set fire to the mill that day, or on any other as the wedding of the lord of Tregellas drew near. But no other troubles disturbed the peace of the estate, and all dared hope that perhaps the fire had been an accident, however improbable, after all. The people grew secure and regarded their overlord with respect for the way he had joined with the common folk to fight the blaze. To be sure, he was a grim man, they said, but if Lady Constance treated him with affection—for the castle folk were quick to notice the change in their mistress and spread the word abroad—then he must be a good man. If she looked on him with favor, they had nothing to fear.

Even Constance, busy with the arriving guests and preparations for her marriage, came to hope that Merrick was wrong, and their lives would continue to be as calm and tranquil as possible in these troubled times. Like her doubts, her worries subsided with every moment she spent with the man she was fast growing to love.

Only Merrick, silent and serious except for those brief hours he spent with Constance, believed that this was but a momentary, blissful respite, and the worst was yet to come.

CHAPTER ELEVEN

THE DAY OF LADY CONSTANCE'S wedding to the lord of Tregellas dawned misty and cool for May, but that did nothing to dampen Beatrice's enthusiasm or stem the bride's barely contained excitement. If someone had told Constance a month ago she would welcome this day so eagerly, and be looking forward to the night to come, she would have said they were mad. Or drunk.

Yet as she dressed in a new gown of brilliant royal blue edged with gold, and with a wedding gift from Merrick of a lovely circlet of gold on her head, she felt like a queen. Better than a queen. Happier than any queen had ever been.

During the ceremony in front of their families and assembled guests, Merrick stood beside her looking seductively, incredibly handsome, even though his black wool tunic lacked any embroidery or other embellishment. The unrelieved simplicity suited him, and indeed, seemed to accent his powerful body more than any finery could. Her heartbeat quickened at the sight of him as it always did, and when he had sealed their vows with a kiss, she thought it seemed an age until they could be alone.

Merrick was as reserved as ever, perhaps even more so. She had come to accept that he would always be so when they were in public, and she tried to act dignified and calm, too. No doubt, to many she appeared equally cool and aloof, even though when he touched her, he set her very flesh ablaze.

During the wedding feast of roasted suckling pig, venison, boar and a host of fowl, she remembered all the reasons she had accepted him. The yearning vulnerability in his eyes when he asked her to be his. That he'd called her his weakness. His generosity to Beatrice. His vow to protect the people of Tregellas. Her certainty that women need never fear him.

And she drank only a little wine.

Merrick, meanwhile, conversed with his guests, discussing hunting and the responsibilities of running an estate. She noted he never, if possible, spoke of the king and queen. And when their eyes met, she knew he was as anxious as she to leave the wedding feast.

Before that time came, however, they had to endure the celebrations and toasts in their honor. Henry's slightly drunken voice rose louder and louder, and he made the most outrageous jokes, much to Beatrice's amusement. Ranulf's smile grew rather strained, until he finally whisked Beatrice away to dance. Constance and Merrick joined them, and while Merrick was a fine dancer, his mind was clearly not on the dance. Or the music.

Neither was hers.

The uncles, nearly as far in their cups as Henry, got

into a heated discussion about the breeding of horses, and only the intervention of Alan de Vern prevented them from coming to blows. As the steward separated them, he winked at Constance, then steered them to different sides of the hall. Sir Jowan flirted outrageously with Demelza, who flirted outrageously back, while Kiernan sat sullenly in the corner, pouting over his wine.

Then, at last, it was time for the bride to retire. Although she'd been anticipating this moment for hours, Constance flushed scarlet as she hurried toward the stairs to Merrick's bedchamber—now hers, as well—trailed by Beatrice, who could scarcely breathe for giggling, and accompanied by what was surely far too many maidservants.

Beatrice giggled and chattered merrily as the servants prepared Constance for her bridal night. Although most of her comments were innocently intended, the maidservants exchanged looks that gave everything she said a hidden, lustful meaning.

Constance didn't know whether to laugh or send them from the room.

"Oh, I hear the men!" Beatrice suddenly cried, jumping up and oversetting the stool upon which she'd been sitting. "They're coming, they're coming! Quick, Constance, to bed!"

She eagerly shoved her silk-clad cousin toward Merrick's bed, newly made with fresh white linen and strewn with herbs intended to be both sweet smelling and conducive to conception.

Horrified that the men might see her in her shift, Constance practically dived for the bed and scrambled under the covers in a most undignified manner. That made Beatrice giggle more, until Constance feared the girl would collapse.

Then Beatrice was forgotten as Merrick appeared in the door, with Henry, Ranulf and several other gentlemen behind him.

A laughing Henry shoved the bridegroom through the door. "Here he is, my lady, and none the worse for drink, I assure you."

Merrick might have been perfectly sober—and Constance believed he was, for he'd barely touched his food and drink at the wedding feast—but Henry and the others were not.

Henry's eyes gleamed mischievously. "I've been giving him lots of excellent advice," he assured Constance, swaying a little. "I don't think you'll be disappointed."

Blushing, Constance glanced at her husband to see how he was taking this good-natured teasing.

He barely seemed to hear. Instead, he strode over to the carafe on a side table and poured himself a drink.

"Wheest, man, now's not the time to get into the wine," Henry said in a loud whisper. "You don't want to be limp."

Ranulf took hold of Henry's arm. "That's enough out of you," he chided, his words slurring slightly. His reddish brown hair was disheveled to an astonishing degree, making it look more ruddy and him more foxlike than ever. "Merrick knows what he's about. He first dipped his wick months before you and—"

As he realized what he'd just said, and when, and where, Ranulf's face turned red and his eyes went wide as cartwheels. The uncles, who'd entered after the others, looked equally shocked at his crude revelation. Sir Jowan, however, blinked stupidly, as if he didn't understand at all.

It would have been comical, except that…it wasn't. Constance didn't need any reminders that Merrick had been with other women. Of course, she would have been more shocked if her husband had been a virgin, but she didn't want to hear about his past escapades on her wedding night—or at any other time.

Merrick's deep, gruff voice suddenly filled the chamber. "I believe my bride and I should be alone."

Beatrice giggled, then hiccuped loudly. Her father, frowning, took hold of her arm. "Come along, Beatrice," he said, pulling her out the door.

Lord Algernon and Sir Jowan followed, both trying to exit at the same time. Lord Algernon muttered a protest, and Sir Jowan his apologies, bowing and gesturing for Lord Algernon to go first. Lord Algernon suggested Sir Jowan lead the way.

This went on for another few moments, until Ranulf pushed his way between them.

That left Henry.

"Well, Merrick," he said, regarding his friend with a slightly stupid grin, "you've done it and well, too. I never thought you'd be the first of us to be married. I always thought it'd be Ranulf, for all his protests and claims that he could love no woman well enough to wed." He beamed at Constance, then spoke to Merrick as if he forgot she was capable of hearing. "Now, before I forget, remember what I told you about—"

Merrick pointed imperiously at the door. "Out!"

Henry blinked. "God's blood, man, there's no need to shout." He backed toward the door. "Just wanted to remind you that since this is her first time, you should—"

Merrick started walking toward him. With a comically exaggerated look of fear, Henry turned and fled, his laughter echoing down the stairs.

"May he trip and break his neck," Merrick muttered as he closed the door.

Constance was sure he didn't really mean that, but she wasn't about to chastise him. Indeed, she wasn't sure what to say or do now that they were alone, and married.

Merrick marched to the side table, where he downed the wine he'd poured. Then he added some more into his goblet.

Was he going to get drunk *now*?

He raised the goblet, then hesitated and glanced at her. "Would you like some wine?"

She shook her head.

Still holding his drink, he sat on the stool in front of her dressing table and put the goblet on the table without drinking from it.

Aware of her rapidly beating heart, mindful of every kiss and caress they'd already shared, Constance wondered why he wasn't getting undressed. He'd seemed very keen to make love with her before their union was blessed by the priest.

Perhaps his friends' remarks bothered him. "Weddings seem to inspire a certain ribald revelry," she noted. "I hope you didn't take offense."

"Henry has a loose tongue."

It was probably better not to discuss Henry. "Does Ranulf really claim he'll never love a woman well enough to wed?"

"So he says."

"Why not?"

Merrick shrugged. And still he sat on the stool.

Chewing her lip, Constance wondered what was wrong, and what, if anything, she ought to do.

As the silence continued and Merrick kept staring at his wine, she grew impatient, and then a little annoyed. If he didn't want to marry her, he could have broken the betrothal. She'd certainly given him cause, at least in the beginning. And hadn't he been anxious, almost desperate, for her to accept him? So what was his reason for this hesitation now? Or was this an attempt to increase her anticipation for what was to come?

Perhaps it was a way to prove who was truly in command in the bedchamber.

If so, had he not learned she was no mild maiden to sit quietly by and wait to be told what to do?

She rose and went to the side table where the carafe and another goblet glimmered in the flickering candle-light, moving slowly, very aware that the glowing night candle beside the bed would make her gown virtually transparent. The coldness of the stone floor made her nipples pucker, as they did when he caressed them.

Merrick glanced at her. She saw his surprise and then desire, enflamed in a moment.

Even though her hands trembled a little, she picked up the carafe. "Perhaps I will have some wine."

Merrick slowly got to his feet. "Constance…?"

"Yes?" she inquired, raising the goblet to her lips and sipping the rich, red drink.

"I've heard the king is on his way back to England, and the earl of Cornwall with him."

Constance felt a stab of irritation. This was their wedding night—why did he have to speak of the king and the earl of Cornwall?

Maybe she ought to remove her gown completely.

Merrick walked over to the window. He opened the linen shutter enough to see out over the walls of Tregel-las. He took deep breaths of the salt-tinged air, as if he was finding it difficult to breathe. "Since the earl is my liege lord, I expect we'll be summoned to Tintagel."

"Do you have an objection to answering the sum-mons?"

"No." Merrick turned and looked at her, his expression frustratingly inscrutable. "But I would prefer to stay here."

She didn't understand his reluctance unless, she

thought with better humor, he would be sorry to leave her for even a short time. "It would be your duty to go, and I could go with you. Alan is quite capable of running Tregellas for a few weeks."

"That is not what troubles me."

She thought of the fate of his cortege when he was a boy. "Is it an attack on our party you fear?"

"That, and other things."

"We'll take a large escort. Ranulf can lead—"

"Ranulf should stay here to protect Tregellas."

"Very well. But if we take sufficient men, we should be safe."

He didn't meet her gaze. "It isn't only concern for our safety that makes me uneasy," he confessed. "I have no love for the nobility. Too many of them are greedy and ambitious, seeking power at any cost."

"You don't have to love them. You need only tolerate them."

"Is that what you've been doing with Kiernan, tolerating him?"

Was *that* why he'd not come near her? Had she not made her opinion of Kiernan clear? What more assurance could she give him?

She answered bluntly, and with indignation. "I resent your implication, my lord. I told you I have no deep feelings for him. I've hardly spoken to him at all since..." This would not be a good time to mention her conversation with Kiernan in the chapel. "Since he arrived with his father. Beatrice has spent more time in his company than I have. I thought you believed me when I said I cared nothing for him in that way."

Merrick ran his hand through his long hair. "I did. I do."

"Then why accuse me?"

"I didn't mean to. I just…"

"What?" she demanded. "What are you trying to do? Enrage me? Upset me? On this, our wedding night? I believed you wanted me, my lord. Was I wrong? Would you rather we had not wed? Would you like to leave me, my lord, and have our union annulled?"

Instead of answering her heated questions, he crossed the chamber in two long strides and pulled her into his arms. His lips took hers with fiery, fierce passion, robbing her of breath and thought. His hands stroked her body, raked her unbound hair, aroused and enflamed her desire until she had to hold on to him or sink to the ground.

Still kissing her deeply, he picked her up and carried her to the bed. After he laid her upon it, he stepped back and started to strip off his clothing.

"I take it, then," she asked breathlessly, "that you don't want to annul our marriage?"

Bending to pull off his boots, he raised his eyes and looked at her. The intensity of his desire made her blood throb with expectancy.

Swallowing hard, she moved back and sideways on the bed, to make room for him, her husband.

He straightened. He wore only his breeches that clung to his powerful thighs, and she could see that he was as aroused as she.

"Take off your shift," he ordered. "I want to look at you."

Taken aback by his brusque command, she swallowed hard as her trembling fingers fumbled trying to undo the drawstring at the neck of her shift.

She heard him remove his breeches and toss them aside. She felt the bed dip when he knelt beside her. He put his hand over hers and held them still. "If you would rather leave it on…?"

She didn't know what to do.

Merrick removed his hand and cursed softly as he swung himself around to sit on the edge of the bed. In the dim golden light of the bedside candle, she could see several small scars crossing the skin of his broad back. His shoulders rose and fell with a sigh. "I'm sorry."

"For what?" she asked warily.

"For frightening you. That was the last thing I wanted to do."

She was unprepared for the remorse in his voice. "I was just caught unawares. And you were so—" she struggled to find the word "—forceful."

He sighed again and answered without looking at her. "I'm a stern, grim man, Constance. If it's a merry husband that you seek, I am not he."

"I want more than merriment," she said, meaning it. "I have no desire to be married to a man little more than a jester, like Henry."

"I am too serious, too harsh. I can't say sweet words of the sort women like to hear."

"You mean you don't utter flattering nonsense or empty promises under the guise of love." She clasped her hands, her heart aching with dread. "Is that all, Merrick? Or have you reconsidered? Do you no longer want me for your wife?

"To be with you is all I've ever wanted," he replied, his deep voice hoarse with longing, his eyes full of anguish, as if he feared she no longer wanted *him*. "But I don't deserve you."

"Why not?" she asked wonderingly. "You are a lord, a mighty knight, champion of tournaments. I doubt there is a better man in England, and if we speak of deserving, perhaps it is I who don't deserve *you*."

His face flushed as he looked away. "You can't mean that."

"But I do," she insisted. "You are everything I've hoped for when it came to a husband. I wanted a man I could respect and who respected me, who made me feel loved and cherished and desired. Who made me feel safe. You do all that, and more. You stir my heart, and my desire, more than I could ever dream, and you need no words to do it."

How he looked at her then! Relief, happiness and something that caused her blood to pulse with excitement mingled in his eyes. He reached out to touch her cheek, sending shivers of longing through her. "How I wish I could find the words to tell you how I feel about you, to say how much I need you, how much I want you."

She had no difficulty with the drawstring of her shift now. "Show me instead," she whispered.

CHAPTER TWELVE

MERRICK NEEDED NO FURTHER urging. He eagerly began to strip off his wedding clothes as Constance blew out the candles set on the table and in the candlestand, all save one beside the bed.

Standing beside it, she gave her husband a brazenly seductive smile. "Before I extinguish the last candle, I want to admire my husband as he wishes to admire me."

Facing her in all his masculine magnificence, Merrick's eyes were dark, exciting pools of desire. She ran her gaze over him slowly, from his wide, intelligent brow, dark, passionate eyes, angular cheeks and sensual lips to his broad shoulders and slender torso. He had a few scars there, ones she'd touched lightly when she'd caressed him before. Dark hairs curled around his nipples and met in the center of his chest. They began again at his navel, and went lower, surrounding his shaft that stood in bold announcement of his desire. His legs were long and muscular, lean and strong from hours on horseback.

"Do I meet with your approval, my lady?" he asked, his voice a husky whisper.

She regarded him with blatant admiration. "You certainly do." She rose, letting her shift fall to the floor and puddle at her feet. "And I, my lord? Do I meet with yours?"

His hungry eyes devoured her. "You are the most beautiful woman I've ever seen."

"And I'm yours," she murmured, stepping forward and wrapping her arms about him. "Your wife."

"Mine," he murmured as he bent his head to brush his lips over hers, teasing and tempting, as their bodies met. "I scarce dared to dream…"

His words drifted away as he kissed her.

Dared to dream what? she wondered as she sank into the haze of desire. That they would be wed? That she would be his? But that had been planned for years and years….

Then she stopped wondering, aware only of the feel of his skin—so much of his skin—against hers. It was like being next to the heat of an open flame. Her breasts pressed against his chest, and his aroused shaft slipped between her naked thighs. His whole body tensed, as if the sensation took him by surprise.

Yet only for an instant, for in the next, he was helping her down upon the bed. His knee slid between her legs to guide her, while his strong arms eased her onto the coverlet and pillows. He sank down, too, his body covering hers as he kissed her.

She could sense him restraining his need, wondering why, until he told her. "Have no fear, Constance," he murmured as his lips journeyed to her ear, his breath warm on her cheek. "I'll make sure you're ready for me."

"I'm ready for you now," she whispered, certain that she was.

"Not yet," he said, his lips sliding lower while he raised his hips and shifted his weight onto his arms. "Not quite yet."

He leaned on one hand, freeing the other to stroke her, beginning with her leg. He brushed light, leisurely caresses upward from her knee to her thigh. He skimmed the place where her thighs met, and that alone was enough to make her whimper. Then he continued until he reached her breast. He gently cupped it a moment, letting the weight rest in his palm, before his fingertips danced slowly around the soft curve and glided toward her nipple. She gasped when he caressed the now stiff peak, then moaned when he lowered his head and sucked her nipple into his warm, wet mouth.

She wiggled and squirmed with the pleasure of it, lost to the myriad sensations created by his lips and tongue and fingers.

His mouth left her breast to again capture hers, this time with a fierce and hungry need. She could feel his control slipping away from him, knew he couldn't wait much longer. She didn't want to wait, either. He was her husband, and she his very willing bride.

She parted her legs and bent her knees, silently inviting him to take her, ready to gladly sacrifice her maidenhead to his questing manhood.

"Not yet," he murmured, raising his head to smile at her.

"Now!" she ordered.

His eyes flashed fire but, smiling devilishly, he shook his head and stroked her belly. Lower. Then lower still. "Not yet."

"Please, Merrick!"

"In a moment."

"You, sir, are…" She threw back her head with a low groan as he pressed the heel of his hand between her thighs, where she was moist and throbbing. "The devil," she finished, panting.

"I don't want to hurt you," he murmured as he bent again to pleasure her breasts.

"Liar!" she gasped as ripples of pure need seemed to spread from his tongue, until her whole body felt enflamed. "You're hurting me now."

He stilled and looked at her, his expression appalled.

"You're wounding my pride by making me beg."

That brought another disarmingly wicked smile to his face. "Would you rather *I* begged?"

Wondering if he could possibly be serious, if this proud, stern nobleman would ever really beg for anything, she nodded.

As his finger slid into her cleft, he looked into her eyes. "Please, Constance," he whispered with a tenderness and yearning that touched her heart, "let me love you."

How could any woman resist such a plea from such a man? "Oh, yes," she sighed. "Yes! Love me *now*!"

He said no more and waited no longer. He positioned

himself between her legs, his hips against hers, his hands beside her head. She grabbed his shoulders and when she felt the head of his shaft against her, pushed forward. His eyes widened, but she didn't care if he thought her wanton or impatient—for wanton and impatient she was.

There was a moment's resistance until the membrane gave way and he was inside her. The pain was sharp, quick, like a cut of a knife. Again he stilled, and looked at her.

"Don't stop," she whispered, clutching the bedsheets in her fists. "Please…don't stop!"

"As you command, my lady," he rasped and then, with a low growl of pure animal pleasure, thrust again.

She raised her head and, wrapping her arms about him, found his nipple and laved it with her tongue as he had hers. His breathing and his quickening thrusts encouraged her, and she became even bolder in her ministrations.

Until the sensation of his thrusting shaft, the anxious need of her own body, consumed everything else. She fell back, pulling him with her, holding him close as she locked her legs about him and licked and kissed every inch of his skin she could.

The tension within her was like a thread being pulled tighter and tighter. She clenched her teeth, bunched the sheet in her hands, panting hard.

And then…the straining need snapped and she rose, lifting her shoulders without even being aware of what she did, and crying out with release. She bucked as he jerked, and his groans joined with her cries as he, too, reached completion.

After the release dissipated, she relaxed, flat on her back, still panting, still slightly throbbing, aware of his weight on her, and his chest rising and falling as he breathed heavily. She stroked his sweat-damp hair until he shifted away from her.

He fell against the pillows and stared up at the canopy over the bed while she turned to nestle against him. "How soon can we do that again?"

"How soon?" he asked, looking at her with surprise.

She toyed with the dark hairs around his nipple. "Yes."

"Are you…are you not sore?"

She hadn't stopped to think about it. "Well, yes, a little," she confessed.

He levered himself up onto his elbow and looked at the sheets, which were smeared with blood from her lost maidenhead. He lay back down and studied the canopy again. "I think no more tonight, my lady, tempted though I may be."

"Your wife is here, Merrick, not hovering somewhere over the bed," she reminded him. "Or are there more important matters deserving of your attention at this time?"

He gave her a rueful smile—a new expression she'd never seen on his face before, and one that delighted her. "Forgive me. I was just thinking that I don't deserve this happiness."

"Yes, you do," she said firmly. Then she had a moment's doubt. "You *are* happy?"

His answer was another long and passionate kiss.

Smiling, Constance snuggled against him, sighed and closed her eyes. "I'm very happy, too, my lord."

LONG AFTER CONSTANCE DRIFTED into blissful, sated sleep, Merrick lay guiltily awake, his beloved bride beside him.

He'd thought he loved Constance with all his heart before they wed. Yet now, having experienced the most exciting, blissful physical union of his life, he loved her even more.

That made his deceit even worse. By not being honest with her, he'd stolen something he could never return, and she could never recover. If she learned the truth, she'd surely think him a base, selfish and disgusting scoundrel, a man who'd tricked her into disgrace and dishonor.

She must never find out the truth. He had to be more on his guard now than he'd ever been, lest he betray himself. And lose his beloved forever.

WHEN CONSTANCE SLOWLY surfaced into consciousness the next morning, she immediately remembered she was married. Sighing and stretching, she reached for Merrick, ignoring the brief, sharp pain between her legs—a small price to pay for the glorious lovemaking she'd shared with him last night.

Her husband wasn't in the bed.

She raised herself on her elbow and discovered that he was fully dressed and looking out the window. Wondering what he was doing, she wrapped the top sheet around her and started to get out of the bed.

He turned and gave her the ghost of a smile. "There's no need for you to rise so early. Stay in bed and rest."

There were dark circles under his eyes, and his cheeks seemed drawn. Or maybe it was a trick of the early morning light. "Why don't you come back to bed and rest with me?" she suggested. "You look tired."

That brought a more natural smile to his face. "If I am, it's because of you."

"I'll gladly tire you out some more. Or is there some pressing business that calls you from our bridal chamber? Did I not hear that you'd excused all but the most necessary watches and patrols today? A wise notion, my lord, considering that most of the men will be the worse for celebrating last night." She patted the place beside her. "And you were so generous, many in the village will be the worse for celebrating, too. Surely there can be nothing vital to take you away from me this morning."

He took a few tentative steps toward the bed. Her body warming as she thought of his kiss, his touch, she smiled enticingly and pulled the sheet slowly from her breasts. "Take off your clothes, my lord, and come back to bed."

He hesitated, and a look of doubt crossed his dark features.

"If you fear to hurt me again, I could pleasure you as I did that other day," she proposed.

With a low moan he scrambled onto the bed, grabbing her and pushing her back onto the coverlet. She eagerly welcomed his embrace, laughing and kissing him at the same time. "I know you're a conscientious overlord, but is not leaving your bride at first light too extreme?" she said before he covered his mouth with hers for another passionate kiss.

"I try to be conscientious in all things," he said, his voice low and seductive as his hand moved down her belly.

She laughed again. "Sit up a moment, my lord."

"Why?" he murmured, nuzzling her neck, which sent the most delicious shivers through her body.

"Because you're wearing too many clothes."

"Ah."

He sat back on his heels and allowed her to lift his tunic and tug it over his head. Then his shirt followed and she ran her hands over his chest. "Lie down, my lord," she commanded.

His eyes glowing with desire, he obeyed. She shifted closer and kissed his lips, letting her tongue swirl around his, then plunge inside his mouth as her hand eagerly explored his naked chest. She encountered his breeches and, still kissing him, tugged the knot of the drawstring loose. She slowly insinuated her hand inside, and found his rapidly swelling shaft.

He gasped when she took hold of him, then sighed as she began to stroke him. Excited herself, Constance slid her leg over his thigh and inched closer. Her breasts, their nipples taut, grazed his chest as she continued to plunder his mouth. Her strokes increased in tempo and she pressed her body closer.

There was no pain now, only that wondrous throbbing between her thighs. Perhaps it wouldn't hurt if she were to take him inside. Perhaps it was worth finding out.

She let go a moment to pull his breeches lower, freeing him. She eyed his engorged manhood greedily, remembering how it felt when he thrust inside her.

As she straddled his hips, Merrick opened his eyes. "What are you…?"

She leaned forward to brush her lips across his, and her breasts across his chest. "Loving you," she murmured.

She slid her mouth from his to kiss his collarbone, then tease and lick his nipples, all the while aware of his shaft hard against her and the few drops of moisture from its tip.

He was more than ready, and so was she. She rose, took him in her hand and guided him to her.

Worry clouded his face. "Are you—?"

"Sure," she confirmed, raising herself a little more. Then she lowered herself.

Tight. It was tight and, yes, she was a little sore, but he felt so…good. She gritted her teeth to keep any sound from escaping her lips, lest he think she was in too much pain to continue. She didn't want to stop, not now, as she rocked forward, her own desire propelling her and overcoming the remnants of the pain.

Merrick emitted a low growl as he grabbed her hips, helping her to move, showing her how to increase his pleasure. His legs twisted and shifted, as if he were too aroused to lie still.

Now completely caught up in their mutual excitement, Constance grabbed his hands and held them over his head. She wanted to be free, to move as she must.

Merrick moaned, but he made no effort to pull his hands from her grasp. Instead, it was clear her action enflamed him yet more. His hips rose and fell, thrusting and bucking with her motions. His breathing grew hoarse, rasping in his throat, while she panted heavily. He was near the brink. She could feel that moment coming....

And then it did. With a groan, his body spasmed, filling her, his seed spilling onto her thighs.

His powerful climax sent her over the edge to her own ecstasy. As she cried out, the waves of throbbing release rolled over her, leaving her spent and sweating.

She slowly, carefully climbed off him, to lie at his side and catch her breath.

"God's wounds," Merrick muttered as he sat up and looked at her with both wonder and concern. "Did that not hurt you more?"

She gave him a satisfied smile. "Perhaps, but I couldn't help myself."

"I should have helped it," he muttered as he got to his feet. He started to tie his breeches, then growled an oath.

"What is it?" she asked, levering herself up on her elbows.

"I've still got my boots on."

Although he was obviously annoyed, she had to laugh. "You only got a bit of mud on the coverlet. It will simply have to be washed."

Which reminded her that soon enough, the uncles and probably some of the other noblemen would be arriving to check the sheets for the telltale signs of her lost maidenhead. She was glad that there was plenty of evidence for them to find. She knew there were those who believed she'd managed the late lord of Tregellas with more than soothing words. Now they would have proof that she had not.

His breeches tied, Merrick put on his shirt and tunic, then went to the wash table and poured water from the ewer into the basin. Bringing the basin and some linen, he returned to the bed.

She sat up, intending to wash herself, but he shook his head. "Let me."

She bit her lip as she lay down and let him wash away the evidence of their passion, flinching at first when the damp cloth touched her skin.

He glanced at her, worry in his eyes.

"I'm not in pain," she assured him. "It's only that the cloth is cold."

He finished quickly. When he took away the basin, she rose and put on her discarded shift, then her bedrobe. As she combed her hair, she asked, "How long do you think it will be before the proof is sought?"

Merrick gave her a questioning glance.

"The sheets. I fear our uncles and the others may not be early risers after a night of such festivity."

Merrick let out his breath slowly. "I suppose I must stay here until they do their duty."

His tone dismayed her a bit. "Only if you wish," she said, trying not to sound hurt.

He came to her and ran his hands through her hair before raising a lock to kiss. "I would gladly spend all day with you, Constance, every day. And not just in bed."

"Then why not linger a little longer?" She thought of something else. "Are you hungry?"

He smiled slowly. "Not for food."

As her blood warmed again, she couldn't resist teasing him. "For conversation, then? About what, my lord? The king and his court? The hall moot in a fortnight?"

They were interrupted by a tentative knock at the door.

Constance wrapped her bedrobe about her more tightly and stood by the window as Merrick went to the door. He opened it to reveal two very bleary-eyed, unsteady noblemen. Behind Lord Carrell and Lord Algernon were Sir Jowan and Sir Ranulf. There were more people, too, but she didn't want to take an inventory of those who'd arrived to witness the evidence of her lost virginity, with one exception. She didn't see Kiernan, and was glad. Casting her mind back, she didn't recall noticing him in the party that escorted Merrick to his bedchamber last night, either.

"We've come…" Lord Algernon began. He stopped, swallowed and swayed a little before continuing. "We've come to examine the…" He fell silent and turned a little paler.

Merrick opened the door wide and gestured for them to enter, then moved out of the way.

Although this was to be expected, Constance blushed and stared at her feet as they went to the bed.

"Satisfied?" Merrick asked evenly.

"Yes, absolutely," his uncle quickly replied, shuffling backward.

Still blushing, Constance let out her breath and raised her eyes—to encounter the unexpected, unwelcome, angry gaze of Kiernan. Pressing her lips together, she met his glare with one of her own. It wasn't as if she'd done something shameful and dishonest. She'd made love with her lawful husband. She'd married in accordance with the betrothal contract, and she didn't regret it.

Kiernan's face reddened, but he continued to stare at her until Merrick stepped between them. He ushered the men out of the door, exchanging a few quiet words with Ranulf.

When they were gone, Constance sank onto the stool near her dressing table, wincing a little. Perhaps they shouldn't have made love a second time so soon.

"Are you unwell?" Merrick asked.

"A little sore."

He went to the side table, poured a goblet of wine and wordlessly held it out to her.

"No, thank you," she said, picking up her ivory comb.

"That was necessary."

"I know."

A strong, firm hand took the comb from her and, to her surprise, Merrick began to run it through her hair. She closed her eyes, enjoying this unexpected intimacy, as well as the gentle tugging sensation on her scalp.

"Are you going to let that boy upset you?" he asked after a moment.

"If you mean Kiernan, I was simply taken aback to see him here this morning."

"I was glad. Now he knows that we are truly wed and he has no hope at all. You are mine, in every way."

She opened her eyes and studied her husband's reflection in the silver plate in front of her. "Yes, I'm yours, to do with as you will," she said slowly, a sliver of her old fear returning.

"Bound to me, for good or ill."

That, too, was true, and more dread filled her. "What ills are you expecting?"

"Rebellion. War."

She stared at him, aghast, fear for her own fate submerged beneath a greater worry. She'd thought he'd meant conflict between them, or differences of opinion, not war. And although she was well aware that there were tensions and conflicts at court, she didn't want to believe he was right. War was a brutal, ugly business that led to death and destruction, sometimes for very little gain. "Do you truly think it will come to open rebellion?"

"I fear it might, and if it does, I'm tied to both the king and the earl of Cornwall. I'll be forced to break my oath to one of them in favor of the other, and if my choice fails…"

He didn't have to finish. She knew the result. He would lose all, including his life.

"I didn't mean to frighten you, but you wanted to know what ills I spoke of."

She rose and clasped her hands in the sleeves of her robe. "Yes, I did."

As it had last night, that haunted look came to his dark, intense eyes. "Now, are you sorry we're married?"

"No," she answered firmly and sincerely. "I will only regret marrying you, my lord, if you treat me as if I have no mind or heart, that I am no more to you than a means to breed sons. I will be sorry we wed if you ignore me or belittle me, and especially if you treat me with disrespect. But if you treat me as a trusted friend and love me as you did last night, I will be more than content. As for your oath of loyalty to two different men, you aren't the only nobleman in the kingdom to face such a dilemma. Sir Jowan is likewise sworn to both the earl and the king, and there are many others."

His expression changed to one that thrilled and relieved her. "I would have you more than content," he murmured, kissing her tenderly.

Sorry she had married him? If he was this way always, how could she be sorry? "I wish you hadn't stayed away from Tregellas for fifteen years," she said with a sigh of both regret and desire.

"I wish now I had not. But I was afraid to see you again."

"Afraid?" she repeated incredulously, drawing back to stare at him in wonder. "To see me?"

"I was afraid you'd tell me you didn't want to marry me."

Still holding him loosely in her arms, she gave him a wry smile. "I didn't want to marry you," she confessed. "I hated you when we were children. But then you came home and were so different from what I expected."

"How am I different?" he asked, a furrow forming between his brows.

"Your looks."

"I'm older."

"No, it's more than that. You're taller than I expected and your eyes…"

His lips grazed hers. "You've changed, too. You used to be so timid."

"You used to be a horrid little brat," she said, leaning forward to kiss him. "I could never love that boy, but I could love you. I do love you."

His dark eyes were questioning pools of limitless depth.

She had said it, and it was the truth. "Yes, Merrick," she said quietly. "I love you. If I didn't love you, I would never have married you."

As he looked at her, his gaze unwavering, her heart sank. Had her revelation been unwelcome to him? Had he believed she felt something less?

She could tell nothing from the glittering orbs gazing back at her. "I realize you may not love me," she said as disappointment filled her, "that you married me because of the contract, but I hoped...I still hope that someday..."

He grabbed her and held her close. "Oh, God help me," he murmured, his lips against her hair. "Constance, sweet Constance, I've loved you since I was ten years old and saw you sitting in that hay field. I've only ever wanted happiness and good fortune for you, and if instead I cause you to be unhappy, if I bring misfortune to you, I will curse myself forever."

Joy and relief filled her as they kissed, tenderly at first, until passion flamed. "I hope to bring only good things to you, too, my lord."

"You've already made me happier than I deserve to be," he said.

He kissed her again, long and passionately, until he reluctantly pulled away. "And if I don't go now, I may never leave."

"Perhaps that's my evil plan, my lord," she teased, no longer afraid of him, or the future. "Maybe I seek to ensnare you with my desire."

"Alas, I must resist," he replied as he reluctantly started for the door.

He gave her that small smile that made her knees weak. "For now."

CHAPTER THIRTEEN

A FEW DAYS LATER, MERRICK looked up from the parchment he'd been reading and smiled as Constance peered into the solar.

As always, his heart thrilled just to see her face but, also as always, that feeling was swiftly followed by guilt that could only be assuaged by pleasing her any and every way he could.

"I thought Alan and Ruan were never going to leave," she said as she entered the chamber. "You must have had much to discuss."

"We did. This is a larger estate than I remembered," he admitted, leaning back in his chair. He held out his arms and she, understanding his unspoken request, settled onto his lap.

"Have you come any closer to discovering who set the fire?" she asked, toying with a lock of his long dark hair.

He wondered if she had any idea how even that simple intimate action thrilled him, or how distracting the weight of her was on his thighs and shaft, but decided it was far too delightful a torment to enlighten her. "I'm sure Alan is doing his best to find out who set it," he replied, caressing her cheek. "I'm less sure of Ruan's enthusiasm, but it may be too late to learn much. The malcontent may be far away by now."

She brushed her fingertips across his soft lips. "Peder hasn't heard anything, either."

He gave her a rueful smile. "I thought sharing such information with 'them at the castle' went against Peder's notion of honor."

"This is different," she said. "The fire caused trouble for everyone, not just the king or the lord of Tregellas."

He nuzzled her neck, inhaling the clean, warm scent of her. "How is the old fellow?"

"Well, although I hope he's not summoned to fight any more fires."

Merrick hoped so, too, and that Peder would continue in good health for several years yet. "Let's pray we have no more such disasters." Of any kind, he added silently, concern momentarily dimming his pleasure.

"With my dowry, we have enough to pay for the repairs to the mill, have we not?"

"Yes, thank God."

"Has Ranulf made any suggestions as to who might take his place?" she asked, pressing kisses on her husband's cheeks and chin.

He tried to concentrate on her questions. "One or two. It seems there was a Scot he thought would be a good choice, but when he suggested it to the fellow, he refused. Then, yesterday, the Scot and his woman left Tregellas."

Constance frowned at that news. "I wonder why?"

Merrick shrugged, not particularly worried about a mercenary who decided to seek employ elsewhere, even if he was a good soldier. Thanks to the ongoing strife in the land, there were always plenty more. "Who knows? Perhaps he was not the sort of man Ranulf believed he was and didn't like being singled out."

"You mean he might have been outside the law?"

His lips traveled from her cheek to her shell-like ear. "It wouldn't be the first time a thief or murderer has hidden in the ranks of foot soldiers. The king of France regularly empties his prisons when he has a war to fight."

"Maybe my uncle or yours could send someone from their castle."

"I'll consider asking," he murmured, not wanting to think about soldiers and fighting and the deeds of kings while they were alone.

"If we were in difficulties, I'm sure we could get money from our uncles." She sighed and tipped her head back as he continued to kiss her. "But I'm glad they've gone home."

"I'd be more glad if Beatrice had gone with them."

Constance sat up straighter. "She's not so very much trouble, is she?"

Merrick couldn't resist teasing her. "Not when she's quiet."

Constance clearly wasn't amused. "She's not talking nearly so much these days," she noted, frowning. "I never thought I'd miss her chatter, but I must confess this new reticence makes me worry. She used to tell me everything, no matter how unimportant and now, well, she doesn't."

Merrick wished he'd never mentioned Beatrice. It was as if a bucket of cold water had been tossed over his head...or almost, for Constance still rested on his lap. "That could simply be a sign she's getting older, or has learned how to behave more like a lady and less like a giggly little girl. She *is* old enough to be married, Constance."

"I'm well aware of that. I just hope she's not hiding something serious from me while she's in our care."

Merrick hated to see Constance worry. He kissed her furrowed brow, as he would kiss away all her troubles if he could. "I know that you love her, and fear for her. But let me say again, you have no reason not to trust Henry."

"I never said a word about Henry."

"You didn't have to. I've seen the way you watch him whenever he's talking to Beatrice, but I assure you, he'd never attempt to seduce a young woman in my family or under my protection."

"I'm trying to be less suspicious." She hesitated and he wondered what else was bothering her, until she spoke. "Is it true he has a mistress in London?"

God's blood, how had she...? "Who told you that?"

"Beatrice."

"How did she hear it?"

"She guessed from things Henry's said in conversation."

Henry should learn to keep his mouth shut, especially when in the company of so inquisitive a young lady. "He's never actually told me that he has," Merrick admitted, "which is not to say he doesn't."

"Wouldn't he confide in you?"

"All men have secrets, even the best of friends," he replied.

But this conversation was veering in a dangerous direction, so he sought to turn it elsewhere. "For instance, I would never tell Henry you came to my solar today and most brazenly seduced me away from my duties," he said as his hand meandered toward her breasts and he again pressed his lips to the bare skin of her neck, hoping to distract her.

"I'm relieved."

She was annoyed.

He stopped kissing her and regarded her warily. "What's wrong?"

"Nothing."

She was a woman and a newly wedded wife. They had just been discussing another man's illicit liaisons. It didn't take a seer to figure out what was upsetting her. "I don't have a mistress, Constance, and never have," he said truthfully. "No other woman has ever held my heart."

She smiled happily, then with seductive intent as she wiggled suggestively on his lap. "You accused me of attempting to brazenly seduce you, my lord, but I must point out, we're married," she purred as she ran her hands up his broad chest. "I don't think we can call it seduction, then…do you?"

"Whatever we're doing, it'll be our secret," he murmured as his breathing quickened and his shaft eagerly responded to her words, her tone and the movement of her warm body against his.

His hand glided along her arm, then upward to her breast. She shifted, and the friction of her body against his hardened shaft made her whimper and shift again, while he continued to gently knead her breast and explore her mouth with his tongue.

She broke the kiss and he groaned like one severely wounded. "What's wrong?" he gasped.

"We had best cease for now, my lord," she said as she ran her finger over the plane of his cheek and down to his jaw. "This is not the place for what I have in mind."

He could think of no better place for what *he* had in mind. Well, for what he had in mind, almost anywhere would do, as long as they were alone.

"The table is large and strong, and not liable to break," he offered, his voice husky with yearning. "Or we could stay in this chair," he suggested, caressing her.

"Really?" she whispered as the excitement took her. "It seems a sin…."

"I recall, my lady, that we've sinned before."

"So we have," she agreed, her eyes shining with anticipation. She ran her tongue lightly over her lips as if in silent invitation—and he needed no other.

He set her on her feet and, with one swift motion, swept the parchments from the table. Holding her around her waist, he pressed kisses to her lips and cheeks, guiding her backward.

As his tongue teased and tormented, drawing forth her desire, his hands cupped her buttocks and lifted her so that she was sitting on the edge of the table. Her arms around him, she wrapped her legs around his hips and pulled him forward, until his manhood was against her, ready for the pleasure to come.

He pushed up her skirt and shift, and in a whisper, his breathing already ragged with need, asked her to untie his breeches. She needed no second urging, but quickly did as he requested. When he was free, she grabbed his broad shoulders to steady herself.

This was no leisurely, gentle coupling. With one swift thrust he was inside her, encircled by her moist warmth, tight around his shaft. She pressed her mouth against his neck, muffling the cry of exultation as he drove home. Then again. Withdrawing a little, he plunged inside once more as the sensations spurred him.

She clenched her teeth and, breathing hard, stifled the cries of ecstatic completion as they came together, the tension snapping and their muted cries filling the air.

Leaning against her, spent and sated, he closed his eyes and held her to him. Constance. His love. His wife.

His weakness.

THAT NIGHT, A HAND COVERED the old man's mouth, waking him instantly. Unable to see, Peder immediately started struggling and trying to bite, kick or punch whatever stinking thief was holding him down.

"It's me!" a voice he hadn't expected to hear again hissed in his ear. "Talek."

When Peder stopped struggling, Talek cautiously removed his hand. Peder sat up, peering in the dim light from the glow of what was left of his fire in the hearth. Talek's clothes were stained and soiled and torn in places, as if he'd lived rough on the moor or in a cave, and he reeked of ale.

"What are you doing here?" Peder demanded. "What if somebody's seen you?"

"Nobody saw me," the former garrison commander mumbled as he hunched by the fire, his arms wrapped around himself, his hands filthy, his nails broken. "By God, I wish I'd gone to France when I had the chance. I could have met Pierre at the cove last time he came. But now that bastard in the castle's got patrols all over the road and in the woods since the fire. I can't get near the sea."

Peder shifted so that he was warmed by the heat from the hearth, and so that he could see Talek better. He didn't need to smell him any better to guess part of the man's trouble. Talek's hands also trembled like a sot's, and his eyes were bloodshot. "I thought you were going to stay close by in case Lady Constance needed your help."

"And I did, didn't I?" Talek grumbled. "But she's gone and married the bastard, hasn't she? No point in staying here and risking my neck for her anymore. So now I need your help. I've got to get a ship to France or somewhere—anywhere—else." He scowled darkly. "If that bastard finds me, I'm a dead man for sure."

"He didn't kill you before."

"Likely because he didn't want to upset Lady Constance more than he did. But now that she's his wife, he probably doesn't give a damn if she'll be angry or not. He'll kill me as soon as look at me."

"I would have believed that once, but now…?" Peder shook his head. "He's not given us any cause to think he's a heartless brute like his father."

Peder tilted his head to regard his friend. "Where exactly were you when the mill was set on fire?"

"Nowhere near," Talek answered. "I was in the wood, in the cave where you hide your tin."

"No, you weren't," Peder slowly replied. "I was there making sure my cache was still safe when I saw the flames." The old man's eyes seemed to bore into those of the former garrison commander. "I'm only going to ask you this once more, Talek, and you'd better tell me the truth. Where were you when the mill caught fire?"

"All right…I was drunk," Talek muttered, looking away. "Drunk as a lord, drunk like Wicked William. Aye, and I was angry, too. Angry and stupid." He bowed his head and mumbled, "I never would have done it if I'd a been sober. I just wanted to make a bit of trouble for him before I left, that's all. I swear on my sainted mother's life."

Peder got to his feet and glared at Talek. "*You* did it? You set the mill on fire?"

"No!" Talek cried, jumping up. "Just the shed. That's all. It just…it just got out of hand and —"

"Out of hand!" Peder retorted. "*Out of hand?* You destroyed it, man, and it'll be weeks before it's right. What the devil got into you?"

"I wanted to pay him back! Twenty years—twenty years I served Lord William. Did his dirty work. Guarded his brat of a son. Twenty years and he sends me away—"

"You drunken fool! You hurt everyone in Tregellas more than him. He can buy what he needs, but the rest of us can't. What about all the farmers who lost their grain? All the women who have to grind their family's wheat by hand if they're to have any bread? I should take you to the castle and throw you into the dungeon myself."

Talek's hand went to his sword and his eyes gleamed fiercely. "I wouldn't try it, if I were you. And I wouldn't tell anybody you seen me. In fact, old man, you should help me get clear away, because if I get caught, it'll be the noose for you. I know where your cache is, and all about Pierre. If I have to, I'll tell that bastard in the castle everything I know."

Peder's hands, calloused and still powerful despite his years, balled into fists. "You would, too, wouldn't you? You'd betray us all."

"If I had to. Now give me what money you've got and get me out of Tregellas."

Peder shook his head. "I won't lift a finger to help you."

Talek drew his sword. "You'd better, old man, or I'll run you through." He stuck the point of his sword on Peder's chest, then reached out to grab Peder by the arm. "If you won't help me flee willingly, I'll just have to take you with me."

The old man twisted away and dived for his bed. From under his pillow he pulled out an Italian dagger Pierre had given him, long and sharp and thin. As Talek raised his arm to strike with his sword, Peder turned and shoved the dagger upward with all his might into Talek's stomach.

The sword fell to the ground with a clang. Clutching at the dagger, Talek staggered backward, stumbling over a stool and falling against the wall of the cottage.

Shaking, Peder rose and went toward him, keeping well away from his feet.

"You bloody bastard," Talek whispered, blood bubbling on his lips. Then he smiled—a terrible, cruel smile. "Now I'll never tell you where your grandson's bones lie."

With a cry of despair, Peder threw himself down beside the wounded man. "Where is he? For God's sake, tell me! Let me bury him in the churchyard. If you've an ounce of pity…"

"What pity did you have for me?" Talek demanded as the blood trickled down his chin and stained his tunic.

"No churchyard for him, like your daughter. The daughter you think's such a saint. She's burning in hell now, though, isn't she? She probably would have anyway. She was a whore—or as good as. She didn't put up much of a fight when I held her down so Wicked William could have her."

Another cry issued from Peder's lips as he rose and grabbed the hilt of the dagger protruding from Talek's gut. He yanked it out, then plunged it into the man again, right through his heart.

Talek's legs kicked once before he lay still.

Panting, Peder staggered back. He ran a quivering hand over his sweating forehead, then dropped the bloody dagger on Talek's body. He made his way to a cupboard and found the bit of wine he kept for special occasions. He pulled out the stopper and drank deep. Then he wiped his chin and leaned back against the cupboard. He closed his eyes and waited for his racing heart to slow, his mind to clear.

What was he going to do? He felt no guilt for what he'd done. Talek had met the fate he deserved and he was glad he'd been the instrument to mete it out. God would surely understand and forgive. But how was he to explain Talek's presence in his cottage? The lord of Tregellas would wonder why the man would come there, unless he knew Peder would give him help or sanctuary. Even if he explained that he'd killed Talek because he'd been threatened, and that Talek had set the fire, would he be believed? Lady Constance would trust him, but that Merrick?

His hatred for the lords of Tregellas was too well-known. Merrick might even believe *he* had set the fire, either alone or with Talek, and was using the man's death to cover his own guilt.

Besides, why not leave the lord to puzzle over who had done it? Let it trouble his mind for as long as possible, as *his* mind was forever troubled by the disappearance of his grandson—and never more than now, when it seemed it was no accident after all.

Peder spit into the fire to clear the bitter bile from his mouth.

Lady Constance, though…she didn't deserve to live with the dread that they had an unknown enemy, perhaps in their very midst. If he could find a way to tell her, she could keep a secret…

But would she? Maybe she'd feel duty bound to tell her husband.

No, better to keep Talek's death and crime a secret, known only to himself.

Peder opened his eyes, and the first thing to meet his gaze was Talek's bloody face, his lips twisted from his death throes.

As Peder started forward, he prayed. Not for forgiveness. Not for mercy.

That God would someday show him his grandson's remains, so he could bring them home for a decent burial. And for the strength to move the body of a lying, treacherous snake.

CHAPTER FOURTEEN

THE DAY OF THE HALL MOOT, THE sky was a dull gray
ceiling of clouds. If the weather worsened, they would
go inside, Constance knew, but otherwise, the hall
was too small for the crowd now waiting with hushed
expectancy for the proceedings to start. Even Beatrice
was quiet, although that was getting to be far from unusual. Henry had declared he would be bored with
such business, and had gone off to hunt. Ranulf was
in the ward, working with the new troop of archers.
Merrick had decided that Welsh long bows could be
an asset, and had set about finding a man to teach a
select group, as well as getting the bows and arrows
for them.

Constance slid a glance toward her husband as he sat
beside her on the dais erected in the courtyard where he
would make his judgments, and grant or refuse requests.
Just as she'd always hoped, they'd talked at length about
the conflicts likely to be brought before him. He'd asked
her about the people involved and sought her advice.

She knew him well enough now to see the signs of
tension in his neck and jaw. In a way she was glad, for

that implied a lack of certainty, not an overweening arrogance and belief that he was infallible.

She put her hand on his forearm and gave him an encouraging smile. His grave expression didn't change, but his muscles relaxed.

Fortunately, all the serious cases were swiftly dealt with. Merrick listened carefully to those with complaints and those who sought to defend themselves against them, then rendered his decisions quickly, and with firm purpose. This was a far cry from the stannary courts of the tinners, which were notorious for long-winded speeches and a longer wait for judgment. Perhaps in future, Constance mused, some of the personal disputes that could be settled by stannary courts would be brought here for a speedier resolution.

Finally all that remained was Merrick's approval of Annice and Eric's marriage. Since there was no question that Merrick would give his consent, Constance anticipated a quick conclusion to the hall moot. Then she and Merrick could—-

A flicker of movement in the shadows of the stable caught her eye, and a glimpse of a familiar face made her catch her breath.

What in God's name was Kiernan doing here? As a neighbor, he would have been welcome to witness the proceedings, so why would he hide like an outlaw or thief?

This was Kiernan, she reminded herself. He was young and passionate and, she knew from long acquaintance, stubborn. It could be that he still harbored feelings for her and merely wanted to see her again. Or maybe his presence had a more sinister motive...

Eric came forward, holding Annice's hand. Annice flushed with a becoming modesty, and didn't raise her eyes as Eric announced, "My lord, I've come to ask your permission to marry Annice, the chandler's daughter."

Constance glanced again at the alley. There was no sign of Kiernan. Maybe she'd been wrong, and it wasn't Kiernan at all. The alley was dark. It could have been someone else.

Even if Kiernan was still angry and unhappy, he would surely never resort to violence. He would sulk and mope and glare, but he would never burn a mill or...

She suddenly realized the yard was completely silent and that Merrick hadn't yet given his answer to Eric.

Eric's smile had disappeared. Annice openly wept and the people in the assembled crowd began to mutter with confusion and impatience.

What was Merrick doing?

Her husband got to his feet. "I will speak to Annice alone."

Constance gaped as he held out his arm to Annice as if she were a lady. The young woman's hand trembled as she placed it on Merrick's arm, and tears fell on her cheeks as he led her a little distance away, where they could speak quietly without being overheard.

Fear and doubt grew as Constance watched them converse, Annice with her head bowed and Merrick leaning forward as if eager to catch every word. It was a disconcertingly intimate pose, and Constance was hard pressed not to squirm with dismay, or give any other sign that she was disturbed. After all, there was a crowd to see her, too.

Again she glanced at the alley, and saw no one.

At last Merrick escorted Annice back to the dais. He put his hand over hers—another intimate gesture—then faced the assembled crowd. "I forbid the marriage."

Constance stared in stunned disbelief. Annice gave a sob, pulled away from Merrick and fled through the equally shocked, surprised crowd.

"My lord!" Eric cried in dismay. "Why, my lord, why?"

Merrick's face darkened with scorn. "You dare to question my decision?"

Angry murmurs rose from the crowd. Men and women exchanged fearful or angry looks—expressions Constance well remembered from the days of Wicked William. In her mind's eye she could see his father dragging that poor girl toward his bedchamber, treating the women of Tregellas as his possessions, to use at his will.

"Why not give an explanation, my lord, as to why you have forbidden a marriage long in the making?" Constance asked, seeking an answer that would calm her fears, too.

Merrick's great dark eyes were as hard as coal when he looked at her. Then he addressed the angry crowd, speaking loudly so that his words carried to the far wall and the soldiers standing guard, his voice cold as the bitter north wind. "The hall moot is over. Go home."

He started to leave the dais.

"He's robbed me!" Eric shouted. "He's had her! He's just like his father!"

Drawing his sword, Merrick charged toward the distraught young man. "Do you question my honor?"

Constance ran between them. "My lord!"

Breathing hard, Merrick kept his fierce gaze on Eric as if Constance wasn't there. His hand gripped the hilt of his sword, white-knuckled, the sinews raised and tense. "If you make such an accusation again, I'll kill you."

"Eric has a right to know why you refuse permission," Constance asserted. And if Merrick didn't reveal it, more than Eric would wonder why.

"I refuse to allow them to marry," Merrick retorted. "That is all I'm going to say. It should be enough." He raised his voice again. "That should be enough for you all."

His sword still held in his hand, he wheeled and marched into the hall.

Constance didn't hesitate for a moment. She hurried after him into the hall, and up the stairs to his solar. Although the door was closed, she burst into the chamber without seeking his permission.

His hands balled into fists, Merrick stood at the window. He had to have heard her enter, yet he neither turned nor gave any other sign that he knew he was no longer alone.

"Why did you refuse them permission?"

His face was a hard mask when he finally faced her. "Because I couldn't, in good conscience, grant it."

"In good conscience?" she repeated. "Why would approving the request of two people who want to marry trouble your conscience? Everyone knows they were just waiting until Eric's father gave him the smithy."

"Did Annice *look* like an eager, happy woman?" Merrick's expression grew grimmer still. "I can tell when somebody is trying to hide something, and she was not acting the joyful, anxious bride. She never looked at Eric, never raised her eyes."

She thought of Annice in the yard. Was what she'd assumed Annice's becoming modesty really something else? Yet surely his decision was based on more than that. "What did she say to you?"

"That is between Annice and me."

His words were like a slap in the face and hurt worse. "You won't even tell your wife?"

"Annice asked me to keep her reason secret. I gave her my word that I would."

If he thought that would satisfy her, he was wrong. "If no more explanation is forthcoming, my lord," she said, her voice firm and completely under control, "the people will think you want Annice for yourself. Even if your father had never been lord here, plenty of other Norman noblemen have taken women, regardless of betrothal or marriage or their will. How else *could* it look when you stand whispering with her in front of everybody and Annice runs away in tears? What else are we to believe but that there's something more between you?"

Merrick's cheeks flushed. "In spite of what I told you

about honoring vows and the way I've treated you, in spite of everything I've done, you think I could be such a lying, lustful hypocrite? That I would come between two people who truly wish to wed?"

His angry words tore at her heart and made her feel guilty for accusing him, and yet… "That's how it looks, my lord."

His eyes flared with rage and he made no effort to hide it. "Clearly I *was* a fool to think I could ever earn the trust and respect of my people, or my wife. I will forever only be the son of Wicked William, no matter what I do." He closed on her and his voice rose in anger. "Or are you glad to be able to accuse me because of a secret you bear?"

"What?"

"I saw Kiernan lurking in the alley like a lovesick boy."

"If he came here to see me, he *is* a lovesick boy—and no more to me than that! I'm an honorable woman—"

"And I'm an honorable man," he retorted, "yet apparently you don't believe I am. Why should I believe *you*?"

She was blameless in this, and sorry if she'd accused him falsely, but she wouldn't abase herself before him, or any man. The inner armor that had protected her for so long, that had enabled her to withstand Lord William's rages, that she thought she would no longer need, returned—hard and cold and as strong as the man facing her. "Because I give you my word."

"So although my word isn't good enough, yours is?"

"If I've misjudged you, I'm sorry, but you'll get no

more apology from me," she declared. "I vowed years ago that no man would make me beg for mercy, so if you think I'm going to grovel before you and plead for forgiveness, you're mistaken. But if I discover you've been unfaithful, then you'll have broken our marriage vows, and I'll consider myself no longer bound by them. In the meantime, I'll do my duty, as I have always done, including in our bed."

Having made her feelings plain, Constance started for the door.

"For God's sake, she begged me to refuse!" Merrick cried.

Shocked as much by his tone as his desperate words, Constance hesitated, then turned back to see Merrick throw himself into his chair. His elbows on the table, he cradled his head in his hands and didn't meet her questioning gaze. "She found out that he'd dallied with another woman in Truro while swearing to love and be faithful only to her. When she told him what she'd learned and that she wouldn't marry him, he got angry. He said he wasn't going to let her spurn and embarrass him."

Merrick's fingers curled into fists as he raised tempestuous eyes to glare at her. "So he forced himself upon her. He *raped* her—and he still thought she would want to be his wife. She doesn't, but full of shame, she saw no other choice."

Gasping for breath, Constance felt for the nearest chair and sat heavily, while Merrick shoved back his chair and got to his feet. He started to pace like an anxious soldier on duty who expects to be attacked at any moment. "I told her the shame was his, not hers. I offered to take Eric into custody and have him brought before the king's justice on a charge of rape, but she wouldn't hear of it. In spite of what I said, she blames herself and begged me not to tell anyone what happened." Merrick halted and regarded Constance with a steadfast, determined expression. "He probably thinks he won't be punished because she won't accuse him openly." He struck his open palm with his fist. "But by God, as I live, one day he'll pay."

Appalled at Eric's act, full of pity for Annice and regret for her accusations, Constance rose and went toward her husband. "Merrick, I'm so—"

He held her off with an outstretched hand. "Sorry?" he demanded. "Sorry you didn't have faith in me? Sorry you so easily believed the worst of me? Sorry you made me break my word and tell you what Annice begged me to keep secret?"

The accusing voice, the expression of rage…

She'd seen it before, lived it before. Never again would she stand helpless and afraid facing a lord of Tregellas. "I told you, Merrick, that even if I'm sorry, I won't grovel."

Merrick pointed imperiously at the door. "Go."

With her head held high, Constance walked out of the chamber and slammed the door behind her.

In the next moment she heard another sound she remembered all too well. Merrick had thrown a goblet against the wall.

MERRICK STOOD BY THE ARCHED window of the solar, his back to the door, staring unseeing into the courtyard.

He was guilty of many things, yet never had he wanted Annice—or any other woman—as he'd wanted Constance. Never would he betray Constance for any other woman. He'd thought she knew that and believed him. Trusted him. Yet in spite of all her apparently sincere words of love, despite marrying him, she still didn't trust him.

Perhaps this was his punishment at last—to have Constance for his wife, to know a short time of bliss, then have it all ripped from him, and while trying to do right.

Maybe there was nothing he could ever do to be absolved of his sins.

He heard the door open, and for a brief instant, hoped Constance had returned. But a man's familiar footsteps heralded a different visitor.

"For God's sake, Merrick, what did you say to Constance?" Henry demanded. "She looks like death. Did you quarrel? Was it over that woman? Did you explain why you stood whispering to the chandler's daughter as if you were lovers conspiring to rendezvous?"

He slowly turned around, his hand tightening on his sword hilt until his knuckles were white as he fought for control.

"I thought you knew me better, Henry," he said, trying to keep the despair from his voice. To pretend he was strong. To remember that he was a mighty lord, and not a frightened little boy alone in the woods. "I would never betray my vows to my wife."

"What did you expect?" Henry asked incredulously. "What do you think the villagers made of that cozy little tête-à-tête? And then your announcement that they couldn't wed?"

Merrick's jaw clenched as his restraint dwindled. "I expect them to believe me an honorable man."

"What, you think you've won their trust in a few weeks after years of abuse at your father's hands?"

His temper burst, raging like a river bursting through a dam. "I'm not my father!" He slammed his fist on the table. "How many times must I say it?"

Shocked at his outburst, Henry backed away and made placating gestures. "All right, you're not your father and there's nothing between you and that woman. Of course *I* believe you, but then, I'm not your wife. It'd only be natural for her to be jealous."

"She has no reason to be jealous of me," Merrick snarled.

"She's a woman. They need very little reason."

"I don't need any advice about women from *you*," Merrick retorted, struggling to regain mastery over his anger, in spite of Henry's infuriating observations.

Henry couldn't possibly understand. To him, women were toys, amusing playthings put on this earth to entertain him. He had no idea what it was like to truly love a woman, to love her so much he'd do anything to have her, even if it meant keeping a terrible secret for years and years. To live with the fear that one lapse, one inadvertent word, would tear her from him and make her hate him forever.

"Well, you'd better listen to somebody, or you're going to lose her," Henry said.

She might already be lost to him, Merrick realized, and pain, like the grip of bony dead fingers, squeezed his heart.

"Go away, Henry." He wanted to be left alone to deal with this agony in his own way, as he had for fifteen years.

"Do you think telling me to leave is going to change anything?" Henry asked quietly.

Of course not, and he knew that better than Henry. He wasn't a fool—and Henry was no virtuous priest to counsel him.

Merrick's temper flared again and his hands balled into fists. "No, because you'll talk and talk and *talk* whether I listen or not, offering your unwanted advice, as if you're the world's greatest lover and all the rest of us are dolts."

Henry flushed. "I'm only trying—"

"I don't give a rat's turd for what you're trying to do!"

Pain came to Henry's eyes, but Merrick was beyond caring.

"Why are you still in Tregellas, Henry? Do you see your chance to make a good marriage? Beatrice is young and silly, but what is that to a great lover like you? You'll either teach her well, or satisfy yourself with another despite your marriage vows."

Henry blanched. "I have no such—"

"So why haven't you left? Have you stayed to offer

me advice I don't want? To live off my land, eating my food, drinking my wine, making eyes at my wife?" Merrick's dark brows lowered ominously as a new source of fury arose, one he'd been burying for weeks. "Maybe it's Constance you really want, not her cousin."

"Merrick, you go too far."

"Do I?" he charged, now certain he'd been tricked by a serpent in their midst. The deceiver deceived—a fitting retribution.

"I haven't forgotten we swore an oath that we would trust each other, fight for each other, guard each other," Henry returned. "Have you? You must have, or how else could you say such things to me, or demean Ranulf as you have, treating him like your lackey or a common mercenary? He's your *friend,* for God's sake, and so am I. That's why I'll tell you the hard truth, whether you want to hear it or not."

"And only you know the truth?" Merrick demanded with a scowl, hatred growing from his anger. How could he have been so trusting? So blind? Thank God he'd never told Henry his secret. "You know it all, don't you? Well, you don't know *me.*"

"No, Merrick, I don't believe I do," Henry said, slowly shaking his head. "Not anymore. And I wonder how well you know *me,* if you think I'd try to steal your wife."

"I've seen you chase after other men's wives. I've seen you catch them and heard you brag of your conquests, as if cuckolding another man is an accomplishment to be proud of."

"I swore no oath of loyalty to those men, and the wives I won were willing—nay, eager—to join me in my bed."

"Oh, it's all their doing and none of yours?" Merrick scoffed. "A convenient excuse for a dishonorable man."

"So that's what you truly think of me," Henry said quietly—too quietly—as he walked toward the door, mercifully leaving at last. He put his hand on the latch, then looked back at Merrick over his shoulder. "I'll be gone before dark."

"Good," Merrick snarled as the door closed behind his former friend.

Then the lord of Tregellas sat in his father's throne-like chair and stared at the door, unseeing, alone with his turbulent thoughts.

SOMETIME LATER, FOR MERRICK had lost all track of time and shouted at a quaking Demelza who'd come to tell him the evening meal was being served, he looked up and focused on the man who'd entered his solar uninvited. "Are you aware that Henry's left Tregellas?" Ranulf inquired.

Ranulf…his friend…whom he'd made garrison commander…temporarily. He couldn't trust him, either. He wanted to, but that would be a mistake.

"Yes, I told him to go," he replied, finding it unexpectedly difficult to get the words out. Or to see Ranulf clearly. "I don't want to talk about it."

"God's wounds, you're drunk!" Ranulf exclaimed, for once in his life completely surprised.

"Am I?" Merrick replied, dazed, as if he'd taken a

hard blow to the head. He stared at the goblet in his hand. "I must be," he muttered, shoving it away. "That would explain... That's not good."

Ranulf had come to the solar with the firm purpose of finding out why Henry had left Tregellas with barely a farewell. He still had that intention, but seeing Merrick like this, he resolved to take a slightly different course.

He picked up the silver goblet lying on the floor. "What happened to this?" he inquired. "Did you throw it at Henry? Or did it levitate over here and fall?"

Merrick's only answer was a scowl.

So he *had* thrown it. Another surprise. Merrick was normally the most self-possessed man Ranulf knew.

"I saw no mark on Henry's head, so I suppose you missed," he remarked, setting the dented goblet on the table beside Merrick's empty one. "Probably more because of your poor aim than lack of intent. I've never seen you throw anything except a spear, and that badly."

"What do you want?" Merrick demanded. "Just t' annoy me and question my decisions?"

Ranulf raised a quizzical brow. "I haven't said one word about any recent decisions of yours. Did Henry? Is that why he's gone?"

"I don't have t'explain myself to you, either." Merrick pointed a wobbly finger at the door. "Get out!"

Instead of leaving, Ranulf perched on the edge of the table and crossed his arms while continuing to regard his friend with his usual sangfroid. "I daresay it was about that woman who was supposed to marry the smith's son. I gather the smith's son and the Queen of the May have been intending to wed for a long time."

Merrick leaned back and regarded Ranulf through bleary, bloodshot eyes. "I don't want her. I never have."

"More than one wouldn't blame you if you did. She's a pretty woman."

Merrick stood up so fast, his chair fell over backward, and he had to hold on to the table to steady himself. *"I don't want her!"*

He reached for the hilt of his sword and tried to draw it out, but the damn thing stuck. "I'll kill any man who says so!"

Ranulf watched as his friend struggled for a moment, then gave up.

"I don't want her," Merrick muttered, splaying his hands on the table, head bowed. He drew in a ragged breath. "Why won't anybody believe me?"

"I don't think Henry would accuse you of wanting that woman when you're married to Lady Constance," Ranulf said.

Merrick went to sit down and nearly fell before he realized his chair wasn't there. Ranulf hurried to right it, and when it was back in place, Merrick sat heavily.

"He said that'd be how it'd look to everybody," Merrick grumbled.

"Everybody who doesn't know you well," Ranulf agreed. Yet that alone wouldn't be enough to make Merrick over-imbibe after all these years. "Did he suggest it might look that way to Constance, too?"

"He didn't have to. She'd already said so."

"So you quarreled with your wife over this woman and then argued with Henry, and now he's left Tregellas."

Merrick glumly nodded. He thought of the accusations Henry had leveled at him with regard to Ranulf, then told himself Ranulf wouldn't have to suffer being garrison commander much longer. Soon he'd find somebody trustworthy enough to fill that place. Eventually.

"It's not surprising to me that people aren't sure what to make of that decision. You offered no explanation, and you're a damned cipher most of the time."

"I can't tell you why," Merrick muttered.

"Have I asked? I'm sure you had good cause, and one that didn't begin and end with lust. But I've known you since we were both ten years old—they haven't."

"They shouldn't accuse me of lusting after other women."

"Plenty of men do, and then there's your late, unlamented father."

"You don't have to remind me."

"Apparently I do. You may be asking too much of your wife and these people if you expect them to accept you on faith so quickly."

"That's what Henry said."

"He's right."

"I didn't want Henry's advice and I don't need yours, either," Merrick growled.

"Because you're doing such a fine job on your own."

The last thing Merrick needed was Ranulf's sanctimonious sarcasm. "You can go, too."

"If I do, who'll lead your garrison?"

"Somebody," Merrick mumbled, frowning.

"You're not going to get rid of me that easily. As it happens, I'm enjoying myself—and as you yourself said, you need a man you can trust in charge of your soldiers. I also swore an oath of loyalty to you, and I intend to keep it."

"So did Henry," Merrick reminded him.

"I'm not Henry's keeper."

"You're not mine, either."

"No, I'm not. But I *am* your friend, and until you tell me to my face that I'm not needed here any longer, I'll stay."

Merrick leaned forward and buried his head in his folded arms on the table as his eyes filled with weak, foolish tears of gratitude.

"Am I still your friend?"

Merrick nodded in response, afraid his voice would betray him.

"Good. Now stop drinking and when you're sober, go speak to your wife."

CHAPTER FIFTEEN

IN SPITE OF HIS INTENTION TO follow Ranulf's advice, Merrick didn't seek out Constance until the hour grew late and he could find no more excuses not to retire. Instead, maintaining his usual stoic demeanor, he checked the new swords the armorer had made. He gave the guards the watchword for the night, paying no heed to their attempts to avoid his gaze. He got some food from the kitchen and ignored Gaston's wary expression and that of the servants cowering in the corners.

By the time he headed for their bedchamber, he was perfectly sober and capable of having a rational discussion with his wife, if she wasn't already asleep.

If she was? He'd crawl into bed beside her warm, soft body, conquer the needs of his own and deal with the trouble between them in the morning.

He walked slowly up the stairs, as if he bore a great weight on his back. Images of his bride danced in his head as he lifted his feet. Her bright eyes. Her smile. That look of sultry invitation. The low growl as the moment of ecstasy took her and she writhed and bucked...

She wasn't asleep. She sat at the table bearing the

polished silver plate that acted as her mirror, combing her long, marvelous hair that fell about her like a golden drapery. Her thin white shift hid nothing and stretched tight across the curves of her breasts.

His breath caught in his throat, as if he were a boy again beholding the girl he would never forget. She was so beautiful, so perfect.

And he was so undeserving. He always had been.

"Close the door, please. There's a draught."

Commanding himself to remain calm, to remember that if anyone was in the wrong, it was he, he silently did as she asked.

She rose and faced him, her expression almost a blank as she ran her gaze over him.

Almost.

Whatever she thought of his decision, she still wanted his body.

It would be enough. It must be enough. He'd done what he'd done, and there was no way to undo it without telling her the truth. What good would that do now? They were married, man and wife, for good or ill.

She untied the drawstring of her shift and let it fall to the floor. Her nipples tightened in the cool air, but otherwise, her skin seemed to glow with heat in the light of the candles as she stood motionless, her eyes telling him…nothing.

If she stayed still, he would interpret that as rejection. If she made no effort to close the distance between them, he would go.

She stepped over her discarded shift and bent to pick it up, her hair flowing about her luscious body in a tantalizing curtain. Straightening, she laid her garment over the stool. "Are you staying, my lord?"

God help him, how could he tear himself away when she stood before him naked and beautiful?

"Do you wish me to?" he managed to say, his voice hoarse as he tried to control his growing desire while betraying nothing of his feelings.

She started toward him. "This is your bedchamber, my lord. You have every right to stay."

Yes, he did, and as she came closer, he felt his control slipping away with every step.

She was his wife. She hadn't barred the door, or ordered him to go. She was offering her body to him.

But even as his reason drowned beneath desire, he knew things were far from right between them. The perfect union they'd shared since their wedding had been marred. Tainted.

She stopped inches from him. She was so lovely with her shining blue eyes. Her lustrous hair. Her warm, full, rosy lips.

With a moan of surrender to the longing he couldn't overcome, he tugged her to him and kissed her, his passionate need unleashed.

She made no effort to resist as he swept her into his arms and carried her to the bed. She uttered no sound of protest as he set her down.

If this was the only way he could show his need for

her, so be it. Because he did need her. More than she would ever know.

But there were no soft words, no gentle caresses, in spite of his intentions. Seemingly, she wanted none as she clutched at him with frenzied passion, her hunger spurring his own. Hoping this meant she did trust him, he tried go slowly, to be tender.

He couldn't, not when she moved as she did, pulling him to her and into her as if she couldn't wait. Or didn't want to.

It was over in a moment, yet not before her cries of ecstasy filled the chamber, as did his own. He fell against her, breathing hard, when he was finished. Perhaps now all would be well again…or so he hoped, until she squirmed and twisted so that he had no choice but to move away from her. Then she turned her back to him.

Oh, God, had she offered herself only because she craved his body?

He rose abruptly and dressed. Without a word he left the room.

Once outside their chamber, he splayed his hands against the cool stone wall and hung his head. Then he let his breath out in a long, shuddering sigh before pushing himself off the wall.

He was the lord of Tregellas, not a little boy alone and frightened in a wood. And Constance was the lady of Tregellas, whether that pleased her.

Or not.

AFTER MERRICK HAD GONE, Constance closed her eyes as another wave of shame, of dismay, of acute disappointment washed over her. Yes, he wanted her still, but not as before. Before, there had been gentleness and kindness; there had been affection and joy.

Despite her resolution not to beg his forgiveness, she'd tried to show him that she was sorry for her accusations, but she'd been so tense, so anxious, she could hardly speak, and her words had sounded cold, even to herself. So she'd deliberately enticed him and given herself to him eagerly.

He'd taken her as if she were the lowliest whore in London. There were no words of forgiveness, or understanding. No tender endearments, no whispers of entreaty.

She had become his woman, to use when and where and how he pleased. She was his chattel, just as she had always feared.

"BY ALL THE SAINTS IN Christendom, I could hardly believe it when I heard, but if you're here, it must be so!" Lord Carrell exclaimed as he sat beside Henry in the main room of a tavern in Truro a se'ennight after Henry had left Tregellas.

Henry gave the man a carefree smile and raised his mug of ale in a salute. "Greetings to you, too, my lord. What brings you to this cheery place?"

He laughed softly at his own joke, for in truth, this tavern was far from the finest establishment in Truro. It had the benefit, however, of cheap lodgings and a relative lack of fleas.

Lord Carrell looked upon him with pity. "I must say, Sir Henry, it's a sad, sad day when a man of your birth and skill must take shelter in a place like this."

His pride pricked, Henry shrugged as if Lord Carrell's observation didn't disturb him. "It was my choice to leave Tregellas."

Lord Carrell gave him a sympathetic smile. "So I heard, but a man like you must have plenty of friends who will offer you their hospitality, if Lord Merrick won't."

"I do," Henry retorted. "I'm on my way to..." He tried to think of a lord who might indeed welcome a penniless but valiant knight, even one with a reputation for being less than chaste where the daughters of the household were concerned. "My brother's," he said, although the last place he wanted to go was Scotland.

"Ah well, Lord Merrick's loss will be his gain. Given the troublesome nature of the Scots, I'm sure he'll be glad of your assistance."

Henry frowned into his mug. Nicholas didn't want or need his help.

Lord Carrell shook his head and heaved a sigh. "I fear I've been sadly disappointed in my nephew-in-law."

Henry perked up.

"I had such hopes that under the tutelage of Sir Leonard he would become a just and honorable man, but alas..."

Henry frowned. "What makes you think Merrick isn't honorable?"

Lord Carrell covered his mouth with his fingertips and looked contrite. "I fear I've said more than I should."

Henry sniffed. "Well, you don't have to tell me he's not." He fixed a determined gaze on Lord Carrell's face, barely visible in the dimness of the low-ceilinged tavern. "Did you know we swore an oath, him and me, to be brothers-in-arms and faithful to death? And what does he do but cast me out."

Lord Carrell drew back in surprise. "He cast you out?"

"As good as," Henry confirmed with a nod of his head. "And me just trying to help the ungrateful bastard." He raised his mug and took a drink, then wiped his lips with the back of his hand. "I tell you, it'll be a cold day in hell before I ride to his aid. He can rot for all I care."

"I was aware he was not winning over his tenants, but I had no idea he would actually break an oath."

Henry shifted uneasily. "I can't say he broke it, exactly."

Lord Carrell didn't seem to hear that qualification as he worriedly chewed his lower lip. "Now I wish we'd delayed the wedding of my niece until we knew him better. If she suffers because of him, I'll never forgive myself. The poor girl deserves better. She spent so many years in thrall to Lord William." He sighed again. "She deserves someone more like you."

Henry recognized flattery when he heard it. "I don't think you'd have been anxious to have her marry a penniless knight."

"I have many castles. One could easily be given over to a relative."

"You would grant me a castle if I served you?"

"I'd be delighted to have such a man as yourself swear fealty to me, and give you a castle to hold in my name."

Henry toyed with the mug and didn't answer.

Lord Carrell leaned in so close, Henry could tell he'd dined on fish that day. "I think, Sir Henry, that you're also concerned for the welfare of my beautiful niece. This way, you would be nearby, should she require assistance."

Henry slid his mug from one hand to the other and back again.

"And if, perchance, Lord Merrick should perish sooner rather than later, she would be free to wed again, to a man loyal to her uncle."

"Or Merrick might live to be eighty," Henry observed. "Tell me, Lord Carrell, do I look like a man whose loyalty can be purchased with a castle?"

Lord Carrell moved away, farther along the bench. "I meant no disrespect, and if I was wrong about your feelings for my lovely niece, I beg your pardon." He rose. "I bid you good day."

Henry grabbed the man's tunic and pulled him back down. "How large a castle and how many men would I have in my command?"

"ALAN DE VERN TELLS ME YOU wish to see me, my lord," Constance said coolly as she entered the solar a few days later.

She always spoke to her husband coolly now, when she spoke to him at all. The only warmth between them came at night, when they shared a bed. Yet even though he made love with her, there was no real intimacy anymore. She was sadly sure their lovemaking served no purpose now but to get her with child so she could bear him a son.

So far, that had not been successful, and when her flux had commenced a week ago, she'd lain awake a long time worrying about what would happen if she didn't conceive. In spite of his vows, would he send her away and take a mistress? Even an illegitimate son was better than none. Would he be content to let his uncle and his uncle's children be his heirs? Would he grow to hate her? Would he become bitter and resentful, cruel and vicious, as his father had before him?

His father. How she wished he'd died when Merrick was a boy. How different things might be.

"I've had a message from the king," Merrick said, pointing to a parchment in front of him. "He congratulates me on my marriage and trusts I'll soon have the smuggling here under control."

Constance stiffened ever so slightly, as she always did when he spoke of smuggling. Thankfully, no smugglers had been captured since he'd arrived, although whether it was because they'd stopped, or were waiting for him to lessen the patrols, she didn't know. She hadn't gone into the village recently to find out, because she hadn't wanted to see Annice, or Eric, or even Peder.

"What can you tell me about the smuggling activity around Tregellas?"

"That it's been going on for centuries and will be difficult to stop," she replied.

He regarded her steadily, without passion. "Please don't play the ignorant woman with me, Constance. You know this land, these people too well, and they trust you. I'm sure you know who's engaged in smuggling and what beaches they use, and when. Who are they, Constance?"

She returned his gaze with one equally dispassionate. "As you gave your word to Annice, I gave my word to my friends—good people who feel cheated and oppressed by a king who uses their money to live in splendor, or to wage his wars in France. They would willingly pay what is honestly asked, but as it is now…"

"They hold themselves above the law. In many ways they already are, yet that's not enough to satisfy them."

"Is it so difficult to understand that when they see how men who also mine tin, yet who happen to live in Devonshire, are taxed at a much lesser rate, they feel they're being exploited?"

"I swore an oath to my king that I will uphold his laws."

"*You* swore. *I* didn't. And my friends' trust means as much to me as your friends' does to you, so don't ask me to betray them. If Henry or Ranulf broke the law—"

"I would consider our oath broken and I would ensure that justice was done." He leaned back in his chair and crossed his arms. "If you knew who set fire to the mill, would you tell me that?"

"Yes," she answered without hesitation. "There is no justification for such an act."

"Even if it was a friend?"

"Yes."

His face inscrutable, he gestured at another scroll. "I've also received word that we can expect a visitor shortly—Lord Osgoode, who's returned to England with the earl of Cornwall."

Constance's brows rose. This was the first she'd heard that Richard was back in England. It would also be the first time they'd entertained so important a guest since she'd been married.

"I trust you'll do all that's necessary to make him comfortable and his stay in Tregellas a pleasant one."

"As you know your duty, my lord," she replied, "so I know mine."

Merrick picked up his quill and looked at the accounts on the parchment before him. "Good day, Constance."

She turned and left the chamber without another word.

RANULF SMILED AT BEATRICE fidgeting nervously at the door of the stable. "Is there something I can help you with, my lady?"

Beatrice looked around as if she were afraid of being seen. "May I speak with you?"

His first instinct was to say that he had something

more important to do, which would include almost anything else. But she looked so worried, he decided to indulge her. After all, he could always walk away.

"Certainly, my lady." He tossed his horse's reins over the wall of the stall and joined her in the doorway. "I gather it's something important."

She nodded and glanced about furtively. "Yes."

If she was trying to be subtly secretive, she was failing miserably.

"Can we not go to the chapel, or somewhere more private?" she whispered. "What I have to say is not for servants' ears."

Ranulf wondered if she thought to flirt with him the way she had with Henry, or even had something more intimate in mind. If that was her only aim, he'd quickly disillusion her. Henry had been amused and acted the honorable gallant; Ranulf had no patience for giddy girls who wished to try out their powers on men. He'd been the butt of that sort of sport once, and it would be the last time. "I don't think that would be wise."

Her eyes widened. "But I don't want…that is, it's about…" She dropped her voice so that he could barely hear her. "It's about Constance and Merrick."

"What about them?"

Beatrice blushed and bit her lip. Then she glanced around again and whispered, "Constance is very unhappy."

This wasn't news to Ranulf. Anyone with half a mind would have realized that something was seriously amiss between Merrick and his bride.

"Is Merrick unhappy, too?" she asked.

"Merrick doesn't speak to me about his feelings."

"But you know him better than anybody else. Can't you tell?"

Of course he could, but he wasn't keen to discuss his concerns with Beatrice, who probably couldn't keep a secret to save her life. "Whatever is between them, is between *them,* my lady."

Beatrice's bright eyes filled with tears. "I only want to help," she murmured, sniffling. "I can't bear to see Constance so miserable. She's endured so much already, and she was so happy on her wedding day and now…"

The last thing Ranulf wanted was for anyone to think he'd made Beatrice cry. After a quick glance around the yard to ensure no one was watching, he hustled the girl into the lane between the stable and the armory, so they couldn't be seen from the yard or the wall walk.

"I would help if I could," he told her honestly, "but Merrick hates advice, no matter how well-meaning." He wondered what had prompted Beatrice to speak to him about the troubles between the lord of Tregellas and his wife. "Has Lady Constance said anything to you about what's happened?"

Beatrice mournfully shook her head. "Not a word. It's like when Wicked Will—I mean, Lord William was alive. She wouldn't say much about him, either." The girl's eyes filled with tears again. "I thought those days were behind us."

Her shoulders started to shake as she began to sob in earnest.

Ranulf reached out and awkwardly patted her on the arm. "There, there. I'm sure it will be all right. Husbands and wives quarrel all the time. My parents certainly did."

"I don't remember my mother," she offered. "She died when I was very small." She sniffled and regarded him piteously. "It's been days since the hall moot and it's just as bad as ever between them. Merrick barely speaks to Constance."

Hoping to make Beatrice feel better, Ranulf tried to make light of the situation. "Merrick barely speaks to anybody."

That earned him a teary glare from Beatrice. "It's not funny and if you think it is——"

"No, I don't," he hastened to assure her, slightly ashamed that he'd given the impression he didn't care about his friend's happiness.

"Then what can we do? There must be *something*," she pleaded, looking up at him with her big blue eyes, her lips half parted, her high rounded breasts rising and falling.

Feeling like a disgusting old lecher for noticing that, he tried to concentrate on the issue at hand. "I think we should leave Constance and Merrick to sort out their own troubles. However well-meaning, I doubt any good can come of us interfering directly. The best thing you can do is stay close to her, so she knows she has a friend nearby."

"As you'll stay by Lord Merrick?" she asked softly. "So that he knows he has a trusted friend nearby, too?"

As if against his will, his gaze fastened on her full, soft lips. He leaned toward her, then remembered who they were, and where, and drew back as if she had the plague. "I won't leave Tregellas until Merrick has a trustworthy garrison commander. Now I give you good day, my lady."

With that, he headed for the armory, getting away from Lady Beatrice and her big blue eyes as quickly he could.

Before he again forgot that he was Merrick's trusted friend, and she was sweet and pure.

CHAPTER SIXTEEN

OVER A FORTNIGHT HAD PASSED by the time Constance stood beside her husband on the dais in the great hall and watched Lord Osgoode saunter toward them. He was not a small man, but tall and broad, with iron-gray hair and a wide and smiling face. His clothes, like his accoutrements, were colorful and expensive, as befitted a man of great wealth and influence at court.

Merrick was not nearly so finely dressed, although he wore his best clothes: a rich, black-and-gold brocade tunic that she'd made for him in the first happy days of their marriage, a white linen shirt laced at the neck, fine woolen breeches and polished black boots.

She wore a gown of emerald cendal, embroidered heavily at the neck and down the long cuffs. Beatrice, who seemed like a shadow of herself these days, had pleaded an aching head and begged to be excused. Ranulf was leading a patrol at the north end of the estate.

"Greetings, my lord," Merrick said as the nobleman reached the dais. "Welcome to Tregellas. Please sit and take your ease."

Lord Osgoode smiled expansively, so that his eyes

were nearly invisible in his fleshy face. "I thank you, my lord." He turned to Constance. "And this would be your bride, I assume?"

"I am, indeed. You must forgive my husband his lapse of manners. We are but newly wedded, my lord, and I think he sometimes forgets me."

"If I had such a wife as you, my lady, I would be unable to put her from my mind for even a moment," Lord Osgoode replied with the smooth flattery of a courtier.

The vein in Merrick's temple started to throb.

Ignoring her husband, Constance gestured at a high-backed chair near the hearth. "Please, do tell us how the earl is faring."

"He's very well," Lord Osgoode replied as he sat on the cushioned seat. "And very pleased by this marriage, as well as the reports he's received of your rule, my lord."

Merrick's eyes narrowed a little. "Reports?" he queried as he, too, sat on a chair facing their guest.

"Naturally the earl's concerned about his vassals and how they're managing their estates. He's been in communication with your uncle, and yours, too, my lady. They've both spoken very highly of your management, my lord."

"I'm pleased I meet with their approval."

Lord Osgoode chuckled and reached for the wine proffered by Demelza. "Come, man, surely you're clever enough to realize that even if the earl of Cornwall is not *in* Cornwall, he keeps himself apprised of what transpires here. He would be a lax overlord otherwise."

Merrick inclined his head in acknowledgment.

"But let's not speak of politics when there's a lovely woman with us," Lord Osgoode said, smiling at Constance.

She didn't want the conversation to lapse into mere meaningless gossip. "I'm always happy to hear the news from court."

"Alas, I've not been paying attention to the latest fashions," Lord Osgoode said with a chuckle. "I haven't taken stock of what fabrics are in favor, and which are not, or how veils and wimples are being worn this year."

Constance clenched her teeth and reminded herself that most men thought as Lord Osgoode did.

"That's not what my wife meant," Merrick said. "She's well aware of the tensions at court. Anything of note you wish to say to me, you may say in her presence."

This was so unexpected, Constance started, then tried to act as if that was perfectly normal.

Lord Osgoode frowned. "But she's a woman."

Merrick's expression didn't alter by so much as the lift of an eyebrow. "I'm well aware of that, my lord."

"Women do not understand the business of men."

"This one does."

Lord Osgoode laughed again, and the tension drifted away. "Ah, you newly wedded husbands! How quick you are to believe the best of your wives."

Constance clasped her hands tight in her cuffs. "My

husband is a shrewd and generous man, my lord, who appreciates that to make a wise decision, one should hear many opinions, even those of a woman. It makes no sense that women who are capable of managing a large household should be considered unable to comprehend the conflicts and problems that arise in running a kingdom."

Lord Osgoode regarded her with a mixture of awe and surprise. Then he smiled again, as an indulgent parent would to a child who's said something unexpectedly clever. "A kingdom is somewhat larger than a castle, my lady, and servants are hardly comparable to lords and knights."

"If the king is allowed to ignore Magna Carta, there would be little difference."

Lord Osgoode sucked in his breath and turned amazed eyes to Merrick.

"My wife enjoys a spirited debate," he said evenly, "and sometimes seeks to arouse dissent in order to ensure a lively discussion. I assure you she does not necessarily speak for me, or that her opinion will be the same tomorrow."

She was about to refute his lie when a glance from him silenced her. And from the expression on Lord Osgoode's face, she decided she would do well not to boggle his mind further with her political observations.

The nobleman reached into the pouch attached to his belt. "The earl summons you, my lord, to his seat at Tintagel. Will you go?"

Merrick accepted the sheepskin scroll and answered without breaking the seal. "Of course."

Then he opened the letter and, after reading it, passed it to Constance without comment.

As she perused the missive that was both congratulatory and an order to attend the earl in Tintagel without delay, Merrick addressed Lord Osgoode. "I see you're surprised that my wife can read, my lord. As it happens, my father came to depend on Lady Constance a great deal in his final days, so it was a good thing that she learned."

Although these were the first complimentary words he'd spoken since their quarrel, she kept her eyes on the parchment before her.

"I'd heard something of that," Lord Osgoode said, and there was an implication in his tone that was all too clear. She could easily guess the sort of rumors that had traveled to the earl of Cornwall's household about Wicked William and his ward.

"My father was a terrible and despicable lecher," Merrick said, his voice stern, his expression even more so. "That is no secret to anyone. But if anyone claims he had improper relations with my wife, I'll gladly meet him on a field of combat."

He was so quick to defend her honor, yet he couldn't bring himself to speak to her, and when he made love to her, it was as if his mind had left his body, leaving only his passionate desire to spur him to do his duty.

Lord Osgoode clearly wasn't sure what to make of

Merrick's brusque defense. She feared he'd made a mistake upsetting the earl's envoy, until his shock turned into an indulgent smile.

Whether this signaled a true change of heart or was merely diplomatic tact, however, she wouldn't care to wager.

"Forgive me if I've offended you, my lord," Lord Osgoode said with an apologetic nod of his head, his deep voice soothing. "Youth sees slights where none were intended. I assure you, my lord, no one suggests your wife is anything but beautiful and virtuous."

Constance finished reading the earl's letter and handed it back to her husband. For a brief moment their fingers touched—hers trembling, his cool—and she had to fight the desire even that slight contact elicited.

"The earl commands us to be there in a fortnight," she noted. "Are all his loyal vassals summoned, too?"

"Yes, my lady," Lord Osgoode replied.

"That will be quite a large number, then. I wonder where the earl intends to house us all and who will be responsible, as he has no wife…yet."

Lord Osgoode's brows rose.

Constance smiled sweetly. "A great lord like the earl cannot go without a wife for long. I thought he might be promised to another by now."

"No, he's not," the nobleman replied, "although there are many noblewomen being offered to him. I believe there may even be those attempting to bribe the king to order him to marry their sisters or daughters."

"The king's brother would be a great prize, especially as he has the king's ear," Constance agreed. "I can only hope the wife he chooses will be good for him, and thus good for England."

Lord Osgoode's narrow eyes narrowed even more. "I'm not sure I take your meaning."

Merrick shifted in his chair. Obviously he wasn't pleased with her comments, or perhaps he was concerned that she was saying the wrong things to this man.

She realized he might be right. What, after all, did she know about Lord Osgoode, other than that he represented Richard? Perhaps Merrick had met him before and was trying to warn her.

Perhaps her pride had led her to say too much already.

Seeking to avert any danger from Lord Osgoode's assumptions, she gave him a bright smile. "I merely meant that if Earl Richard is happily wed, he will be more content, and thus more likely to remain at home, and that's surely better for England."

She patted Merrick on the knee. He stiffened beneath her touch, but she ignored his response to concentrate on the earl. "I wish all men and women were as happily married as my husband and I, or the king and his queen. Henry and Eleanor are very happy, are they not?" She gave Lord Osgoode a flirtatiously pert look. "And he informs her of the affairs of state, does he not? And asks her opinion, too, or so I've heard."

Lord Osgoode laughed. "Touché, my lady! Yes, he does, although some would say she is too involved in the affairs of state—but then, he is young yet and, as you say, happily in love."

"So of course he wishes to please her in all things," she said brightly, like the happiest of brides.

Having played her part long enough for now, she decided to decamp and leave Merrick to deal with Lord Osgoode. "As delightful as it is talking to you, my lord, I must beg your leave to be excused to see that your chambers are ready. I thought you would be too fatigued for a feast tonight in your honor, so I've planned one for tomorrow. I hope you approve, my lord?"

"That sounds most excellent, and I appreciate your concern for my fatigue," Lord Osgoode replied.

"Would you care to bathe?"

"That, too, would be most welcome after my long ride."

"Then a bath shall be prepared, and a maid sent to serve you."

Lord Osgoode's eyes gleamed. "I give you my thanks for your kind hospitality, my lady."

Obviously he had one opinion of what the maid's service would entail; Constance had another, which is why Demelza would be sent to attend him and not one of the younger maidservants.

Nevertheless, she acknowledged his gratitude with a nod of her head and left the hall to see that all was ready.

"HOW ARE YOU FEELING NOW?" Constance asked Beatrice as she entered her bedchamber after she had seen to Lord Osgoode's comfort.

Beatrice moved to sit up against the head of her bed. She was pale, and had dark circles under her eyes. She'd been listless and very quiet the past few days, and hardly touched her food. Today she'd taken to her bed. Being busy with her duties and preparing for Lord Osgoode's arrival, Constance had assumed it was nothing serious, but now fear hardened into a knot in her stomach. "Would you like me to send for your father? Or Maloren?"

Beatrice immediately shook her head. "Maloren's chatter would only make me feel worse. I think a good night's sleep would cure me completely. The willow bark potion helped. The ache in my head is nearly gone. What's Lord Osgoode like?"

Somewhat relieved, Constance shrugged and sat on the bed at her feet. "A bit too smug for my liking, as many courtiers are."

"What news did he bring?"

"Merrick's been summoned to Tintagel."

"Will you go, too?"

"I have too much to do here," she replied, although that wasn't precisely true. Under Alan de Vern's supervision, the household could run quite smoothly for several days. "Is there anything you need? Anything I can get you to make you feel better or rest more easily?"

Beatrice looked down at her hands folded in her lap. "I can't fall asleep, and when I do, I have terrible dreams. Then I wake before dawn and can't get back to sleep."

Perhaps her poor cousin was merely exhausted from

a lack of sleep, Constance thought hopefully—although that was also worrisome.

"What's troubling you? What's upset you so much that you can't sleep?" she asked gently, hoping it wasn't anything to do with the absent Henry, even though she'd kept a close eye on Beatrice and seen nothing to make her suspect there was any need to worry about her honor.

Beatrice raised her eyes, and the look she gave Constance was so adult and so shrewd, Constance instinctively tensed.

"What's happened, Constance?" she asked. "You were so happy after your wedding, but now—"

"There's nothing the matter with me," Constance lied. Beatrice wasn't normally so perceptive, or at least, she hadn't been.

"Yes, there is," Beatrice replied fervently, her expression telling Constance that she was determined to find out what had gone wrong between her cousin and her husband.

Constance rose. She wasn't going to discuss Merrick, or her marriage, with Beatrice, who couldn't possibly understand. "I'm sure all marriages have their moments of disagreement and anxiety."

To her chagrin, Beatrice threw back the covers, got out of bed and followed her. "I know you quarreled with Merrick after the hall moot, and Henry argued with Merrick before he went away, probably about you."

"Merrick's dispute with Henry had nothing to do with me," Constance replied, hoping that was true as she busied herself tidying the dressing table, although she'd never learned what they'd fought about. Merrick had never told her, and Henry hadn't given her any reason for his sudden departure.

"I'm sure you never encouraged Henry," Beatrice said, coming beside the table. "He's the sort that would expect all women to be attracted to him, and can't conceive that they aren't. It's better that he's gone."

Constance stopped tidying to stare at her cousin, appalled anyone—even Beatrice—would think she was upset about Henry. "Whatever difficulties I may be having with my husband, they have nothing to do with his friend."

"Is it Annice?"

Constance started for the door. "I don't wish to discuss this."

Beatrice ran around her and blocked her way. "I was at the hall moot, Constance," she said, her voice trembling, her eyes filling with tears. "I saw what happened. I'm not surprised you quarreled with Merrick about it. I've lost hours and hours of sleep trying to figure out why Merrick did what he did. I even went to Annice to try to get an answer, but she wouldn't even talk to me. Still I'm sure—sure!—Merrick's done nothing dishonorable. He loves you."

"Whether he loves me or not," she said coolly, "I never claimed he was unfaithful to me. I happen to know he had another, very good reason for refusing to allow Annice and Eric to marry."

"What was it?" Beatrice implored.

"Please don't ask me anything more about that," Constance replied. She was sorry she'd said as much as she had. She couldn't explain Merrick's decision without revealing Annice's secret, and he'd given his word. It was bad enough he'd broken it to tell her; she wouldn't betray Annice's confidence further. "Let it be enough that I'm quite certain he has no lascivious interest in Annice, or any other woman in Tregellas."

"What about in London?"

"He says he has no mistress anywhere, and I believe him."

"Then why can't things be as they were?"

Exasperated with her cousin's questions, Constance lost her patience. "Because they can't," she snapped.

Beatrice stared at her, shocked, then she started to cry. "I only want to help."

Constance immediately regretted her harsh response and spoke more gently. "I appreciate your concern, Beatrice, truly I do. But if there are…difficulties…between Merrick and me, *we* must work them out. Marriages are transactions, in a way, so you can't expect to be blissfully happy all the time." She couldn't keep the bitterness from her voice. "If you can be happy in your marriage at all, you should thank God."

"Is there nothing I can do?" Beatrice asked plaintively.

Constance wiped away her cousin's tears with the edge of her cuff. "No, and perhaps for you, it will be different."

"I think it would be better not to marry at all," Beatrice said, weeping softly. "I'd rather live and die celibate than suffer as you're suffering now."

Constance hugged her cousin. And made no reply.

"I ASSUME OUR GUEST HAS retired?" Constance inquired that night when Merrick came to their bedchamber. In spite of her attempts to feel nothing when she was with him in order to lessen her anguish, her heartbeat quickened as he began to disrobe and fold his clothes with deliberate care.

"Yes, he has."

"Have you ever met him before?"

"No."

She should have known it was useless to seek a conversation with her husband. Yet even so, there were some things she needed to know. "When do you leave for Tintagel?"

He tossed his shirt onto the chest nearby, leaving him half-naked. "*We* depart in two days."

She had no desire to be dragged all over Cornwall however he wished. Chattel or not, she would assert some degree of independence. "I can't. I can't leave Beatrice."

Sitting on their bed, Merrick started to remove his boots. "Is she seriously ill?"

"No, I don't think so." Since she had no desire to go to Tintagel with him, she decided not to tell him that she thought Beatrice's trouble was more a product of her anxious mind than a physical ailment. "Yet while she may not be in any great danger, she should stay here until she's feeling better, and it would be improper for her to remain in Tregellas if I'm away. Normally I would ask her father to come, but since he's probably been summoned to Tintagel, too, we have no choice."

"I want you with me in Tintagel," Merrick said as if he hadn't heard her. He rose and started to untie the drawstring of his breeches.

She turned away and resumed combing her hair. "And I told you, my lord, why I cannot go."

"I'll send a message to Lord Carrell. His daughter is his responsibility, not ours. He can send someone to fetch her home."

"She shouldn't be forced to travel."

"I thought you said she's not seriously ill."

"I said I don't *think* she is, but I'm sure a journey wouldn't help her feel better."

"It is my express order that you accompany me to Tintagel," Merrick commanded as, naked, he threw back the coverlet. "I have need of you."

"What, to warm your bed?" she retorted even as she tried to stem her growing desire. "Heat a stone and put that at your feet."

He got into the bed and covered himself. "To tell me what other men's wives and daughters have heard about the situation between the king and his barons."

"You want me to *spy*?" She lifted her chin defiantly. "Like Peder, I will not."

"I want your help."

"To listen at doors, or try to discern a dollop of useful information from hours of meaningless gossip?"

He raised a coolly inquisitive brow. "This seems a sudden change of attitude, my lady. I thought you would leap at the chance to go to Tintagel, the better to express your political views to a larger audience. You certainly seemed anxious enough to wag your tongue in front of Lord Osgoode, even if your ideas make him suspect that the lord of Tregellas is plotting treason."

Guilt washed over her as she thought of what she'd said to Lord Osgoode upon first meeting him. Yet it couldn't be as bad as Merrick was implying. "Surely he doesn't think that. Besides, what I said about the king is true," she finished defensively.

"In *your* opinion," he retorted. "To some, it's treason, and most men will assume I share those opinions, because no woman would dare espouse a view opposite to her husband's."

"*I* would."

Merrick climbed out of bed. "Yes, you would—whether or not it would make trouble. But men like Osgoode don't know you're the exception."

"That's not my fault—"

"For God's sake, woman, are you a fool?" he demanded, glaring at her, his hands on his hips although he was still unabashedly naked. "Whether you like it or not, that's the way of the world and by vainly, arrogantly expressing your views before a man we don't know, you've put us all in danger."

"I have not," she countered, fighting back tears of both anger and dismay, telling herself he was wrong. He had to be. She'd always tried to protect people, not endanger them. "You made it clear to Lord Osgoode I don't speak for you."

"You made me give him an excuse, and he seemed to accept it, but men like that forget nothing. If I do anything—*anything*—that seems even a little suspicious, he'll remember and take the tale to court.

"And even if I agree that you're right and Henry is a bad king, would you have me risk my life, yours and that of everyone in Tregellas to find out? Are you really so certain Richard would do better? If you are, you have a very rosy view of mankind. He could turn out to be a good deal worse."

With that, Merrick tugged on his breeches and grabbed his boots.

Although she was taken aback by his harsh words, she heard the truth in them. What was she really asking for when she spoke of deposing the king?

Yet even so, her pride rose up as Merrick marched haughtily to the door. She wouldn't beg. Even if he was right, she wouldn't plead with him to stay. "Where are you going?"

He looked at her over his shoulder, and a more blood-

less, cold expression she had never seen. "To sleep elsewhere." His lips jerked up in a scornful smile. "Afraid
to be alone, my lady? Perhaps you can get some solace
from Kiernan, or some other nobleman who spouts soft
words and empty endearments."

Shocked, appalled and, most of all, indignant, she
grabbed her ivory comb by the bed and threw it at his
head with all her might.

The missile missed him by mere inches. Instead, it
struck the door and shattered.

"I see you learned something from my father after
all," he growled as he opened the door. "In two days, my
lady, and whether you want to or not, you'll go with me
to Tintagel, and Beatrice will go home."

CHAPTER SEVENTEEN

"EXPECTING TROUBLE, ARE YOU?"

"Always," Merrick replied, regarding Ranulf with cold composure as they stood together in the armory. His cortege was to leave for Tintagel at dawn the next morning, and he wanted to make sure all was ready.

"Tintagel's not that far," Ranulf noted. "Are you sure you need so many men in your escort? Between Lord Osgoode's soldiers and ours, that's over fifty."

Ranulf's words brought no comfort as that old, familiar, hated fear gripped Merrick again. A journey. A road. A wood. The dying. The dead. And blood upon the ground.

He forced the memories away. "I *want* that many men. Or do you think I'm leaving Tregellas too unprotected?"

"God save you, no. This place is so well fortified, a band of children could hold it against an assault."

Ranulf's confidence brought no relief, either.

Merrick went over to a stand holding several simple iron swords, their hilts wrapped with leather strips. So many weapons. So many soldiers. So why could he never feel completely safe? "The men will be ready to go at first light?"

"Absolutely. Will your wife?"

Merrick closed his eyes a moment, remembering their last argument. His anger. His harsh words. "Absolutely."

"I thought perhaps you might want her to stay here."

"No. Another pair of ears, especially for what the women are saying, will be valuable."

"Does she know what you want her to do?"

She knew. That didn't mean she would do it. Yet rather than answering, Merrick grabbed one of the swords and took a few practice swings.

"I was afraid you didn't care what she thought about anything after the hall moot."

Ranulf was trying to sound nonchalant, as he always did, but Merrick wasn't fooled. The very fact that he was saying anything at all about Merrick's relationship with his wife after their last confrontation on that subject revealed a deep and genuine concern.

No matter how well-meaning he might be, Ranulf would never understand, any more than Henry could.

So Merrick didn't reply, hoping Ranulf would take the hint and speak of something else.

He didn't.

"Is all well between you, then, despite appearances?" he inquired as he leaned back against the rough stone wall and crossed his arms as if he intended to stay until he had some answers.

If it was to be a contest of wills, Ranulf was going to lose, Merrick thought, disgruntled, as he made a defensive feint.

"You're happy together?"

Merrick turned and aimed a blow at an imaginary opponent.

"That's just what I thought. All is *not* well, and hasn't been since the hall moot. In fact, I'd say you're the most miserable man in Tregellas."

Merrick decided to answer that, or who could say what other conclusions Ranulf would reach? "You're wrong," he said as he replaced the sword.

Ranulf's eyes widened with exaggerated surprise. "Oh, so you're stomping around like an enraged bull and growling at everybody because you're deliriously happy, and Constance is floating about like a disheartened ghost because she's blissfully content."

"My wife doesn't *float*," Merrick retorted. He nodded at stacks of thin wooden shafts on a nearby shelf and sought to focus Ranulf's attention elsewhere. "Are those arrows ever going to get feathered?"

"Tomorrow, and don't change the subject," Ranulf countered. "Are you going to talk to Constance and smooth things over, or are you going to let the ditch between you widen until you can't bridge it at all?"

First Henry, now Ranulf. Who would be the next to offer him advice? Beatrice? "My relationship with my wife is none of your concern."

"Yes, it is," Ranulf replied, "when you're ruining it."

Merrick marched toward the door. "I'm not going to talk to you about my marriage."

Ranulf intercepted him. "Well, you'd better talk to

somebody—preferably your wife, and the sooner the better."

Merrick's brows lowered as his patience deserted him. "For a man whose own history with women is not the best, you have a lot of gall."

"I've learned from my dismal history with women," Ranulf answered, genuine sorrow in his hazel eyes as he put a hand on Merrick's arm. "Believe me, Merrick, keeping your feelings to yourself and expecting a woman to somehow read your mind is a very serious mistake."

Everyone was always so sure they were right. That they knew what he should do—when they understood *nothing*.

"I don't expect Constance to read my mind," he shot back as he pulled away. "I expect her to believe that I'm an honorable man, since I've given her no reason to think otherwise."

"And so you're going to sulk until one of you is dead?"

Merrick's temper flared. "I'm not sulking!"

"All right," Ranulf agreed with a shrug, apparently unaffected by his anger. "You're not sulking. You're brooding. Moping. Use what word you will."

Merrick pushed past him. "This is pointless."

Again Ranulf blocked his way. "It would be pointless if I didn't believe you cared about her. But you do—more than I've ever seen you care about anything or anybody."

Friend or not, Merrick wasn't going to talk about his wife with Ranulf. "Let me pass."

"For God's sake, Merrick, if you love her, make peace with her!"

"Do *not* tell me how to live my life!" Merrick snarled. "You're the commander of my garrison, not my overlord."

"I thought I was your friend."

Ranulf's quiet words hit Merrick like a blow to the chest. He'd lost Constance. And Henry. Would he now lose Ranulf, too?

But he couldn't be honest with his friend, no matter how much he wanted to be. He might reveal too much.

"Make sure the men and the baggage carts are ready at first light," he said, walking around Ranulf.

As Merrick opened the door, Ranulf sighed heavily. "And Lady Beatrice?" he asked. "How many men should escort her home?"

Merrick briefly checked his steps. "Ten."

"Then ten it shall be, my lord," Ranulf murmured as Merrick closed the door.

CONSTANCE HAD BEEN UNHAPPY for days, but now, seated on her mare in a drizzling rain, her cloak providing little in the way of shelter, she was utterly wretched. She wished she could have stayed at home, where she would at least be warm and dry, as well as not having to dread what might happen at Tintagel.

The women would surely marvel at her husband's good looks and proud bearing, and make jokes and sly innuendos about his abilities in bed. Maybe one of his former lovers would be there, to whisper to other women and smile knowingly and try to catch his eye.

The men would look at her with speculation, just like the few who'd visited Tregellas before Merrick arrived, making her feel like a head of livestock to be judged.

The talk would surely turn to the way the newly wedded couple rarely spoke. How the lord of Tregellas ignored his wife. How she kept her distance from him. Some of the women might try to take her place, at least in his bed. Some of the men might assume she would be anxious for a sympathetic ear, hoping that "comfort" might lead to adultery.

If she'd stayed home, she wouldn't have to endure that.

If she'd stayed home, Beatrice wouldn't have had to leave, either. Her poor cousin had sobbed so piteously as she got into the wagon to return to her father's castle.

Ranulf's friendship with Merrick seemed to be suffering, too. As Beatrice had taken her farewell, he'd looked as grim as death.

The faces of the villagers they'd passed confirmed that whatever goodwill Merrick had earned, he'd lost it. Only the bevy of workmen repairing the mill had paused in their tasks and nodded a simple greeting as the cortege went by—but then, they were getting well paid by the lord of Tregellas.

Once in Tintagel, she would have to guard her tongue, whether she wanted to or not. Merrick was right. Most men would assume her opinions were also her husband's, and so she would have to take care not to embroil them in the turmoil of the court.

Fortunately, it was also the way of the world, or at least of men, to consider women little more than silly children. All she had to do was chatter like Beatrice and give several contradictory opinions about the state of the realm for Lord Osgoode and everyone at Tintagel to assume she was an empty-headed ninny, trying to sound less ignorant than she was. Thus far, she'd been successful. Lord Osgoode now thoroughly patronized her.

What Merrick thought of her new behavior she didn't know. Although he had never again spent the night away from her, and the telltale bits of chaff in his hair the next morning had told her he'd probably slept in the stables after their most recent argument, he seemed more of a stranger to her now than he ever had.

She sighed heavily. Every hope, every dream of happiness and security she'd had, was in ruins, like the mill. Shattered, like her comb.

Her gaze moved to Merrick, riding at the head of the column in full chain mail, his shield on his left arm, his sword at his side, his mace tied to his saddle. His posture was so straight, so stiff, so apparently ready for battle.

"I wonder if the rain will cease or get worse before we reach Tintagel," Lord Osgoode speculated beside her.

Constance stopped looking at her husband and tittered. "I hope better, or I fear my gowns will be ruined and I'll look a complete fright."

"I'm sure you are never anything less than beautiful," Lord Osgoode assured her.

Constance struggled not to betray any scorn, but this man made Henry look an amateur when it came to meaningless flattery. "Is it much farther? I fear I'm not well traveled. I've never ridden past Lord Carrell's holding."

That was quite true, and she had the aching legs and sore back to prove it.

"I doubt we can reach it today," Lord Osgoode replied. "I understand there's a monastery not far from here that offers lodging to weary travelers. I'm sure your husband will stop there for the night to let you rest."

Constance feared Merrick didn't care one jot about her discomfort or fatigue.

Lord Osgoode tilted his head and looked up at the sky. "I do believe the rain is stopping."

He threw back his hood. "Ah, that's better," he said, inhaling deeply. "There are times I regret I don't have more estates in the south of France. The weather is so much more pleasant. You and your husband must visit me there."

"Oh, I'd love to! It must be delightful to be so rich and travel! I fear I seem woefully ignorant to you."

"A woman of such beauty has no need to be clever," Lord Osgoode replied, giving her a condescending smile. "Nevertheless, you're quite well-informed about the situation at court."

She grinned sheepishly. "I confess I care little about such matters, my lord. However, I've discovered that the best way to get my husband's attention is to feign an interest and ask lots of questions."

God help her, even Beatrice never sounded so silly.

"I hope he appreciates your efforts."

She giggled and lowered her eyelids to feign a modest blush. "Oh, yes, indeed. I am well rewarded."

She slid a scrutinizing glance at the nobleman riding beside her from beneath her lowered lids.

Lord Osgoode didn't look overly pleased by that answer. Perhaps he hoped she was frustrated and so lacking for affection she'd be an easy target for his oily charm.

Lord Osgoode kneed his horse closer and she anticipated more empty flattery. "If it does come to rebellion, many men are going to wonder which side your husband will support."

So, he thought to get information from her. Even if she did know her husband's opinion on this vital matter, she wouldn't share that knowledge with Lord Osgoode, especially after Merrick's warning.

Instead, she widened her eyes with bogus dismay and very brightly said, "I have no idea. He's never told me."

There was a flash of annoyance in Osgoode's eyes, but in the next moment he was once again the placid, genial companion. "Let us hope that no choice need be made, especially as it seems your husband has quite enough to deal with on his estate. The fire at the mill was most unfortunate."

"Yes, it was. Thankfully, the repairs should be finished before we return from Tintagel. It was kind of Sir

Jowan to send us his mason. He's a rough and crude sort of commoner, but he seems to know what he's about. At least, I hope so."

"And you still have no idea how it happened?"

"No. Merrick's been trying to find out, of course, but alas! To no avail."

"At least your husband's been successful at stopping the smuggling. It's a pity he hasn't captured some of the outlaws, though, so that their punishment could set an example. Peasants and villeins require a strong hand, or they begin to think they have more rights than they do. These tinners, for instance. I don't know how the Cornish lords put up with them."

Ahead, Merrick raised his hand to halt the cortege, giving her an excuse not to answer. It was getting nearly impossible to hide her true feelings and guard her tongue.

"I wonder why we've stopped," Lord Osgoode muttered as he nudged his horse closer to the front of the cortege.

She was curious, too, so she did the same. Lord Osgoode repeated his question when they reached her husband, who was staring ahead at the thick wood of oak and ash.

"This would be a fine place for an ambush," he replied.

It was not his words so much as his tone that made her shiver with sudden fear.

"What fools would ambush us, my lord?" Lord Osgoode asked incredulously. "We have over fifty men."

Merrick twisted in his saddle as if he wanted to see

his men and confirm they were there before he answered. Constance had never seen his face so pale, his eyes so bright.

"Obviously you've never been ambushed, my lord, and all around you slaughtered," he answered. "I have, and I will take no chances."

That silenced Lord Osgoode.

Whatever Merrick was thinking or remembering, his voice was firm and steady as he called for the master-at-arms and ordered him to have the mounted men break into three groups—one to ride in front, one to ride beside Lady Constance and Lord Osgoode, and one to ride at the rear.

Once all were in position, he raised his hand and signaled them forward.

MERRICK HAD RISKED DEATH and injury many times in tournaments and training. He'd fought at Sir Leonard's side during some skirmishes with a disloyal castellan who had refused to give up a keep when Sir Leonard put a new man in command. On those occasions he'd felt not fear, but a grim determination to prove himself.

Yet those battles had been on open fields, or in the case of the castellan, on the wall walks and in the wards of a castle—open areas, not enclosed by trees.

Sometimes it took only the scent of damp foliage to bring back the terror. The memories of the screams of injured and dying men. Sir Egbert lying on the ground, staring at the sky with dead, wide-open eyes. The fiercely scarred leader of the soldiers, tough and frightening himself, shouting his orders, trying to turn his horse. Then shrieking as his arm was sliced from his body. The servants slaughtered where they stood, regardless of rank or age. The boy his own age, his neck slashed and his tunic stained with blood. Everywhere, the blood.

And then running through the trees, the underbrush scratching and tearing, until he fell exhausted and could run no more.

Merrick gripped his drawn sword tighter and tried to put those thoughts from his mind as he rode into the wood. He had won tournaments. He was a good fighter, and well armed. It would take bad luck, or a mistake on his part, for him to fall.

His horse could fight, too, with teeth and hooves. He had many other soldiers with him. Even Lord Osgoode would have been trained to defend himself.

Yet in spite of all his silent reassurances, sweat trickled down Merrick's back, making the padded gambeson he wore beneath his mail stick to his skin.

Because greater than his dread of the dark, damp wood was his fear for Constance's safety, perhaps her very life. He silently cursed his stubbornness and vain pride that had insisted that she come. He should have let her stay in Tregellas, where it would be harder for an enemy to hurt her. Even if it looked odd, or made the earl and other noblemen speculate, he should have insisted she remain behind.

How much farther to the end of these woods?

The master-at-arms had told him there was a monastery not far from here. If they made it out of these woods safely—*when* they made it out of these woods safely—they would stop there, so Constance could rest. She'd not uttered a single word of complaint, but he was sure she was tired and probably sore. The groom had told him, in answer to his question, that Lady Constance was a good rider, but rarely ventured far. She'd likely already been longer in the saddle then she'd ever been in her life.

He never should have married her. He never should have made her the wife of a man detested and mistrusted by the villagers and tenants, so that there would always be the dread that they would rebel.

He never should have asked her to betray the trust of those same villagers and tenants. Or else he should have told her how pleased and relieved he was when she had not, for otherwise, he could never trust her, either.

He did trust her, as much as he trusted anyone.

Which was never, ever completely. He didn't dare. His secret was too terrible. His friends would despise him, the earl would strip him of his estate and Constance…she would rightly wish him straight to hell.

Merrick's horse skittered nervously. He'd been gripping too hard with his knees. He relaxed his hold and looked ahead.

In the distance the road began to widen and the trees thinned. Thank God. Not long now.

The memories receded, back into the place where he

kept them, along with the fear of discovery that haunted him night and day. He even ventured to half turn in his saddle—to encounter Constance watching him intently.

He faced forward immediately and cursed himself for a fool. He was a hundred ways a fool, and if he needed any proof, he had only to look at the woman he was making miserable.

At last they came out of the wood. Broken, rocky moor stretched toward the sea to their left. The land to their right had been cleared for pasture from the road to the top of a ridge running parallel to the muddy track. Beyond the field, the forest continued. A stone cottage and some outbuildings were not far off. The turn for the monastery should be in about another mile or so.

Merrick ordered the men to sheath their swords, and so did he.

As they rode on, the air was very quiet and still, the only sounds that of their cortege: the creaking wheels of the baggage carts, his men's marching feet, the horses and their jingling accoutrements. At this time of day the men were too tired for much conversation. Nor could he hear the soft murmur of Constance's voice, and the lower tones of Lord Osgoode as he spoke to her.

She'd been acting unlike herself since he'd chastised her about her remarks to Osgoode. Even if he did fear being accused of trying to rob the king of his birthright, and although he didn't trust Osgoode, he shouldn't have lost his temper. Despite that, Constance had apparently agreed that he was right and sought to repair any damage she might have caused by acting like a simpleton. Only a man of Lord Osgoode's prejudices wouldn't see that she was merely acting like a fool. He'd caught Ranulf staring at her with blatant bafflement, and Beatrice had looked puzzled, too.

There was no activity at the farm ahead.

Where was the farmer? His wife? Children? Not even a dog barked a warning that a mounted party approached on the road.

Merrick turned his head to look at the field—and his blood froze.

Ambush!

Not in the woods, as he'd feared. Here, where he thought they'd be safer. A force that easily matched his own was galloping out of the forest and down the ridge. With lances.

Lances that could pierce mail and take a man down with a single blow—and they had none.

In the next instant the lances were forgotten as he heard Constance's warning cry.

Nothing else mattered but her. Not his own safety, or anyone else's. Whether the attackers would merely take her prisoner or murder her, he neither knew nor cared. She was his wife, his beloved, and he would let no man harm a hair on her head.

He shouted for the master-at-arms, and as he did, he realized the men were already forming into battle lines, while a group of about twenty circled Constance and Lord Osgoode.

Thank God for Ranulf's training!

He shouted at them to take his wife and Lord Osgoode to the monastery, no matter what else happened.

Raising his sword, his reins in his left hand, his shield raised, he roweled his horse to a gallop and led the charge. He swung his sword at the first lance he could, the blow shattering the tip. He recovered quickly enough to swing at the mounted man, but missed and nearly overset himself by leaning too far forward.

He regained his balance and with a sharp nudge of his knees, turned his destrier. Three of his mounted men had fallen, two of the attackers.

He quickly searched for Constance. He spotted Lord Osgoode and their guards, fighting with a will against a group of nearly the same number.

Where was Constance? Oh, God, where—? There! She'd broken out of the fighting group and was riding down the road, her scarf gone, her unbound hair and cloak streaming behind her.

"Fly, beloved, fly!" he shouted at the top of his lungs.

Then his heart leapt into his throat as one of the attackers broke off from the group around Osgoode and rode after her.

Merrick recognized him at once. He'd seen him in tournaments, watched him practice, knew the way he sat his horse as well as he knew his own name.

"*Judas!*" Merrick screamed, the word torn from his heart as he spurred his horse forward. "Traitor!"

Death was too good for Henry.

Six other mounted men appeared in front of Merrick, two with maces, the rest with swords that flashed in the sun emerging from behind the clouds.

With an enraged bellow, Merrick charged the nearest man, swinging his sword like a madman, albeit one with incredibly good aim and years of training. His horse, excited by the battle, snapped and bit at anything that got in its way.

Merrick's opponent was no novice, but even so, he was no match for a furious Merrick, either. The wrath seemed to fairly pour out of the lord of Tregellas and he fought with an almost supernatural power.

His enemy's companions, seeing his difficulties, pressed closer. Merrick's horse, enclosed, reared back, kicking. Merrick's sword flashed silver in the sunlight, then glistened with blood as one by one the men surrounding him fell, to be trampled by the hooves of his horse.

After the last man shrieked and tumbled from his horse, a bruised and bloodied Merrick raised himself in his stirrups.

Constance! Where was Constance?

There, lying on the ground with Lord Osgoode kneeling beside her.

Not taken. Thank God. Not taken.

But oh, God, if she was dead…

He kicked his horse into a gallop and rode toward his fallen wife, barely noticing that his men had succeeded in repelling the attack.

When he reached Lord Osgoode he brought his horse

to a halt so swiftly, it sat back on its haunches. He jumped from the saddle and threw himself to his knees beside his pale and motionless wife, everything else forgotten as he stared, horrified, at her white face. "Dead?" he croaked, his throat almost clenched shut with fear.

"No, not dead," Lord Osgoode said. "She fell trying to escape. I don't think any limbs are broken, but I fear she struck her head."

Merrick turned to ice inside. A broken limb could be mended. Tears in the flesh could be sewn. But a wound to the head... Sometimes they were nothing, sometimes they were a slow death. "And the man who tried to take her?"

"I'm sorry to say he escaped, my lord."

Merrick rose. "Not for long and never from me," he said, and his voice made Osgoode shiver.

"Take my wife to the monastery," Merrick ordered as he mounted his horse, his face grimly set, resolve hardening his heart.

He was going to find Henry, who would then discover just how merciless the son of Wicked William could be.

CHAPTER EIGHTEEN

THE VOICES WERE MUTED, AS IF they were under water. Or she was.

"It would be best, my lord, if you didn't disturb her," a man said. She didn't recognize his voice, but he sounded learned. Middle-aged.

"I must see her."

That was Merrick. He was alive! Thank God. But she'd never heard his voice sound like that before. Distraught. Upset.

"My lord, please. I've given her a potent draught and we should—"

"Will she live?"

Of course she would. There was no need for him to worry…although it was comforting to think he did worry about her. She was just tired, so tired she couldn't open her eyes.

"That is in God's hands, my lord."

"I *must* see her before I leave."

Now he was angry. Impatient. The old Merrick.

Where was he going? To Tintagel? Weren't they already there?

Where *was* she?

Maybe if she slept, she'd be more alert when she awoke….

A hand took hold of hers. A rough, calloused hand. A man's hand. Merrick's hand, grasping hers so very gently.

"I'm so sorry," he whispered, his voice low and rough, nearly breaking.

Sorry for what? For quarreling? So was she…

She wished she wasn't so tired. Wasn't there something she had to tell him? Something important?

"Constance, my love, my love, if you die, I'll never forgive myself."

She attempted to open her eyes, but couldn't. She wanted to open them. What was wrong that she could not?

She tried to tighten her grasp, to move her fingers, but she couldn't do that, either.

"I never should have married you."

She lay completely still, too shocked to try to move again.

"I've lied to you, Constance," he whispered, his voice in her ear as he leaned close, his breath warm on her cheek. He smelled of sweat and leather and…blood.

The battle. They'd been in a battle. There was something important about the battle….

He rested his forehead on her shoulder. "I never should have put you in danger."

Her heart ached to hear the pain in his voice. If only she could say something to comfort him. Perhaps if she slept a bit first…. And then there was that other thing, some important thing…

"I've lied to you, Constance," he whispered, and her shoulder grew damp. Was he…was he *weeping?* "I had no right to marry you. No right to claim Tregellas."

She must be dreaming. She had to be dreaming.

Yes, that was it. She was asleep and having a nightmare.

"But I've held your image in my heart for so long, loved and cherished you for so long…and when I saw you again…when I could marry you and have you for my wife…I was too weak to release you."

Release? She didn't want to be released. She wanted only to sleep a little while, to ease the soreness in her head.

"When you wake up, when you're better, I promise before God I'll go to the king and the church and anywhere else I must to end our marriage, so that you can be free again, as you should be. I've sinned a great sin against you, Constance, and I hope…I pray…that someday you'll forgive me."

She tried once more to open her mouth, to say his name, but she was drifting back into that dark oblivion. She mustn't. Not yet.

"My lord, I beg of you, please!" the unfamiliar voice pleaded softly from far away. "You must let your wife rest."

She fought hard to speak, to open her eyes. "Hen…ry," she whispered.

Merrick sucked in his breath and his hand released hers.

Hc had heard her. She wanted to say more, that Henry had tried to help her, but the effort of speaking had taken what remained of her strength.

"My lord, please!"

"I'm going. Do everything you can, Father. Send word to me at Tintagel. I have business there that cannot wait."

"The other man you brought, my lord. He's hurt and should be—"

"He should be dead and he soon will be, but not before I'm finished with him."

"May God have mercy on his soul," the other man said sadly.

The last thing Constance heard before she lost consciousness was her husband's grim response. "May God have mercy on us both."

"MY LADY?"

Constance's eyelids fluttered open. Her head still ached, but not so much. She looked at the lime-washed walls around her bed, felt the rough, simple linen against her skin and the scratchy wool blanket, noted the crucifix on the wall opposite— and realized Ranulf was bending over her. "Where's Merrick?" she whispered.

"Tintagel," hc replied, his expression grave as he sat on a stool beside her bed.

"Here, my lady, drink this."

She hadn't realized another man was there, but she recognized the voice from before. He'd bccn the other man in the room when Merrick was with her. A sad, distraught, then grimly resolute Merrick.

She turned her head, to find a pleasant-looking, tonsured monk offering her a cup.

"This is Brother Paul," Ranulf explained. "He's the physician here and has been taking care of you. You fell from your horse."

"Yes, I remember." She put her hand to her head, then frowned as she remembered more. She struggled to sit up, aided by the physician. She took the cup and sipped the soothing mulled wine as Ranulf watched anxiously.

"Why are you here?" she asked Ranulf as she handed the cup back to the monk, her hands trembling slightly. "Is there trouble at Tregellas?"

Ranulf shook his head. "No. I came to find you, my lady."

"Merrick sent word that our cortege was attacked?"

"No. Henry sent word it was about to be."

She sat up straighter. "Henry came out of nowhere and grabbed my horse. He tried to help me get away."

"Perhaps this can wait until another time, Sir Ranulf," Brother Paul suggested. "The lady is still not well—"

"I'm well enough," Constance insisted. She turned her full attention back to Ranulf, her aching head forgotten. "Henry knew about the attack?"

"Yes, but I gather his rescue wasn't completely successful, or he would be here, too."

"I don't know what happened after I fell." She

frowned, struggling to remember the first time she'd come to consciousness. "Merrick was here. He said…"

He'd said he'd lied. He'd said he had no right to marry her. "I tried to tell him Henry was there, but I couldn't."

"You were seriously hurt, my lady," Brother Paul said softly. "You need to rest."

"I appreciate your concern, good brother, and I'm grateful for your help, but I'm sure you can understand that I must know what happened," she said before again addressing Ranulf. "Where's Henry now?"

"I don't know. I came here as soon as I got his message. He said you would be here, waiting for me."

"Why did he not send a warning to Merrick? Why to you?"

"He feared that Merrick wouldn't believe him."

"And you would?"

"I have no reason not to, and I didn't quarrel with Merrick. Henry planned to save you during the attack and bring you here, where I would find you. Later, I was to go to Merrick and tell him what Henry had learned. Henry thought Merrick would be more inclined to believe him after the attack."

"What about Merrick? What if he'd been hurt or even killed?"

Ranulf made a little smile. "Having seen Merrick fight, Henry didn't think that likely."

Constance wouldn't have shared that confidence, although it seemed Henry and Ranulf were right. Merrick hadn't been killed. "What had Henry learned?"

Ranulf started to rise. "The details can wait until you're feeling better."

She put her hand on Ranulf's arm. "I want to know everything now."

Ranulf glanced at Brother Paul.

"Even if you go," Constance threatened, "I won't rest for wondering what you were going to say." She softened her tone and her expression. "Please stay, Ranulf." She looked beseechingly at the monk. "Brother Paul, have mercy and let him."

"Very well," the physician reluctantly agreed. "But if you feel tired or dizzy or faint, he *must* go."

"I give you my word that he will," she promised.

"Perhaps, my lady," Ranulf said with a significant look, "it would be better to keep this conversation between the two of us, as it touches on serious political matters."

"I think that would be wise," Constance agreed, even as she wondered what exactly he meant by serious political matters. "If you don't mind, Brother Paul? You may leave the door open and watch from the corridor. Ranulf will summon you if I feel sick or faint."

Her words might have been conciliatory, but her tone was not. Recognizing the commands for what they were, or perhaps not wishing to become involved in any political troubles, Brother Paul rose and quietly departed the chamber, leaving the door ajar.

"Now then, Ranulf, tell me all," Constance said with both anxiety and impatience.

"Henry's message said that he had discovered a conspiracy."

"Against the king? Or the earl of Cornwall?"

"Both—and against you and your husband."

She could easily understand why his enemies would want Merrick dead, for he would be an implacable foe. "But why me?" she wondered aloud. "Am I not more valuable alive, to hold for ransom or to ensure my husband's silence or cooperation?"

"If this were strictly a political conspiracy, yes."

Constance shifted. "It's not?"

Ranulf shook his head. "I regret being the bearer of such news, but greed as well as ambition inspire your enemies."

"Who are they?" she demanded.

"Your uncle, and Merrick's."

"Lord Carrell?" It was like getting another blow to the head. Dizzy, she closed her eyes and willed herself not to swoon.

She heard Ranulf rise.

"No!" she cried softly, grabbing his arm. "I'm all right. Please stay."

"You're ill, my lady. I told you too much too soon. The rest can wait."

Her grip tightened on his arm like a vise. "Please!"

Ranulf reluctantly sat back down. "Apparently Lord Algernon wants Tregellas, and Lord Carrell has agreed to help him in this quest."

Lord William had often claimed that Algernon begrudged him Tregellas and would stop at nothing to get it. So Algernon might be involved, but… "My uncle would never hurt me."

Ranulf raised a brow. "Yet he left you in the care of a man who, I gather, was only slightly better than Caligula."

"I was betrothed to Lord William's son."

"Before Lord Carrell had a daughter of his own. After she was born, the bargain couldn't be broken without penalty."

She was well aware of that—and that her uncle could be miserly.

"Perhaps he even hoped your future father-in-law would do his work for him and kill you in one of his rages," Ranulf suggested.

That would explain why he'd left her in Tregellas all those years, no matter what Lord William did.

"If Merrick and I are both dead, Lord Algernon will inherit Tregellas, but why would my uncle want him to have it?"

"So that his daughter may marry the lord of Tregellas instead of his niece."

She gasped as the answers to other questions fell into place. Why he'd never arranged a marriage for Beatrice or even mentioned it. The looks the two older men sometimes exchanged, their whispered conferences. And yet… "There's no reason she couldn't marry Algernon now."

"Except that Lord Algernon doesn't yet possess Tregellas, and all that goes with it. He gets Beatrice and a blood bond with Lord Carrell only *after* he has inherited the estate."

It sounded incredible, yet she could believe it. "How did Henry come to find this out?"

"After he left Tregellas he encountered your uncle, who'd heard of his quarrel with Merrick. Your uncle offered him a place. Finding both your uncle's manner and offer suspicious, Henry accepted. He discovered evidence of a conspiracy, including some very incriminating letters. I've seen them, and I fear there's no doubt of your uncle's guilt, my lady."

"How did Henry get these letters?"

"It would probably be better not to ask," Ranulf replied with the hint of a smile. "Henry's very adept at getting around a castle without being seen."

While on his way to amorous assignations, no doubt. "However he came by the knowledge, I'm grateful."

Ranulf's eyes gleamed like jewels. "What Lord Algernon doesn't seem to realize is that if Beatrice is widowed, her father will as good as control Tregellas and all the power that goes with it."

Regardless of Ranulf's presence, Constance threw back the covers and started to get out of bed.

"What do you think you're doing?" Ranulf demanded, too shocked to be polite.

"We must go to Tintagel at once." She had to see her husband as soon as possible, and not just to tell him what Henry had learned. She had to know what Morrick meant when he'd told her that he'd lied and he would release her from their marriage.

"The moment I got Henry's message, I sent a warning to Merrick of the plot against you."

Constance wasn't comforted. "You obviously don't know my uncle. *If* the messenger has reached Tintagel safely, *if* he gets the message to Merrick, my uncle is still clever enough to have the earl believing Merrick is the real conspirator, planning treason against the king. Or he'll throw the blame onto Lord Algernon entirely. We must go to Tintagel. Where's Henry now?"

"I have no idea. He told me only that he would try to get you to the monastery. He didn't say what he planned to do after that."

"Then we'll pray he's safe and find him later."

A BUCKET OF ICE-COLD WATER landed on Henry, soaking his soiled, torn clothing and the dank straw upon which he lay. Coughing and spluttering through bruised and cut lips, he cried out as other pain assailed him when he moved—from his ribs, his wrists enclosed in iron fetters, his legs in chains...

Somebody kicked his ankle, hard. "Wake up, you lump of dung."

He opened his swollen eyelids as best he could, to see Merrick glaring at him like an avenging angel in the flickering light of a torch, his drawn sword clutched in his other hand.

Merrick, who'd ridden him down like a stag and cornered him. Who'd ferociously attacked and wouldn't listen as he tried to explain—

Merrick kicked him again. "I know you're awake."

Holding his side, Henry tried to stand.

Merrick shoved him down to a kneeling position. "You have no right to stand before me, you traitorous dog."

"You don't understand—"

"The hell I don't! I saw you with my own eyes try to steal my wife."

"No," Henry protested, his voice hoarse with thirst and pain.

Once more Merrick struck him with his booted foot. "Liar! Base, vile liar! Dishonorable viper!" He bent over, so that his accusing, glaring eyes were looking directly into Henry's. "There is *nothing* you could have done that would make me hate you more."

"I swear—"

"What, you would make another oath?" Merrick replied scornfully as he straightened. "What happened to the one you already swore, that you would be my loyal brother to the death?"

"I've kept—"

"By lusting after my wife? By trying to kidnap her?" Merrick brought the tip of his sword to rest just under Henry's left eye. "Death is too good for a man like you."

"Listen to me!" Henry pleaded, desperation lending him strength. "I was trying to save her."

"From what?" Merrick demanded. *"Me?"*

"Lord Carrell," Henry replied, gasping with the effort. "And Lord Algernon. They planned the attack, not me."

The tip of the sword bit into Henry's skin. "Is there no end to your wickedness that you'd accuse our own relatives?"

"It's true," Henry insisted. "And Lord Carrell and Lord Algernon are not just *your* enemies—they're plotting against the king, too. I have proof, letters Carrell was sending north to other traitors."

"How did you come upon these incriminating letters?" Merrick sneered. "Did Lord Carrell ask you to deliver them?"

"No—he had other work for me to do." Henry pressed on before Merrick spoke again. "He heard we'd quarreled and he sought me out. He offered me a place in his service. I felt in my bones there was more to it, that he wasn't to be trusted, and he soon proved me right. He all but offered me Constance if I would serve him."

"Liar!"

"Ask Ranulf if you don't believe me. I sent him a message, telling him everything. He was to meet Constance and me at the monastery near here after I'd taken her there. Then we would both come to tell you what I'd learned. He's got the letters, too, so he would know I was in earnest, and to keep them safe. He should be at the monastery. Wait for him before you kill me, Merrick, please!"

Again the sword nipped, and a slow trickle of blood ran down Henry's cheek, to fall and mingle with the other blood already staining his tunic. "Why send this proof to Ranulf and not me?"

"Because I thought you'd be more likely to believe it if Ranulf was already convinced. But you must believe me. Lord Carrell and Lord Algernon are your enemies, not me!"

"What a convenient way to purchase more time— blaming others. Although what good you think it's going to do you, I can't guess. Have you any notion where you are?"

Henry looked at the damp stone walls around him. "A dungeon."

"You're in Tintagel. The earl of Cornwall himself is going to pass judgment on you. You might as well stop lying, Henry. It's not going to save your miserable life."

"For God's sake, I'm telling you the truth! Your uncle wants Tregellas."

"And he simply came out and told you, just as Lord Carrell blithely offered you my wife?" The sword moved to Henry's throat. "I should kill you right now."

"I'm not lying! He didn't offer me Constance like a merchant making a trade. He implied she could be mine if you were dead. But that was just a ruse to get me to serve him."

"And apparently a good one."

"He was sure that because we'd quarreled, I would be against you."

"Not surprising, given that you've betrayed me."

"But I didn't! I was angry, yes, and upset with you,

but I'd never betray our oath, or our friendship. I agreed to serve him to protect you!"

"And thus you led a force that attacked me, my men and my wife."

"Because if I didn't, I couldn't have saved Constance!"

"You planned to save her by abducting her and taking her where? And doing *what*?" The sword tip was against Henry's chest now. "I saw how you looked at her, Henry."

"She's a beautiful woman, and, yes, if she were free, I'd do everything I could to get her into my bed. But I swear to you, Merrick, I'd never try to seduce your wife."

"Perhaps seduction was not your aim."

Henry's eyes widened with shocked dismay, then his face twisted with anguish. "God, Merrick, you don't think I'd rape her?"

"For all I know, you could be capable of anything."

"For God's sake—and the sake of our friendship all these years—*listen* to me! Carrell doesn't just want you dead. He plans to kill Constance, too."

"Why? What purpose would her death serve?"

"That way, Algernon would inherit Tregellas. Then he's to marry Beatrice, so that Carrell and Algernon would be bonded by blood."

"A fine story," Merrick said through clenched teeth. "A very pretty tale."

"I knew you could protect yourself in a fight, so I was trying to get Constance to safety. I would have succeeded, too, except that she fell."

The sword pressed harder against him. "Yes, she fell and now lies unconscious. If she dies, I'm going to kill you myself. Very, very slowly."

Henry's already pale face blanched beneath the filth. "I swear to you on my life, Merrick, I was trying to get her to safety."

Merrick drew back, a look of complete disgust on his face.

His voice nearly gone, Henry choked back a sob of anguished despair. "Can you so easily believe I'd betray you? Do you truly think me so completely without honor?"

Merrick shouted for the guard to open the door.

"For the love of God, Merrick, you have to believe me!" Henry cried as the massive door creaked open. "They're conspiring against you—and against the king, too! Once they have Tregellas, they're going to lead a rebellion." He raised his shackled hands and clasped them together, pleading. "Wait for Ranulf. For God's sake, Merrick, wait for Ranulf!"

Merrick went out without a backward glance and the door clanged shut behind him.

CHAPTER NINETEEN

THOUGH SHE WAS MINDFUL OF Brother Paul, who'd insisted on coming with them to Tintagel, Constance nudged her horse to a slightly faster walk as she, Ranulf, the priest and their armed escort rode through the narrow valley leading to the earl's fortress. In the near distance she could see large stone walls whitened with lime and an arched gate flanked by square towers.

At least the weather was good; had it been otherwise, she would have had more difficulty convincing Brother Paul to let her leave the monastery. Even so, the cool breeze coming off the sea whipped her cloak about her, and poor Brother Paul, farther back on his donkey, looked as if he was shivering.

She raised her voice to call out to Ranulf, so that the knight riding in front of her could hear her above the wind and the waves crashing against the cliffs. "Those are the outer defenses?"

Ranulf let his horse drop back until he was beside her. He nodded. "That gate guards the bridge to the island."

"It seems a very defensible place."

"And an easy place to which to lay siege," Ranulf answered, clearly not overly impressed. "One need only block that gate and set up a blockade, and you could starve out the garrison in a few weeks."

Constance hadn't considered that aspect of the location. "Then why would the earl choose such a place for a fortress?"

"Can you not guess, my lady?" Ranulf asked with a sardonic smile.

"Because King Arthur was born in Tintagel?" she ventured. Like anyone who'd been in Cornwall for more than a week, she was well versed in the tales recorded by Geoffrey of Monmouth about the legendary king.

Ranulf's smile became more natural. "Exactly."

"Richard wasn't born in Cornwall."

"No, but this place does convey a certain fame by association. Richard is an ambitious man."

"I hadn't considered Tintagel in that light." She gave Ranulf a wary glance. "How ambitious is the earl? Do you think he'll ever rebel against his brother?"

"No."

Constance recalled her husband's fears. "Merrick thinks he might."

"Merrick sees danger around every bush and shrub, my lady. And in truth, given that he's the lord of a great estate, he must be prepared for war. I have no such responsibilities, so I can afford to think of conflict only in terms of whether or not I may gain an estate. Merrick must think in terms of protecting what he already possesses."

By now they'd reached the outer gate. Ranulf identified their party, and the gates swung open to allow them to enter. From there, it was a rather precarious ride across the narrow bridge and through yet another gate before they entered the main yard, which was a-bustle with servants and soldiers, an indication that the earl was in residence.

Brother Paul looked about him, both amazed and impressed. Meanwhile, Ranulf swung down from his horse and hurried to assist Constance, who didn't refuse his help. She wasn't feeling sick or dizzy, but she wasn't about to risk swooning.

Ranulf called for a groom and issued a few brief orders to his men. He spoke to the groom when he appeared, then returned to Constance. "It seems we've arrived at a good time. The nobles are gathered in the hall. I was afraid Merrick might be out hunting or otherwise away from the castle."

"Let's not waste another moment," Constance said, heading for the large building that had to be the hall.

As they entered, Constance paid no heed to the size of the chamber, or the banners hanging from the beams, or the tapestries. Her attention was on the group of men seated and standing near the hearth at the far end.

"Constance!"

Merrick shoved his way through the group and rushed toward her, a smile of such joy on his face, she could scarcely believe it was the same man.

And then she was in his arms, engulfed in his embrace. "Constance," he whispered. "You're alive! Praise God, you're alive!"

"I suggest you loosen your hold and let her breathe," Ranulf remarked behind them. "She's not quite completely recovered."

Merrick gasped and quickly let go of her.

"I have a slight ache in my head, that's all," Constance assured him, thrilled by this reception.

"Thank God you're here," Merrick murmured as his gaze searched her happy face.

Ranulf tapped Merrick on the shoulder and nodded at the group of men watching them. "Have we interrupted a counsel?"

Merrick forced his attention away from Constance. "Yes. Come, I'll introduce you."

Ranulf didn't immediately follow. "Where are Lord Carrell and Lord Algernon?"

Constance quickly surveyed the gathering, seeking their villainous relatives. She couldn't see the uncles, but a frowning Kiernan was among the group, his father beside him.

Merrick's brow furrowed. "They *were* here."

"They can't be permitted to leave," Ranulf urged. "They're conspiring against you and the king and the earl."

Merrick's eyes flashed. "What evidence—?"

"Henry sent me letters that he intercepted bearing Lord Carrell's signature and seal. They're damning, Merrick."

"Your father often accused his brothers of wanting to

steal Tregellas," Constance added, "and being willing to do anything to get it. I thought it was just his usual raving, or suspicions deepened by his final illness, but I believe Henry has indeed discovered proof of a conspiracy."

"Henry attacked—"

"He was helping me escape from the fighting, trying to take me to a safe place. I wanted to tell you in the monastery, but you left before I was able."

Merrick blanched. "Oh, God. What have I done?"

"Lord Merrick," called out a tall, well-made man seated on a brightly cushioned chair. "Are you not going to tell us who these people are?"

Constance had never met the earl of Cornwall, but she was sure she was looking at him now.

"Yes…no…I must go, my lord," her husband replied, more incoherent than Constance would ever have believed possible. "You must excuse me."

He turned on his heel and ran out of the hall. As Constance and Ranulf stared after him, Kiernan's voice broke the shocked silence. "That is Lord Merrick's wife, my lord, and that other fellow is his garrison commander."

Pride and anger fired in Constance. Taking Ranulf's arm, she advanced toward the earl and the other powerful noblemen gathered around him.

"I am Lady Constance of Tregellas, my lord earl," she announced. "And this is my husband's most loyal and trusted friend, Sir Ranulf. We come to bring you proof of a conspiracy against you and your brother the king."

A SOUND OUTSIDE THE CHAMBER caught Henry's ear. Lifting his head, he listened closely. Was it a jailer bringing food? Guards coming to take him to his execution?

A slow, torturous death more like.

Maybe it was just the rats. If they were looking for food, they wouldn't find any here, unless they considered *him* food.

Henry curled his lip in disgust, making it bleed again. He licked away the warm, coppery liquid and decided that if he had to die, he wasn't going to be gnawed by rats first.

He got to his feet and grabbed the waste bucket, throwing its contents as far across the small chamber as he could. Thus armed, he flexed his knees, trying to loosen the stiff joints.

A key turned in the rusty lock.

Not rats, then. He swiftly put down the bucket within arm's reach, sat and lowered his head as if he were asleep. If the guards were coming to take him to his death, the moment his shackles were uncoupled from the wall, he'd grab the bucket for a weapon and try to escape. Better to die fighting.

Lord Carrell came into the chamber, his nose wrinkling with the stench.

What did *he* want? Not to confess, of that Henry was certain.

He hated to think he might die while this blackguard lived, but he showed no sign of despair or dismay when he spoke. "Greetings, my lord traitor. Have you perchance come to join me in confinement?"

"Still the charming knight, are you?" Lord Carrell retorted, his words slightly muffled by the cloth he pulled out of the sleeve of his long tunic and held over his nose.

"A true gentleman is always a gentleman, regardless of his circumstances," Henry replied. "Of course, you're no gentleman and likely never were, treacherous snake that you are."

"Say what you will, I'm free and you're going to die," Lord Carrell sneered. "Your former friend is most determined to have you brought before the king's justice at once. Stand up."

Henry's blood chilled in his veins, but he made no effort to move. "If you don't mind, my lord, I prefer to remain seated."

"Stand up or I'll have the guard drag you up by your hair."

"In that case…" Henry rose, glad his recent activity had eased his stiffness so he didn't look weak in front of the dishonorable offal before him. "Now, then, my lord, what brings you to my abode?"

Lord Carrell shook his head. "Men like you never learn, do they?"

"I'm actually quite accomplished."

His enemy's brows lowered. "You can stop trying to play the merry rogue with me. It's not working. Your friend wasn't fooled, was he? He still thinks you're a lying, despicable dog."

Henry's jaw clenched ever so slightly. "For now. He'll discover the truth when Ranulf arrives."

Lord Carrell's eyes flared with surprise. So Ranulf still had not come. He hadn't had a chance to tell Merrick about the letters, or show him the proof that he—Henry—hadn't betrayed him. That was why he was still here.

"My own plans may have gone a little awry, but not so badly as yours, my lord," Henry said, hoping Ranulf would get there soon. "Alas, my lord, I fear your messenger to your confederates in the north never made it past the boundary of your estate. The poor fellow was intercepted and strongly encouraged to give up his pouch. Then it was sent along to Ranulf. Your plans have been thwarted, my lord, and in a little while, you'll be here instead of me."

"You strutting ass!" Carrell growled. "Do you really think you can defeat me with nothing but a few letters?"

"Considering what's in those letters, I'd start praying for mercy right now, if I were you."

Carrell's lip curled. "You're so very clever, are you?" He began to twist the cloth in his hands until it was like a coiled rope. "How unfortunate for you that all your shrewdness isn't going to prevent you from succumbing to your wounds before you're brought before the earl of Cornwall to spread your lies."

As he started toward Henry, the younger man lunged for the bucket. He struck Carrell on the side of the head. Carrell staggered sideways, his hand to his face as he pulled a dagger out of his belt. Henry swung the bucket again, striking his enemy's hand. With a curse, Carrell let go of the dagger, which fell into the fetid straw.

"Guard! Guard!" he shouted as Henry tried desperately to reach the blade.

Carrell realized what he was doing and scrambled to get the weapon first. Henry tugged on his chains, paying no heed to the pain in his wrists, but the dagger was too far away.

The door opened—and Merrick rushed into the room. He instinctively kicked the dagger away from both men.

"He tried to kill me!" Carrell cried, his cheek red and bruising as he rubbed his equally bruised hand.

"I was defending myself," Henry said, panting, as he got to his feet. "I have evidence of his treason."

"I know. Ranulf has come."

As Henry slumped against the wall with relief, Carrell massaged his left arm. "This alleged proof is a lie!" he exclaimed. "Those letters are forgeries."

"Bearing your signature? Stamped with your seal that never leaves your finger?" Henry demanded.

"Anyone may copy a seal," Lord Carrell snarled, his complexion gray and his lips turning blue. "He's lying, I tell you! Trying to save himself!"

"That will be for the king to decide, but I fear he will not take your side, my lord," Merrick said. "There is too much evidence against you, including the word of Sir Henry."

With an enraged snarl, Carrell charged Merrick, trying to push him out of the way so he could get out the door. He might as well have tried to move a mountain. Merrick grabbed him by the shoulders, turned him around and pinned Carrell's arms behind him. "There will be no escape for you, my lord."

Carrell grimaced as if in great pain. Then he collapsed in Merrick's arms.

Merrick shouted for the guard and when the man came, wide-eyed, the lord of Tregellas laid the unconscious nobleman on the floor. "Fetch help and tell whoever comes to take good care of him. I want this man alive to stand trial. But first, give me the keys to these fetters."

The guard fumbled to untie the huge ring of keys from his leather belt, then tossed them to Merrick before he rushed out of the cell.

"I was afraid you were going to kill me before Ranulf got here," Henry said, still panting, as Merrick unlocked his chains.

Merrick looked Henry in the eye. "I might have," he admitted. He put his shoulder under his friend's arm. "May God forgive me."

Henry leaned on him heavily. "And Constance?"

"Well. She came here with Ranulf."

"Thank God for that. I truly tried to help her, Merrick."

"I know," Merrick replied. "Don't talk anymore. Brother Paul, a physician, has come from the monastery with Constance and he can tend to you. He's very skilled."

"Good. I think you might have broken a rib or two."

"I'm so sorry, Henry. Please be quiet and save your strength."

Henry grinned as they started up the steps and out of the dungeon. "I'll forgive you as soon as you get me some wine."

ALTHOUGH SHE WAS IN BED IN A finely appointed chamber, Constance wasn't asleep. Brother Paul had insisted she rest, and the earl had made it very clear by his peeved expression that he really didn't want her in the hall as they discussed the treachery of her uncle and Lord Algernon.

Perhaps he didn't like it when the queen insisted on being part of her husband's political discussions, either.

In truth, she was glad to get away. It was nerve-racking being near Merrick, yet unable to speak to him privately.

What lie had he told her, what could he have done, that could make such a man sound so remorseful, so anguished? Her mind conjured a host of answers, each more terrible than the next.

A knock sounded on the door, which creaked open a little. "My lady?"

God help her, Kiernan. Was he always going to be a thorn in her side, appearing when she least wanted to see him?

She would feign sleep. She closed her eyes and took deep, slow breaths. She heard the door begin to close....

"What are you doing outside my bedchamber?" Merrick demanded, his voice a little muffled because he, too, was in the corridor.

"I came to see Lady Constance," Kiernan replied, sounding tense but determined. "Will she be all right?"

"Brother Paul believes she will soon be completely recovered. So now you may go."

"I was at the hall moot—"

"I know. I saw you there."

Kiernan drew in his breath sharply. "So help me, my lord, if you've taken a mistress—"

Constance threw back the covers and started to get up. Kiernan had caused her a great deal of trouble, but for the sake of their past friendship, she would help him if she must.

"I have not taken a mistress. I am too content with my wife to crave another."

She froze near the door and held her breath to listen.

"It was Annice's decision not to marry the smith's son," her husband explained.

"But Constance looked so—"

"Constance knows why I made that decision. More than that, I will not say."

"If you ever hurt her, my lord—"

"I would rather die than cause her pain." Merrick's voice grew accusing. "What about you, Kiernan? Are you a spiteful man? Would you destroy a mill to ease your wounded pride, no matter who might suffer?"

"No, by God, I wouldn't!" Kiernan cried, and if ever a man sounded truly aghast at an accusation...

"Constance thought you wouldn't stoop to such an act. Neither do I."

There was a moment's silence, and she would have given much to be able to see them instead of only listen.

"Our estates adjoin, Kiernan, and I hope for peace between our families. I know that you care a great deal for Constance, and that she was glad of your friendship. No man knows what the future holds, and she may have need of friends in the days to come. It would do my heart good to think she has one in you."

"I…my lord…I will always be her friend," Kiernan stammered, obviously as taken aback as she by Merrick's words. "If she needs anything…anything at all…she has but to ask."

What future was Merrick talking about? Why did he think she would need a friend?

"I believe I've misjudged you, my lord," Kiernan said.

"Others have done so before," her husband answered. "Now, if you'll excuse me, I want to see my wife."

BY THE TIME MERRICK CAME into the room, Constance was sitting up in bed, her heart pounding, her curiosity roused to an almost unbearable degree.

Yet even so, as he ran his gaze over her, her body reacted instinctively, as if it were his hands and not his eyes, and she was naked, not clothed in a thin silk shift.

"I hope I haven't disturbed you," he said.

"No."

"Does your head still hurt?"

"No."

He nodded and started to leave.

"Merrick!"

She scrambled out of bed and reached for her bed-robe, ready to ask about that lie, until he regarded her with those cold, dark eyes.

"Where's Henry?" she asked, desperately seeking something else to say.

"Now that his injuries have been attended to, he's in the kitchen, eating." Merrick hesitated a moment, and his expression clouded as he continued. "It's been a long time since his last meal."

"He's cleared of all suspicion?"

"Yes."

"He must understand how it looked."

Merrick didn't meet her steadfast gaze. "I should never have doubted him."

She clutched the bedrobe about her. "What of Lord Carrell and your uncle?"

"They are on their way to the Tower, well guarded and in chains."

"What will happen to Beatrice?"

"Her family is to be stripped of all lands, but she may retain her title, and I've asked that she be placed under my protection."

This unexpected act of generosity only added to the puzzle that was her husband.

What kind of man was he? An evil blackguard guilty of some heinous sin, or a generous nobleman who would take pity on a young woman who might suffer because of someone else's treason?

She had to find out. She couldn't live another mo ment with that question on her mind. "What did you mean in the monastery when you said that you had lied and would release me from our marriage? Have you committed some foul crime?"

She waited, poised between hope that he was innocent of anything terrible and fear that he was not.

Merrick stood as still as a statue, his face like a stone effigy's. Then he slowly turned on his heel and went to the door. He put his hand on the latch.

Constance wouldn't run after him and beg for an answer. "I can't live with uncertainty and dread, as I did when your father was alive," she said, her heart a dull, cold ache of disillusion. "If you won't tell me, I'll imagine the worst and seek to have our marriage annulled."

Merrick bowed his head. His shoulders slumped. For a long, long moment she watched and waited, not daring to breathe as he stood motionless, the very image of forlorn misery.

Then he shuddered, as if he was shaking off some great weight. After the spasm passed, he turned back, his eyes full of such anguish and remorse, they were almost unrecognizable. But the tight resolve of his jaw— that bespoke her husband, as did the deep furrows of concern upon his brow.

When he finally spoke, his voice was almost unrecognizable, too, full of raw emotion and ragged sorrow. "I *have* lied to you, Constance. I've lied to everyone."

He spread his hands in a gesture of submission and his expression settled into hopeless despair. "I'm not Merrick."

CHAPTER TWENTY

"I'M BREDON, THE SON OF TAMSYN. Peder's grandson."

Impossible! He couldn't be. Bredon was dead. He'd drowned. He was dead. Drowned.

As her mind struggled to understand not just what Merrick had said, but his remorseful attitude, Constance felt for the end of the bed and sat heavily. "But he…he died! Everyone knows he drowned in the river."

Merrick shook his head. "No, I did not."

"But…if he didn't die—"

"I didn't."

"Then what happened? You…you're…how did you come to be Merrick?" She gasped and covered her mouth. "What happened to *him*?"

"*He* died. In the ambush on the way to Sir Leonard's." He took a deep breath, then the words seemed to fairly pour out of him, like a stream in flood in the spring. "I went fishing at the river, and a man came to me there—a nobleman, dressed in such finery as I had never seen. He asked me if I wanted to meet my father, and like the curious child I was, I said yes. That man was Sir Egbert.

"But he didn't take me to my father. We rode a long way, to join a cortege. There was another boy there—Merrick. My height, my coloring. They put me in his clothes, and he wasn't pleased about being dressed in mine.

"Sir Egbert told me I was going to get to ride a pony—and whatever happened, I was not to say a word."

Merrick looked without seeing at a tapestry on the wall of a group of ladies seated in a garden. "After the attack, I fled until I could run no more, and the next day a patrol from Sir Leonard's castle found me.

"I was too exhausted and terrified to explain what had happened. Since I was dressed like Merrick, and there was no one to say otherwise, they assumed I was the heir of Tregellas. Yet…" His words trailed off as she stared at him, still too shocked and dumbfounded to speak.

Merrick finally fixed his steadfast gaze on her. "Bredon's body was never found, was it? And he disappeared just after Lord William's son was sent north to be fostered."

"Yes—but…but you knew the castle the day you arrived. You never asked where the solar was."

"An educated guess. Norman castles are much alike."

"You recognized Sir Jowan."

"A lie."

"And Talek?"

"Him I did know, from when he'd come to the village with Lord William's noble son. My mother warned me to stay far away from them both, and I did."

She studied his face, his hands. "You look like Lord William."

"I may not be Merrick, but I am Wicked William's son. Although my mother wouldn't admit to anyone else whose get I was, she told me, swearing me to secrecy. She wanted me to know I had the blood of nobles."

"So you switched places with Merrick?"

Merrick grimly nodded. "Although I didn't know it then, I later realized that if we were attacked, I was to be a decoy. The real Merrick was dressed in my clothes and put among the servants with the baggage carts, presumably for his safety."

"Instead they killed everyone except you."

"Everyone but me." He took another deep, shuddering breath. "When I understood their mistake, I was afraid to tell the truth. What if Sir Leonard thought I'd lied on purpose? What if they believed I'd been trying to trick them? I was so frightened, I didn't know what else to do, except become Merrick and pray that Lord William wouldn't come. If he did, I'd try to escape, somehow."

"But he didn't."

"No. When I realized he wasn't going to, I felt a little safer—but never completely."

"Is that why you didn't speak for so long after the attack?"

He nodded. "I didn't understand the Norman tongue, so I didn't dare talk until I learned enough to get by, and when I thought I could sound like a Norman nobleman's son. It was weeks before I ventured even one word, and then I was afraid to say much."

No wonder he was so reticent, even now.

"Later I couldn't risk going home in case my ruse was discovered, although I sorely missed my poor mother, and Peder, who was like a father to me. I knew they would be worried about me, wondering what had happened. If only I could have found a way to tell them."

He bowed his head. "When you told me my mother had killed herself believing I was dead…" His voice dropped to a tortured whisper. "Now she suffers in eternal torment because of my lie."

Constance rose and put her arms around him and held him close. "We will have prayers and masses said for her," she promised. "I'm sure God will understand. She was as good as murdered by the men who stole her son and made her believe that he was dead."

Merrick gripped Constance tightly, as if he were falling and she the rope to save him.

"You are too good for me, Constance. Far, far too good," he murmured before he pulled away and walked to the delicately arched window.

When he faced her again, he cleared his throat and his voice was stronger, firmer, when he spoke. "I had decided before I returned to Tregellas that I would break the betrothal and set you free. It was no more than you deserved. But I discovered I had not the strength. I did remember you sitting in a hay field—that was no lie— and when I found a woman the same and yet, oh, so different, I could not give you up. But never, ever was I so tempted to reveal my secret as when I was with you in the first days of our marriage, and never was I more ashamed of my great lie.

"Yet what would become of us, of me, if I told you? I feared you would hate me for deceiving you. So rather than reveal my secret, I tried to keep my distance, and even to push you away before I told you what I'd done."

He looked at her with bleak, pleading eyes. "In spite of all my resolve, I was too weak to stay away from you. Even after we quarreled, I simply couldn't resist the need to be with you. To touch you. Kiss you. Caress you. To show you how I truly felt, no matter how I behaved toward you.

"But I love you, Constance. I would have done anything for you—except tell you the truth, because it meant I might lose you. I was wrong to deceive you, and, worse, my actions put you in danger. As Merrick's wife, you were in harm's way. If you'd not been Merrick's wife, you would have been safe."

He took hold of her hands and gazed at her with all the intensity of his passionate nature. "You must be safe, Constance, and you should be free. You were married to a base pretender under a false pretext, and no law will uphold our deceitful union."

Her heart swelled with sympathy. With compassion. With love. "Do you truly love me?" she asked softly.

He looked down at their clasped hands. "I've loved you since I was ten years old, and I'll love you until the day I die."

"What will become of you if the truth becomes known?"

He shrugged.

This air of defeat was at least as distressing as his revelation. Where was the strong, decisive warrior? She must get him back. "Who do you suggest I marry, my lord?"

He dropped her hands and stepped back as if she'd hit him. "What?"

"Surely if you're so eager to be rid of me, you must have some idea who you think will make a good husband for me. Henry, perhaps, although he has no land? I would suggest Ranulf…except his position is the same. Sir Jowan? Or would you have me wed one of the queen's French relatives, who knows nothing of this land or Tregellas? Because if I'm no longer married to you, the king will probably marry me off to a member of his wife's family. A fine fate," she said grimly, "and after you've spoiled me for another man by making me love you so much, my heart will surely shrivel and die if you leave me."

As his wife's smile lit her features and her brilliant blue eyes shone, the mighty lord of Tregellas's face flushed and he stammered, "That's not…I…you still love me?"

"Yes, I still love you, with all my heart." She took his hand and led him to the bed, sitting upon it and pulling him down beside her. "But there's no need to give up Tregellas, my beloved lord, because whether you're Merrick or Bredon, it's rightfully yours as Lord William's only surviving son. Didn't you read your father's will? Your father said that if he died without legal issue and his illegitimate son by Tamsyn was found alive, he was to inherit Tregellas."

Merrick—Bredon—stared at her with dumbstruck disbelief. "Algernon said my father never made a will."

"He lied, my love, blatantly lied, and had I known of this sooner, I would have realized he was not to be trusted."

Although she could easily believe Algernon had lied to Merrick, another explanation came to her. "Or perhaps he truly didn't know," she mused aloud. "He was in York when your father had it written, and it could be your father never told his brother because he hated him. Maybe he thought if Algernon knew about the will and its contents, he'd try to steal or destroy it."

"Maybe he already has," Merrick suggested, as if he didn't dare to hope.

"I doubt it. Your father kept the key to the chest holding the important documents on a chain around his neck, and the solar locked, too, when he wasn't there. Algernon would never have had the chance to take it from the room before you came."

Merrick gave her a look of bleak dismay. "If I'd known what was in that chest, I would have kept it locked, too. And the solar. But I haven't. It's possible Algernon found it after I arrived."

"But there's a copy in the cathedral in Canterbury, and another in Westminster," Constance hastened to assure him. "Your father sent them there for safekeeping. Remember, he trusted no one. And even if Algernon somehow managed to have them destroyed, Alan de Vern witnessed it, and the scribe who wrote it still lives. I'm sure that poor man remembers every word. Your father was not an easy man to please."

Despite her revelations and assurances, Merrick still didn't look relieved, or joyful. He was puzzled, confused. "Lord William acknowledged me? Did he not believe I'd drowned?"

She shrugged her shoulders and wished she knew what had been in his father's mind. "I don't know. He never spoke of Tamsyn's son, not once in all the years I was with him." There was one reason she could give that made sense of the will of the late lord of Tregellas. "I suspect it's more likely that he was trying to make trouble for Algernon, whom he loathed and believed was conspiring against him—which, we now know, he was. By putting that clause in his will, Algernon would have to go to great lengths to prove that you were dead. It would tie him up with legalities for months."

She gripped Merrick tighter at the thought of so much malignant hate, pondering what else Wicked William might have done. "I fear your father may even have planned your abduction, using an innocent child to protect his own son, or taking you to torment your mother and grandfather. Peder made no secret of his hatred for Wicked William."

"If my father knew about the ruse, would he not suspect it was the impostor, and not his son, who'd survived?"

Her heart ached because of what she had to tell him, but she had known his father well, as he had not, and she wanted no more secrets between them. "Perhaps he did know, and didn't care. He gave no sign of affection toward Merrick while he was alive, although he was his son. He loved nothing except his castle and his money, and he feared nothing more than losing them, even to a son. It wouldn't surprise me to learn he had wanted you both dead. By killing everyone in the cortege, he would do away with both his sons and Egbert, leaving only Algernon to fear. That would also explain why he sent his brother with the cortege instead of taking his son himself."

Merrick sucked in his breath. "There were accidents when I was training and in tournaments. I often wondered...feared... He must have been mad."

She looked into her husband's eyes and spoke firmly. "Whatever he was, you're the lord of Tregellas by right of birth, for there is no other living child of Lord William. And more, you're the lord of Tregellas because you deserve to be."

He still looked uncertain. "I hope the earl thinks as you do, and the king."

"You're going to tell them? There's no need—"

"Yes, there is," he insisted. He brought her hands clasped in his to his chest and regarded her with grim determination. "As I love you, Constance, I won't lay the burden of living with this lie on you."

"But I gladly accept it," she replied, not understanding why more people needed to know. Those who hadn't known Wicked William might question why he'd lied for so long.

Then another explanation came to her and it made her gasp with dismay. "Or do you fear I'll betray you?"

"I know you won't," he said softly, and with a sincerity that reassured her. "Yet I also know what it is to live with the dread that one slip of the tongue, one incautious word, will be your ruin. Most of all, I fear that you'll come to resent having to keep this secret and, therefore, me."

"I won't," she vowed.

"I wish I could be as certain of that as you, but I would always be seeking the signs that you grow weary of that cross, as I've watched for signs that people suspected I was not nobly born for fifteen years. I'm going to tell the earl of Cornwall the truth. And Peder, too. I especially want him to know his grandson is still alive."

When Constance saw Merrick's firm resolve, she knew nothing she could say would dissuade him. This, too, was part of the man she'd married. "I'll go with you when you speak to the earl, to tell him that whatever happens, I'll still be your wife. I love *you,* whatever your name may be."

"And if he imprisons me for my ruse?"

"Then, my lord," she said, as resolute as he, "the earl had best be prepared for the battle of his life. You are the rightful heir of Lord William, and not only do I love you, I care about the people of Tregellas. I would go to war to win you your lawful rights and keep Tregellas out of the king's—or the queen's—hands."

At last he smiled, and in a way she'd never seen before, as if he had lost a heavy load he'd carried for too long, and was finally free. "I think you could defeat even the king and all his counselors. With you by my side, how can we lose?"

"Then you'll fight for what is yours in law?"

"Yes," he whispered as he leaned in to kiss her.

Excited passion flickered through her body as it had when they'd first married. The desire that she had tried to stifle in more recent days broke free. She laughed with the joy of it, even as they kissed.

He drew back, puzzled.

"I'm happy."

He smiled slowly, wonderfully. "I'm happy, too. Truly happy."

"And come what may, I am yours forever, Mer   Bredon."

"As I am yours," he whispered, his voice husky with need as his hands opened her bedrobe to reveal her thin shift. "And I have been Merrick for so long, I hardly recognize my rightful name. I'll feel like you're talking to somebody else if you call me Bredon."

She shrugged off her robe. "Very well…Merrick."

THEY MADE LOVE SLOWLY, TENDERLY, with soft words and gentle endearments. As if a gate long closed had swung open, Merrick said all the things he'd yearned to for so long. Of Constance's sweetness. Her gentleness. Her beauty. Her knowledge of healing. Her concern for others.

His admiration. His respect. His desire. His love.

And she, in turn, revealed how he impressed her with his intelligence, his justice, his competence, his skill in bed and out of it.

They spoke until their passion made all words superfluous, for their bodies, their lips, their hands said even more as they touched and kissed and loved.

Yet afterward, although they were exhausted, neither one slept well.

There could be no real rest until the earl of Cornwall knew the truth, and they their fate.

RICHARD OF CORNWALL FROWNED as he looked from Merrick to Constance and back again when they stood before him in the great hall of Tintagel. "You are not the lord of Tregellas but some *impostor*?" he demanded. "And you've pretended to be Lord William's son for *fifteen years*?"

"He may not be Lord William's legitimate son," Constance declared, determined that Richard understand what was most important, "but he *is* Lord William's son. According to the terms of his will, Lord William's illegitimate son takes precedence over anyone else except his legitimate son, who was killed fifteen years ago."

The earl regarded Merrick with a steadfast gaze that was not unlike her husband's. "Then why the ruse?"

"Because I didn't know the terms of my father's will and because I was a frightened child when I first lied about who I was. Then I feared it was too late to tell the truth."

"But now you will?"

"Yes, my lord. Now I will. Now I have. Would you rather I had continued to lie to you?"

The earl leaned back in his chair. "No, I would not, and I must admit I see no reason you would come to me with such a story if it weren't true. I've also heard of Lord William's…peculiarities…and thus I can well believe he was mad enough to make such a provision in his will. And however skeptical I might be had this story come to me another way, the fact that you've come to me yourselves stands in your favor."

Constance slid a glance at her husband, whose face, not surprisingly, betrayed nothing. The tension in his body and the way he gripped her hand told her another story.

"I'm also well aware of your loyalty to me and to the king, as well as your skill in battle," the earl continued. "It would be foolish of me to lose such a capable commander, especially if your father's will is as you say."

Squeezing Merrick's hand, Constance started to smile with relief.

"However, I will agree to allow you to remain the overlord of Tregellas on one condition."

Her smile disappeared as dread replaced relief.

"I would ask that you tell no one else the truth. The kingdom is in enough turmoil, and I need a strong right arm. Besides, you've managed to keep this secret for fifteen years. Surely you're used to it by now."

Merrick's expression grew as sternly determined as she had ever seen it. "My lord, I've kept that secret for too long as it is. I no longer wish to bear that burden, or force my beloved wife to carry it, as well. And my grandfather yet lives. I'd like him to know me—truly know me—while he can."

The earl frowned. "You would disobey me in this?"

"If I must."

Richard rose, and both were reminded that this man, too, was the son of a king. "You would give up Tregellas? You would become nothing more than a nobleman's bastard?"

"If I must."

"And what of your wife? Will you condemn her to a life of poverty and uncertainty, too?"

"Whatever my husband's fate," Constance said without hesitation, "he already knows I'll share it, and gladly. But I warn you, my lord, that others know the terms of Lord William's will. There was a scribe who wrote it and he yet lives. There is Lord William's steward, Alan de Vern, who witnessed it. If you attempt to give Tregellas to another, I'll fight you tooth and nail in the courts."

The earl's brows rose. "You will?"

She moved closer to her husband. "With my husband's help, of course. Other nobles who fear that the king is loath to follow the law of his own realm will surely be most interested in the outcome."

Richard frowned as he studied her. "Is that a threat, my lady?"

"However you wish to consider it, my lord, you must know that I'm right. Your brother the king has already angered many of his nobles by trying to ignore the provisions of Magna Carta. Would it be wise to raise more suspicions in their minds by attempting to deny my husband his rightful inheritance?"

The earl looked at Merrick. "Your wife is a shrewd and very well-informed woman."

Merrick smiled. "She's also very stubborn and can be most determined."

"I can believe it," the earl muttered. He thought a moment, then said, "Fortunately, I happen to agree with her. There's no need to change the lordship of Tregellas—provided those *are* the terms of the late Lord William's will. Therefore, I will go with you to Tregellas and see this unusual document for myself. If it is as you say, then I see no reason to disinherit you, or for the truth to remain hidden. But if it is not…" He pinned his gaze on Merrick. "You alone shall suffer for your lie."

Constance stepped forward. "My lord, I—"

The earl swept past them. "I will hear no more about this until we reach Tregellas."

CHAPTER TWENTY-ONE

THE NEXT DAY, EARL RICHARD rode at the front of the group traveling to Tregellas, with Merrick and Constance on either side of him. Henry and Ranulf were behind them, and then the other nobles, including Sir Jowan and his son. Lord Osgoode had elected to remain in Tintagel, cosseted by his mistress who'd been waiting there for him.

Brother Paul had thrown up his hands when Henry insisted upon leaving and claimed he didn't understand young people anymore. They all seemed anxious to disobey his sage advice.

However, no priestly admonition was going to convince Henry to stay in Tintagel. He wanted to get away from that castle as soon as possible.

"I tell you, nothing will surprise me after this. *Nothing*," Henry said to Ranulf. "Next thing you know, the king will abdicate and join the church."

"If that happens, heaven help the church," Ranulf replied with a wry grin.

"I suppose it does explain a few things about Merrick, though," Henry mused a moment later.

"Yes, it does," Ranulf agreed. "His confounded silence, for one thing. It also makes his refusal to even discuss rebellion against the king more understandable."

Henry grimaced with pain as he shifted in his saddle. "How's that?"

"Feeling guilty because he believed he'd already stolen one man's birthright, he had no desire to help steal another's."

Henry let out a low whistle, then winced, his lips not yet healed. "God's wounds, you're right." He nodded at Constance. "At least whatever difficulties he was having with his wife seem to have abated. Do you suppose he apologized?"

"I don't know," Ranulf replied. "But they're certainly happy."

"Indeed they are. He's as blissfully besotted as my brother, and that's saying something."

Ranulf thought they had talked about love long enough. "So, are you still determined to leave us at the next crossroads?"

"I've put off a visit to my brother long enough."

"Merrick's truly sorry he accused you of betraying him."

"So he's said."

"Do you forgive him?"

"I'm here with him now, aren't I?"

Ranulf raised a skeptical brow.

Henry frowned. "He's no very gentle interrogator."

"He was upset about his wife."

"That I understand, but he was so quick to believe the worst of me."

"Perhaps because you never seem to take anything seriously."

"I take our oath seriously," Henry replied. He slid his friend a questioning glance. "Do *you* trust me?"

"Yes."

Henry gave a small sigh of relief, then said with a hint of pique, "That's more than Merrick does. He never really trusted us, did he? Or he would have told us the truth."

"I think he did trust us, as far as he was able."

"Which wasn't very far."

"Would you have told anyone such a secret, thinking you could lose everything?"

Henry shifted in his saddle again, but this time his discomfort was mental, not physical.

"No, I didn't think so," Ranulf said, "and neither would I."

They rode in silence for a while, each man wrapped in his own thoughts, until Henry spoke. "You're staying on as garrison commander in Tregellas?"

"For now."

"I wouldn't wait too long before I asked for permission to marry Beatrice, if I were you."

Ranulf started and his horse whinnied in protest. "What?"

Henry's eyes shone with amusement. "You know you want to."

"Don't be ridiculous," Ranulf huffed. "She's too young. And she talks too much."

Henry twisted in his saddle to look behind him at the rest of the cortege, then at his friend. "Young Kiernan seems to have gotten over his infatuation with Lady Constance. I wouldn't be surprised if his affections started drifting to a certain talkative young lady who, I point out, is *not* a child and who, I believe, is beginning to resemble her beautiful cousin more every day."

Ranulf's jaw clenched. "I wish you'd keep your outrageous speculations to yourself."

"You could lose her if you don't put a little more effort into the wooing."

"Shut your mouth," Ranulf growled, "or broken ribs or not, I'll knock you off your horse."

"Oh, very well," Henry said with a short laugh. "You have absolutely no interest in the lively, lovely little Lady Bea—and I'm going to swear off women for the rest of my life."

"WELCOME HOME, MY LORD, MY LADY. Earl Richard, you honor us," Alan de Vern declared as the cortege entered the courtyard of Tregellas the next morning.

The earl dismounted at the same time as Merrick and looked around the yard. "A most impressive fortress. I think I've been too long in France. I should pay more heed to what's afoot in Cornwall."

A pale and anxious Beatrice hurried over to Constance the moment she was off her horse. "I hope you don't mind that I've come here, despite what my father…despite my father," she said worriedly, "but between Maloren's weeping and his leman's cursing, I couldn't bear it there."

"I'm glad you did. You'll always be welcome in my home," Constance assured her.

Beatrice smiled tremulously as a tear rolled down her cheek. "Thank you. I'm more grateful than I can say. If there's ever anything I can do to repay you for your kindness…"

Constance gave her a warm, comforting smile. "You can promise me that you'll always come to me when you're troubled. I love you like a sister, Beatrice, and sisters should always help and succor one another."

Beatrice embraced her, weeping softly. As she stroked her cousin's back, Constance looked for Merrick. Ranulf had his back to them, giving orders to the soldiers of their escort, but a glance over his shoulder told her he had witnessed Beatrice's distress. She gave him a smile, too, to assure him Beatrice was welcome in Tregellas.

Then she spotted her husband striding toward Alan, with the earl right behind him.

"You received my message?" Merrick asked the steward.

"Yes, my lord," Alan replied, shifting anxiously as his gaze flicked from Merrick to the earl and back again. "Alas, my lord, I could not find the will."

Alarmed, Constance stepped away from Beatrice. "It wasn't in the chest in the solar, in that cedar box?"

Alan shook his head. "There was no cedar box, my lady."

Despite her dismay, Constance's mind worked swiftly, seeking an explanation. "Perhaps one of the servants moved it when they were cleaning the solar before Merrick came home. I'll ask Demelza—"

"Was the box carved with a pattern of leaves and vines?" Merrick asked

"Yes!" Constance exclaimed, relieved. "You've seen it?"

"Ruan has such a box. I noticed it in his house when I was talking to him about the mill repairs."

The earl tapped his foot impatiently. "Who is this Ruan?"

"The bailiff, my lord," Merrick replied. He swiftly scanned the courtyard. "He's not here."

He gestured for Ranulf to come closer. "Take ten men and go to Ruan's house," he said to his friend. "In the lower room there's a shelf near the hearth. At the back of it, you'll find a carved cedar box. Inside it there may be a sealed document. Bring them both to me—and Ruan, too."

"I'll go with him," Constance offered. "I know exactly what it looks like."

"We'll *all* go," the earl declared. "I'd like to get this matter settled as quickly as possible."

Thus it was that the villagers of Tregellas saw the lord of Tregellas and his wife hurrying through the village with another, obviously noble man at their side. Lady Beatrice, the steward and some soldiers were also in the party heading for the bailiff's house at the end of the green. Those shopping in the market or manning their stalls immediately abandoned what they were doing to follow, each asking the other if they knew what was happening.

When they reached Ruan's large house, Merrick rapped sharply on the bossed door. "Ruan!"

He listened a moment, then drew back and shoved the door open with his broad shoulder. As the crowd's curious muttering grew, Merrick marched into the house and dragged out a struggling, protesting Ruan by the collar of his tunic.

"Ranulf, see if you can find that box," Merrick said as he ran a scornful gaze over the terrified bailiff.

Ranulf disappeared inside the house. "What were you hiding under the floor, Ruan?" Merrick demanded.

"N-nothing, my lord—only the money I've earned."

"Why were you trying to go out the back when your lord was calling for you?"

"B-because I heard the mob and didn't know—"

"Why they were coming here. Did you fear your dishonesty had finally been discovered?"

"I've earned everything you'll find in my house!" Ruan protested. "Every ha'penny."

"We'll see."

Quaking with fear, Ruan asked piteously, "What are you…what are you going to do?"

Merrick fixed his cold, implacable gaze on the bailiff. "That will depend on what we find in your house."

At those words, spoken in such a tone, Ruan started to struggle more fiercely. "No! No! It's not fair!"

He might have been a doll for all the difference his agitated motions made to the man holding him by the collar. When Ruan realized his efforts were futile, he went limp.

"Do you think it was easy being bailiff here, with your cursed father for a master?" he pleaded, sobbing. "Do you think I enjoyed having to enforce his orders and then listen to the tenants complain? To have mud and worse thrown at me? To be scorned and reviled?" His self-pity shifted to rage. "And for what? A few miserly coins and the back of his hand when he was in one of his rages!"

He pointed a shaking finger at Constance. "Ask *her* how it was!"

"Yes, I was here and know how it was," she replied, sad to see any man, even Ruan, reduced to such a state. "But if you found the position so odious, you were free to go."

"Did you also *earn* the right to steal the late lord's will?" Merrick asked with slow, stern deliberation.

"I took no will!" Ruan protested. "Why would I want that?"

"Because there was more in that box than a will," Constance replied. "Lord William kept some jewels and gold coins in it, too, as I remember."

Ranulf appeared in the door, an open cedar box in his

hand. "There's no jewelry or coins in here now," he said. He reached inside and pulled out a scroll. "But there is this."

"Give it to me," the earl commanded. He took out the dagger he wore in his belt and slipped it under the wax seal Constance recognized as Lord William's. While Ruan continued to whimper, Richard unrolled the parchment and started to read.

Constance held her breath, praying the will was as she'd remembered, fearing it wasn't, or that what the earl held was some other document.

After a long moment when the whole crowd seemed to be holding its breath, Richard raised his eyes. "It is just as you say, my lady. Even if he's not the earl's legitimate son, your husband is the rightful heir to Tregellas."

The villagers turned shocked eyes onto Merrick.

"I'm not Merrick," he announced, his voice loud in the silence. "I'm Bredon, the son of Lord William and Peder's daughter, Tamsyn. I was taken from the riverbank and put in Merrick's place in the cortege. He was killed, but I—"

Suddenly a shout such as Constance had never heard, of joy and anguish, of happiness and dismay, rose from the back of the crowd. Then Peder shoved his way forward.

"My boy! My blessed, blessed boy!" the old man cried. Tears streaming down his cheeks, he reached out and took Merrick's face in his hands. "When you talked to me at the smithy, I thought… God help me, I thought

I was going mad. But the look in your eyes…I'd seen that look a hundred times in Tamsyn's…. Bredon, my boy—is it really you?"

Merrick put his hands on his grandfather's shoulders. Now she could see the resemblance between them. Their brown, resolute eyes. Their height. The shape of their jaw. "Yes, Grandpa, it's really me."

"And you're not drowned?"

Merrick shook his head. "No, Grandpa, I didn't drown," he softly, gently answered.

The earl cleared his throat. "This is all very touching, but I'm tired and thirsty and could use some wine. Shall we retire to your hall, my lord? Your dear wife looks tired, too, and so does this elderly fellow who, I take it, is your grandfather?"

"I'm perfectly fine!" Peder declared, clinging to his grandson as if he feared he'd disappear again.

"Constance should rest," her husband said to him. "So come, Grandpa. Come home with me."

"IT'S LIKE SOMETHING OUT OF A minstrel's tale," Beatrice said as she watched Constance prepare for bed that night. "He's like a sort of prodigal son, only he wasn't really. It wasn't his fault he went away. And then he didn't dare come back."

She sounded almost like the Beatrice of old, but there was a look in her eyes that told Constance her girlish innocence was gone. She was a woman now, and one who would carry the burden of her father's shame for the rest of her life.

Until, perhaps, she found someone to take that burden from her, or gladly share it.

"I'm glad the earl's put you in our care," Constance replied. "I can always use your help."

"I'm very grateful. Anything I can do to help you, you have but to name it."

Constance stifled a little smile, thinking she would welcome another pair of hands or assistance with the servants in a few months, when she would be busy with a new and wonderful concern. But she'd not yet told her husband, so she didn't want to tell Beatrice, either. "Thank you. I hope you'll have a fine husband and a household of your own someday."

Beatrice's cheeks reddened and she crossed to the window, looking out at the night sky. "I'll never marry. I'm the dowerless daughter of traitor."

Constance went and put her arm around her cousin's slender shoulders. "You're the cousin-by-marriage of the lord of Tregellas. And we'll gladly give you a dowry."

Beatrice shook her head. "I can't ask that of you."

"You're not. I'm telling you how it will be," Constance replied with a smile. "If there's a man you wish to marry and he shares that desire, we'll do everything we can to make the marriage."

"You really are too good to me," Beatrice whispered as she hugged her cousin.

A deep, slightly husky male voice interrupted. "Have we not had sufficient tears today?"

Constance looked over her shoulder at her husband standing on the threshold of their bedchamber. Whatever his name was, the very sight of him made her heartbeat quicken and her body warm with desire.

"It was a rather unusual homecoming," Constance remarked with a seductive little smile that, judging by the look that came to her husband's face, had exactly the effect she was aiming for.

Beatrice hurried to the door. "I'll leave you now," she murmured, then she ran from the room, weeping.

"I regret that the sight of me makes Beatrice burst into tears," Merrick remarked as he came farther into the room.

"She's rightly upset about all that's happened and worried about her future. I told her we would provide her with a dowry."

"We will?"

"She must have one if she's to marry well. You do want her to marry well?"

"I would have her wed tomorrow if I could."

Constance frowned. "Don't you like Beatrice? Or is it because of her father's crime that you—?"

"I'm the last person to blame a child for the sins of the father," Merrick said, "and I do like her. It's just that she always seems to be so anxious or upset when she's near me. As Henry once so memorably remarked, I don't bite."

"But you *are* intimidating. And don't tell me you don't know that. In fact, my imposing lord," she said, insinuating her arms around his waist and giving him a very impertinent grin, "I think you're very well aware of how you're perceived, and cultivate that reaction, too."

Merrick didn't smile in return. "It does keep people at a distance."

"There's no more need for that, is there?" she wheedled.

He kissed her lightly, and then he smiled. "No—except for my enemies, or those who might become my enemies."

"Of course. You may be as stern and forbidding to them as you like."

"I'm glad I have your permission, my lady," he replied.

There was something in his response, beneath the jovial banter, that disturbed her. "What is it? Did Earl Richard say something to trouble you?"

"Not the earl," Merrick replied as he stepped away from her. "My grandfather had some news for me today. Talek set fire to the mill."

Constance sat heavily on the end of the bed. She'd been wrong about that, as she had about so many things.... "Because you dismissed him?"

"Yes."

"You'll have to find him and bring him to justice."

"Justice has already been meted out. Talek's dead, by

my grandfather's hand. It seems Talek was guilty of other crimes, as well. If my grandfather hadn't killed him, I would have."

Constance looked down at the floor. Talek had been a friend to Peder, too, and if Peder believed Talek guilty, he probably was. "How did Peder find out?"

"Talek confessed. Then he threatened my grandfather with…" He eyed his wife speculatively. "How much *do* you know about the smuggling around Tregellas?"

"Enough to guess what Talek's threat might have been." Talek likely claimed he would expose Peder's illegal activities. "But the taxes really aren't fair and—"

"I'll do all I can to change that." Merrick's eyes glimmered with satisfaction. "But if my patrols have no luck catching tin smugglers, well…this is a difficult coast to guard."

Constance regarded him warily. "Are you telling me, my lord, that you'd let tinners get away with breaking the king's law?"

"As I have broken the law against participating in tournaments, perhaps?" he countered, smiling at her surprise. "My love, not only would I, I have. Remember that I grew up here with a grandfather who's been smuggling for years. I know every cove, every beach. Which ones they use, which ones they don't. So if my men have had no luck…" He shrugged, and grinned with roguish delight.

Constance laughed merrily and shook her head.

"There may be no end to the things I'll discover about my husband."

"But those are the only laws I'll turn a blind eye to," he said firmly, sounding more like the man who'd arrived in Tregellas all those days ago.

"Those are the only ones I'd care to see broken," she agreed. "Although, if I had my choice, I'd prevent you from going to tournaments. You could get hurt."

"But then you'll tend to me, won't you?"

"Well, my lord, when you put it like that…"

Instead of smiling at her response, however, he remained grave as he took hold of her hands. "Peder had other news. It seems Eric was caught trying to force another girl in Truro. He's in prison there now."

"Good!"

"At least he didn't get Annice with child." Merrick's face clouded for a moment. "I didn't mean to speak of such matters tonight." He let go of her hands and patted his tunic. "I've brought you a gift to…to make up for many mistakes."

"I made mistakes, too."

"Not like mine." He lowered his voice and spoke in a seductive purr. "Will you come and get it?"

She gave him a sultry smile in return. "It's in your tunic, not your breeches?"

"Your impertinence continues to astonish me, my love," he replied with that devastating little smile that nearly made her forget what she was about.

"Your *body* continues to astonish me," she whispered as she insinuated her hand into his tunic.

"Beware. It has teeth."

She stopped and looked swiftly up at his face. His smiling, handsome face. "But it shouldn't hurt you," he said. "I hope you like it."

"I'm sure I will," she replied as she reached farther inside, taking her time and moving her hand over far more of his broad chest than was strictly necessary until she felt something enshrouded in velvet cloth. She drew it out and regarded him quizzically, then unwrapped a beautiful comb of horn, the top wonderfully carved with tiny flowers.

"Oh, Merrick, it's lovely!" she cried, running her fingertip over the carvings.

"May I?" he asked, holding out his hand.

She gave him a puzzled look, then she understood and, smiling, went to the stool at her dressing table. He followed and began to comb her thick, luxurious hair that he'd admired from afar all those years ago.

Leaning back, Constance closed her eyes. "I hope you really don't mind Beatrice being here. She's much quieter than she used to be."

"It's not her chatter that troubles me. She can be quite amusing. I'm just not looking forward to all the young swains we'll have to accommodate when they come seeking her out. She's becoming a very beautiful, charming young lady."

Constance opened her eyes, to see her husband's rugged chin. "Beautiful? I know she's a pretty girl, but..."

Merrick leaned forward and kissed her forehead. "You see her with the eyes of a cousin. I see her with a man's eyes, and believe me, my beloved, she's fast turning into the sort of woman men will fight over. Have you never noticed how much she resembles *you*?"

In truth, Constance hadn't. "Perhaps she does, a little," she mused. "Her hair is darker than mine and her eyes a deeper blue."

"No woman will ever be as beautiful to me as you are, but she's going to be very lovely indeed. I would rather not have lovesick young men coming to blows in our hall."

"Perhaps we should think of finding a husband for her ourselves then," Constance proposed.

"Kiernan seemed quite attentive during the evening meal."

Constance turned so fast, the comb caught in her hair. "Ow!" she cried, putting her hand to her head as she gave him a dumbfounded look. "Kiernan?"

"What's wrong, my love?" Merrick replied as he worked to extricate the comb without snapping any of the teeth. "He's young, he seems honorable and an alliance with his family would be advantageous."

"He's just...he's just not the sort of man who'd be

right for Beatrice," she said, knowing her excuse was feeble, but certain in her heart that Kiernan couldn't make Beatrice happy.

"What sort of man *do* you think Beatrice should marry, besides a very patient one?"

Although his tone was teasing, Constance answered seriously. "A man who'll love her as she deserves to be loved."

"Have you any candidates in mind?"

She hadn't before, but now one came to her, and although she surprised herself with her instinctive choice, the moment his name popped into her head, she felt it was right. "Ranulf."

That took Merrick aback—literally. *"Ranulf?"*

"She thinks he's hiding a broken heart. That's why he's so cynical about love and romance." Constance gave her husband another insolent grin. "There *is* something about a man with a secret."

"She may be willing, but Ranulf? He always claims he'll never love any woman well enough to wed."

"And you have no idea why?" Constance asked with a puzzled frown.

Merrick kissed the tip of her nose. "If I knew, I'd tell you, but I don't. Even Henry can't get him to say anything more than that."

"Well, if he's not willing, what about Henry?" she suggested. "I think I've been very wrong about him."

Her husband sighed and his expression grew troubled. "As was I. I fear Henry's never going to forgive me for accusing him of betraying me and trying to do you harm."

"I'm sure he will, in time."

"I'll live in hope," he said as he sat on their bed. "I wish I'd told both my friends the complete truth long ago."

"I wish you'd told *me* sooner," she said as she sat beside him. "It would have saved me much distress. Promise me there'll be no more secrets between us."

He tucked a lock of her hair behind her ear. "I promise."

"So now I'll tell you *my* secret."

Worry darkened his features. "Your injury isn't more serious than Brother Paul—?"

"I'm with child."

Merrick stared at her incredulously.

"You're going to be a father," she said, smiling with all the happiness she felt.

His eyes bright with joy, Merrick cried out her name and hugged her close. "I can't believe it!"

She pushed him away a bit so she could breathe. "Have we not made love often enough?"

"Yes, but…oh, Constance, my love, my heart! I don't deserve this, too!"

"Of course you do," she replied, pretending to be indignant. Then her expression softened, and so did her voice. "You deserve to be happy, husband, for the sake of all that you've endured, the burden you bore, the pain you suffered. I'll do all I can to help make you happy, God willing, for the rest of my life."

"God be praised, you've already given me more than I ever hoped to have. Constance, this is wonderful! I'm so happy. And you—are you well? Should we send for Brother Paul? Or a woman skilled with such things? A physician?"

She put her fingertips against his lips to stem his anxious questions. "I've never felt better or happier," she assured him, smiling and loving him with all her heart. "I've found such love and contentment as I never hoped to have. Now, please, stop talking, my dearest, and make love to me."

His deep, full-bodied laugh filled their chamber. "That's the first time in my life I've ever been asked to be quiet." Then his voice dropped to a low, intimate whisper as he leaned close to kiss her. "Since I want nothing more than to please you, I'm eager to obey *both* requests, my most beloved lady."

* * * * *

Be sure to look for Margaret Moore's
upcoming historical romance
HERS TO COMMAND,
the next book in her new medieval series
BROTHERS-IN-ARMS,
Coming in February 2006
only from HQN Books!

MARGARET MOORE

77003 BRIDE OF LOCHBARR	___ $6.50 U.S.	___ $7.99 CAN.
77040 LORD OF DUNKEATHE	___ $6.50 U.S.	___ $7.99 CAN.

(limited quantities available)

TOTAL AMOUNT	$ _____
POSTAGE & HANDLING	$ _____
($1.00 FOR 1 BOOK, 50¢ for each additional)	
APPLICABLE TAXES*	$ _____
TOTAL PAYABLE	$ _____

(check or money order—please do not send cash)

To order, complete this form and send it, along with a check or money order for the total above, payable to HQN Books, to: **In the U.S.:** 3010 Walden Avenue, P.O. Box 9077, Buffalo, NY 14269-9077; **In Canada:** P.O. Box 636, Fort Erie, Ontario, L2A 5X3.

Name: _____

Address: _____ City: _____

State/Prov.: _____ Zip/Postal Code: _____

Account Number (if applicable): _____

075 CSAS

*New York residents remit applicable sales taxes.
*Canadian residents remit applicable GST and provincial taxes.

HQN™

We *are* romance™

www.HQNBooks.com

PHMM1005BL

Join top authors for the ultimate cruise experience. Spend 7 days in the Mexican Riviera aboard the luxurious Carnival Pride™. Start in Los Angeles/Long Beach, CA and visit Puerto Vallarta, Mazatlan and Cabo San Lucas. Enjoy all this with a ship full of authors and book lovers on the **"Authors at Sea Cruise"** April 2 - 9, 2006.

Mail in this coupon with proof of purchase* to receive $250 per person off the regular **"Authors at Sea Cruise"** price. One coupon per person required to receive $250 discount. For complete details call **1-877-ADV-NTGE** or visit **www.AuthorsAtSea.com**

PRICES STARTING AT $749 PER PERSON WITH COUPON!

Proof of purchase is original sales receipt with the book(s) purchased circled. Prices are applicable for new, hed and inside cabins.

MIRA® HQN™

Carnival. The Most Popular Cruise Line in the World!

GET $250 OFF

Name (Please Print)

Address _____ Apt. No. _____

City _____ State _____ Zip _____

E-Mail Address

See Following Page For Terms & Conditions.

For booking form and complete information go to www.AuthorsAtSea.com or call 1-877-ADV-NTGE

Prices quoted are in U.S. currency.

AAS05A

Carnival Pride^{SM}
April 2 - 9, 2006.

7 Day Exotic Mexican Riviera Itinerary

DAY	PORT	ARRIVE	DEPART
Sun	Los Angeles/Long Beach, CA		4:00 P.M.
Mon	"Book Lover's" Day at Sea		
Tue	"Book Lover's" Day at Sea		
Wed	Puerto Vallarta, Mexico	8:00 A.M.	10:00 P.M.
Thu	Mazatlan, Mexico	9:00 A.M.	6:00 P.M.
Fri	Cabo San Lucas, Mexico	7:00 A.M.	4:00 P.M.
Sat	"Book Lover's" Day at Sea		
Sun	Los Angeles/Long Beach, CA	9:00 A.M.	

ports of call subject to weather conditions

TERMS AND CONDITIONS

PAYMENT SCHEDULE:
50% due upon booking
Full and final payment due by February 10, 2006

Acceptable forms of payment are Visa, MasterCard, American Express, Discover and checks. The cardholder must be one of the passengers traveling. A fee of $25 will apply for all returned checks. Check payments must be made payable to **Advantage International, LLC** and sent to: **Advantage International, LLC, 195 North Harbor Drive, Suite 4206, Chicago, IL 60601**

CHANGE/CANCELLATION:
Notice of change/cancellation must be made in writing to Advantage International, LLC.

Change:
Changes in cabin category may be requested and can result in increased rate and penalties. A name change is permitted 60 days or more prior to departure and will incur a penalty of $50 per name change. Deviation from the group schedule and package is a cancellation.

Cancellation:
181 days or more prior to departure	$250 per person
121 - 180 days or more prior to departure	50% of the package price
120 - 61 days prior to departure	75% of the package price
60 days or less prior to departure	100% of the package price (nonrefundable)

US and Canadian citizens are required to present a valid passport or the original birth certificate and state issued photo ID (drivers license). All other nationalities must contact the consulate of the various ports that are visited for verification of documentation.

<u>We strongly recommend trip cancellation insurance!</u>

For complete details call 1-877-ADV-NTGE or visit www.AuthorsAtSea.com

---

MIRA®   HQN™

For booking form and complete information
go to **www.AuthorsAtSea.com** or call **1-877-ADV-NTGE**

Complete coupon and booking form and mail both to:
Advantage International, LLC,
195 North Harbor Drive, Suite 4206, Chicago, IL 60601

Prices quoted are in U.S. currency.

AAS05B